Ran

THE
SECRET
SEA

BARRY LYGA

FEIWEL AND FRIENDS

NEW YORK

A FEIWEL AND FRIENDS BOOK
An Imprint of Macmillan

Our books may be purchased in bulk for promotional, educational, or business use. Please contact your local bookseller or the Macmillan Corporate and Premium Sales Department at (800) 221-7945 ext. 5442 or by e-mail at MacmillanSpecialMarkets@macmillan.com.

Library of Congress Cataloging-in-Publication Data
Names: Lyga, Barry, author.
Title: The secret sea / Barry Lyga.
Description: First edition. | New York : Feiwel & Friends, 2016. | Summary:
  "Three friends find themselves plunged into a world of quantum physics, a
  rare disease that only affects identical twins, and a mysterious fact about a
  real-life global catastrophe"—Provided by publisher.
Identifiers: LCCN 2015022201| ISBN 9781250072832 (hardback) |
  ISBN   9781250086808 (e-book)
Subjects: | CYAC: Adventure and adventurers—Fiction. | Family life—Fiction.
  | Friendship—Fiction. | Heart—Diseases—Fiction. | Science fiction. |
  BISAC: JUVENILE FICTION / Action & Adventure / General. | JUVENILE
  FICTION / Science Fiction.
Classification: LCC PZ7.L97967 Sec 2016 | DDC [Fic]—dc23
LC record available at http://lccn.loc.gov/2015022201

Book design by Liz Dresner

Feiwel and Friends logo designed by Filomena Tuosto

First Edition—2016

10 9 8 7 6 5 4 3 2 1

mackids.com

For Morgan. Because it's her favorite.

THE SECRET SEA

PROLOGUE

Look up.

Look down.

Look all around.

All around, there is the world and there is the dark, and there is something else besides, something I have brushed up against and experienced but cannot explain or understand.

And he . . . he has been asleep too long, able to dream only of himself, while I have been awake longer than I thought possible.

I wish I could say I've been looking for you, Zak, that I have been on a quest, but the truth is, I've always known where you are. I've always been there. Watching you, trying to speak to you, desperate to steal even the smallest moments of your attention.

Look up. I'm there, against the ceiling, along the sky.

Look down. I'm there, on the floor, on the ground, gazing up at you.

Look all around. I surround you. I envelop you. I am in the air you breathe.

For years, I've tried to break through. Beat my fists against the invisible walls between us and screamed to you.

You've only ever heard whispers.

Until now. Now...

Look up. Look to the sun. The sky and the stars. There are worlds awaiting.

Look down. This earth, this soil, is not a conclusion. It is not *all*.

Look all around. There are people beyond people, Zak. There is something *else*, something *extra*, and you are closer to it than you realize.

But it, too, is closer to *you*.

It lurks and looms. It hides in the sunlight and laughs silently.

Zak.

Oh, Zak.

If only you knew.

If only you could *see*.

Zak.

Look *up*.

PART ONE

ZAK

ONE

Zak Killian knew it was crazy, but there were days—like this one—when he thought he might have a guardian angel.

He knew there was no such thing, of course. Guardian angels were superstition, like black cats causing bad luck. "Garbage," his dad called it. "Nonsense."

Still, even though he knew it was either garbage or nonsense, Zak couldn't help occasionally fantasizing that there was someone—some*thing*, maybe?—watching over him. Trying to protect him from harm.

It could only "try" because it was an angel, ethereal, incorporeal. It couldn't touch the world or interact with it. It could only advise him, whispering in a voice high and breathy. Warning him away from danger. It had never steered him wrong, this disembodied voice.

This voice that sounded like his own.

The voice sounding like his own sort of made sense if you stopped to think about it. Which he often did, like today, on the subway on his own for the first time.

He had finally persuaded his parents to let him take the subway to school when it started again in the fall, and this day was his summertime dry run. His parents were so overprotective it was ridiculous. Probably because he was an only child.

Well, and there was his health problem, too.

Zak placed one hand on his chest and the other tight against his ear. He listened to the thrumming, rushing bellow of his heart. So like the ocean.

He couldn't hear or feel anything amiss, but his doctors assured him there was indeed something wrong with his heart. "Nothing we can't control," they said. "If you listen and take your medicine and watch your diet, you're going to live a long, happy life."

Now he closed his eyes for a moment, letting the rocking motion of the subway soothe him. It was like a boat, in a way. With his eyes closed, he could almost hear gulls screaming against the wind, the *snap-hiss* of sailcloth. . . .

The train squealed and ground to a halt, jolting him out of his fantasy. And good thing, too. He'd been dreaming of boats for a month now. How weird was *that*? To the best of Zak's knowledge, he'd never been on a boat in his life. After the third or fourth dream of riding the waves, he'd asked his mother.

"Mom, have I ever been on a boat?"

Zak's mother had been packing her suitcase for the week she would spend out of the apartment while Dad lived with Zak. At first, distracted, she'd misunderstood, saying, "You want a *boat*? What on earth do you need a boat for?" And then, before he could clarify, she'd blown a stray golden-brown hair out of her eyes and chuckled and said, "No, wait, I'm sorry. I didn't—have you ever been on a boat?" She planted her fists on her hips like a comic book superhero, something she often did when she was deep in thought.

"I don't think so," she said after a moment or two. "There was one time when you were little—we were going to take the ferry to Governors Island, but . . ." She drifted off and shrugged, her expression sad.

Zak wondered if "we" included his father, or if they'd been fighting and divorce-bound even then. At twelve-going-on-thirteen, he was old enough and wise enough to recognize when he shouldn't push her for more information. He didn't need the whisper of a guardian angel to know that much.

So. No boats. What accounted for the dreams, then?

That question would have to wait. The train had stopped, and Zak had to get off in lower Manhattan. This wasn't his final stop, but it was where he needed to transfer from the 6 train to the R, which would take him back home to Brooklyn. The 6-to-R routine would be his daily commute home once school started up again in a few weeks. Today, he'd managed to get from Prospect Park in Brooklyn all the way to Wellington Academy in midtown Manhattan with no glitches. Now it was just a matter of reversing the route.

He shuffled out of the train with a cluster of commuters and made his way to the far end of the platform. When he arrived at his final destination, he would want to be on the first car because that would get him closer to the exit that was nearest to home. He was proud of himself for figuring this out. His dry run would be a total success.

"They call it a dry run," Dad had told him, "because fire-fighters used to practice drills without using water. So that was a dry run, and when they needed to use water, that was a wet run."

Dad was full of obscure facts like that. It came with being a history professor.

But his dry run hadn't been totally without glitches.

After arriving at Wellington Academy, he'd lingered for a few minutes, not wanting to turn around and go home after just arriving. He was alone in the city for the first time ever. So he'd wandered into the bodega across the street from Wellington Academy. It had a sign that read MOST EXCELLENT GOODS AND FOOD, which sounded—let's be honest—pretty freaking awe-some. He and Moira and Khalid had wanted to go inside for as long as they could remember, but they'd always been accompa-nied by parents or teachers, none of whom ever wanted to slip inside and sample the possibly forbidden delights of the store.

This had been his chance.

He'd gone inside and roamed the store's aisles for a couple of minutes . . . which was all the time it took, because the place was tiny and packed tight. Disappointingly, there was nothing really "most excellent" about the goods or the food. It was all stuff you could find in any store.

Still, he'd fished around in his pocket for a buck's worth of quarters and bought a small bag of gummi bears. Then, satisfied with his rebellious individuality, he'd left the store and headed back to the subway.

No.

The voice of his guardian angel. The voice of his garbage and nonsense.

Standing by the subway entrance had been a tall man in a long black coat. There was nothing strange or off about him, but when Zak had focused on him, the voice—so high, so young—had said again, *No.*

Maybe there *was* something wrong about the man. The black coat, in such hot, humid weather . . . And why was he just loitering by the subway? He didn't look like he was waiting for someone. Usually people fiddled with their cell phones or read a book or did *something* while waiting. This guy was just . . . *there.*

Zak had gnawed at his lower lip, then he'd waited for the light on Lexington Avenue to change and crossed the street to enter the subway there instead. As he waited for the train, he'd looked around for the man in black. Nothing. He'd felt a well of relief when he got on the train and the doors closed safely behind him.

And now, standing on a different platform, Zak heard the voice again. It said . . .

Well, that was crazy. What did *that* mean?

The sound of the train interrupted his thoughts. It was coming down the tunnel, but something sounded wrong. Instead of the clanking bash of the subway, that mechanical and rattling echo, he heard something different. It was a whisper rising to a roar.

Run, the voice in his head said again. It didn't shout; it just insisted. *Run now.*

He couldn't help it—a charge of absolute terror ran through him, borne on the words from the guardian angel. Something was coming. Something awful.

"Get out of here!" he yelled to the others on the platform. "We have to get out of here! Something's going to—"

Something splashed against him. His calves and shoes were suddenly cold and wet.

He looked up just in time to see a gushing wall of water filling the subway tunnel.

And then the screams started.

TWO

Zak would have stood frozen, rooted to that spot on the plat-form, if not for the guardian angel's voice continuing to urge him on. He spun and dashed around a column, then scrambled up the steps as fast as his legs could churn, leaving wet footprints on the concrete. At the top of the stairs, he paused for a single instant to catch his breath, then launched himself through the turnstile and fled up another flight of stairs and into the summer sunshine.

He realized that he had no idea where he was. Somewhere in lower Manhattan. On his way to Wellington Academy, he'd stayed underground in the subway station the whole time. Now he hadn't just lost his bearings; he'd never had them to begin with.

Pacing in a widening circle, he scanned the area for a cop, a firefighter, anyone with any kind of authority. No one else had run with him up the stairs. No one else had followed.

All that water . . . All of those people, drowning right now . . .

"Help!" Zak screamed to the pedestrians all around him. "The subway's flooding! Help!"

Most of the people on the sidewalk—even the ones not on their cell phones or plugged into earbuds—ignored him. Of the ones who didn't, most glanced in his direction, then kept walking.

But one guy—a big guy in jeans and a white T-shirt—stopped and cocked his head at Zak.

"What did you just say?"

"It's flooding down there!" Zak could hardly catch his breath. "A huge wave just came down the tunnel and—"

That was enough for the man, who pulled his cell phone from his pocket and ran to the subway entrance. He paused halfway down the stairs to turn back and point a threatening finger at Zak. "Do *not* come down here!" he ordered, then continued down the steps, barking into his phone the whole time.

Zak was trapped in a nightmare, one of the really bad ones where you're experiencing one thing but you're aware of something terrible and awful happening at the same time, not far away. Up here, in the open air, it seemed like just another too-hot summer day, with everyone going about their business as usual. Down below . . .

He tried not to picture the platform overrun with water. Tried not to imagine dead bodies floating up near the ceiling.

The sensation of being on a boat rushed him, and he swayed, grabbing the stairwell handrail for balance. He could feel water in his lungs. . . .

How long he stood there, clinging to the handrail, he did not know, but when he opened his eyes, the man who'd run into the station was coming up the stairs, glaring at Zak as though Zak had personally run his puppy through a shredder.

"How bad is it?" Zak choked out.

"Not bad at all," the man said, fuming. To his phone, he said, "Yeah, never mind," then slipped it into his pocket.

Never mind? What was wrong with this guy?

"Are you crazy?" Zak demanded. "People are dying! Aren't you, like, a cop or something?"

"No, I'm with Con Ed." When Zak said nothing, the man said, "The power company. I saw nasty stuff a while back when Hurricane Sandy hit Manhattan. I thought we were seeing something like that again. Thanks for getting my heart rate up, kid."

"What do you mean? Do something!"

"There's nothing *to* do, and you know it." The man kept coming up the stairs until he towered over Zak. "This stuff isn't funny."

Only he didn't say "stuff."

Zak trembled. He didn't understand what the man was getting at. He'd *seen* the water with his own eyes. Heard it with his own ears. He'd . . .

"You know what? I'm gonna teach you a lesson," the man said, and then clamped his fingers around Zak's wrist and dragged him down the stairs.

Zak thought of screaming but was too surprised to do so.

Down in the tunnel, where he'd expected to see a dirty aquarium of death, he saw instead the receding lights of the N train and some leftover straphangers loitering on the platform.

On the dry platform.

Well, *almost* dry. Where Zak had been standing was a shallow puddle, steadily fed from a smallish stream of water overhead.

"But—" he began.

"But nothing. This how you get your kicks when school's out for the summer? Joking about this?" The man pointed up.

Zak followed his gesture. Above them a pipe sagged slightly, broken at a weld seam. That was the source of the water.

A broken pipe.

A broken *pipe*?

"But I saw—" *And my guardian angel said . . .*

"Ever hear of the boy who cried wolf? Do they even teach you stuff like that these days?" Again, he didn't really say "stuff."

"What's your name?" the man demanded. "Where are your parents?"

In mere moments, Zak went from terror to relief and back to terror. At first he'd been afraid that the man would hurt him. But people who are going to hurt you don't usually want to call your parents. And then he realized that he was about to be in a huge amount of trouble.

The next thing he knew, the Con Ed man was dropping him off at home. And the next thing he knew after that, he was sitting in the living room of his apartment with his parents staring at him from the sofa.

It was weird seeing his parents in a room together. Each week they exchanged grim little smiles and terse words of advice as they swapped out of the apartment where Zak lived, but that was the sum total of their interactions these days. Until now, when Zak brought them together.

"What went through your head?" Dad asked. He was the more even-keeled one. The calmer one. Professor of history and

African American studies. Mom had the temper. "A little thing like some water and you go screaming about a flood? Are we supposed to let you go to school on your own when you can't even keep your wits about you when a pipe breaks?"

I saw it! Zak wanted to say, but didn't. Because, yeah, he'd seen the platform about to flood—had seen it with his own eyes.

But he'd also seen it utterly *not* flooded with those same eyes. As much as he wanted to believe that the station—and everyone in it—had been in danger, he couldn't deny the evidence.

"You can't go panicking like that," Mom said. "Your heart can't handle that kind of stress."

"I thought . . ." He stopped. He didn't know what to say. "I guess I thought I saw something. I made a mistake."

"You thought. You saw. Something." Mom. Biting into her words like undercooked pasta.

"You know those signs everywhere? 'If you see something, say something?' I thought I saw something."

"You thought you saw a *flood*, Zak. Not a package or a suitcase left on the platform." Dad folded his arms over his chest.

"No one thinks they see a flood," Mom said, not even looking at Dad. "You don't say, 'Is that a flood over there? Oops, no.' What's really going on here?"

Zak struggled. He didn't know what to say. He'd never been a good liar—Moira had a much better imagination, and Khalid was more convincing—so he usually tried to stick to the truth. But the truth wasn't going to help him in this case. He'd already told them everything except for—

Run. Run now.

—the bit about his guardian angel's voice. And he didn't think that part would help him.

Besides, his guardian angel had been totally wrong this time.

Garbage and nonsense. Dad was right.

"I thought I saw a flood," he said, his voice shrinking with every word. "I don't know what else to tell you. I thought the tunnel was flooded and it was coming toward us. Why else would I go running like that?"

Mom muttered something in Spanish, which she usually did only after being on the phone with La-La. The words were unfamiliar to Zak, whose Spanish was passable, so that meant they were probably swear words.

Dad shot a glare at Mom. He didn't speak much Spanish, but he knew the bad words pretty well.

"Am I punished?" Zak asked, even though he knew the answer already.

"Are you kidding me?" Dad asked. "I can't believe you even need to ask that question."

"You are so punished," Mom said, "that I don't even know what the punishment *is* yet. I am—" She broke off, sighed, then said, "*We are* so angry at you right now that we can't even begin to imagine an appropriate punishment."

So maybe we just skip the punishment this time, Zak thought, but was way too smart to say out loud. His parents wouldn't appreciate the humor. Not now.

"Go to your room," Dad ordered. Zak nearly jumped out of his chair at the opportunity to get away from his angry parents. "Your mother and I will figure out a fitting punishment."

"And then we'll *double it!*" Mom shouted as Zak disappeared into the hallway.

Zak flung himself onto his bed with all the outrage he could

16

muster. He didn't *deserve* to be punished. He'd *seen* something. He'd *heard* something.

If there really was a flood, they'd be singing a different tune, he thought. *I would probably be on TV as a hero for running and getting someone. And my parents would be all, "Oh my God, Zak, we thought we would lose you! You were so brave! We're so glad you got away!"*

Yeah.

If there had been a flood.

But there hadn't.

There *had* been water, though. Right? The voice had told him to run *before* the pipe sprayed him. There was something going on, something strange, something he couldn't identify. Even if he'd imagined the flood, he hadn't imagined the pipe and the water.

What's happening to me? Zak thought.

He rolled over onto his stomach. Even though it was still early, he was suddenly very tired, and the muted back-and-forth of his parents' voices through the wall lulled him to the edge of sleep.

And his guardian angel's voice—a sad, yearning, almost desperate whisper just as he drifted off: *I'm sorry.*

Or maybe he just imagined that.

THREE

I'm sorry was the most the guardian angel had ever said. It was actually a complete sentence. Usually, it was just a word or two, like *Run!* or *Run now!* Simple things. The voice couldn't—or wouldn't—say much. Sometimes Zak wasn't even sure it was a voice so much as a sense of the word, the underlying imperative of it.

But as he woke in the middle of the night, he heard words—more than one or two—jumbled together, as though fighting each other for primacy.

—free—

He blinked sleep out of his eyes.

—God—

God?

—Zak!

He sat up straight and slapped at the light switch, turning on the lamp, a scream tucked right behind his lips, eager to explode forth.

His name. It had said *his name.*

And for the first time, the voice was familiar. Not merely as the voice of his guardian angel. He'd always known and trusted the voice. And now he knew why.

—the secrecy—

"Tommy?" he asked the empty room. And a chill raced up his spine before evaporating at the base of his skull.

Tommy. Tommy, his imaginary friend. Tommy, who had gone away around the same time Moira's family moved to Brooklyn from Dublin. Zak had—if he was being honest—pretty much forgotten about his invisible buddy until this very moment, this moment of late-night/early-morning darkness and solitude. Being alone was nothing new to Zak. He hated it, hated the isolation and the sense that the world could have vanished outside his door and he wouldn't know. Maybe it came from being an only child.

But there was a special kind of aloneness that only filled the wee hours and that only happened to children, although Zak was too young to understand that. Children know true isolation in a way that adults have forgotten, forgotten like scraped knees and loose teeth and . . .

And imaginary friends.

He shook his head. It was crazy. Tommy had been a figment of his imagination, nothing more. This kind of thing happened to only children, he knew. It was no big deal. Tommy, like most imaginary friends, eventually went away once Zak had actual friends to play with. He'd known Khalid forever, but they'd only started school together when Moira's family arrived. And they'd become an inseparable trio and Tommy had gone away.

And now he was back.

—God—

Zak spun around in bed. The voice had been right behind—

—free—

He turned again. Nothing. No one there. He rolled out of bed and stood in the center of his room. He realized he was panting. He touched his chest by reflex; his heart pumped normally.

I'm losing my mind.

Nothing. No answer from the air.

"Tommy?" he whispered again. "Tommy, is that you?"

Zak!

—free—

Beware!—

—secrecy!

The chill was back, this time spreading down along his shoulder blades. Why was he so scared? Tommy had been his friend.

Yeah, and then you stopped talking to him. Maybe he's really, really pissed.

That thought pummeled his chest; his heart thudded. He suddenly pictured a ghostly imaginary friend, angry and plotting revenge, coming back after years in limbo with . . .

With what? With a ghost knife? What could a ghost do to him, anyway?

"I'm sorry," he said, not realizing how similar to his guardian angel's voice his own sounded in that moment. "I'm sorry, Tommy."

Was his guardian angel really an angel? Was it looking out for him, like when it warned him away from the man in the black coat? Or was it tricking him, like when it told him to run from the flood that wasn't there?

Was it even—he shuddered—making him *see* things? It was one thing to hear an occasional voice or experience a sense of something. But to see a wave of water where there was none . . .

Am I losing my mind? Am I going crazy?

No. He couldn't be. The pipe. The pipe had burst. Far from a flood, sure, but it was water from nowhere, like the flood he'd seen.

Unless it was just a coincidence. That was possible.

Maybe I am crazy.

His heart pounded. He was supposed to tell his mom or dad if he felt something—*"Anything at all!"* they'd insisted—wrong in his chest. He didn't think this qualified. It was just plain old fear.

I'm not running to them like a baby. It's all in your head, Zak. That's all it is. It's all dreams and . . . and garbage and nonsense, like Dad says.

He left the light on and crawled back into bed. Somehow, he sensed that he was alone again, and suddenly he was very tired.

Free. God.

What did it mean?

He fell asleep wondering.

It's all in your head, he'd thought. But then again, crazy people had it "all in their heads," too, didn't they?

Zak didn't think he was going crazy, but he also thought that crazy people probably didn't think so, either.

He fidgeted with his breakfast. Dad had made huevos rancheros. The only time Zak got anything remotely Latin to eat was when Dad was cooking; Mom "refused to be a stereotype." She made killer lasagna and chicken parm, but she didn't know an enchilada from a taquito.

Dad didn't have the cultural baggage, and he'd worked his way through college as a short-order cook in a Mexican restaurant in Greenwich Village. The huevos were particularly spicy today, just the way Zak liked them, but all he could manage was to push the eggs around in the bean sauce, thinking about the voice in his head, thinking about Tommy again for the first time in forever.

"Something wrong?" Dad asked, sliding into a seat across the table with his own plate of eggs.

Zak considered telling his father what he'd heard. But he figured after the disaster on the subway platform (or, rather, the *non*-disaster), that Dad was fed up with hearing about things Zak had "imagined."

"Nothing," he muttered.

Dad sighed. "You know, you can be angry at your mom and me for punishing you, or you can think about what you did wrong and maybe direct some of that energy toward not getting punished again in the future."

Dad was big on "directing energy" to the right places. Zak was tired of it, honestly. When he'd gotten up this morning, he'd been surprised to find Dad in the apartment at all—it was Mom's turn this week. But Dad was on summer hours from the university; he could work from home. Zak's punishment was a week's grounding, so Dad would stay here, work from home, and make sure Zak went nowhere and had exactly zero fun.

Three more weeks until school started, and one-third of them was now a total waste.

Stupid guardian angel.

"Want to talk about it?" Dad asked. "Maybe tell me why you lied?"

Zak shrugged. There was no point to the talk. If he told his dad the truth, Dad wouldn't believe him anyway—he'd already proved that by punishing Zak in the first place. So his only option other than just keeping his mouth shut was to *really* lie this time and come up with some reason why he'd told the "story" about the subway flooding.

Nah. Better just to say nothing.

"You know, Mom and I are just worried—"

"You're *always* worried," Zak snapped. "That's all you *ever* do. Well, I'm fine. My heart is fine. I'm not *dying* or anything. I'm *fine*."

Ah, crud. It had felt good—amazing, really—to go off on Dad like that, but there would be a price to pay. Zak managed to keep staring at Dad for a few seconds but quickly felt hot shame along his cheeks; as if controlled by some external force, his eyes drifted down to his plate. He'd stirred the huevos rancheros into a tumorous mass of black sludge.

Dad cleared his throat. "Well, fine. And if you're not going to finish those huevos, just put your dish in the sink and head to your room."

Zak did as he was told. His bedroom was cramped and small, but it was *his*. He was surrounded by the things he loved—old books, toys that he was too old for but secretly still adored, his iPad, his Xbox. Being confined to his room for a week wasn't as big a torture as his parents liked to think it was.

A moment later Dad appeared in the doorway, arms folded over his chest. He pursed his lips, then held out a hand.

Zak sighed and handed over his Xbox controller.

"And the iPad," Dad said.

Zak surrendered the iPad, too.

"What am I supposed to do all day?"

"Read a book," Dad suggested, and closed the door.

Read a book. Yeah, right. Usually, Zak loved reading, but he'd read every book in the house (even a few of the adult books he

23

wasn't supposed to read), and he didn't feel like rereading anything. He could have finished up his summer reading list, but that felt less like fun and more like work. Besides, he didn't want the silence. He was petrified of the quiet, all of a sudden. Quiet meant that he would hear the voice if it came back.

When it came back. He somehow knew that it would definitely, definitely come back. And for the first time, that frightened him. He'd thought he'd understood the voice, the guardian angel. It had made him feel not just special but also powerful. For his whole life, his parents had treated him like something made of filament, like one of those lace cookies that fell apart if you picked them up too fast.

One more reason he hated solitude: nothing to do but to think. About his parents and their coddling. About his heart.

"You're delicate," they told him. *"Your heart isn't like other kids'. You have to be careful."*

Being alone sucked. When other people were around, he could sink into them, enjoy them. But when he was alone, he suffered a powerful, painful sensation that something was missing. It throbbed like a missing limb. He'd read that people who had arms or legs amputated could still feel them. That was how Zak felt when he was alone—as though something had been cut off him and stolen away, but he could still sense its weight. And he needed it back.

"You're all we have"—another one of his parents' favorite pronouncements.

He was tired of being all they had. Tired of being told to be careful. He felt fine. Sometimes he had little hiccups in his chest, but no big deal. Doctors and parents didn't know everything.

They didn't *need* to know everything.

He took his daily verapamil pill and settled in for the long, boring wait. The room was too quiet. Out in the living room, Dad would be propped up on the couch with his laptop, pecking away, his computer glasses perched comically at the end of his nose. Zak wanted to open his bedroom door just so that he could hear the occasional clack of the keys.

But then he had a better idea. He rummaged in his nightstand drawer and came up with his old iPod. It was three or four years old and didn't really hold a charge anymore. He'd stopped playing with it when he'd gotten the iPad.

But as long as he left it plugged in, it should work. He fired up the video chat app.

Zak's best friend was Khalid, and his other best friend was Moira. He hoped that he would never have to decide which one was his *best*, best friend, because that choice was impossible. He'd known Khalid longer—he couldn't remember *not* knowing Khalid, in fact—but Moira was, well, she was Moira. She was smarter than any three kids at Wellington Academy combined . . . *and* she had the highest Xbox Live Gamerscore of anyone he knew, under the Gamertag DeadSeriousIrishGurl.

Years ago, the first time he'd visited Moira at home, he'd asked for a glass of water. Her mom, Mrs. O'Grady, had said, "Sure, laddie," and Zak had felt as though he'd heard English being spoke for the first time. That night, he'd asked his mother why Mrs. O'Grady spoke the way she did.

"She's from Ireland, *cariño*." For once, the pet name from childhood hadn't bothered him; he'd been too distracted. "It's just her accent. The same way La-La has an accent."

"La-La's from Puerto Rico, not Ireland."

"Different island is all." Mom had shrugged and then settled in as Zak peppered her with a million questions about Ireland, the Irish, and red hair and green eyes.

The next day, he'd overheard his mother on the phone with La-La. "Oh, it's definitely puppy love. Totally harmless at this age. It's actually sort of cute."

His cheeks had flamed at her words. It was ridiculous. *Puppy love*. His mother was clueless. Sure, he *liked* Mrs. O'Grady. What wasn't to like? She was sweet and kind, with a cheerful smile and impossibly red hair and bright green eyes. And that lilting brogue. He couldn't help it—he just liked being around her and hearing her voice. Moms didn't know *everything*.

Moira could imitate her mom's brogue—she had lost her traces of Irish accent after a year or so in the States—and occasionally said, "Sure, laddie," in that special way when Zak asked a question, but he was reasonably certain she was just kidding around, not outright mocking him.

If he wanted to figure out the voices in his head, Moira was the one to call, the supergenius. But if he just wanted a sympathetic ear, it had to be Khalid.

He tapped Khalid's name, and a moment later Khalid grinned out of the screen at Zak.

"Zak Attack!" Khalid hooted, and in that instant, Zak knew that he wouldn't say anything at all about the dreams, the voices, the subway.

Khalid's enthusiasm was like lighter fluid on kindling—once he started talking, it was impossible to be upset or melancholy. Within seconds of seeing Khalid on the tiny iPod screen, Zak had forgotten all about the previous night's "visit." When Khalid suggested they hang out, Zak shrugged it off with a short excuse about being grounded, offering no details. And the great thing about Khalid was that he never asked for details.

"I assume you don't deserve your punishment," Khalid said.

"Thanks for that."

"Team Zak one-double-oh."

Khalid was fond of saying "one-double-oh" instead of "one hundred percent." He thought it made him cool. Sometimes Zak agreed and sometimes he didn't. Right now, he did.

"Can we Xbox it?" Khalid was saying.

"No, Dad took the controller."

Khalid pulled a face. "Man, it sucks that your dad's a gamer, too. Otherwise, he probably wouldn't have even *thought* of that. You know what you need to do?"

"What do I need to do?"

Chortling, Khalid said, "Once you're a free man again, we'll go to the game store and buy another controller. And you hide it in your room somewhere. So the next time you're grounded, your dad will take the controller that's sitting out, and then you can use the hidden one, and we can totally gang up on Moira on Live."

"You're an evil genius," Zak said in awe.

"Moira may hog all the As, but I'm devious," Khalid said with modesty. "I should be a supervillain."

"You totally should be."

They spent some time figuring out what kind of supervillain Khalid should be, and then Zak heard his father stirring out in the hallway. He signed off quickly and shoved the iPod under his bed just as Dad knocked on his door.

"Yeah?"

Dad opened the door and poked his head in. "What are you doing in here?"

"Nothing." Which wasn't a lie; at that precise moment, Zak wasn't doing anything at all. Dad hadn't said, "What *were* you doing in here?"

"I thought I heard you talking."

Zak shrugged. Not a lie because, well, no words. You couldn't lie without words, right? Let Dad draw his own conclusions.

"I know you're angry at your mom and me right now, but trust me—you're getting off easy. If you'd pulled this on your grandfather . . ."

Zak tuned him out. When Dad started talking about growing up in Harlem in the eighties, Zak lost interest. Whatever.

". . . so this is why we had to do this. Do you understand?"

Zak shrugged again. He knew his parents hated when he did that.

"Not talking? Fine. Maybe you'll talk to the doctor."

The *doctor*? "I'm not sick."

"Oh, he *does* have a voice!" Dad shook his head. "Not Dr. Shamir. This is someone else. Someone to talk to about what you did yesterday."

"What doctor?"

"Her name is Melinda Campbell," Dad told him, "and maybe you'll be willing to tell her what you wouldn't tell your mother and me. We're going tonight. Your mother is coming here after work, and we'll go together. So"—he checked his watch—"get a shower and something to eat."

Zak grumbled his way through a shower and a late lunch, then retreated to his room again to await Mom's arrival. What was the deal with this doctor, anyway? He retrieved the iPod from its hiding place and did a search for *melinda campbell* and *doctor* and *new york city*.

The first hit showed a white woman, maybe Mom's age, maybe a little older.

CAMPBELL, Melinda, MD, PhD, it said.

And under that:

Specializing in childhood traumas and disorders. Available by appointment only. Contact Youth Psychiatric Services at . . .

There was an e-mail link, as well as a phone number, but Zak had stopped reading.

She wasn't just a doctor. She was a psychiatrist. His parents were taking him to a head doctor.

His parents thought he was crazy.

FOUR

Dr. Campbell's office was in the Village, so they had to walk to the F train. It was August-hot, but the temperature between Zak and his parents was frosty. No one spoke except to point out when a light had changed.

Two blocks before the subway station, Zak steeled himself. He would have to go down into the subway for the first time since the previous day's vision of flood and death. His parents would be watching him carefully, he knew. He didn't want to do or say anything that would make them think he was any crazier than they already did.

It was one thing to suspect himself. It was another thing to have his parents think he was a nut job.

As they took the first steps down into the subway, Zak forced himself not to look around. Then he wondered if that was strange, so he looked around a little bit—what he hoped was a normal amount.

Dirty tiled walls. A sign reminding people that rat poison had been dispersed in this station recently. A slew of posters—for movies, books, TV shows, plays, college courses—some of which had been defaced with random mustaches and an assortment of body parts. People milling about, restless in the heat and humidity.

Down on the tracks, a rat poked its nose at a crumpled Doritos bag, clearly not affected by the poison.

Nothing strange.

No flood.

No voice.

And then.

—secrecy—

Zak blinked and composed himself. He would not—he could not—betray any hint of hearing Tommy to his parents.

Don't—

—tell—

No kidding.

"There's no reason to be afraid," Dad said suddenly.

"She's just going to talk to you," Mom added.

"I'm not afraid," Zak said a little too quickly.

"You looked a little tense."

Silence, Zak realized, was his best defense. He crossed his arms over his chest and stared at the rat, which by now had forced its snout into the Doritos bag and was no doubt scarfing down whatever crumbs remained.

The F clanked and rattled into place at the station. Zak settled in.

The train pulled out, swaying that way subway trains did, in that way Zak imagined boats did. He closed his eyes and reached out for the feel of the breeze, the creak of the masts.

For the voice.

He couldn't help himself. Once, he'd scraped his arm on a rough tree in Prospect Park, tearing a patch of skin from his elbow almost up to his shoulder. It hadn't been *that* bad—Mom called it a "surface abrasion"—but it had been broad and almost epically tender for a few days. And yet, he'd been unable to keep from running his fingers along his arm's textured surface, despite admonitions to leave it alone, despite the tickle that crossed the line to pain without warning.

He sought out the voice for the same reason, for the same unknowable reason. He couldn't help himself. If it *was* Tommy . . .

The subway moved to and fro, its rhythm somehow liquid. No voice, but he could swear he heard . . .

The cry of a gull . . .

A gull? What's a gull? How do I know?

A bird. A gull was a bird.

No. That was the squeal of the brakes.

But it wasn't. It was a bird. Screaming and squawking as it flapped its way between the masts. The sails cracked in the wind, their snaps like whips.

"You keep a-skylarkin'," a voice bellowed, *"and I'll have ye keel-hauled right quick!"*

Not *the* voice, but a voice that filled him with a familiar dread. He flinched.

The ship rocked to port. The mainmast creaked.

"Trim the sails!" the voice barked. *"Trim 'em, and trim 'em good, God blast yer eyes! Ye whistled for the wind, and ye got it, so trim 'em!"*

Something was in his hands. A rope, rough and thick and heavy. It burned his fingers as it slid through them.

The ship rocked again, listing to starboard this time. Above, the clouds angered to purple, and rain lashed down from a suddenly split sky. And then the ship's hull juddered, as though it had dragged along the ocean floor, but they were miles from land in any direction. The ship vibrated once more, shaking him, threatening to knock him down, and a voice said, "Zak. Zak, get up, we're here," and the ship was gone, the sea was gone, it was just him and his parents and the F train.

"I'm okay," he said immediately, blinking away the dream. His parents shared a significant look that Zak knew translated, roughly, to:

Are you going to ask him?

You ask him.

I don't want to ask him.

I'm not going to ask him.

Mom relented. "Are you getting enough sleep at night?" she asked.

"I'm fine," he insisted, shoving his way out of the train. He wasn't sure, though.

Out of the subway, they emerged at Sixth Avenue and West Fourth. They crossed the avenue and passed Christopher Park on their way to Dr. Campbell's Perry Street office.

"It's interesting to watch the evolution of neighborhoods," Dad was saying. He couldn't help himself—he always had to fill uncomfortable silences. He was so used to lecturing all the time. "It used to be that the Village was its own sort of enclave, but recently SoHo has started making inroads. When you don't have any sort of definitive boundaries for things, history becomes the only dividing line. And people don't pay much attention to history. So you get overlap and bleed-through. The Village was originally—"

"Not. Now," Mom said in a brittle tone. Dad frowned but stopped talking.

Zak liked lower Manhattan, the Village especially. It felt like it was part of a different world from the rest of Manhattan, which was set off in a rigid grid of streets intersecting avenues. The Village was a ramble of streets that crisscrossed and ran diagonally and wound around parks and blocks—rhombuses and triangles and the occasional trapezoid, not squares and rectangles.

Secrecy—

Don't tell . . .

Free . . .

Zak ignored the voice, concentrating on walking straight ahead. Dr. Campbell's office was a second-floor walk-up over a flower shop. From the outside of the building, Zak expected something dark, walnutty. *Baroque* was the word Moira used to describe old-fashioned rooms with wood paneling and brass ornaments. Zak prepared himself for something seriously baroque.

But Dr. Campbell's waiting room was, instead, white-clean—sharp lines, no nonsense. Fresh white walls that gleamed. Shining black and sparkling chrome accents.

Zak waited—alone—in the outer office while his parents went in first for a few minutes. He barely had time to pick up a weathered old iPad tethered to the coffee table, when the door opened and his parents came out. Dr. Campbell stood in the doorway, smiling.

She wore a gray skirt with a light green shirt and an expression that was supposed to be reassuring. But Zak knew her job was to rummage around inside his head. He didn't relish the prospect. What was in his head was *his*, and he didn't intend to give it away.

"Zak?" she said. "Do you mind if we talk a little, just you and me?"

He absolutely minded, but his parents' faces reminded him that he had no choice in the matter. He went inside.

The inner office was also painted white, with a glass-topped desk in one corner. There was a sofa against the opposite wall, under a window, and a comfortable chair facing it. She directed him to the sofa. He sat down and pressed himself into a corner, then folded his arms over his chest.

Dr. Campbell sat in the chair and propped a notepad on her crossed legs. She smiled again at Zak, but the smile only reminded him of the bleached bones of the Jolly Roger, the flag pirates flew on the high seas. She was so very, very white, even in the late heat of August. Didn't she ever go outside? At all?

"Zak," she said calmly, "what we have here is a dilemma. You know what that means, right?"

He bristled. He wasn't an idiot. "No kidding."

The smile again. He didn't like it. Not at all. "You know that I'm going to talk to your parents. That's sort of the whole point of you being here. But because you know I'm going to talk to them, you're not inclined to tell me certain things, are you?"

He shrugged. He hadn't planned on telling her much of anything anyway. There was nothing *to* tell her.

She went on. "So, here's the deal: I'll only talk to your parents in generalities. I'm not going to tell them specifics. So, for example, let's say you've been thinking a lot about red apples. And you can't stop thinking about them. I'll tell your parents that you're having obsessive thoughts and that it has to do with food and I'll recommend some steps they can take to help you and some things you can do, too, but I won't mention red apples, or even apples at all. Is that okay?"

Zak shrugged again. Whatever.

"Zak," she said, tilting her head the way people did with puppies and babies, "this goes a lot better if you speak up. I'm really just here to help you."

"I don't need help." There. How did she like that for *speaking up*?

Don't tell—

"Why do you think you're here, then?"

"My parents made me come here."

"You know why, right?"

He heaved out the most annoyed, exasperated sigh in his arsenal.

"It's about what you said you saw in the subway yesterday. Why would you lie about something like that? Unless . . ." She paused, tapped her notepad with her pen. "Unless you *did* see it."

He had seen it. Of course he had. But he knew that only crazy people saw things that weren't there. And he wasn't going to let her call him crazy.

So he said nothing. He frowned and looked out the window. Perry Street bustled below him in the early evening light.

Dr. Campbell let the silence hang for a moment. "You have a heart condition," she said out of nowhere. "How do you feel about that?"

Without meaning to, Zak put a hand against his heart. It was still thumping away reliably, as usual. He hated being reminded of it.

"I'm fine," he told her. "I feel fine. My real doctor says I'm fine."

"I didn't ask how you felt. I asked how you felt *about* it."

"Does it matter? I can't do anything about it."

She actually laughed at that—a short, huffed "Ha!" that pleased him for some reason. She seemed to relax a bit, and her smile became warmer and more genuine. "This is true, Zak. Very true. You have a great perspective on it."

He hadn't expected a compliment. He uncrossed his arms and put his hands palms-down on his knees. "I don't have much of a choice. It's my heart. It does its thing and I do mine."

"So, if you've come to terms with your heart condition, then is there something else bothering you? Talking about it doesn't always make it go away, but it can make it better."

Secrecy—

Don't tell—

He couldn't tell her about the guardian angel. He wouldn't. That was a step too far. But it was true that things were bothering him, and maybe she was right—maybe talking about them would help a little bit.

"I've been having weird dreams," he admitted. "About boats."

"Boats?" She said it with such incredulity that he expected her to write it on the notepad and circle it with big, overlapping loops. But she just kept tapping the pen on the pad. "What about them?"

"Old boats," he said, warming, leaning forward. It *did* feel good to talk about it.

He told her that he'd been dreaming of boats—sailing ships from olden times—for weeks now. Sometimes the skies were clear and the dreams were just pleasant, if confusing. Other times, though, like on the subway, the sea churned and roared like a thing alive. That was when the dreams took on the character of nightmares.

"And the weird thing"—he'd almost said *crazy thing*, but he wanted to avoid that word—"is that I've never been on a boat in my life! So how do I even know enough about them to dream so much?"

Dr. Campbell nodded. "That's a great question, Zak. And we've run out of time, so we're going to talk about it next time, okay?"

Zak checked the clock on the wall. To his shock, they *were* out of time. He'd been talking to Dr. Campbell about his dreams for almost an hour.

She held the door for him as he exited to the outer office. His parents arranged for another appointment in a few days' time, and then they all left together, and it felt almost normal. He even waved good-bye to Dr. Campbell on the way out.

Zak had the feeling that things would be different now. Talking about the dreams *had* made him feel better. And that night, he didn't hear the voice and he didn't even dream about boats.

He did, though, wake up in the middle of the night.

Outside.

In lower Manhattan, far from his home in Brooklyn.

With cops surrounding him slowly.

FIVE

The world filtered in too slowly and too quickly at the same time; Zak was overwhelmed by the input, the noise, the sights, the smells. The feel of hard concrete under his bare feet. The warm breeze ruffling his pajamas.

He was outside. He had gone to sleep in his bedroom, and now he was outside.

"... seriously, kid..." someone was saying, but Zak brushed it aside, chasing something else, another voice, *the* voice—

—*look up*—

It was speaking to him, so clear and so strong for the first time *ever*, and he strove to listen, pushing past the other voices.

"—Bellevue?"

"Get me a car—"

Zak flicked his eyes left and right. Three cops, arrayed around him. Moving slowly, unthreateningly. No one had drawn a gun. Not yet.

Outside. Definitely outside. There was a chain-link fence in front of him. Construction equipment all around.

And a sign. 9/11 MEMORIAL MUSEUM, with an arrow pointing off.

Too much happening all at once. He staggered, and one of the cops moved forward as if to catch him, but he regained his balance and righted himself.

"Kid, just take a deep breath and—"

Why wouldn't they just. Shut. Up. For a minute. A single minute. He needed to hear—

And the gulls cried again, so loudly that Zak gasped and jerked his shoulders in shock. The sky above was black, star-speckled, but it was also—somehow, at the same time—clouded and roiling with incipient rain. The mast creaked; the sails cracked.

It happened right here, Zak realized. *This is where the boat was.*

But how was that possible? He looked around, ignoring the cops, and was stunned when he looked past the fence to find the looming, lofty height of the Freedom Tower. He had sleep-walked to lower Manhattan, to Ground Zero, to One World Trade.

—look up—

I was on the train going under *this spot before. When I had the dream.*

He knew it like he knew his own heart: The boat had been here. Someone had whistled for the wind, God blast their eyes, and the wind had come and—

Impossible. How could it be? A boat *here?* It was too far from shore, from both the East and Hudson Rivers. A boat couldn't get here.

"Kid," a cop said, coming closer, "if you don't start talking to us, we're going to have to—"

Zak ignored him, straining for the only voice he cared about.

40

And it came to him. Came hard and powerful, like someone had cranked up the volume on Zak's psychic earbuds.

I am in darkness.

Darkness and quiet.

For so long.

And then there is light.

And then there is loud . . .

Zak screamed at the sudden clap of thunder that exploded between his ears. He dropped to the sidewalk and slapped his palms to either side of his head. The world had erupted in a fountain of light and sound, roaring out of a dark silence that had been both perfect and infinite. He whimpered.

Look up.

Look down.

Look all around.

Oh, Zak.

"That's it," a cop said, and Zak felt hands on him. He didn't care.

If only you could see, Tommy said.

And then, *Help me, Zak,* and it occurred to Zak for the very first time that maybe he himself was the guardian angel.

Wind whipped past him, and the wind had shape, had form, somehow, and it *slithered* more than blew, with an almost tactile, greased sensation, like having oily feathers dragged along his body. He caught a glimpse of blue, gold, and red before the colors flickered into darkness.

"Are you Tommy?" he asked, on his knees, gazing up at an image that flickered back and forth between the Freedom Tower and a sailing ship's crow's nest. When he received no response, he shouted, "Is that who you are? Are you back? Is it you, Tommy?"

Don't tell. They're lying—

—secrecy—

Only the voice didn't say *secrecy*, Zak realized as the police handcuffed him. It had *never* been saying *secrecy*.

Secrecy was a blur, two words merging.

Secret.

Sea.

Secret Sea, said the voice again as Zak was hauled to his feet by two police officers and carried to a waiting ambulance.

SIX

They handcuffed him gently, and they handled him gently, too. No bruises; not even any sore muscles.

As they pulled him away from the World Trade Center, the voice became softer, the image of the storm-mottled sky weaker. He closed his eyes tight, trying to focus beyond the voices of the cops, beyond their hands on him, trying desperately to hold tight to the voice and the ship and the storm.

Close by, there was a police station. Or a police office. Or a police bunker. Zak wasn't sure what the correct term was. By the time they got him there—and, truthfully, it was a matter of minutes, if that long—Zak had calmed considerably. He was a child in the arms of men with guns and nightsticks. At first he'd thrashed against them, mad for the voice, desperate to return to it. But it was ridiculous to fight them. He went limp and they carried him off and now he was in a small, badly lit room with pockmarked greenish walls. It smelled of old cigarettes, older coffee, and body odor.

There was a steel loop bolted to the table, where, he imagined, they could attach a prisoner's handcuffs, but they had removed his cuffs when they brought him in here.

He was alone. He cradled his head in his hands.

Think, Zak. Think it through.

Alone again. He gritted his teeth together.

The voice was gone, but his memories of it lingered, like a strong after-scent of perfume. Or sea air.

A boat. There'd been a boat at the World Trade Center. He was sure of that.

He was equally certain that the voice he'd heard—the voice he'd *been* hearing—was that of Tommy. His imaginary friend, no longer imaginary? Speaking of a secret sea, warning him not to tell. Talking about

—look up—

Yeah, that.

He looked up from the table. There was a window cut into the wall opposite him, looking into a room much like this one. A boy of Zak's age stared through the window. The boy wore a Teenage Mutant Ninja Turtles pajama shirt much like Zak's. He had a thatch of thick, black curly hair that needed to be cut, eyebrows that were a little too bushy, and a complexion like candied walnuts. He was startlingly familiar, and Zak felt a flush of embarrassment an instant later when he realized—*duh*—that the kid was, in fact, himself. That was no window—it was a mirror.

He'd seen enough cop shows to know that someone was watching from the other side.

Didn't recognize myself. Didn't recognize my own reflection. That can't be good. That has to be a sign of serious crazy.

The door opened, and a woman in a police uniform entered. She glanced at the mirror, then sat down across from Zak.

"Hi, there. My name's Judy. What's yours?"

Her nameplate read JEFFERSON. Judy Jefferson.

He shrugged. "Zak." He wondered exactly how much trouble he was in. If they didn't know his last name, they couldn't call his parents, right?

"Zak. Zak what?"

He said nothing.

"Zak, I can't have you shutting down like this. Do you know how you got here?"

"The police brought me."

"Right, right. But do you know how you got to the World Trade Center?"

He shrugged again.

"We have some video footage and eyewitness testimony. . . ." She walked him through what the police knew—he'd emerged from the A train over on Fulton and walked, barefoot, to the World Trade Center, where he'd stopped. Some late-night pedestrians had seen him and summoned a police officer from a nearby kiosk. "You were very lucky," she summed up. "You could have gotten hurt. Or *been* hurt."

Zak grimaced. He was all too aware of what could have happened to him. His parents drilled the dangers of the city into him at every turn, more so now that he would be traipsing off to school by himself every morning.

"Has anything like this ever happened to you before?" Judy asked. Translation: *Are you always crazy, or is this a special occasion?*

Better not to say anything, maybe. He folded his arms over

his chest and tried to think. Was there any way to get out of this without landing in serious trouble? Probably not. Once the police were involved, *serious trouble* seemed to be a bare minimum. But he had to try. If he could talk his way out of here and get home before Dad woke up and realized he was missing . . .

The door opened just then, and a man in a rumpled business suit stepped inside. He nodded to Judy and then stood near the door, saying nothing.

"Is there maybe someone I can call for you?" Judy asked. "Mom or Dad? A grandparent?"

Gnawing his bottom lip, Zak pondered. He couldn't just sit here all night and into the morning. He had to say *something*. But the idea of waking up one of his parents right now . . . No way. He had to avoid them.

"You could call Khalid," he blurted without thinking. But, yeah, that made sense. Khalid could get *his* parents to help out.

"Khalid?" Judy and the business suited guy exchanged a glance. "Who's Khalid?"

"Khalid Shamoon," Zak said. "I can't remember his phone number." Which was true—Khalid's number was programmed into Zak's cell and into the landline at the apartment. "It's probably under his father's name. Ozzie Shamoon."

"Ozzie," Judy repeated.

"It's his nickname. Short for Osama."

Judy's eyes widened, and the man by the door snorted a snort that seemed to say, *Are you kidding me?* But he walked out, leaving Zak alone with Judy again. She asked if he was hungry or thirsty. He asked for a glass of water, and a uniformed police officer brought one a minute later, without Judy's moving a muscle. Zak knew he was being watched through the mirror, but this proof of it was still unnerving.

He waited for the man in the business suit to return, but he didn't. The next time the door opened, it was Zak's dad, bleary eyed and wearing jeans with a T-shirt and an expression that told Zak that the police were the very, very least of his problems.

Of course Mr. Shamoon had called Dad as soon as he heard from the cops. Of course. Just like a grown-up. You couldn't trust anyone over eighteen. That was the kid code. He wasn't angry at Mr. Shamoon for tattling on him; he was angry at himself for thinking Mr. Shamoon wouldn't in the first place.

Dad signed some papers and talked to some cops and then hustled him into a cab outside. Zak felt a strong tug in the direction of the Freedom Tower and had to clutch the frame of the cab to force himself inside.

The sky was just lightening over the East Village as they drove across town toward the East River. Dad told the driver to take the Manhattan Bridge, then sighed heavily. Zak waited for him to say something, but nothing came. The silence was awful.

"Are you going to tell Mom?" Zak asked after an extended quiet.

Dad laughed without mirth, a short, miserable bark. "Am I going to tell Mom? Are you really asking me that, Zak? Of *course* I'm telling your mother. What do you think this is? Some kind of guy thing? I let you run around the city at all hours and keep it between us? Are you crazy?"

Dad's tone—acerbic and angry—hurt almost as much as his last question. Zak wanted to snap, *You're the one who's making me see a shrink—you tell me if I'm crazy!* But instead he pulled himself into a ball and huddled against the door, as far away from his father as possible. He'd never heard his dad so upset.

"What were you thinking?" Dad insisted, glaring at Zak. "What made you think you could just sneak out of the house and gallivant around the city like that? What are you *doing*, Zak? What is going through your mind when you pull something like this?"

Zak could have answered, but he was afraid the answer would only make things worse. Because telling his father that he hadn't "pulled" anything, that he hadn't thought he could "just sneak out of the house," that he hadn't made any decisions at all . . .

That would be like admitting to his father that he *was* crazy. Might as well ask to be fitted for a straitjacket and locked up in Bellevue, where they sent the crazy people.

"This isn't cool, Zak," Dad said, his eyes troubled, his expression pained. "Your mom . . . This is going to kill your mother. Of all the places in the city to go, you had to go to Ground Zero. The place she hates more than anything else in the world."

Right. Mom's brother. He'd died there way back before Zak was born, back in 2001, when what was now one tower had been two. Twins. Zak had seen them on old TV shows and in old movies. Mom's brother had died—

Tomás.

Mom's brother . . . Zak's dead uncle.

His name had been Tomás.

"You mean Uncle Tomás, right?" Zak asked, his voice barely a whisper. He was hoping to be wrong. He was hoping that he'd remembered the name wrong, that it wasn't Tomás. . . .

"Yeah, Tomás." Dad was wistful, for a moment bled of his anger. Remembering.

Tomás. Thomas. Tommy.

Zak held his head in his hands. *What is going on? What's going on in me?*

SEVEN

His parents usually argued quietly, and Zak was pretty sure they thought he couldn't hear them at those times, even though he could.

Now, though, they weren't even trying to be quiet.

Two days after his sleepwalking experience, through the closed door of Dr. Campbell's office, Zak could hear his mother's voice—high, trembling—competing with his father's—deeper, slower. They'd been yelling at each other for a good five minutes straight, according to the clock on the wall.

"—can't even keep him in the *apartment*, much less the borough!" That was Mom.

"*You* try watching a kid when you're asleep at three in the morning!" Dad.

They went back and forth. Accusing. Defending. Zak put his hands over his ears, but he could still hear them. Maybe he should have told them the truth. Maybe he should have told them about Tommy, the voice, the boat, the dream. The sleepwalking. But every time he considered it, the truth seemed too enormous and too fluid to contain, as if he'd tried to gather the ocean in his arms and lift it up out of the world.

He couldn't tell them anything, so he'd told them nothing. And so they argued.

They were arguing because of him. When they'd divorced, they spent a lot of time telling him it wasn't his fault. He'd gotten used to hearing them argue, dismissing it as Parent Stuff. But this time it *was* his fault that they were yelling at each other. His fault and nothing more.

Dr. Campbell interrupted them. Zak could hear her voice, low and murmured, but he couldn't make out the words. His parents' voices eventually went mute, and a moment later the door opened.

Mom's makeup was a mess, cried into a frozen mask that made Zak think of old Native American warriors he'd seen in movies. Dad's eyes were bloodshot. They both looked like they wanted to be anywhere but in Dr. Campbell's outer office, anywhere but near each other and Zak.

"Zak? Come on in and let's talk a bit, hmm?" Dr. Campbell beckoned from just inside the door.

Zak had to force himself to stand, to walk past his parents. They'd never hit him or spanked him, but these days he figured he was headed in that direction. He probably deserved it, too. If he had a kid who'd done what he'd done, he'd seriously consider giving him a good smack.

Inside, with the door closed behind him, he was still keenly aware of his parents just on the other side of the wall. The wastebasket was filled with tissues.

He took the sofa again. Dr. Campbell sat across from him. She drew a deep breath and then smiled at him.

"So, we decided to go walkabout, eh?"

Zak wasn't sure what that meant; he shrugged.

"Walkabout is something the Aborigines do in Australia. They leave their villages or their towns on foot, and they wander in the wilderness until they have a vision from what they call Dreamtime."

Zak startled at the description, then tried to mask his surprise. That sounded scarily like what had happened to him. Except he hadn't intended to "go walkabout." It had just happened to him.

Dr. Campbell noticed his reaction, though. "Is that what happened, Zak?" she asked very softly. So softly, he knew, that his parents wouldn't be able to hear. "Were you looking for something?"

He said nothing.

"Was there something you needed to find?"

Still nothing.

"Did you find it?"

The cry of the gulls. *Trim the sails!* The storm overhead.

The Secret Sea.

Tommy.

What could he tell her?

He couldn't tell her anything.

Don't tell. That's what the voice said, the voice of his imaginary friend, or maybe the voice of his long-dead uncle, dead before Zak was even born.

"I don't know what you're talking about," Zak said quietly.

Dr. Campbell nodded slowly and wrote something on her pad for the first time.

———

At home, decisions were made outside of Zak's earshot, and the next thing he knew, Dad was packing up, even though he still had four days left in his week. Mom was taking over.

"Bedroom. Now," she said as soon as Dad left.

It was two in the afternoon. Zak didn't protest. He resisted the urge to slam his door.

He scrounged for the old iPod and plugged in the earbuds. A moment later, his best friend's long, thin face filled the screen.

"Hey, man, what's going on? You still grounded?"

"They have to invent a new word for what's happening to me. *Grounded* doesn't begin to cover it. Tell your dad I'm sorry I woke him up the other day."

"He was already up. For *Fajr*."

That was even worse; he'd interrupted Mr. Shamoon's morning prayers.

"Hey, look, Khalid, can I—"

"Oh, hey! Moira's on! Hang on!"

Before Zak could say anything else, a still image of Moira popped up as she loaded into the conversation. Zak couldn't help himself—he grinned as soon as he saw her. That was his default reaction to Moira, and even as depressed as he was at that moment, he still grinned.

An instant later, the image moved and she was on with them.

"Now, laddie," Moira said, mimicking her old Irish brogue, "why are ye misbehavin' so? Don'tcha want to be playin' and gambolin' with your wee friends in these fine summer days before school's startin' again?"

She was laying it on pretty thick to amuse him. It wasn't

53

quite the same as Mrs. O'Grady, but it still made him feel a lot better. "I'm trying, believe me. I'm trying."

"What *happened*?" Khalid asked. He was always the one who put the camera too close to his face; now he was so eager and so excited that he had positioned it mere inches away, and Zak and Moira had a distressingly close look at his upper lip and nostrils. "I heard Pop and Mom talking about it, but I didn't get the whole thing."

"What did they say?"

Khalid's image moved in a way that made Zak think he'd shrugged. "Not much. Just that maybe I shouldn't hang with you so much for now."

Not much. Not much? That was everything!

"Fortunately, we're not listening to parents these days, are we?" Moira chimed in.

"Why start now?" Khalid asked.

Zak could only nod. His throat had clogged, and he couldn't speak.

"So, you went to the tower," Moira said. "What's going on, Zak?" Her voice had lost its playfulness. Khalid would be concerned but never let on; Moira wasn't afraid to get serious.

Zak shook his head and swallowed down the ball of hot emotion that had congealed in his throat. "I don't know," he whispered. "I didn't mean to do it."

Khalid furrowed his brow. Moira frowned. "What do you mean?" she asked.

"If he doesn't want to talk about—"

"Was I asking you, Khalid?"

"I think I sleepwalked." He was grateful to Khalid for trying to spare him, but also grateful to Moira for making him talk about it. He had the two best *best* friends in the world. "I don't remember anything before waking up there."

His friends absorbed that for a moment. If *that* freaked them out—and it should, shouldn't it?—then what would they say if he told them the rest? If he told them about Tommy and Tomás and the boat and the gulls and the storm and the sky?

"Well, that's new," Khalid said.

"Are you sure you sleepwalked?" Moira's bottom lip was chapped and rough from her constant gnawing at it; she had it between her teeth now as she thought through the situation. "Maybe someone came and *took* you—"

That was even scarier than the idea that he'd sleepwalked! "No. The cops have video of me going in and out of the subway."

All three fell silent and pondered that. Zak decided to risk a little more.

"Do you guys know anything about boats?"

"My people have the ship of the desert, the camel!" Khalid chortled in a very broad, fake, heavy accent, clearly glad for an opportunity to joke.

"I mean real boats, like sailing ships."

"Why?" Moira asked.

"Well, this might seem crazy, but I just have this feeling that there was a boat there."

"Where?"

He hesitated but then told them: "Where I was. At the tower."

If they'd all been in the same room, he was certain that at this point Khalid and Moira would have exchanged a worried look. Instead, they both just nodded on his screen and looked away from their cameras for a moment.

Before anyone could speak again, Zak heard his mother's

tread on the creaky hardwood floor outside his door. He signed off quickly and hid the iPod just as Mom opened his door.

"Dinner," she said, clearly leaving him no other option.

Dad had made empanadas and left them in the fridge the day before, so Mom heated them up for dinner. She sat at one end of the table and picked and pecked at her food, a sight that set Zak's parent alarm off. Mom couldn't live with Dad or love him anymore, but she'd always liked his cooking. *"On our first date,"* she'd told Zak once, years ago, *"your father cooked chicken mole and brought it to my apartment in the Village. He thought it was the way to my heart, and I guess he was right. It was the most romantic thing I'd ever seen."*

"Hey, Mom?"

At first he thought she hadn't heard him. She just kept poking at an empanada. But she finally looked up at him, her eyes tired and dull.

"What, Zak?"

He'd meant to ask her something, but her expression prompted an apology instead. "I'm really sorry."

She nodded as if she didn't quite believe it. "I appreciate that, but what I want is less an apology and more an explanation."

"I don't have one."

She threw her fork down in disgust. "Why would you do that, Zak? Leave the house and go into the city like that?" She stared at him, and he was helpless under her angry gaze. Clearly, she expected him to say something, and when he didn't, she picked up the fork again and savagely stabbed at her food. "Is this what they warn parents about when they talk about kids becoming teenagers? Because this is *crazy*, Zak. This isn't just acting out or being disrespectful. This is *dangerous*. This involved the police. You're all I—we—I have left. You could have been hurt. You could have been killed. Do you even understand how serious this is?"

"I understand," he said quietly. Because he did. Better than *she* knew. Because he knew more than she did.

Chowing down, Zak barely tasted Dad's cooking as his mind spun wildly, trying to think of a way out of his situation. She was deeply focused on him right now, and she would take whatever he said very seriously. He might be able to learn something.

"I have a question," he said, picking his words carefully. "Can I ask it?"

"I can't believe you're *speaking*. Yes."

"It's about Uncle Tomás."

The stricken look that crossed her face pained him. He felt as though he'd pressed a scalding-hot iron to her flesh. So many years later, and her brother's death still slashed at her like a sword.

"What about him?"

"You miss him, don't you?"

Mom grimaced as though hit with a migraine. "I miss him like . . ." Her lower lip trembled. "When I was . . . A while back, before you were born, your dad and I moved from the Village to Brooklyn. And I messed up and left a box of kitchen stuff in the old apartment. Nothing expensive, just some dishes. But one of them was a serving dish that was just the right size."

Zak wasn't sure where his mother was going with this, but he said nothing and let her continue.

Wiping at the corners of her eyes with her napkin, she said, "By the time we'd unpacked in the new place, I remembered the box, but it was too late. It was days later and it was gone. And every time I have people over, I think of . . ." She sighed. "I miss him so much, Zak."

"Did he *give* you the dish?"

"No. No, it's just that . . . That's how I miss him. Like that dish you forgot to go back for, the one that would be perfect for guests right now."

It made no sense. It was actually ridiculous, but his mother seemed near tears anyway. He didn't want to press her, but he had to.

"Did he . . ." *Careful, now. Think about this.* "Did he have a boat? Or did he go out on a boat?"

Mom's pained expression melted into a mix of disbelief and exasperation. "What on *earth* are you talking about?"

Great.

"What is *with* you and boats?" she asked, and he knew then that Dr. Campbell had told his parents about his dreams. Which was fine. She'd said she would do as much.

"I don't know," he said lamely.

"Well, here's what I know: Dr. Campbell is worried, and your father and I are worried, and we're running out of options very quickly. You're exhibiting signs of . . . Look, Dr. Campbell wants more intensive therapy sessions with you."

He shrugged. Fine. Whatever.

"And she's also putting together a recommendation for some medications."

Zak tried not to let his expression betray his surprise and dismay. Drugs. Great. Just *great*. More meds, in addition to the verapamil he took every day for his heart condition. Who knew what these new drugs would do to him? Wasn't there a chance they would just make him worse?

There were any number of kids at Wellington Academy who headed to the nurse's office each day to pop some kind of pill. ADD, ADHD, bipolar disorder, whatever. There was a medication for everything, even for the things that didn't bother the kid in question.

He'd known many of those kids before they started the meds and now after. None of them had volunteered for the drugs or asked for them. There wasn't necessarily something *wrong* with them afterward, but there wasn't necessarily something *right*, either. They were different kids now.

Maybe that's what I need. Maybe I need to be a different kid.

Would that mean sacrificing his friends? The things he loved? What would he be like, and would he like himself, and would he even be able to tell the difference?

I don't think I want to find out.

But he knew that if the decision was made, he wouldn't have a choice.

———————

Later, his iPod pinged from its hiding place under his pillow. He swiped it on and discovered a text message:

Check this out, it said, followed by a link to a website and Moira's usual sign-off: *xox*.

He tapped on the link and stared, dumbfounded, at the headline to the article that popped up: *Secrets of WTC Shipwreck Sleuthed Out*.

EIGHT

Maybe Zak wasn't so crazy after all. The ship was real.

When the site of the World Trade Center was excavated after the buildings were destroyed, a sailing ship was found there.

Underground.

Under. The. Ground.

It dated back to the eighteenth century, sometime in the late 1700s . . . right around the time of the American Revolution. The article was a bit long and boring for him, but one thing he got out of it was that the ship was a little . . . weird. He didn't quite understand all of it, but apparently the ship's construction didn't quite match the typical details of the time period. It used nails instead of something called wooden trunnels, for instance.

But, whatever. Who cared? It was *real*.

So. If I'm not crazy about this, then maybe I'm not crazy about the other things, either.

Which meant . . . which meant that the voices in his head,

the dreams, the visions . . . They might not be inventions of his own mind.

They could be *real*.

And that, Zak realized with a shudder, was actually more frightening than the idea that he was losing his mind.

"Garbage. Nonsense," Dad always said. If it wasn't proved by a scientist in a lab somewhere, Dad would have none of it. Zak had always thought that attitude made a lot of sense.

Until now.

But there's some physical evidence, right? This isn't like astrology, where you can't prove anything. I imagined a boat and—poof—there's a boat.

So what about the dreams, the voice, the visions? If they were just as real as the ship, then what *were* they?

Had his uncle's spirit somehow brought him to the tower? Was Uncle Tomás the "Tommy" of Zak's childhood?

That almost made sense—he'd been a little kid when he'd spoken to Tommy. A young child starts hearing a voice . . . You don't think, *Oh no! A ghost!* You think, *A friend! A friend only I can see.* And everyone else thinks it's an imaginary friend, and that's that.

Which meant . . . which meant that Tommy had been with Zak for a long, long time. And maybe Tommy—Uncle Tomás?— had somehow prodded Zak to sleepwalk to where the twin towers had fallen.

He wished he could talk to someone about all of this. Wished not to be alone, wished to have someone to tell. A brother or a sister or even a close cousin. Because while it would be good to bounce this off Khalid or to dig into the impressive nuggets of knowledge in Moira's massive brain, he was pretty sure that even his best friends would rat him out to an adult if he said, *So, guys, I'm pretty sure the ghost of my dead uncle has been trying to communicate with me from beyond the grave and sent me to the Freedom Tower to learn about the boat buried under there.* Yeah, if he were in their shoes, he'd go running to his parents, shouting *Zak's crazy!* for sure.

In bed, he stared up at the ceiling.

"Tommy?" he whispered to the empty air. "Uncle Tomás?"

Nothing.

"If you're there, I need a little more, okay?" He paused. "I need another vision or another dream. I found the boat, but I don't know what to do next." For a while now, he'd been desperate to avoid the dreams and the voice. Now he steeled himself for them. He craved them.

"I'm ready," he told the spirit he now believed—knew—to be surrounding him. "I'm ready for whatever's next."

———————

I was in darkness.

Zak grumbled in his sleep.

Secrecy.

Secret Sea.

—look up—

He rolled over.

Zak!

He shot upright in bed. The voice was right next to him. And he looked over.

Zak!

It was above him. He looked up.

ZAK!!!

Behind him. Below him. Everywhere he looked, nothing. But it was all around him.

I'm still dreaming, he thought. *Dreaming I woke up. But am I dreaming the voice, or is the voice in my dream?*

Zak, don't trust him!

It was weak, fading.

Don't trust him! You can't—

"Who? Don't trust who?" Before, it had been "they" who were lying. Now Zak wasn't supposed to trust "him."

He has been asleep too long. The voice was like a dying breeze, fading in twilight. *And I . . .*

And it was gone like sunshine.

Zak! it screamed, its return as sudden as its disappearance was gradual. *Zak! You have to come back to the ship! You have to unlock the secrecy and the Secret Sea! Do it! Tell no one!*

Zak groaned and rubbed his eyes. *Was* it a dream? Or was he really awake? He tried to pinch himself to find out, but his skin refused to cooperate, slipping out from between his fingertips.

A dream, to be sure.

Why was his heart pounding so, then?

Just a dream. Just a dream.

Something slapped against his window and he gasped. Turned to look.

It was something heavy: cloth, wet. It battered against the window over and over, buffeted by a sudden gust of air.

"Ye whistled for the wind. . . ."

It was a flag. He couldn't make out the colors or the pattern; it kept whip-snapping in a ferocious wind. He clambered out of bed and pressed his nose to the glass. A storm slashed the sky, and the apartment—the building—rocked and heaved as if in an earthquake.

Or on the sea. I'm back on the boat. My whole bedroom is on the boat.

He spun around and his bedroom was gone, replaced with curved, timbered walls, a low ceiling, flickering torchlight. The timbers creaked and complained; the floor tilted.

You have to return to the tower, Zak, the voice told him. *You have to unlock the secrets and set them free.*

The floor shifted under him again. Zak lost his balance and collapsed, thinking, *A dream. At least it's just a dream.*

He awoke on the floor.

Fell out of bed, that's all. Tossed and turned and fell out of—

It was a wooden floor, unlike the carpeted one in his bedroom, and he panicked, remembering the ship. He knew he wasn't dreaming any longer, couldn't believe he was somehow *on* the boat now, and that's when he realized the wooden floor was very even, very regular. Not rough-hewn.

And it wasn't moving.

It was the hardwood floor in the bedroom that his parents switched off using.

His body ached. He pushed to his feet and glanced around. Sleepwalking again?

Great.

Sunlight poured in through the slats of the window blinds. The apartment was quiet. Still. As though the air had tired itself out and given up moving. It lay warm and languid all around him.

He explored quickly. It was past nine in the morning, and Mom was nowhere to be seen, but he did discover a note from her:

Zak—

Had to go in to work for a meeting. La-La is on her way.
Go nowhere.

Underlined twice. Just in case he didn't get it.

He went to his room and got dressed, thinking. It must have been a life-or-death (more likely a job-or-else) meeting to get Mom out of the apartment, under the circumstances. And his grandmother was on the way over to babysit because Zak was now officially unreliable, dangerous, etc. He was a Bad Kid, and you didn't leave Bad Kids unattended. Who knew what they could get into?

Like sleepwalking . . .

He'd sleepwalked to the tower, and there had been some reason for that. Now he'd sleepwalked to his parents' room.

Why?

He went back in, fully aware that he was racing a clock that ticked down to a deadline he couldn't see. Who knew when La-La would arrive? Still, he had to figure this out.

Immediately, he realized what was happening. Near where he'd woken up, his parents' safe squatted in a small niche between the wall and the dresser.

The safe was only a foot wide, tiny but heavy. It was grayish green, with rounded corners and a black pug nose of a combination lock on its door. As a child, Zak had been curious about the safe, had spent time twirling its dial like safecrackers on TV, but to no avail. His parents had chuckled at his interest. "There's nothing fun in there, big man," his dad used to say. "Just insurance papers and birth certificates and passports."

And right now . . . it was open. The door was just slightly ajar, a black crack waiting to admit light.

Had Mom left it unlocked when she went to work? No. Zak knew that—somehow—*he* had opened it. The same way Tommy/ Uncle Tomás had jogged him from his bed and steered him to the spot where the mysterious eighteenth-century ship had lain buried for centuries, the spirit had this time led him here and guided him through the proper twirls and twists of the combination lock.

Hurry! It was no voice but his own. *La-La'll be here soon!*

He opened the safe and peered inside. No gold bars and stacks of cash, like in the movies. As Dad had promised, there was just a pile of papers and file folders and a few thin envelopes.

He riffled through as quickly as he could. He didn't know what he was looking for, but he figured that anything remotely interesting would have to jump out at him from this heap of *boring.*

First, he found an envelope labeled *Zak*. It contained some old report cards and some medical records and his birth certificate: *Zakari Malcolm Killian*. No big deal. There were a *lot* of medical records—a log of every doctor's visit Zak had ever had for the heart condition that lived in his chest.

But then, under that, was another envelope. Identical. For some reason, Zak's hand shook as he drew it from the safe, as though his hand knew something his brain didn't.

Tommy was printed on the envelope, in Mom's very steady, very neat handwriting.

Wait, what? Is this . . . Did they call Uncle Tomás "Tommy"?

He opened the envelope and slid out the few papers within. Medical stuff again. It made his eyes want to bleed, so he shuffled the documents aside.

Birth certificate.

Thomas Oscar Killian.

What?

The birthday was the same as his own. April 27.

The. Exact. Same. Day.

Oh God.

Thomas Oscar Killian was born at 3:32 in the afternoon on April 27, approximately three minutes after Zak.

Zak's head swam. His vision blurred, refocused, blurred again. This was . . . this was impossible. This couldn't be happening.

One of the medical papers caught his eye. *TTTS?* stood out in large letters, scrawled in red pen. Underneath, someone with different handwriting and a black pen had written *(Twin-to-twin transfusion syndrome)*.

I don't . . . I don't understand. I don't understand.

A twin? A twin brother? Named Tommy? Zak's arms raced with gooseflesh, and his teeth began chattering on their own. He was suddenly freezing in the middle of August, sitting in the sunlight from the window.

Where *was* his brother, then? Where was Thomas Oscar Killian? Why were they keeping his brother from him? Why didn't anyone ever talk about him?

What in the world was happening to his life?

That phantom sense he'd always had, that sense of something carved away from him, amputated—it always lingered, but now it was stronger, so powerful it hurt. He could barely breathe.

He couldn't bear looking at the birth certificate any longer, so he shoved it back into the envelope and beheld the last piece of paper from the *Tommy* envelope.

CERTIFICATE OF DEATH was stamped officially across the top. Zak didn't want to look farther down, but his eyes were already skipping ahead, heedless of the demands of his brain, his heart, his soul.

Thomas Oscar Killian had died at the age of two and a half, of kidney failure.

No, Zak thought, and then couldn't think anymore. His brain refused to cooperate, refused to form words as his brother's death date seemed to come unmoored from the paper on which it was printed and to float into the middle space between him and the death certificate.

Dead.

His heart jumped. That was normal. Everyone's heart skipped a beat occasionally, even Zak's.

But this time, when it jumped, it didn't come back down. It just kept rising, pressing up high in his chest until the pressure became more than he could stand, and he realized that something was wrong, something was quite desperately *wrong,* and he gurgled something that might have been *Help,* but there was no one to hear, and the next thing he knew, he was facedown on the floor and the world was shrinking into utter darkness.

NINE

Zak?

Tommy? Tommy, is that you?

Zak, can you hear me?

Am I dead? Is that what happened? Am I dead like you?

Zak, can you hear me?

Yes! Yes, I can hear you!

If you can hear me, you have to understand: You can't trust him.

Trust who? Who are you talking about? What's happening?

Look up. Look down. Look all around. The answers are hidden, but they *are there.*

What? What do you—

Whatever you do, Zak . . . Whatever you do, never, ever go into—

"He's awake!" a voice said as a burst of intense light blinded him.

"No!" Zak screamed. "Tommy! Tommy, what were you saying! Tommy!"

"Put him back under!" someone shouted. "Now!"

"Tommy!" Zak thrashed against the hands that held him down. "Tommy!"

And then the world went dark. Which was fine.

But quiet, too.

Which wasn't fine.

Tommy? Tommy, are you there?

And then everything—even Zak himself—went away.

TEN

He woke and then he slept again, but the sleep was dreamless, voiceless, Tommy-less, and so it felt nothing like sleep. It was, instead, a great blank stamped into him, a void. An abyss.

Being awake took on the character of dreams instead. Sometimes he couldn't open his eyes, his lids too heavy to move. Voices drifted around him, snatches of sound on the air.

La-La.

Mom.

Dad.

Other people.

Just like in a dream where no matter how fast you run, you can't make any headway, the harder Zak tried to focus on the voices around him, the less he heard. And then he would slip again into the void.

Sometimes his eyes fluttered open and he would glimpse a blurred snapshot of the world—a face, haloed with curls, maybe his grandmother, maybe not. His dad? Who knew? He couldn't tell, and then the weight of his eyelids would win again and back to the void, back to the abyss.

Maybe that was better.

Because when he was awake, he thought of Tommy. In those brief lucid moments before sinking into the quicksand of unconsciousness, he would think of his twin, of the piece of him that had been missing without his realizing, and he wondered how he could not have known. If he'd been missing an arm, he would have known, right? And yet he'd been missing an entire person from his life and he hadn't realized.

Or maybe he had. Maybe that's why there was the imaginary friend, the voice, the dreams. The aching sense of solitude when forced to be on his own.

Sometimes when he opened his eyes, there was no one. No voices. No blurry faces peering down at him. He was alone. Again. This time, more alone than he'd ever been, which was a considerable amount. He had thought that the loneliness of an only child of divorced parents was as intense as could be experienced. But a single piece of paper had taught him otherwise. True loneliness proceeded not from being always alone but rather from being partnered . . . and then losing that partner.

He hadn't even known that Tommy had existed, but now all he wanted was his twin back.

Every time he opened his eyes, they were wet with tears. In the abyss, in the formless void, Zak wept for his dead brother.

That had to mean something.

ELEVEN

He finally opened his eyes for more than a few seconds. Enough time to clear them of sleep gunk.

He was in a hospital room. Clean, but in that shabby way hospital rooms have—there are stains even bleach can't completely eradicate, and the walls of Zak's room bore their dingy ghosts. The smell of antiseptic soap and starch lingered, and the air hung paralyzed.

The bed was too stiff in some places, too soft in others, and no matter how Zak positioned himself, he couldn't find a spot that felt right. Add to that the wires that unspooled from stickers on his chest to a monitor, and the IV tube that kept getting caught on the bed railing, and it was impossible to be comfortable for more than two minutes at a time.

How do they expect people to get better when they can't even relax?

He suffered flickering, choppy memories of doctors and nurses clustered around him, of his parents peering down at him, their faces creased with worry wrinkles, expressions desperate and terrified. Someone had, he believed, tried to explain to him what had happened—a "cardiac event." Those words lingered in his recent memory. *Cardiac event.* That sounded scarily like something that happened to old people, and it had happened to him.

"You're going to be okay," someone had said at some point, and he wasn't sure he believed it.

He put a hand over his heart. According to the monitor, it was loping along just fine, but he didn't really believe it was still in his chest until he felt its thrum with his own fingers.

His mouth tasted stale. Gummy. He couldn't reach the bedside tray, where a pitcher and glass rested tantalizingly, mockingly.

The door to his room opened, and to his surprise Dr. Campbell entered, followed by his parents. Mom and Dad had bags under their eyes and looked so much older than usual.

He couldn't quite believe his eyes—they were holding hands. Mom had obviously been crying, and Dad wore beard stubble.

How long have I been here?

Dr. Campbell stood at the foot of his bed. Mom and Dad split and took seats on either side of him; Mom took his hand, and Dad rested a palm on Zak's shoulder. It was creepy that no one said anything.

"Do you need anything?" Dr. Campbell asked.

"Thirsty." His voice croaked and cracked. His throat hurt.

Dr. Campbell poured a glass of water and handed it to him. He drank it as quickly as his sore throat would allow, then held it up, signaling for more. She refilled and he sipped at it this time.

"Zak, I've been speaking with your parents, and I've asked them to talk to you. I've asked them to be very honest with you, and they've agreed. They're not going to talk about your . . .

walkabout. Or anything like that. They just want to tell you some things. And I think maybe..." She cut her eyes left and right, taking in both of them. "I think maybe they might even want to apologize."

His parents nodded in miserable synchronization.

Dr. Campbell settled into a seat in the corner of the room. Zak looked from Mom to Dad, then back. They both stared down at the floor, neither one willing to speak.

"Someone has to talk," Zak said at last.

Bobbing his head, Dad said, "I don't know what you saw or read—"

"I know about my brother."

Dad blew out a trembly, shuddering sigh. "Yeah. Okay. Look, we..."

"You were sick," Mom said abruptly. "When you were in the womb. Both of you. You had something called TTTS."

"Twin-to-twin transfusion syndrome," Dr. Campbell chimed in quietly. "It affects identical twins. Very rare."

"I don't know how to explain this," Mom said helplessly. "It's like..." She drifted off and gave Dad the *You take over* look.

"You and your brother shared everything in the womb," Dad said. "And there was a connection between the two of you. A very special one. But what happened was..."

"One twin begins to take blood from the other," Dr. Campbell said very calmly. "You know about blood transfusions, right? This is similar, except it's accidental. One twin absorbs blood from the other."

Zak had a mental image of two babies in a belly, one of them drawing blood from the other, growing larger as the other shrank.

"I sucked out his blood?" he exclaimed, horrified. "Like a vampire?"

"No!" Mom shouted, and flung her arms around him. "No, never think that! You didn't do *anything*."

"This is why we didn't tell you," Dad explained. "We were worried you would blame yourself. It was an accident of nature. No one *did* anything. It just *happened*."

"Never, ever blame yourself for this," Mom whispered in his ear.

"You both had health problems when you were born," Dad said. "Your heart condition, from too much blood in the womb. And Tommy had kidney problems from too little blood. We thought we might lose one of you, or even both of you, but we got lucky." He looked away, his jaw trembling. "For a little while."

Zak was uncomfortable in his mother's awkward embrace; he pushed her off him. "But then Tommy died. And you just pretended he never existed."

And then it was like Zak could rewind his life and watch it again, only this time through a different camera angle. His sixth birthday party, when he'd turned a corner at the restaurant and seen La-La sobbing in Mom's arms for no apparent reason. His mother's seemingly bizarre, overwrought annoyance at every mention of his imaginary friend. The way his father would turn and gaze lingeringly at dual baby carriages on the street.

You're all I—we—I have left, Mom had said to him.

Have left.

Left.

All that remained. Zak was what was left after Tommy died. Everyone knew and everyone mourned.

Everyone in his life had missed Tommy. Except for his own twin. Because they'd lied.

Lied, like Tommy had promised.

Zak had spent his life thinking he was alone. And then he wasn't.

And then he was.

Don't trust him, the voice had said.

More like "don't trust them."

Mindful of the tubes and wires attached to him, he folded his arms over his chest, wishing he could make himself disappear. He wanted to be away from his parents, probably forever. Never to see them again. He'd thought he'd been angry at them in the past, when they'd punished him or denied him something, but that was kiddie anger. This—this emotion he was feeling now—he knew that this was adult anger.

"You've been lying to me. My whole life."

"We thought—"

"Michael." It was Dr. Campbell. Zak had been so wrapped up in his outrage that he'd forgotten about her. She said his father's name again and came over to the bed. "Let me handle this part.

"I've known you much longer than the past week," she told Zak. "Your parents brought you to me soon after Tommy died. They wanted to know how it would affect you, what it would do to you." She shook her head and opened her mouth to continue speaking, but she couldn't. Rummaging in her purse, she produced a tissue and dabbed at her eyes.

"I owe you an apology, too. God, Zak, I'm so sorry. I'm so, so sorry. I told them . . . I told them that you probably wouldn't remember Tommy at all. That your memories of him would fade. Clearly, I was wrong. You've been remembering him, and it took the form of your imaginary friend, your sleepwalking . . . and then you learned about him the worst way possible."

"We really were going to tell you," Dad said in the least convincing tone ever. "When you were older."

"How old do you have to be to know about your dead twin brother?" Zak asked with an acidity he'd never dared before with his parents.

"We were worried about your heart," Mom whispered. "About something exactly like *this*—"

"I deserved to know!" Zak shouted, and the heart monitor beeped and pinged warningly. The three adults all hissed in a panicked breath, and Zak felt a surge of warm power at the thought of the terror he'd just instilled in them. "I deserved to know. You let me go around thinking I just came up with the name *Tommy* on my own, letting me think he was just my imaginary friend. And you all got to keep this secret to yourselves and never bothered to tell me the most important thing in my *life*."

"I understand you're angry—" his dad began.

Zak shook his father's hand off his shoulder. "Angry? Are you kidding me? You've been lying to me my whole life, and you think you can just say you're sorry and it's okay?"

When he was younger, Zak had accidentally spilled purple Kool-Aid on his mother's favorite skirt. He'd apologized lavishly and profusely, but she'd remained upset. Eventually, after his umpteenth apology, she'd said, "Zak, it was my favorite. . . . *Sorry* doesn't actually fix anything. Sometimes *sorry* isn't enough."

He'd never understood that. Sorry had always been enough. Until now. His parents and Dr. Campbell could apologize until the end of time, and it wouldn't be enough. If it wasn't enough for a skirt, then there weren't enough *sorry*s in the world to fill the hole left by his twin. Until that moment on the floor at home, that moment when he'd seen the birth certificate, he'd never realized that the gap in his life hadn't always been there. He'd thought he just hated being alone, that it was as simple as that. But no. Something vast and important had been missing. The world had been incomplete.

Something had been taken from him that could never, ever be returned.

Unless.

"Don't tell."

"Zak, can you hear me?"

Unless there was still a way to be with Tommy after all.

TWELVE

They left him staring at the water-stained acoustic ceiling tile above him, willing Tommy's voice to return. His efforts, his strains, rewarded him with precisely nothing.

He'd thought his life was a good one. A full one. But now he knew the truth—it was a life of lies, and only half a life at that. A life of fractions. He was a fraction. Exactly one-half of what he was supposed to be.

Tears came on unexpectedly. For himself? For his brother? Probably for both. He'd never really known his brother, but the ache and the sorrow and the loss were all too real for him. Zak couldn't shake the notion that there should be a hand to clutch, eyes to gaze into. That there was a half of him missing.

Missing. Or taken away.

When the door opened, he thought for sure it would be his parents again; he'd been rehearsing an agonized rant of epic proportions, eager for the moment when he could let loose on them. Instead, it was Khalid, followed steps later by Moira, and all of Zak's anger was quenched by sheer joy and relief at the sight of his friends in the flesh. Even the hollow soreness in his chest—a pain literal or figurative or both, he couldn't tell—lightened some.

"Whoa!" Khalid exclaimed. "You *are* life-sized! I was starting to think you'd been shrunk down to fit in a video chat screen."

Khalid grinned broadly, his eyes no doubt dancing behind the sunglasses he wore. He'd recently started wearing them every time he left the house, no matter where he was. Even in movie theaters. He insisted it was the coolest thing in the world, and that even if it wasn't, "I'll *make* it cool." He came close and clasped, then reclasped, Zak's hand in a complicated ritual that was more a dance move than a handshake.

Moira rolled her eyes, whether at Khalid's comment, his sunglasses, or his handshake, Zak couldn't tell. Probably all three. Her hair had been cut recently, right around her ears, with sleek, shiny strands of it flying away every time she bobbed her head. She wore a pair of heavy-framed glasses and a painfully bright T-shirt with the words *100% GEEK* and *100% GIRL* inscribed across it, as well as a cluster of overlapping pins on her right shoulder that looked like the beginning of a growth of multicolored plate-armor. One of the larger buttons was a new one that Zak hadn't seen before. It read *I like you ironically.*

"How did you guys get in here?" Zak asked as Moira came closer. She wasn't much for shows of affection, but she did brush a stray hair from his forehead.

"We used the door," Khalid said in a tone of overwrought concern, pointing. "Did they operate on your *brain*, man?"

Moira sniffed. "As usual, Khalid's being a moron. We basically threw fits until our parents let us come to see you. The doctors didn't want to let us in, but we guilt-tripped your parents."

"And *then* we used the door," Khalid reminded them. "The door was important to the plan, and I don't understand why you're downplaying it. Without the door, we literally would not be here."

Moira sighed in aggravation and awkwardly crossed her arms over her chest. "How are you, Zak? Really."

"I'm okay. The doctors say I'm going to be fine."

Khalid perched with one hip on Zak's bed. "Did you seriously have a heart attack?"

"I think so. Or maybe not. They called it a 'cardiac event.'"

Khalid tilted his shades down and looked out over the top. "That sounds fun."

"Totally. Want to try one?"

"Maybe later."

"Is this connected to your sleepwalking?" Moira asked abruptly.

Zak startled, and his heart monitor emitted a sharp bleat. He'd almost forgotten that Moira was there. When she wanted to, she could be so quiet and still that it was easy to overlook her, especially amid Khalid's antics. But she stood right next to him, gazing down at him with concern.

"What makes you think—"

"It's a weird coincidence," she interrupted, "that an otherwise normal, healthy person would suddenly have two medical crises in a row. Maybe there's a connection."

"Science Girl rides . . . again!" Khalid sang.

Moira ignored him and touched Zak on his shoulder, where

Dad had hours before. This time, Zak didn't mind so much. "What are they saying? Have they told you anything?"

Zak drew in a deep breath. *An otherwise normal, healthy person*, Moira had said. But she didn't know.

"Don't tell."

That was fine advice for ghosts. But Zak was alive and had friends.

"I need to tell you guys something," he said. "Something big and serious."

"I live for big and serious," Khalid said, leaning forward eagerly.

Zak started to talk.

He told them everything.

Every. Thing.

He was tempted to hold back some of the details, some of the crazier things. But it was all connected—his brother, the World Trade Center, the ship, the sleepwalking, the "cardiac event," the voice, the dreams. The flooded subway that suddenly wasn't. Trying to talk about one part of it without talking about the rest of it would be like walking on a single stilt—good luck keeping your balance. And your perspective.

As Zak spoke, Khalid paced, never taking off his sunglasses— he was deeply committed to the weird experimental theater of his own life. But Zak could tell from his cheeks and eyebrows that his eyes were growing wider and wider as the story went on. Moira stood completely still the whole time, staring through her thick lenses at Zak, her arms folded uncomfortably over her chest. *I like you ironically* kept flashing at Zak.

"That . . . is . . . crazy," Khalid said when Zak finished, and Moira immediately and quite seriously slapped the back of his head. Hard. Khalid yelped.

"Don't call Zak crazy," she remonstrated.

"I didn't call *him* crazy! I called his *story* crazy."

"Either way."

"It's okay," Zak said quietly. "I know how it sounds. And I wouldn't blame you guys if you didn't believe me, but don't tell my parents, okay?"

"We believe you," Moira said. "Well, I do."

"You don't think I'm nuts?"

"Of course not," Moira said. "How could you have opened the safe without knowing the combination? A ghost actually makes sense. And besides—the boat was right where you said it would be."

"I just believe you 'cause I'll always believe you," Khalid said. And then he intoned solemnly, "Three Basketeers." When they'd been younger, one of them—probably Khalid—had misheard the title of the famous novel and thought it was about basketball. They'd declared themselves the Three Basketeers, and merely invoking that phrase was like making a promise unto death.

It had been years since they'd described themselves so, one more piece of jetsam heaved over the side of the ship as they raced toward teendom.

Still, the sound of those words instantly sent Zak back to the overseriousness of childhood, the wallowing in personal importance. Moira nodded gravely and said, "Three Basketeers."

"Three Basketeers," Zak answered, completing the circuit. Done.

"Now what?" Khalid asked. He was always eager for action—oftentimes incredibly stupid action, but action nonetheless. He rubbed his hands together. "Do we need one of those, you know—" He held his hands out flat, mimed scrubbing something along a surface.

"A Ouija board?" Moira asked. She'd grabbed Zak's chart from the end of his bed and was flipping through it. "Grow up."

"I don't know what to do next," Zak confessed as Moira fiddled with her phone. "But I know it can't be done here."

"No kidding." Khalid pulled a chair over and plopped down next to Zak. "But how do we get you out of here?"

"And where do we go once I'm out?"

"We get you out of here first," Khalid argued, "and *then* we figure out what to do."

"That doesn't make any sense."

"It makes perfect sense."

"Dude, we have to know where we're going first."

"We're going *out*—that's where we're going." Khalid hopped up from his chair and dashed to the window, dodging around Moira, who was studying Zak's heart monitor intently. "I bet this window . . . Yeah! Check it—there's a roof right down there." He jabbed a finger at the glass excitedly. "I bet we could jump it, easy."

"Jump it!" Zak's heart sent him a warning jolt.

"Or maybe we could make a rope out of bedsheets and anchor it with your IV pole and climb down."

"You're nuts. I'm not doing that. Especially without a destination in mind." He tried to sit up in bed, but Moira was suddenly looming over him, tugging gently at the wires connected to his heart monitor, then poking at the oxygen tube running into his nose.

85

Zak tried to brush her back. Khalid turned from the window in a huff. "Fine. What's *your* suggestion, genius?"

"I think we need to find a way to contact Tommy. And it seems like he speaks to me best when I'm asleep."

Khalid snapped his fingers and pointed. "Quick! Fall asleep!"

"Right," Zak said drolly. "I'm just wondering: Maybe tonight when I sleep, I can try to sort of . . . control the dream. It's called lucid dreaming. My dad told me about it once. Because I was having nightmares. And he said that there's a way you can take control of your dreams and change them around."

"So maybe you can actually talk to the voice!" Khalid said excitedly. "And figure out your next step!"

"Yeah." Zak turned to Moira, who by now had moved to the other side of the bed and was staring at her phone. "Moira? Care to join us here on planet Earth for a minute and tell us what you—"

He broke off as Moira, with no warning, dropped to the floor. A moment later, she popped back up with a plastic sack that she tossed at Zak. It landed heavily on his gut. Inside were his clothes.

"Get dressed," she said. "Your cardiac enzymes are back down to normal levels, your blood pressure is good, and your heart rate is fine. You're mobile. We can get you out of here."

"Like I said—through the window!" Khalid exclaimed.

"The windows don't open," Moira said witheringly.

"I can't just go," Zak said. But the weight of the bag—his clothes, his shoes—tempted him. "I'm on a heart monitor. An alarm will go off."

"I already turned off the alarm. I Googled the manual."

"But where do we go once we're out of here?"

Moira stared. It was the same look she always gave them

when they were all doing math homework together and Zak and Khalid just. Didn't. Get it.

"We have to go to the subway," she said. "Preferably close to the Freedom Tower, but it probably doesn't matter, since you had a vision at the Canal Street stop."

Zak and Khalid looked at each other, then looked at Moira.

"Go on," Khalid prompted. "For the dummies in the room."

"It's obvious—the voice is stronger when you're asleep, yes, but we can't force you to sleep. So we do the next best thing. The voice and the visions are also strong when you're underground. Probably because that gets you closer to where the ship was buried. So we have to take you down into the subway. Duh," she finished for good measure.

"That's amazing," Khalid said in awe. Zak nodded in agreement as Moira began unhooking the various wires from him.

"Puh-lease." Moira sniffed. "Anyone who's ever read a comic book would have figured it out."

Zak nodded slowly and said, "All right, guys. Turn around."

"Why?" Moira asked, annoyed.

"Because in order to get dressed," Zak said with a grin, "first I have to get naked."

Moira's eyebrows shot up, and her face flamed almost as red as her hair. She quickly turned away as Zak peeled back the sheet.

THIRTEEN

Unsteady on his feet for the first time in days, Zak weaved a little. Khalid and Moira persuaded him to try a few practice laps around his room before they would open the door. After three or four turns, he felt confident.

His heart seemed to throb more noticeably than usual. Was it an aftereffect of the "cardiac event"? Or was he just paying more attention to it because it had failed him?

"You getting the hang of this walking thing?" Khalid asked.

"I'm fine," Zak lied. "Let's go."

He anticipated guards shouting and nurses sounding alarms as soon as he left the room, but nothing happened. No one spared a look for the three kids casually strolling down the corridor. Zak suffered a pang of terror as they rounded the first corner, wondering if he might walk into his parents or his doctor or Dr. Campbell. He hissed in a breath and forced himself not to squeeze Moira's hand, which she insisted he hold. But the new hallway was empty, save for an orderly mopping the floor, and they pushed into a stairwell. Soon they were out on the street.

Zak tilted his face to the sun. It was late in the day, but it was summer and the sun, low in the sky, still emitted warm light. After days of air-conditioning, the humidity outside wrapped around him like a living blanket trying to smother him. He breathed through the initial surprise, focused on the heat from the sun, silently ordered his heart to behave.

"Subway's this way," Khalid said. Zak scarcely paid attention. He let them lead him along the sidewalks, enfolded in the damp air that smelled of car exhaust, barbecued chicken kebabs from a nearby food cart, half-melted road tar, and the tang of his own sudden sweat. Buses belched; the sidewalks vibrated with a million footfalls; ten languages spoken at top volume assaulted his ears.

Through it, past it, beyond it, he sought *the* voice, Tommy, his twin. *Come back*, he pleaded. *I didn't know who you were. I'm sorry I let you get away. If you come back, I'll never let you go again. Just come back.*

"Here we go...." Khalid and Moira helped him down the steps into the subway. Zak realized that he didn't have his MetroCard, but Khalid swiped him in, and soon they stood on the platform. Zak gazed around. It was just a subway platform in Brooklyn. Nothing exciting or exceptional about it—rusted overhead steel, trash-strewn tracks, bored commuters loitering. A darting shadow in the distance that his experienced eyes knew—without even seeing it totally—to be a rat, scavenging in the wasteland of the tracks.

Where are you, Tommy? How can you still speak to me?

He stared down at the tracks. A fork lay there. Not a plastic fork dropped from a takeout bag or tossed aside after being used—that would make sense. No, this was a shiny silver fork, clean and new, sitting on the track.

For a moment he forgot why he was here. What on *earth* was a perfectly good fork doing on the subway tracks?

"Here," Moira said. The platform vibrated, and the air went a-roar. Zak thought he was back on the ship, its hull shaking with each crashing wave, but the vision stubbornly refused to come.

They clambered onto the Q train to Manhattan. At this time of day, most straphangers were headed in the opposite direction, coming to Brooklyn from the city, so there was no trouble finding three consecutive empty seats. Khalid and Moira flanked Zak.

"Are you okay?" Moira asked him. She had been holding his hand off and on since they left his hospital room.

Tommy, come back. Please. I need to understand.

"He looks a little pale," Khalid said, worried. The flickering confines of the subway car warped in the lenses of his sunglasses. "Maybe this wasn't such a good idea."

"I'm fine," Zak said. He was close, he knew. Somehow, he could sense that he was close to understanding. Close to Tommy. Again.

"Are you sure?" Moira this time.

"Yes. Trust me."

I'm coming, Tommy. His heart skipped a beat and he froze, but it picked up its reliable rhythm immediately. *One way or another, I guess, I'm coming.*

The train rattled along, making its usual stops in Brooklyn before diving under the East River to trundle toward Manhattan.

The car was eerily silent as only a subway car can be. The noise of the car itself, of its hissing, squealing mechanics, became divorced from the interior, as though it belonged to another world, and the universe within purged itself of sound.

"They must have named him after my uncle," Zak said, needing to break the silence. He felt nothing; he heard nothing. If he didn't talk, he would go mad.

"Named who?"

"My brother. Thomas Oscar Killian. For Uncle Tomás."

"Right," Khalid mused. "Does that mean *you're* named after someone?"

"My dad's stepfather. Grampa Zachary." He'd never really thought about it before, this business of naming people *for* people.

He'd thought his imaginary friend was his dead uncle; now he knew it was his dead twin. But how? Why? There were other dead people in his life—Grampa Zachary, for one—and he'd never received a visitation from any of them. Not until Tommy. Was being twins enough to breach the barrier between life and death?

He wanted to ask Moira. She subsisted on a steady diet of comic books, science fiction, and fantasy novels. If anyone had a theory on this, it would be Moira. But she would probably have *ten* theories, each one with fifteen subtheories, and if asked, she wouldn't stop until she'd expounded on each and every one. So, maybe not.

"What's the plan here, Moira?" Khalid asked. "We're almost in the city."

Zak thought he heard something just then, but maybe it was just his imagination. He'd never really heard the voice when he was trying to—it had always sneaked up on him.

"We need to go to the World Trade Center," Moira said confidently. "If anything's going to happen, it'll be there."

Khalid twisted around to look at the subway map on the wall behind him. "We should have switched to the R or the N," he said. "We're gonna end up too far uptown. But we can hop on the R at Canal and—"

Canal. The Canal Street stop.

"What about the E?" Moira asked. "That takes us right to the World Trade Center."

The Canal Street stop was where he'd seen the flooding. He braced himself.

"Nah, the E doesn't connect up until, like, Times Square. We should just get off at Canal and—"

Moira yelped. "Zak! Stop squeezing—"

But he couldn't help it. His hand had a mind of its own, clenching Moira's hand tightly as the subway car—

The subway car filled with water. Zak's eyes widened, and he strained to hear—

Zak! Zak! Hurry! You have to hurry! Otherwise, it'll be too late!

Stronger, louder than he'd ever heard before.

Tommy! Tommy, listen to me! What's happening?

The car was awash in foaming water. Zak jumped to his feet, dragging Moira up as well, trying to keep their heads above the waterline. How could the car still be racing along while filled?

"Zak! Dude!" Khalid grabbed at Zak's shoulder, trying to pull him back into his seat, but Zak kept his footing. His heart cranked. Stronger. Faster. As the water reached higher and higher, the voice screaming in Zak's mind got louder and louder—*I can't hold on much longer, Zak! You have to hurry! You're the only one who can save me!*—yelling for him to hurry, but the water was so high now that he could barely keep his head above it, and his heart pounded like a drum solo that would never end, but drum solos always ended, and when they did, when this one did, what would happen to his—

And it was over.

As suddenly as it had come upon him, the vision was over. The water vanished in an instant, far too quickly to drain away. It was gone as if—

"As if it was never here," Zak whispered.

"Zak?" It was Moira, her voice quiet and gentle. Khalid was standing, too, one arm around Zak's waist.

"Dude, you're sweating like crazy. You okay?"

He wanted to tell them that it wasn't sweat—it was water. That somehow he'd been submerged.

Tommy? Tommy! Where are you?

Zak, I can't keep holding on. Tommy's voice was weakening. *You have to hurr—*

Gone.

"What happened?" Moira asked, extricating her hand from his now-limp one. Together, she and Khalid ushered Zak back into his seat.

"You guys didn't see the water?" he asked. "You didn't hear the voice?"

"Sure we heard the voice," Khalid said.

"You did?" Zak turned to Khalid excitedly, grabbing his friend by the shoulders. "You heard Tommy?"

Khalid's eyebrows mated in concern. "Tommy? Dude, no. The voice of the conductor." He pointed to the ceiling. "Telling us that Canal is closed for work and we're skipping it."

Zak groaned and slumped back in his seat.

"You heard something?" Moira asked. "And saw something?"

"Yeah. Right while we were going through Canal Street. Under it, I mean." What would have happened, he wondered, if they'd stopped there? What would have happened the other day if, instead of running, he'd stood his ground on the platform? Would he have drowned in a flood no one else could see?

He told them what he'd seen. And heard. Khalid took the unprecedented step of removing his sunglasses. He stuck one arm of the frame in his mouth and gnawed at it.

"Look, this is serious. What are we getting into here?"

Moira pursed her lips, thinking. "What do you want to do, Zak? It's your brother. It's your heart."

There was never a question. "We keep going. We figure this out."

FOURTEEN

They switched trains at Times Square and took the E back downtown. Zak tapped his foot rhythmically on the floor of the train, his body vibrating with urgency and energy. All he could think of was the terror in Tommy's voice, the plea.

"You're the only one who can save me!"

The "only one" part interested him much less than the "save me" part. What did it mean?

Was it possible to rescue Tommy . . . from death?

He wanted to broach the subject with Khalid and Moira but was afraid the very idea of bringing Tommy back to life would be one step too far, even for his best friends. So he sat, silent, between them and tapped his foot and tried to breathe regularly. It was more difficult than he thought breathing could or should be.

At one of the stations with Wi-Fi, both Khalid's and Moira's phones erupted into flurries of bleeps and ringtones as a backlog of messages came through. All from their parents.

Where are you??? Mrs. O'Grady demanded.

Zak is very sick and you have to bring him back to the hospital NOW, Mr. Shamoon insisted.

There were more of them, all in the same vein. Varying levels of plea, threat, and cajoling, with a common note of command. A moment of silence swaddled the three of them, and then Khalid said, "Three Basketeers, baby," and switched his phone off.

Moira did the same. "Three Basketeers," she repeated.

"Three Basketeers," Zak added.

"Team Zak one-double-oh!" Khalid hooted.

Zak knew then that he was the luckiest guy in the world, to have two such friends. Words refused to come, so he just gripped their hands tightly and nodded.

And hoped his heart could handle what was to come. The next vision.

He knew there would be another one. In close proximity to the World Trade Center, especially underground, the visions had come reliably. He both wanted and feared them. They could reveal Tommy to him, answer all his questions, blow apart all the secrets that had begun with his parents years ago.

They could also kill him.

As the train rushed under Manhattan, Zak closed his eyes and tried to conjure Tommy's voice, his presence. It was strange—he had no true memory of his twin, yet he felt as though he could imagine Tommy's presence with ease. It was like leaning on your arm until it went numb . . . and then feeling it slowly come back to life. Tommy was pins and needles throughout his whole being, awakening him from a clotted numbness he hadn't even discerned, because it had gone on so long that it had become normal.

But now . . . now he could feel again.

He and Tommy were like the old twin towers that had once stood at the end of this subway line—so alike on the outside, different on the inside. One with a bad heart, the other with kidneys that wouldn't work. One had died and one had lived, and maybe that was the way it was supposed to be. But maybe—just maybe—there was a way to fix that.

At the Spring Street stop—two away from the World Trade Center—a cop got on their car. Zak had scarcely registered her presence, when Khalid hauled him to his feet and pulled him off the subway just as the doors closed. Moira barely made it out with them.

"What the hell?" she demanded, rubbing her shoulder where the door had clipped her.

"Five-oh," Khalid said, as if that explained everything.

"Police?" Zak asked. He tried to follow along, but they were closer to the World Trade Center now, and his ears were beginning to buzz. Just a bit. Just enough to be distracting. He thought he could hear the scream of a gull, but it might have been the subway train pulling out of the station.

"Look," Khalid said, hustling them toward the exit stairs, "you think it's a coincidence the cops showed up here?"

"They randomly check subways—" Moira began.

"Random, my butt," Khalid interrupted as the three of them went up the stairs. Any static in Zak's ears vanished. "Look, Zak sleepwalked to Ground Zero before, right?"

Moira groaned, getting it. "His parents called the cops when we left the hospital, and they're going to be waiting for us."

"Right. And they're probably staking out the subways nearby."

To Zak, it all sounded remarkably paranoid and, at the same time, highly logical. "So what do we do, then?"

Khalid shrugged. "Go home and play video games?"

Zak ignored his buddy's attempt at humor. He could think only of Tommy's anguished voice, crying out for help. What if his brother was being tortured somehow? Who knew what happened to people after they died? Maybe Tommy was in torment—*had* been in torment for years—and only Zak could save him.

"We'll walk down to the World Trade Center," Zak said. This part of the city was unfamiliar to them all, but getting to the Freedom Tower wouldn't be difficult. It was the tallest building in the city—in the country—and its trapezoidal angles dominated the skyline. They couldn't miss it. "We'll stick to the smaller streets, avoid any cops we see."

"What do we do when we get there?" Moira asked.

It was a good question. Zak pretended to think about it, calling out in his thoughts for Tommy.

There was no answer.

"We'll think of something," he said with a confidence he did not feel. And they turned to the tower and began walking.

"There's a lot of cops here," Moira said nervously.

"There's always a lot of cops here," Khalid shot back.

They were on Fulton Street, near the Freedom Tower. Sure enough, the place was crawling with cops. Zak had last been here a few nights before, when he'd awoken from his sleepwalking adventure. He strained to hear the gull, the lap of waves. Something tickled at him, but it could have been the evening breeze coming down Fulton.

His parents were definitely onto him. Khalid was right—there was always a big police presence in this part of town—but there was a flavor in the air, something almost physical. A wariness. An awareness.

The cops were waiting for something.

For him.

"I think—" he started to say, and then the street vanished, the tower vanished. He was on the ship again. This time he forced himself not to panic, not to gape like an idiot. Instead, he stayed as calm as he could, quelling the lurching spasms of his heart.

But wait—his heart *wasn't* lurching. At all. It felt perfectly fine. Reliable. Not like *his* heart.

Shouts and screams all around him. Orders barked. He looked up. Rain spattered and spit. He looked around. The squeak of pulleys and the creak of wood. He ignored it all and—for the first time in a vision—looked *down*.

At his hands.

They were pale. And definitely white.

I'm not me in the vision! I'm someone else!

With that realization, things changed—he felt as though something slender and scalding hot had slipped into his gut and then split in two, moving up and down at the same time, cutting him in half. He gritted his teeth against the pain, and then the pain was gone and he could perceive both the rocking, storm-tossed deck of the sailing vessel *and* the crowded, humid sidewalk along Fulton Street. Moira and Khalid stared at him.

"He's zoning out again," Khalid said, worried, as if Zak weren't there at all.

"I'm okay," Zak said. His voice echoed weirdly in one ear but not in the other, as though he'd plugged one with cotton. He felt the rope from the ship slip through his hands, as it had once before. "I'm fine."

"Are you sure?" Moira leaned in. "You look pale. You're sweating again."

Khalid came closer, too, and started talking. Zak wished they would both shut up—it wasn't easy, maintaining this connection. On what he thought of as the "ship side," a burly man, naked to the waist and bleeding from a gash along his shoulder, grabbed Zak by the elbow and shouted horrible curses at him, ending with ". . . *and get yer keister up there now, God blast ye!*"

Zak felt that half of himself stumbling along, then climbing a rope ladder. He went dizzy as that half looked up—the rope ladder swayed sickeningly, occasionally slapping against a mast that rose to scrape the bottoms of the thick gray clouds overhead. As Zak climbed higher on the ship side, he found it more and more difficult to maintain a connection, especially with Khalid's and Moira's chatter on the street side. He broke the coupling, staggering on the street side for a moment as if physically shoved.

Khalid and Moira caught him before he could stumble off the curb and into traffic.

Zak, Tommy said, his voice clear. *This is it. You won't get another chance.*

Too many police, he told Tommy, eying the entrance to the subway. There were four cops loitering by the entrance and who knew how many more inside?

It's now or never. I need you, Zak. I can't come to you—you have to come to me.

"We have to go into the subway," Zak said.

Khalid and Moira glanced nervously at the entrance. They could see what he saw, obviously.

"Right . . . ," Khalid said with a smidgen of doubt in his voice. "And this is a good idea because . . . ?"

"I have to do it," Zak said. "You don't have to come with me."

Moira cleared her throat. "And that's exactly why we will."

Zak's own throat needed some clearing. He clenched his jaw, willing the tears clustering at the corners of his eyes to go away, and succeeded for the most part. "Thanks," he whispered.

"Let's go," said Khalid.

They sauntered to the subway entrance as casually as they could, hoping that they were wrong, that these cops were there just because it was part of a normal patrol, not because they were on the lookout for three kids on the run. And they closed in quite a ways before one of the cops tilted his head and nudged his partner, the two of them scrutinizing the trio as they got even closer.

You can do this, Tommy said, and his encouragement actually emboldened Zak and made him wish he could share it with Moira and Khalid.

A moment later, he realized he could—he took their hands in his own and squeezed reassuringly. His heart skipped a beat, then another, then settled back into a normal rhythm. For now.

The first cop nodded curtly and opened his mouth.

The ship side returned then, suddenly, wind howling and rain blowing.

"Run," Zak said, and released his friends' hands and charged straight ahead as fast as he could.

FIFTEEN

It was like running through a museum with only two paintings, copies of which were hung next to each other in an endless gallery of repetition. With each step, Zak moved from street side to ship side and then back again. Hot August night and concrete underfoot became chilly, storm-ravaged afternoon with rickety boards beneath. And over and over again.

He pressed through it, ignored it, focused on charging straight ahead, darting between the cops before they could react. Moira and Khalid were right with him, but he didn't let himself think of them. He could only think of straight ahead, of the subway.

You're doing it! Tommy yelled. *Keep going!*

Zak needed no encouragement—the shouts of the cops behind him were enough to propel him forward at top speed. His heart thrummed in his ears, and he tried not to think of what was happening in his chest as he raced ahead. He scrambled down the stairs, leaping from the third-to-last step to the floor below. Clusters of annoyed commuters shouted in aggravation; Zak flailed wildly, knocking people away, shoving aside the ones who didn't recoil from his pinwheeling arms. Grumbles about "crazy kids" and barks of recrimination filled the air, but he didn't care.

The station was crowded, but Zak was small and wiry and able to slip between people. As he gained the turnstile, he spared an instant to check over his shoulder—the cops were far behind him, larger and having trouble getting through the crowd.

He ducked under the turnstile and felt a trill of exhilaration and guilt at the same time. Jumping the turnstile was *wrong*. But fun. *Oh, man, Dad's gonna kick my butt for this.*

Ha! He had bigger problems. No time for that. They could fine him later, ground him for eternity. If he survived. He scooted along and emerged on the other side of the gate.

The platform! Tommy urged. *Hurry! The police are getting closer!*

He checked in both directions, saw the sign for the platform, the uptown E train. He charged in that direction, once again scattering passengers in his wake.

He caught a flicker from the ship side; there, he'd swung down from the rope ladder as the ship listed dangerously to port. (He didn't know how he knew port was the left side of the ship, but somehow he did.) On the street side, he stumbled to his left with the sway of the ship, then caught his balance and blasted down a flight of stairs two at a time. Rain started falling on the ship side; it was cold and needlelike on his skin, pelting him like tiny hailstones. He left wet footprints on the street side even though it was dry there.

Finally he emerged on the platform. Maybe a dozen people lingered, waiting for the next E to come along. Zak leaned against a column, catching his breath, his heart dashing along like a rabbit running from a Doberman. A man in a suit lifted an eyebrow and made a point of pulling his briefcase a little closer.

I don't want your briefcase, you tool. Tommy! Tommy!

Footsteps clattered behind him, and he dared a look over his shoulder, ready to take off again despite the dangerously rapid pounding in his chest. He would *not* let the cops catch him.

But it was Moira and Khalid, similarly out of breath, racing toward him. They almost collided with him but stopped just in time.

"Well?" Khalid demanded, heaving and wheezing. "Is this the place?"

"Is it?" Moira asked, also short of breath.

Zak didn't know what to tell them. He didn't want to disappoint them, but there was nothing here to indicate that he was in the right place. Whatever the *right place* might mean. He could still glimpse the ship side, where the pale boy whose eyes he saw through was now tugging at a hatch built into the deck of the ship. But that was all.

"I don't know," he admitted. And the crowd clustered along the stairs shouted in outrage.

"Cops are coming," Khalid said. "We gotta do something." He looked down the length of the platform. There was another exit at that end.

"They'll be blocking that side," Moira advised.

Tommy! Tommy!

You have the power, Zak. Not me.

What?

It has to be you. I've brought you this far. You have to come the rest of the way on your own.

Zak pondered for a moment. He'd always been *waiting*,

passively receiving the visions and the voice. But was it true? Could he force it to happen? Could he push forward instead of merely standing his ground?

He imagined for a moment that he heard something else, something new—a far-off cry of anguish. No. It was a gull from ship-side, maybe. That's all.

I can do this. I can do it.

The cops were almost down the stairs, shoving out of the way those people who didn't move at their shouts. Zak grabbed Moira's and Khalid's hands.

"I need you guys." He didn't know how he knew it or why it was true. Only that it *was* true.

"We're here," Moira said, and squeezed his hand.

"Hurry," Khalid muttered, gazing back at the stairs and the cops.

Zak didn't know if he *could* hurry. He wasn't sure exactly what he was trying to do in the first place, so he had no idea if it could be hurried. Maybe it was like baking a pie—you couldn't just turn up the heat to make it bake faster. You'd end up with a burned shell surrounding raw fruit paste.

But maybe . . . maybe it was like a fire hose, and you could open the nozzle wider and let the water fly.

He closed his eyes and envisioned ship-side. The sky was gone now; the version of Zak on that side had gone belowdecks. A barrel screeched as it strained its moorings, then snapped loose from the wall and rolled toward him. Zak dived out of the way; the barrel smashed against a column in the middle of the compartment. Zak had trouble making out the size of the compartment because the only light came from a flickering torch—

A torch that now dropped to the wooden floor. It rolled, guttering.

The ship had juddered, the entire thing shaking and grinding to a sudden halt, as though it had run aground in the middle of the water.

"Zak! They're surrounding us!" It was Khalid, heard as though through a bad cell connection. Somewhere, ghostly fingers tightened on his own.

The rolling torch fetched up against a pallet tied to the deck. A lick of flame lashed its length. Zak drew in a deep breath at the sudden eruption of light and heat in the enclosed space.

Zak knew what he had to do; he had to somehow marry ship side to street side. He could see into both of them, but he could be in only one. If he could make them intersect, then maybe—just maybe—he could cross over. . . .

He opened his eyes and staggered. Ahead of him was the trough beside the subway platform, along the bottom of which ran the tracks for the trains. But overlaying it was the belowdecks compartment on the ship, now ablaze with fire. Zak's heart double-timed, or maybe it was the sensation of his own heart beating alongside the ship-side person's.

Down in the tunnel, the clatter and clang of a train echoed.

"Step away from the platform!" a voice shouted. At the same time, someone yelled, *"Man overboard! Man overboard!"*

Zak's vision doubled as he stared at the overlap of the ship and the subway station. The train grew louder and louder, merging with the creak of the ship and the crackle of the flame until they became a single, pervasive chatter and rattle.

And—

There.

Zak's breath whooshed out of him, and he doubled over as though to vomit, but nothing came out. Khalid and Moira held him steady.

The train was gone. The ship was gone.

A massive wave of water was coming down the subway tunnel. Just like the one he'd seen the other day.

Hurry! Hurry, Zak! I can't wait much longer!

The last time he'd seen this, Tommy had told him to run.

Hurry!

Zak tossed looks over both shoulders. A cop crept closer, one hand on his nightstick, the other reaching out cautiously. Khalid and Moira, within reach, shrank back toward Zak. Nowhere to go. They were caught between the cops and the edge of the platform.

The water rushed at him, a liquid bullet throwing off wavelets, lapping at and overrunning the border of the platform.

Zak! Now!

Moira shrieked as a hand clamped on her. Khalid shouted.

Zaaaaaaak!

Zak took a deep breath and leaped into the water.

SIXTEEN

The water vanished. Zak's legs pumped in empty air above the subway track.

The train reappeared, bearing down on him.

SEVENTEEN

The water returned, bubbling and fizzing around him as he collided with it in midair.

Somehow, somewhere in there, the train hurtled along the track as if nothing was wrong, its headlight wavering and glowing under the water, like an angry, fluorescing lamprey. Zak opened his mouth to scream and swallowed salt water. The train hurtled toward him.

EIGHTEEN

The water was gone again. Zak fell toward the tracks, praying he wouldn't hit the electrified third rail.

NINETEEN

And the water came back. Zak, still choking on seawater, struggled against the flood, thrashing.

There was fire somewhere. Somewhere above. The ship. Part of it had caught fire.

He had to stop thinking of the ship. Of the train. He had to think *between* them. He had to focus. . . .

TWENTY

The world went silent. Zak hung suspended in something that was neither water nor air.

Between. Think between *the ship and the train.*

Something cracked open ahead of him, as though a hole had been torn through his line of sight. He could perceive the edges of it; they crackled and popped with strange energies.

Tommy? Tommy, can you hear me?

Faintly: *Zak! You—*

Gone.

Then back, strong: *Go! Go now!*

There was nothing to push against, nothing to use for propulsion, but Zak nevertheless found himself moving toward the hole. As he approached it, his scalp buzzed with static, and his skin crawled.

And then he was through and

TWENTY-ONE

flailing in the water, floundering and writhing. He was fully submerged and at first couldn't tell which direction was up. He struggled against the force of the water, ready for it to vanish again, figuring that if he could tread long enough, the subway station would return.

But a burn settled into his lungs.

The water wasn't going away.

He kicked, lurching up and to the side. He hadn't had time to inhale and hold a proper breath before being plunged into the water; his vision blurred and he longed to gasp in, but he knew that would be death.

Instead, he kicked again and karate-chopped with his hands, pulling himself along and upward. After a few moments he broke the surface, and his chest inflated with a desperate, instinctive breath. He hacked out some water and phlegmy crud from his throat, spitting it into the foamy green water surrounding him.

And above him . . .

Not the steel girders, pipes, and cables of the World Trade Center subway station. No.

A black, star-speckled sky, stretching in every dimension to infinity.

What?

"Hey!" a familiar voice shouted. "What the *hell*?"

It was Khalid, a few yards to Zak's right. (*No, starboard— you're in the water now.*) Khalid's sunglasses hung comically askew from one ear.

"Khalid! What happened?"

"The flood must have washed us through the tunnels and out through a vent or something into the river."

Moira cut cleanly across the water toward him, her stroke smooth and sure. Zak actually could swim quite well, but the shock of the transition had caught him off guard. He treaded water until Moira reached him. Her glasses ran with trickling speckles of water; she looked at him over the top of the lenses.

"Are you okay?" she asked, now treading as well and flipping her sodden hair back from her forehead.

"I think so. What happened? Are we in the . . . ?" He thought about Manhattan's geography. "The East River? The Hudson Bay?"

Khalid had swum over by then. "Can we figure that out later? I can't keep this up forever, and who knows *what*'s in this water."

True. The waterways around New York weren't renowned for their cleanliness.

"Think you can make it?" Moira asked.

Zak nodded. His answer didn't really matter. Either he could swim or he couldn't. If he couldn't, there was no way Moira and Khalid could tow him to . . .

To . . .

To where?

"I see something over there," Khalid said, hooking a thumb.

Zak peered in that direction. It was dark out, with only a little glow from the buildings ahead, but he could make out what looked like a seawall or a bulwark. It was long and dirty white, with a sketch of vertical lines straight before them. A ladder.

Moira outpaced the boys easily. Zak struggled to keep up with Khalid, his breath coming only with great difficulty, his strokes weak. *You can do this*, he thought calmly. *You can do this.* He didn't know if he was talking to himself generally or to his heart specifically, but he settled into a rhythm of words and actions, encouraging himself as he kicked and stroked. Soon he was at the ladder.

Moira was halfway up already. Khalid grabbed a stringer and drifted off to one side, too exhausted to speak. He nodded, urging Zak toward the ladder. Zak decided not to argue; he wanted out of the water.

He ascended the ladder as quickly as he could, his weight returning, magnified by his sodden clothes. Hauling hand over hand, he eventually reached the top and collapsed to the ground next to Moira, who lay on her back, breathing heavily.

Zak shivered. The night was cooler and drier than he remembered it being before their mad dash into the subway station. Darker, too—twilight had suddenly become late night.

He caught his breath, coughed up some more water and phlegm. Khalid's head poked up over the lip of the seawall, his sunglasses hanging askew from one ear. There was a hum in the distance, and the sound of Moira's breath and the rasp of his own lungs. And then Khalid groaned in complaint as he levered himself off the ladder.

How long they lay sprawled there, catching their breath, he had no idea. He counted the irregular beats of his heart and waited until his chest returned to something like normal (would it ever truly be normal again, though?) before sitting up. Next to him, Moira sat cross-legged on the ground, frowning and squinting as she tried, without luck, to clean her glasses with her soaking-wet T-shirt.

"Where are we?" Khalid asked. He'd tucked his shades into the collar of his shirt and was peering around.

Zak couldn't get his bearings. The skyline was unfamiliar from this angle—he was used to seeing Manhattan from Brooklyn. But then he looked out into the water and caught a glimpse of the Statue of Liberty. He sighed in relief.

"Okay, guys, it's all good. We're probably somewhere near Battery Park. I can see—"

"Guys?" Khalid's voice wavered like sand nudged along by the tide. "Uh, what happened to the Brooklyn Bridge?"

Zak looked in the direction Khalid was pointing. The Brooklyn Bridge was gone.

TWENTY-TWO

They all stared. The familiar lighted span of the Brooklyn Bridge was nowhere to be seen. It should have been easily visible from the southern edge of Manhattan, but instead there was nothing.

"Wait," Zak said after a moment of silent horror. "Wait. I think I see the *Manhattan* Bridge way up there, but there's no . . . This doesn't make any sense."

"You *think*?" Khalid exploded.

Zak waved both hands, trying to silence his friend and pump more blood into his brain at the same time. It was right on the tip of his tongue. . . .

"Where *are* we?" he asked. "Look around. This doesn't make *any* sense. The Brooklyn Bridge should be over *there*." He pointed. "But there's just water."

"No kidding!" Khalid stomped a foot. "What happened to the bridge?"

"It's not just the bridge!" Zak told him. "Look *around*."

And they did.

They stood on a concrete walkway that formed a smooth arc

above the water they'd swum through. The walkway transitioned into a carpet of grass, cut with cobblestone paths, heading off to what Zak presumed was the north. To the south and east was nothing but a railing and water. They were at the very tip of the island of Manhattan.

But given the position of the Manhattan Bridge in the distance, they should have been farther uptown. Somewhere around the World Trade Center.

"It's like the island . . ." Zak trailed off, not wanting to say the word *shrank*.

"It's like someone cut off the end of it," Khalid said, which was just as likely an answer. "What the . . . ?"

He and Zak turned slow circles. The skyline of Manhattan rose up to the north, but it had changed. Gone were the familiar Freedom Tower and the distant spire of the Empire State Building. Instead, even in a city renowned for its tall buildings, the skyline was now replete with megaskyscrapers—a phalanx of one-hundred-plus-story towers arrayed beyond the park in which the three of them now stood. More baffling, in and among the skyscrapers, tubes—roughly fifty stories up—connected various buildings in a zigzag pattern. The buildings and the connecting tubes were lit as though by neon, though not as garish. The light was simple, off-white, and it seemed to fluoresce more than shine.

The entire cityscape had transformed into a gently glowing series of impossibly tall towers, and the island itself had shriveled.

In a panic, Zak spun around, looking east across the river toward Brooklyn. It was still there, hazy in a light offshore fog.

Through the mist, he could make out a vaguely familiar skyline, interrupted by more clusters of too-tall buildings, luminous with that odd sort of light.

"It's been washed away," Khalid choked, pacing the edge of the walkway, glaring down into the water as though he could surface the rest of the island through sheer willpower. "We did something. When we jumped into that water, we did *something*—"

"Stop it," Zak said, grabbing him by the elbow. "We didn't—"

"You don't know!" Khalid shook Zak off and rounded on him, his throat working, his neck straining. Zak had never, ever seen Khalid so angry. He'd never even imagined his friend could get this angry.

"You don't know what happened!" Khalid went on. "We just ran off and hopped into the water, and when we came out, everything was screwed up! The whole southern part of the city is *gone*, man! You think it's just a coincidence? We *did* something!"

Zak opened his mouth to speak . . . and his heart thrummed once in an extra-special way he'd never experienced before. It felt like it was trying to crawl up his throat.

"We didn't do anything." He could only manage a whisper.

"Are you *kidding* me?" Khalid grabbed Zak and shoved him toward the railing. "Look!" He pointed. "That's the Statue of Liberty, way out there. How far is it *supposed* to be?"

Khalid was right. Zak's earlier glimpse had been fooled by his exhaustion and surprise. Now that he really paid attention, he could tell: Liberty Island was so far in the distance that he could barely see it through the late-night gloom. A huge chunk of lower Manhattan was gone. Either that or . . .

"The island moved?" He couldn't believe he was actually saying it, but it was somehow more comforting that the alternative. Even his heart relaxed a little bit at the idea. "Maybe all of Manhattan is still here. The island just *moved*."

"*Just* moved?" Khalid howled. "Do you realize how insane this all is? Do you have any idea—"

"Guys!"

"—how big a freakin' deal this is, no matter *what* happened—"

"Khalid, I don't know what to—"

"—because we *did* something, Zak! We wiped out a whole—"

"—say, but come on, man, we just got in the water—"

"—mess of people. They're *dead* because of something we did—"

"No, no—"

"Guys!" Moira screamed the word this time, and both Zak and Khalid broke off. Zak hadn't realized it, but they'd gotten so close that their noses almost touched, leaning in toward each other, yelling into each other's faces, not even hearing each other. Now, panting, they turned as one to Moira, standing a few yards away.

"Come. Over. Here," Moira said firmly, gesturing.

She waited for them along the railing that prevented people from falling into the water, on the far side of the gap for the ladder they'd climbed. Some sort of granite pedestal stood there. As they drew closer, Zak saw that a bronze plaque had been bolted into the face of the pedestal.

"Read it," she ordered them, and they both leaned in to scrutinize the embossed text.

> HOUSTON CONFLUX
> You are standing at the spot of the world-famous
> Houston Conflux, where the East and Houston Rivers
> meet at the Atlantic Ocean. First sailed by Captain
> Henry Hudson in 1609, the Houston Conflux ...

It went on, but Zak had seen enough. "Houston Conflux?" he asked. "There's no such thing. And it's not the *Houston* River—it's the *Hudson* River. What *is* this?"

"It says here," Khalid said, peering closely at the plaque, "that the Conflux was one of the continent's busiest seaports until 1805, when a fire on the docks wiped out most of the shipping facilities. Shipping moved up the Houston River while repairs were under way, but the War of 1807 interrupted the rebuilding, and eventually plans were scrapped. ..." Khalid cleared his throat. "Okay, so I'm not the best student of history, but I have *never* heard of the War of 1807."

"That's because there's no such thing," Zak said. If there was one thing he knew, it was history. It came from having a history professor as a father. "There was a War of 1812, but not 1807. And there *was* a big fire in lower Manhattan that wiped out a lot of stuff, but it was in 1776, back when the British occupied the city during the Revolutionary War. It doesn't make any sense."

"None of this makes sense," Khalid complained.

"Makes perfect sense," Moira said, her voice clipped. "Alternate universe."

Khalid and Zak exchanged a glance of mutual confusion before looking over at Moira. She wasn't paying any attention to them, focused on trying to peel her T-shirt away from her body and wave it dry in spots.

"Earth to Moira," Khalid said. "Mind explaining?"

She didn't even look at them. "An alternate universe. A parallel earth."

"A what?"

Moira gave up her attempt to dry even the hem of her shirt, but she still wouldn't meet their eyes, instead scrutinizing her water-speckled lenses. "Basic physics. Universes in superposition. This place exists in a different dimensional space than ours, but otherwise is nearly identical."

"This isn't one of your sci-fi books, Moira!" Zak was surprised by the outrage in his voice. Outrage and fear, if he was being honest. Because if this was true . . .

He didn't want it to be true.

"It's not science fiction." If she was upset or scared by his tone, she didn't show it. She sniffed. "There's a whole branch of physics and there's something called brane theory, but I'm not going to bore you guys with it." Her expression said, *You wouldn't get it anyway.* "Physicists have been theorizing multiple universes for decades. The 'many worlds interpretation' of quantum physics."

"Not buying it," Khalid said. "Makes more sense that we did something to flood lower Manhattan."

"Then explain the different skyline." Moira pointed north, to the too-tall buildings with their crisscross of tubes. "Explain what is *obviously* some kind of subway in the sky. Explain the War of 1807 and the Houston River."

Khalid opened his mouth to answer, then gave up, shaking his head. He turned away from the two of them and stared out across what was at least still called the East River. Zak stood between them, not sure what to do. Comfort Khalid? Challenge Moira?

But there was no challenging her. His gut knew what his brain had been denying.

They were in an entirely different universe. A different version of the New York City they'd grown up in, superficially similar, but with enough changes to make it an alien landscape.

No Freedom Tower. And from where he stood, it seemed that the water came up to what would have been Fulton Street in what he now thought of as "their world."

"That's why it's called the Houston Conflux," he muttered. "Different landmark, but named after the same guy."

He glanced over at Khalid, but his best friend had taken a couple of steps away, arms folded over his chest, back ramrod stiff. He clearly did not want to be bothered right now.

"You're the science expert," Zak said to Moira. "How do we get back to our world?"

Moira blinked. Her expression—passive and calm—did not change as she said, "Home? I don't have the slightest idea."

TWENTY-THREE

"You're joking, right?" Zak peered closely at Moira, looking for a hint of a smile or a grin. "There has to be a way home. There's always a way home, right?"

"I don't know what to tell you, Zak. I don't even know how we got here in the first place—how am I supposed to know how to get us home?"

She seemed nonchalant, but Zak had known her long enough that he could detect the slight tremor in her voice, the quirk of her lips, the crinkle of her eyes. And the way she'd been talking since her discovery of the plaque—clipped, brusque.

Moira was terrified and doing her best not to show it.

Happy-go-lucky Khalid was sulking, and supergenius Moira was baffled. It was the perfect time to panic.

Zak ran a hand through his still-wet hair. There had to be some kind of explanation. And if there was an explanation, then there had to be a solution. Right?

Right?

"You have to think," he told Moira. "You have to think harder than you've ever thought before, Moira. We have to figure out how to get home."

She wouldn't look at him, staring instead at the plaque celebrating the Houston Conflux. "There's nothing we can do about it right now," she said, her voice tightly controlled. "So there's no point in panicking."

"Don't you want to go home?"

"Yes," she said, stiff and emotionless, still staring. "But panicking isn't going to get me there any sooner."

Zak clenched his fists. Why did she have to be so infuriatingly rational?

"Well, think, at least!" he barked at her, then went to check on Khalid, who was still staring across the river. Great. One friend was shutting down, and the other was shutting him out.

Khalid spoke quietly, without looking over at him, still staring out at the alien version of Brooklyn. "You think maybe there are versions of *us* in this world? Living across the river in Brooklyn, no clue that we're standing here. Hanging out with their families, just chilling?"

Family . . . Zak shivered as a breeze found him. The air was warm, but as it blew through his sodden clothing, it chilled him. Family. Tommy. In the shock of their arrival in this other universe, he'd entirely forgotten. This wasn't just about getting home; it was about family. Family that had left him, family that had lied to him, family that was gone.

Tommy? He hurled the thought with all his concentration. *Tommy? Can you hear me? Is this what you wanted when you told me to go into the water? Did you want me to come here?*

Nothing. No answer.

Just great. As if the situation weren't bad enough: His best friends wouldn't look at him or even at each other. He was trapped in another universe. And he couldn't sense his twin brother.

He'd never felt more alone in his life. Which was saying something.

He put a hand on Khalid's shoulder. "Hey, man. You okay?"

"Oh, sure," Khalid said with a scarily calm sarcasm. "I'm just wondering if my parents had a boy in this universe. Or if they ever met at all. Maybe my dad never got out of Iran. Or, hey—maybe there *is* no Iran! Who knows, right? What fun!"

"Well, there's a city here, where there's one in our world. So it seems like this universe is pretty similar to ours. I'm sure there's an Iran."

Khalid grunted as he absorbed that.

"I'm sorry I yelled at you before," Zak said. It wasn't much, but it was all he had to offer. He couldn't go through all this alone. And he couldn't let the Three Basketeers break up. Not now. They needed each other too badly.

Khalid groaned. "Yeah. Me too. Crap!" He threw his hands up and turned around for the first time since being captivated by the sight across the river. "My parents were right—I should have stayed home today."

"We should have hung out in my hospital room and watched TV," Zak agreed.

They bumped fists and grinned at each other. "Now we have to get Science Girl to come around."

They stood on either side of Moira, who now sat cross-legged on the ground, manipulating some rocks and twigs she'd arrayed before her, staring down at them as though they held the answers to all the mysteries of the universe (whichever one).

"Hey, Moira," Zak said, "maybe you want to join us here in the real world?"

"One of them, at least," Khalid joked weakly.

Moira said nothing.

"Moira, come on. We can't just stand here all night. We need to figure out what happened."

Moira gathered up the rocks and twigs and stood. She handed Zak a small rock. "Stand like this," she said, positioning him so that he held the rock out at chest height, an arm's length from his body.

Without a pause, she handed Khalid a larger rock and arranged him so that he held his at head height, hovering over Zak's by a foot or two.

"Khalid, the rock you're holding represents our world, our New York City. Zak, you've got this world."

"What are we doing?" Zak asked.

"You said we need to figure out what happened," she told him. "This is what happened."

She took a twig and stretched to balance it atop Khalid's. "This is us."

"Looks just like us."

Moira ignored Khalid's barb. "I can't explain the science behind it. Just trust me on this. Physics tells us that universes exist in great numbers, side by side. Imagine an apartment building with an infinite number of units next to one another, with thick walls so that you can't hear the people next door. You don't even know they're there."

"What's the deal with the rocks?" Zak asked. His arm was getting tired.

"Just trying to illustrate a point, and I don't have anything to draw with. Imagine that apartment building. And one day, you knock down the wall."

"How?" Khalid asked. "Why?"

"Doesn't matter. You knock it down, and you discover another apartment next door, similar to yours but a little different. Like, maybe some of the rooms are positioned differently."

At this point, she reached up to drag the twig along Khalid's rock. "So, this is us, in New York. And we're going along just fine until . . . *something* happens." She knocked the twig off the rock. It dropped and skimmed past Zak's rock, hitting the ground.

"New York is different here," she said. "In our world, there was land. Here, water. So we came through and ended up in the drink. Just like if you knocked down the apartment wall from your bedroom and found yourself in someone else's living room instead. Get it?"

Zak wasn't completely sure he understood, but he got enough of it. As he dropped the rock, he realized Moira was shaking. Just the tiniest bit. She turned back to the pedestal and leaned on it, her hands gripping the edges so hard that her fingers turned even paler than usual. Her face had blanched; her spray of freckles stood out in stark relief. Her body vibrated with some barely contained emotion, and if she'd had the strength, Zak knew, she would have ripped the pedestal right out of the ground.

She whispered something. Zak couldn't hear it, so he said, "What was that?"

"I *am* thinking," she said through gritted teeth. "You told me to think, and I'm thinking so hard, Zak, and I've been thinking this whole time, but I can't figure it out. I can't figure out how to get us home. I'm not smart enough. I can't figure it out. I'm so sorry. I'm sorry, guys. I can't. I'm not—"

Zak pried her right hand from the plaque and held it tightly. "Stop apologizing. It's not your fault. I shouldn't have yelled at you like that. It's not your job to figure out how to get us home."

She finally turned to him. Tears swam in her eyes behind the smeared lenses of her glasses. "Then whose job *is* it?"

"All of ours," Khalid said, and put his hand on top of theirs. "Three Basketeers all the way."

Moira sniffled and nodded. "Three Basketeers."

"Three Basketeers," Zak said. And then, in his mind, *Tommy? You want to be the fourth?*

Again, there was nothing.

Almost nothing.

"Zak?"

Tommy's voice.

In his ears this time, not his mind.

Zak spun around at the sound of his name, seeking something in the enfolding purple dark. He was surprised to realize that Khalid and Moira were glancing around, too.

"Who said that?" Khalid demanded, panicked. "Who *said* that?"

"You heard it?" Zak asked. "You heard it this time?"

"Is that the voice?" Moira asked. "Is that what you've been hearing all along?"

"I think so—"

"Zak!" the voice called again, and they all startled. It seemed even closer, as if it had emerged from the air between them. They stared at each other, then at the ground, then at the sky, but still nothing.

"I'm trying . . . ," it said, and faded.

"What is going *on* here?" Khalid asked. Moira—who had no doubt read of circumstances eerier and more terrifying in her library of creepy sci-fi and fantasy novels—looked thoroughly freaked out. Zak understood—he'd been living with this voice in his head as long as he could remember. He'd become accustomed to it, and even though it had now transferred itself into the open air, it was still the same voice. He had no fear of it, and it did not surprise him.

"Guys," he said, "calm down and be quiet—"

"I think it was from over here," Khalid said, pointing.

"No. It's this way," Moira insisted.

"Guys, just settle down and listen, okay?" He took Moira's hand and grabbed Khalid by the shoulder. "You can't find it, and you can't force it. Just let—"

"ZAK!"

This time the voice doubled in on itself as its volume spiked; it echoed in Zak's mind at the same time as it rang in the air. He hissed in a pained breath and released his friends, clapping his hands to his ears. But that couldn't keep the voice out, as it repeated his name over and over. It was like having nails driven one by one into his skull. He flinched with each repetition of his name, driven to his knees with the pain.

Someone touched him, hands on his shoulders, and a voice shouted, but he couldn't hear it over the voice in his head. Feet padded near him, back and forth, moving as though in desperation, but he couldn't open his eyes to see which of his friends was in motion. The pain was too intense.

"—see it, Zak!" Khalid's voice finally broke through, tinny and small, as if from a great distance. "You have to see it!"

Zak forced his eyes open. Khalid crouched near him,

steadying them both with hands on Zak's shoulders. Moira was running a jagged, zigzagging path from the pedestal to the two of them and back, breathless, staring.

There, in the space between them all, a mist had gathered. Wispy and translucent, it purled and gathered and spread and regathered as if with a mind of its own, floating and grasping from a foot above the ground to six or seven feet straight up. It was a dirty-white color, a sort of grayish pearl, climbing and drifting down over and over as it pulsed in and out.

"What *is* it?" Moira was jogging its perimeter, watching it from all angles, her eyes wide and her expression one of sheer bafflement.

Khalid shook Zak. "What is it, man? What's going on here?"

"I don't—"

But then he did. He did know.

The voice in his head stopped saying his name.

Almost! it cried. *I'm almost there!*

"Tommy!" Zak screamed, and launched himself to his feet. He would have thrown himself at the mist, which had now coalesced into a cloud of writhing, snakelike tendrils of vapor that seemed to boil in the very air, but for Khalid, who held him back.

"We don't know what it is," Khalid cautioned.

Almost there! Don't go! So close!

And then the cloud collapsed in on itself with a strangely soft hissing sound. There was an instant of silence—nothing but Zak's own breath and his heartbeat in his ears—and then the cloud flowered back from its pinpoint of collapse, only this time it had color to it—gold and red and blue.

The eruption of light stunned them all, and they froze there, staring at a silent, contained explosion of fireworks. Its colors washed over them, harmless, until the finale, when a burst of powerful white light forced them all to flinch away and cover their eyes.

"I'm here! I did it!" said the voice.

"It's him," Zak shouted, blinking spots out of his eyes. Fumbling, he managed to grab both Moira's and Khalid's hands, and he squeezed them tightly. "It's Tommy!"

And as his vision cleared, for the first time in his memory, he saw his brother.

TWENTY-FOUR

Tommy looked exactly like Zak, which was no surprise. When he smiled, wisps of smoke peeled away from his lips, as if the mere motion of smiling had cut loose some part of him.

"Zak," he said, and spread his arms wide. More streamers of smoke peeled from him, and Zak realized that if he squinted, he could barely make out the trees of the park *through* his brother.

Zak had lunged forward, but Moira and Khalid held him back. "Dude," Khalid said, "we don't know what's going on."

"I'm not going to hurt you. *Any* of you," Tommy said. "I need your help. We both do."

"Both?"

"How do we get home?" Moira said suddenly.

Zak wrestled himself free of them and approached Tommy. The air grew colder and drier near his brother, and he knew even before he extended a hand that he would feel nothing when he tried to touch him. Sure enough, his hand went through, as though sweeping aside mist from dry ice. "Tommy, what's going on?"

The boy seemed to take a breath. Like a hole blown through smoke by a fan, a section of his chest faded from view for a moment before filling back in. "I'm not sure how long I can sustain this projection. It's difficult. Even here, where the rules are different."

"What rules?" Khalid asked.

"Are the laws of physics different here?" Moira chimed in.

Zak wished they would both just shut up. He was standing mere inches from his brother! Was Tommy not truly dead after all? Or was this alternate universe a place where people from his own world went after they died?

He waved his friends quiet with a look that said, *Stop messing with this!* Abashed, they both fell silent.

Tommy shook his head sadly, the curls of fog that drifted away from him with each motion making him look even sadder. "I'm here, stuck. Unable to leave the physical universe, to move on. Just like poor Godfrey."

Zak peered around, knowing he would see nothing, but straining for a glimpse nonetheless. "Who's Godfrey?"

"He's my friend. He's a spirit, like I am, only he's been trapped for so much longer. He's endured . . . I don't have time to explain it all. Godfrey is from *this* universe," Tommy said, "and he's making it possible for me to manifest like this. He has power. . . ."

"What kind of power?" Moira piped up.

Tommy inhaled again, and a little more of him vanished. "I have to explain everything. . . ." He paused. "No, there is no time for everything. I'll try to explain enough."

"But—" Moira said.

Zak spun around and gave her a death glare. "He doesn't have time for questions! Let him talk!"

"Godfrey was on a ship," Tommy told them, "sailing from the islands to Manhattan City. But a storm surprised them, and they were swamped. They should have been able to press through, but the hull was torn open, even though they were miles from shore."

"Wait a second," Khalid said. "*That* boat? The one under the World Trade Center? That was, like, *centuries* ago."

"The boat crossed over," Moira muttered. "It somehow slipped from this universe to ours, and there was land where they didn't expect it."

Tommy went on as if they hadn't spoken. "He knew a spell, an old spell from the islands. He could live on after death. So he cast the spell and survived as a spirit. Alone until he met me."

Tommy grinned sadly. Zak's throat tightened with horror and memory. Being alone like that would be the worst thing he could imagine. He had thought that *he* had been alone, but there had always been Khalid and Moira. And his parents, he supposed. This Godfrey person had been alone for a long, long time until he'd found Tommy.

"You and I share a special link, Zak. Closer than any other two people in the world, closer even than most twins. United by our birth and our disease. My death was only the beginning for me. Because of our connection, I remained bound to earth instead of moving on like most of the dead. Then Godfrey and I found each other. Two lost spirits, trapped in the land of the living for different reasons. But we realized that we could combine our strength and speak to you. You couldn't *always* hear us, but sometimes you could."

"I thought you were imaginary. Or Uncle Tomás."

Tommy paused and opened his mouth to speak again. Zak

realized, to his horror, that Tommy's feet had dissolved into a chaotic, foggy swirl of colors, and the effect was slowly climbing up his legs. It was as though he were unraveling before their eyes.

"We had to bring you here," Tommy said quickly, aware of his time ticking away. "This world works differently. You would call it magic, but it really isn't. Here, Godfrey and I have a chance to live again."

"How?" Zak stepped even closer, and the conflicted eddies of light and fog that made up Tommy's form became more indistinct. He was fading with each passing instant—Zak had to learn as much as possible. Now.

"We need energy. Power. You'll have to figure out most of it for yourself," Tommy said. By now, he'd unraveled even further— from his chest down, he was a dissipating patch of smoke, rapidly vanishing into the night air. "Godfrey says you'll need something called electroleum. It's a power source, and more. It—"

"It sounds dangerous," Khalid said nervously.

By now Tommy's body had disappeared all the way up to his throat. He was a wispy head floating in the air above a fast-clearing wedge of smoke, with one arm still drifting loose, like a marionette's controlled by a separate puppeteer. "Completely safe. We need a massive energy source. Will free us." He was beginning to sound garbled, like a drowning man calling for help. But panic never touched his eyes. They bore into Zak, drilling deep to plant the importance of what he said. "Rupture walls between life and death," he said. "So much energy. Set us free."

His face and head unraveled then, spinning out into a gentle drift of vapor until there was nothing left of him save for a smear of color on the air.

And then that, too, disintegrated, torn apart by the breeze, and they saw nothing but the night and the sky and the trees and the water, and even in Zak's own mind, they were alone again.

Zak heard Moira and Khalid chattering nearby, but he stayed rooted to the spot where Tommy had manifested and then disappeared. Zak sought any kind of contact—nothing came. He'd been so close! Tommy was . . . well, not *alive*, maybe, but still existing. Still himself. Even on some kind of . . . spirit plane. The idea should have sounded ridiculous to Zak. It was the garbage and nonsense his dad had railed against his whole life. But then again, his dad had also lied to him his whole life. His dad didn't know everything. So who cared what his dad thought.

Besides: His dad was in another universe entirely. Dad—and Mom and Dr. Campbell and everyone else who had deceived him—didn't matter anymore. He had his best friends with him, and he would soon have his twin brother as well.

That was all he needed.

If only he could make contact! As much as he tried, he could detect not even the tiniest bit of Tommy or the mysterious Godfrey. Maybe they'd used too much of their power to speak to him. Maybe it would take time.

Yeah. Time. That's all. It would just take time.

Khalid and Moira approached Zak. "You all right, man?"

"Do you need a second?" Moira asked.

Did he? The sensible thing was probably to sit down and try to clear his mind. But the problem was, his mind felt totally clear. For the first time in a long time, he didn't doubt his own sanity or his own senses. His brother was kinda alive, kinda dead, but it was the kinda-alive part that mattered. Tommy *was*, and there was a way to make him whole again.

"I don't need a minute," he told them. "I need to find out where we are, first."

"One map coming up." Khalid pulled his phone out of his pocket and fired it up. It flickered for a moment, then died.

"Water, idiot," Moira said. "We ruined our phones when we crossed over into the ocean."

"The Conflux," Zak corrected her.

"Right. The Conflux. And even if our phones *did* work, they wouldn't work anyway."

Khalid blinked. "Even *I* know that doesn't make any sense."

But Zak got it. "There probably aren't compatible cell phone networks over here. They might not even use Wi-Fi. Who knows?"

They stared at each other. For the first time, Zak realized, he had no idea what to do next. They'd come over into the water, so they'd swum to shore. And then they'd tried to figure out where they were. And then they'd listened to Tommy.

But now?

There was nothing for them to do.

Nothing at all.

Feeling suddenly exposed out by the Conflux, they retreated from the water's edge, deeper into the park, following one of the pathways. The park was lit by that same odd sort of pale light they saw on the buildings uptown, captured in decorative swirls atop tall poles. It bathed the trees and the pathways with a soft glow that reminded Zak of early, dim sunlight behind curtains.

A little ways in, among a cluster of trees and shrubbery, they found an odd-looking bench on the side of the path. It was made

of something that looked like bronze, with ornate, curling arm-
rests. Zak, exhausted, slumped into the seat.

"You think it's safe here?" Khalid asked.

"We've been here, yelling at each other, for a while, and no
one has shown up," Zak reasoned. "It's probably okay."

"We don't know what or where is safe," Moira pointed out.
"So we should be cautious no matter what."

"Buzzkill," Khalid said lightly, but then made a point of pacing a perimeter, poking into bushes and looking around trees.
Moira followed his example, and once they were reasonably certain they were alone, they both joined Zak on the bench.

"Did we really just see a ghost?" Khalid said. "Because I have
to tell you—this is way freakier than I signed up for."

"There are some theories," Moira said, "that the body's elec-
trical impulses could continue after physical death. It's all sort
of bull, though." She shrugged. "Then again, we're in a whole
different universe. The physics here could be different. *Everything*
could be different."

"But there's still air to breathe," Khalid said. "There's still
trees and buildings. I don't get it. It's a whole 'nother universe,
right? Why isn't it weirder?"

Moira shrugged. "I don't know. If there's an infinite number
of universes, some of them are going to look a lot like ours. Like,
what did you have for breakfast this morning?"

"Oatmeal," Khalid said.

"Sure, okay." Moira nodded enthusiastically, warming up. "So,
somewhere out there is a universe *exactly* like our own with the
only difference being that you had scrambled eggs instead of
oatmeal."

"That sounds like a waste of a universe. And I hate eggs."

"Not in that universe," Moira said. "That universe's Khalid likes eggs. And that's the only difference. But from that tiny difference, big changes can happen. A ripple effect. You eating eggs instead of oatmeal could end up changing the world in big ways."

"I always knew I was important."

"We need to focus, guys." The conversation was interesting, but Zak didn't think speculating about Khalid's breakfast choices was going to help them. "We saw what we saw," he told them. "We're not going to start second-guessing it, okay? We all saw it. We all heard it. It happened. This isn't about theories. It's about what we actually witnessed. Now we have to figure out what to do next. We can't just sit around this place."

"We need a plan," Moira agreed. "We need to figure out a way home."

"First we need to rescue Tommy. And this Godfrey kid, too. He's the one, guys. The one I've been seeing in my visions. He was the kid on the boat, and he's in trouble, too."

Moira gnawed at her bottom lip. "Zak, if we get the chance to go home, we should take it—"

"He's my *brother*, Moira! He was missing my whole life, and now I can get him back. I'm not giving up on that."

"I'm not saying you should. But if we come up with a way home first, we have to use it."

"Says who?"

"Guys!" Conveniently, Khalid was sitting between them, so it was easy for him to lean in and stop their argument. "It's all a moot point right now anyway. We have no idea *how* to get home. All we know is what Tommy told us. Unless you want to roam this world looking for a door back home, the only sensible thing to do is what he said. Tommy said his friend Godfrey has power, right? Maybe we help Godfrey, then Godfrey helps us."

That sounded good to Zak. Moira considered for a moment, then agreed. "In most classic alternate-universe fiction, there's a guide of some sort who appears after the characters cross over, to sort of introduce them to the new world and set them on their quest."

"Well, unless you think that fish I saw in the water counts as a guide, I say we go with Tommy," Khalid joked.

Moira smiled. "I wish I knew how we got here in the first place. We were down in the subway, and then we saw the water—"

"Wait, wait, wait. You guys saw that?" Zak's head spun. He hadn't realized that, for the first time, someone else had seen the sights he'd thought were for his eyes only. The evidence that Something Strange Was Going On was all around them now, but it still made him feel better that Moira and Khalid had seen the same thing he had, in *their* world.

Both Khalid and Moira nodded.

"We were holding your hands," Moira put in. "Maybe that did it. An actual physical connection allowed us to see what you saw. Or maybe we were just so close to the crossover point. . . ."

"Crossover point?"

Moira sighed heavily, then brightened. "Remember when we were talking before, about the apartment building? I said you broke down a wall. But you really shouldn't be able to do that. Not in real life. But in science fiction, there are places where the wall between realities—between apartments—is thin enough that you can travel. Either you break it down or there's some kind of hidden doorway between apartments."

"And one of those places is under the World Trade Center?"

Moira shrugged. "I guess. I mean, how else do you think that boat got there?"

Zak was stunned. Of course. He turned and looked out over the Houston Conflux. Right where they stood (well, close by) was the location of the World Trade Center and the Freedom Tower in their own universe. But here it was just water.

He remembered the juddering of the boat as it tossed in the storm. It had somehow crossed from this universe into their own, running aground because where there was open water *here*, there was land back home. He mentioned this to Khalid and Moira.

"That explains a lot," Moira said. "Like the construction of the boat. In our universe, everyone's baffled by it. Stuff like using iron nails and all that. But maybe *here* that's just how they built most boats back then."

"Eggs-loving Khalid builds his boats differently," Khalid muttered.

"Exactly. Some of the changes ripple out and then just fade away, but some of them ripple out and knock over a boat. Or scare a duck out of the pond. And the changes compound."

"So," Zak mused, "Godfrey gets on a boat somewhere, headed for New York."

"Manhattan City," Moira corrected.

"Right. And there's a storm that threatens to knock the boat over." With his newfound understanding, he ran through the memories of ship-side. "All hands on deck. They were fighting for their lives against the storm." When he tried, he could relive it—the gulls, the wind, the rain. The snap of the sails and the shouts of the captain. "Godfrey tried climbing into the rigging to fix one of the sails, but he got thrown off when the ship moved. And he went belowdecks for safety, and the ship nearly caught on fire. . . ."

"So he cast a spell to protect himself," Moira said.

"That's the part I don't get," Zak admitted.

"*That's* the part?" Khalid spluttered.

"Well, one of the parts. A spell. I mean, you tell me that physics says there are other universes, Moira, and I believe you. But magic spells? Come on."

"Tommy said we would 'call it magic,'" she pointed out. "There was a famous science-fiction writer named Arthur C. Clarke who once said that 'any sufficiently advanced technology is indistinguishable from magic.' If you showed a medieval knight your iPhone, he would think you're a wizard, not just a kid with a phone."

"So it's not *really* magic." That somehow made Zak feel more comfortable, and then he felt ridiculous for finding comfort in such a small thing.

"It doesn't matter, really," Moira said. "All that matters is that he did *something* that allowed him to live beyond the death of his body. Magic spell, uploading his consciousness into the air, whatever. And then the boat came through to our world and wrecked on land and ended up buried."

"Right under what eventually became the old World Trade Center."

"What do you think it was like?" Khalid mused. "Being under there? Especially when the towers came down?"

Zak shuddered. He tried to imagine it—stuck underground for so long, in darkness and in quiet . . . and then, from nowhere, *light* and *loud*.

He *tried* to imagine it but knew his powers of creativity couldn't possibly match up to the reality.

"Do you think he saw them?" he asked. "The people who died that day? He's a ghost, so do you think—"

"Shh!" Khalid said, holding up both hands. His expression was alert and concerned. "I hear something."

TWENTY-FIVE

Now Zak heard it, too—and so did Moira, from the look on her face. It was a rustling in the shrubbery around them ... and then footfalls. With a shared look of panic, they leaped up from the bench and spun in every direction, looking for the source of the noise, just as a man emerged from the greenery across the pathway.

He was tall and broad-shouldered, wearing what they immediately realized was a police officer's uniform, though it didn't match up with any police outfit they'd ever seen. The slacks were gray with a black stripe down the outside of each leg, and rather than a shirt, he wore a sort of greenish tunic with a black bandolier that crossed from left shoulder to right hip. There were pockets along the bandolier, and a slot for a round silvery badge that looked nothing like an NYPD badge. He wore a helmet that reminded Zak of photos he'd seen of English cops—bobbies, they were called.

In his hand, the man held a short, thin tube that at first seemed to be a flashlight. But on second glance, it was obviously much more—it projected light from the end, but there were also two bent, steely prongs jutting from it, like those on a stun gun.

"Well, now!" the man exclaimed. "What have we here?"

Zak and Khalid had jumped up first, and so they got the blast of light in the face first. They flinched at it and shielded their eyes. The cop clucked his tongue in apology and shifted the beam away from them.

"Sorry, boys," he said jovially. "You surprised me, is all. Not a lot of folks come down to the Conflux this late at night. Nothing to see, really."

He had a slight accent that Zak couldn't entirely place. Not broad, but noticeable. A nameplate on the right breast of his tunic read *Ofc. Cheong.*

"We were just killing some time," Khalid said. "You know. Wandering."

Officer Cheong's eyes lit up. "Not from around here! That makes more sense, then. No, no, wait, don't tell me." He held up a hand as though one of them had almost spilled a delightful secret. "Let me guess. I'm pretty good with accents. You boys hail from North Florida?"

Zak and Khalid looked at each other. Khalid mouthed, *Accents?*

Zak shrugged. "Yep, you got us. North Florida."

Cheong hooted and slapped his thigh. "I knew it! Southerners! Come to Manhattan City for a good time, eh?"

Zak grinned his best grin. The officer seemed friendly enough, and maybe he could actually help them out. Regardless of the universe, cops were cops, right? "Say, I was wondering—"

But just as he stepped forward to speak, Officer Cheong's expression changed. The beam of light wavered, then straightened, going over Zak's shoulder.

Landing on Moira.

Zak and Khalid had stood up first and had been blocking Moira from Cheong's view until now. Now, as Moira came into view, Officer Cheong stared with a fury that shocked Zak.

"Hey there, *frau*," Cheong grumbled. "What are you doing here?"

"She's our friend," Zak said.

Cheong's stance had changed. He'd gone from loose and friendly to all business. "Really, now?" he asked. "Your *friend*?"

Moira shrugged. "Well, yeah."

"Hey! When I'm talking to you, I'll talk *to* you," Cheong snapped. "Got it? Until then, you keep your mouth shut."

Any other time, someone talking in that tone to Moira would have been on the receiving end of a blistering Irish retort. But the night and the swim and the crossing of universes had taken their toll, and she just stood there in shock.

"Now, boys," Cheong said, playing the light from Zak to Khalid and back again, "tell me what's really going on here."

Zak's mind went blank. He couldn't come up with a lie or a story or even a question to stall for time. Helpless, he gestured to Khalid, who seemed similarly devoid of words.

"You messing around with someone else's *frau*?"

"I don't know what you're talking about," Zak said, finally relying on complete honesty. He had no idea what was going on or why the man kept calling Moira a "frow."

"Look, if you can't explain what's going on out here, I'm going to have to take her in."

"Are you *kidding* me?" Khalid erupted. Zak winced. He wished Khalid would think before antagonizing the cop in the man's own universe.

"You know how it is, boys," Cheong said gruffly, though of course they hadn't the slightest idea "how it is." He brushed them both aside and clamped a hand on Moira's arm, just above the elbow. "Come along, *frau*. We'll get you home nice and safe, no worries."

Moira snapped out of whatever passive daze she'd been in. She struggled to jerk her arm free, but Cheong held her fast. "Let go of me, you creep!" she yelled. "Get off!"

"Stupid *meid*," Cheong muttered. He tapped the side of his helmet. "PDNY Station Twelve, this is Cheong. I have a loose *frau* down by the Conflux."

Moira couldn't pull away. Her eyes—wide with fear—met Zak's, and without thinking any further, Zak threw his weight at the cop, hitting with his shoulder across the backs of the man's knees. Cheong's legs buckled, and Moira twisted free from his grasp, dodging to one side as the cop dropped his weird flashlight-like object.

"Hey!" Cheong stumbled forward but kept his footing. Zak stood back up and prepared for another tackle attempt, but his heart fluttered warningly.

Spinning around, Cheong pointed a threatening finger. "I don't want to run you in over this, but you guys aren't leaving me much—"

A *sizzle-crack* sounded just then, and Cheong yelped in pain, then dropped to his knees.

Khalid stood next to him with the "flashlight." The two prongs sparked with electricity, and Khalid stared in wonder. "This thing *rocks*."

"Zap him again!" Moira shouted as Cheong fumbled on his bandolier for something.

Khalid shoved the gadget at the exposed flesh of Cheong's neck, below the rim of the helmet and above his tunic's collar. The cop screamed—briefly—and then collapsed.

"Is he dead?" Zak's heart settled down. Mostly. At the sight of the limp form of Officer Cheong, it gave a little halfhearted skip. But wouldn't anyone's, watching a best friend assault a police officer?

"No. He's breathing." Moira shivered. "Good for him, I guess."

"Guys, we gotta get out of here," Khalid said. "He called this in. I bet more of them will be on the way."

Nothing else needed to be said. Without a word, they ran off through the bushes, into the night.

Khalid and Moira were far ahead of him, making good time. Zak did his best to keep up as they burst out of the park and onto a sidewalk, but he was falling behind. He just couldn't run as fast—his lungs burned, and his heart pounded too hard when he put on the speed. The best he could do was keep them in sight.

The street beyond the sidewalk seemed familiar—some of the buildings looked like the ones back home. There were only a few cars on the street, and they all had an odd sort of appearance—too curvy, too *round*. And, he realized, they were almost completely silent. The only street noise was a slow, polite sort of burp as each car passed him. So similar to home but so different. Infinite universes, Moira had said. And this particular "apartment" was decorated a lot like their own.

There were a few people out on the street. Zak paid them no mind as he weaved in and out, trying to catch up to his friends. He was so intent on his task that he tripped over his own feet and nearly collided with a woman who must have been an actress headed to some kind of audition—she was wearing a ton of makeup and an outfit right out of the Victorian age.

He had no time to goggle at her. Moira and Khalid were pulling farther away.

"Wait!" he shouted, but his breath was gone, and so his shout came out as a gasp. Fortunately, they must have realized they'd left him behind; both stopped running, checked over their shoulders, and waved him on.

But Zak didn't catch up to them. This was Canal Street, he realized—some of the buildings were familiar, but he also spied a street sign. It wasn't a reflectorized white-on-green sign, the kind he was used to. Instead, it was a flat gray with letters that glowed softly and seemed to hover just a fraction of an inch above the surface of the sign.

So, if this was Canal and they'd come from what *should* have been Chambers Street, then that meant . . .

Sure enough, he noticed another sign, this one with an arrow. It read:

BROADWAY
CANAL

He gestured for Moira and Khalid to come back to him, and after a moment's hesitation they did so, jogging with an ease Zak envied as he caught his breath.

"What are you doing, man? We have to keep moving. That cop'll—"

He interrupted Khalid. "Look around you. There's not a lot of people out here. But Broadway intersects Canal just a couple of blocks that way." He hooked a thumb. "There'll be lots of people there, and we can blend in."

"Then what?"

A wounded, angry roar came from the park. "Then we figure out 'then what'!" Zak exclaimed, and took off toward Broadway. To heck with his trouble breathing. No *way* he was going to be caught by the cops, not when he had more important things to do. Like rescuing his brother from beyond the walls of death.

They ran down Canal, darting between pedestrians, dashing across streets against the lights, weaving between those odd, silent vehicles. Zak recognized the slope of Canal up ahead. They were almost at Broadway.

Good thing, too. At a shout from Moira, he risked a look over his shoulder. Two cops were chasing them down; one of them had the bulk and heft of Officer Cheong, who probably had taken it personally when Khalid zapped him unconscious.

Zak dug down deep and put on a burst of speed that made his heart complain. He ignored it and pushed ahead. Mercer Street disappeared off to his left, and then it was less than a block to Broadway. Once on Broadway, they could cut uptown and hide in the crowds and among the many alleys and side streets.

Khalid and Moira had passed him and dashed ahead. All of a sudden, they stopped dead in their tracks. Zak nearly crashed between them and kept going, but he stopped at the last minute.

"What are you doing? We have to keep—"

And then he saw what they could see. They'd come to the end of Canal Street.

Which, in this world, led to an actual canal.

TWENTY-SIX

A sign nearby read BROADWAY CANAL and had some information about "services"; Zak didn't even bother skimming it.

Right there, right before them, where there should have been a bustling, busy, too-crowded two-way boulevard that wended through the Lower East Side north to the Upper West Side, was instead a canal—a gentle, wide waterway cutting its way through the city. Gondoliers poled their way up and down the current.

"Oh," Khalid said, and then let loose with an impressive string of curse words, some in English, some in Farsi.

Zak only knew English swear words. He wished he'd picked up some Spanish ones. It seemed like the right time for them.

"Bloody hell," Moira said in her mother's voice.

They stood on a cement platform that ran the length of the canal in both directions as far as they could see. A polished brass railing, lit at intervals with that same odd glowing substance they'd seen everywhere, kept them from jumping (or, more likely, falling) into the canal. Passersby milled about, some of them apparently amused by the three kids who'd just come barreling down Canal Street, others miffed and muttering imprecations. Out on the canal, the gondolas drifted by, all of them decked out with motors, but most of them poled along.

"Now what?" Khalid asked.

Zak checked—the cops were less than a block away. He looked up and down the canal quickly, noticing a break in the balustrade, where a wooden walkway led to a small pier.

"Let's grab a ride!" he said, and darted in that direction. Moira and Khalid followed, pushing their way through the crowd gathered along the canal. Soon they arrived at the pier. A gondola eased its way to the pier with the gentlest bump.

A tall man with a powerful chest greeted them, doffing his beret. "What can I do for you chaps this fine evening?" he asked. "Whereabouts uptown?"

Zak noticed a sign with a list of stops on it. Fortunately, they were all familiar: Fourth Street, Sixteenth Street, and so on. There was a schedule of prices that made no sense—the numbers were all preceded not by the familiar $ but rather by an uppercase S struck through with horizontal lines: S̶.

Yeah, figures the money would be different, too.

"Fourth Street," Zak said. "Fast." He was too afraid to look over his shoulder.

The gondolier smiled and stepped aside so that Zak could board, then froze when he got a clear look at Zak's companions.

"Sorry, chaps. I can't help you."

"You have to!" Zak said.

"Nope. Maybe someone else. Not me." He wielded his pole to block Zak from boarding.

Behind him, Zak heard fast, heavy footsteps on the pier. The cops. More than two of them now, from the sound of it.

"Please," Zak begged, but the gondolier only shook his head and repositioned his pole, ready to push off from the pier.

Just then, Khalid shoved past Zak and leaped onto the gondola, knocking the gondolier off-balance. The bigger man stumbled as the gondola rocked with the unexpected motion. Khalid hit the deck, and Zak got the idea—he jumped, too, followed by Moira, the two of them hitting the gondola a few seconds apart, causing the boat to jitter back and forth. The already-unstable gondolier tipped forward and fell into the water.

"Hold tight!" Khalid yelled. He was over by the motor and fiddled with it for a moment. Zak grabbed hold of the gondola seat; Moira clutched the nearest gunwale. The motor kicked in, lurching them forward. The expected roar of sound didn't materialize; instead, the motor was as quiet as the softly burping cars back on Canal Street.

They shot forward into the canal just as the cops massed on the pier. There were at least half a dozen of them now, including Officer Cheong in the lead. One of them dived into the canal, and Zak feared that the man would catch up to them, but instead of swimming after them, he stroked his way to the gondolier, who had surfaced and was treading water while screaming curses after his fleeing boat.

"Watch out!" Zak shouted. Another gondola was crossing right in front of them, poled along too slowly to divert its course. The gondolier and his passengers—a man and a woman holding hands—stared in sheer terror at the boat bearing down on them.

Khalid did something back by the motor, and their gondola banked hard to starboard, skipping around the slower one. "This is *awesome!*" Khalid chortled.

"How did you know how to start the engine?" Zak yelled.

"There's only one button! I chanced it!"

"Can you keep us going?"

"One-double-oh!"

Zak leaned toward the prow. The gondola was going much faster than he'd've thought possible; its wake rippled outward toward the retaining walls of the Broadway Canal and rebounded. Slower-moving gondolas rocked and threatened to capsize, caught in the overlapping swells. Far back, the police couldn't make any headway, having to dodge a welter of gondolas and waves cramming the canal from bank to bank.

Moira joined Zak up front, peering ahead. Ghostly lights effervesced from lampposts and the sides of buildings. "It's a straight shot," she said. "They'll catch up eventually. There are no bends to hide behind."

Zak checked over his shoulder. The cops were still far behind but were making slow progress through the obstacle course the trio had inadvertently left behind. "We have to get out of here," he said. "If we stay on the open water, we're in trouble."

At the stern, Khalid whooped and hollered over the sound of the water being cut by their hull. Sure, it seemed like fun, but Zak knew that this thing couldn't be outfitted to run so fast for too long. It was a *gondola*. It was for slow movement and short distances. The motor was probably for emergencies and would run out of gas—or *whatever*—at some point.

"We need to get off this thing!" Zak cried out.

Khalid boggled. "Are you kidding me? This is the most fun I've ever had!"

Scrambling to the back of the gondola, Zak managed to crouch down near Khalid. The only sound was the rush of water and the occasional polite eructation from the motor. It was, relatively speaking, eerily quiet.

"They're going to close us off somewhere ahead," Zak explained. "As long as we're on the canal, we can only go in one direction. They probably have boats waiting up ahead already."

Khalid considered this. "I hate when you're right."

"I know, and I apologize."

"So, what's the plan, Stan?"

Moira joined them; the gondola's front end tipped up ever so slightly, and water rained down around them. "We have an audience," she pointed out.

Sure enough, on the raised walkways on either side of the canal, crowds had gathered, pointing and gaping. Zak didn't blame them; it probably looked pretty bizarre from where they stood. Behind them, the police in the other gondolas had threaded the confusion and were speeding in their direction.

"I have an idea," Khalid said.

"Now I'm worried," Moira said.

"Don't worry." And then Khalid steered them right at the retaining wall at top speed.

The purloined gondola struck the retaining wall straight on. Its prow, made of lightweight fiberglass and not designed for a full-speed collision, crumpled instantly, folding in on itself like cheap foil.

As onlookers watched, the gondola's engine flared once, lighting up the night, a flash of daylight in the dark, blinding everyone watching.

And then the crushed gondola sank slowly to the bottom of the Broadway Canal.

PART TWO

ZAK

KHALID

MOIRA

TWENTY-SEVEN

"I thought there would be an explosion."

Khalid was disappointed. On the gondola, he had noticed an area of darkness where one of the oddly glowing lampposts along the canal wasn't working. Taking advantage of the relative dark, he'd shouted for them to leap from the gondola before impact, hoping no one would notice them bailing out in the dark. Now the three of them floated at the opposite side of the canal, clinging to a ladder that was painted red and had an arrow with the word *EMERGENCY* pointing to it. This qualified.

"I don't think they use gas," Moira said. She'd given up on her glasses and tucked them into a pocket somewhere, forcing her to squint to see him. "So no explosion. But you're lucky you didn't electrify the water or something."

"Sometimes it pays not to think ahead," Khalid said smugly.

"Shut up and get up the ladder."

Khalid hauled himself up. There was no one around, everyone having gathered a little way down the canal to gawk at the crushed gondola. He lay prone on the concrete and extended a hand to help Zak up.

But down in the water, Moira was holding Zak under one arm as she fervently clung to the ladder with her free hand.

"He can't do it!" She was terrified. "Khalid, there's something wrong with Zak!"

TWENTY-EIGHT

Zak couldn't breathe. At first he thought it was because he was in the water, but that didn't make sense—his head was above the waterline. Something else was wrong. His lungs couldn't hold the air. His chest refused to inflate.

His hand, gripping the ladder, was numb with a thousand pins. His arm felt a mile long, disconnected from him. How was he even holding on?

Someone was close to him. He could feel the touch of a hand, the press of a body against his. The warmth of it. Voices from far, far away came to him, sounding like the guardian angel who had become his brother, voices summoning him from one world to another, to life beyond death.

"He can't make it up the ladder."

Who was that? It sounded familiar.

"What's wrong with him?"

Is that you, Tommy? he called in his mind. There was no answer. Maybe he'd lost his twin again. Which was worse—to never have him in the first place, or to lose him, then find him, then lose him again? Zak didn't know.

"Help me." Moira. It was Moira's voice. She was struggling with him, pushing him against the ladder. "Climb, Zak! Can you climb?"

He wanted to. He truly did. With his eyes now open, Moira shivered into view before him, hair plastered to her head, face speckled with water and freckles. He tried to talk to her. Tried to explain that there was a pain inside him bigger than the world, and if he could just push it out, he'd be fine, really, he'd be perfectly fine and he'd be up that ladder in a jiff, but the pain refused to budge, nestled—no, *lodged*—in his chest, radiating out to his extremities.

He opened his mouth. Water sloshed in. He tried to speak but only ended up coughing out the water.

"Try this." A voice from above. Again familiar. Khalid. Of course.

Hands on him. Under his armpits. Hauling.

Other hands. Moira's? On his legs, pushing.

His head lolled back and he stared at the sky, which seemed to get closer until everything went black.

TWENTY-NINE

Zak woke up to the sensation that his arms and legs had been taken away. Not cut off or pulled off—there was no pain at his joints. It was as though they'd just disappeared, leaving a disconnected head and torso.

Reflexively, he lifted his right arm and was pleased to see it hover into view. It was numb, as were the rest of his limbs, but at least it was still there and under his command.

"—wouldn't even know where to start," Moira said.

"Well, we don't have a choice," Khalid said heatedly. "He's—hey, he's up."

They crouched down by Zak. "How are you, man?"

Moira took his wrist and felt for his pulse.

Zak took a moment to orient himself. There was some kind of box around his head. When he craned his neck—which took great effort—he could tell that he was lying on his back, his head and shoulders sheltered by a whitish crate of some sort. Outside the crate was an alleyway. Regardless of the universe, all alleyways looked roughly the same, it appeared; this place would have looked right at home back in his own version of New York.

"Where are we?" he asked. Maybe they *were* home. Maybe he'd dreamed all of it.

"Not sure," Moira said. "We had to move quickly. Once we got you out of the water, we ducked into a side street, then kept moving."

"You carried me?"

Khalid shook his head. "You were sorta kinda conscious. We had to support you, but you stumbled along."

Zak nodded and tried for a deep breath that he so achingly needed. It was impossible, his chest protesting even at a shallow one. "Trouble breathing," he managed.

And then he remembered: his verapamil. How long since he'd taken it? They'd probably been giving it to him at the hospital, but who knew how long it had been since his last dose.

"Guys, I'm not good." He knew his condition was bad, but saying so made it worse, and he had to stop not only to take a sip of breath but also to keep himself from panicking utterly. "Can't breathe right. Chest is tight." He felt someone squeeze his hand, and for a vertiginous moment couldn't tell if it was right or left, Khalid or Moira.

"We'll figure this out," Moira promised. "We're going to get help for you."

It was Khalid squeezing the hand. Zak turned to look up at his best friend. "I feel really bad," he said. Tears clustered in his eyes. Normally, he would be ashamed of crying in front of his friends—especially Khalid—but the fear and the compression in his chest drove the shame from him. "Don't leave me, okay?"

"Don't worry—Moira's gonna find medicine or a doctor or something. I'm not going anywhere."

"You have to," Moira said quietly. "You have to be the one to go."

"No way." Khalid thrust out his jaw. "Not a chance. You're the genius, Science Girl. You can find the right pills or the right doctor. My job is to stay with Zak."

Moira produced her glasses from a pocket and stared at the blotchy, spotted lenses for a moment before surrendering and tucking them away again. "Look, every time someone in this world sees me, it gets dramatic. The cop. The gondolier. Maybe it's an Irish thing."

"What are you talking about?" Khalid clearly wasn't interested in the conversation. He wanted Moira off on a medicine quest. Now.

But even in his semi-lucid condition, Zak caught on, dredging up yet another one of Dad's impromptu history lessons. He couldn't summon the strength to explain, but fortunately Moira went on:

"Once upon a time in this country, the Irish were practically slaves."

Khalid's eyebrows shot up. "Seriously? Like, when? Like, back before the Civil War?"

Moira shrugged. Zak knew, though. He remembered his father telling him about the signs that read IRISH NEED NOT APPLY even as recently as a hundred years ago, a generation after the Civil War.

Khalid whistled.

Moira shrugged. "It's my stupid hair. Maybe in this universe, people in America still hate the Irish, and they saw my red hair and flipped out."

"Well, *we* love you," Khalid said.

"Gee, thanks. That's not going to help much, though. You have to be the one to go, Khalid. I can't run around out there without attracting attention. You can. Take the stun-gadget thingy, just in case."

Zak nodded. "It's cool, man," he said.

Khalid clearly didn't want to go, but he bobbed his head as though psyching himself up and smiled grimly. "Okay. If you say so. I'll be *right back*, you got it? Right back."

"What was your medicine called?" Moira asked. "Do you remember?"

Did he remember? Of course he remembered. Taking his pill was a daily part of his life, as much a part of his routine as tying his shoes, pulling on his pants, or using a fork. There had been two names on the pill bottle: the brand name, Isoptin, and the generic name, verapamil. Zak gave both names and watched Khalid mouth them over and over again, memorizing them.

Just as Khalid hopped up to leave, though, he smacked his fist into his palm. "Wait. Wait a sec. What if it's a different name here?"

Zak groaned, but Moira touched his forehead, calming him. "They speak English here," she pointed out, "so the language developed similarly. Most medicines have Latin roots. They probably use them here, too. Even if it's called something different here, a doctor should be able to figure out what we need based on the name. The people look like us, talk like us, live in a city like ours. Some things are inevitable—they'll have a medicine for Zak."

She didn't say, *We don't have any other choice, anyway.* Because it was true, and there was no need to say it. Zak knew that his life depended on Khalid's being able to find the right medicine in an alien world. Soon.

"I believe in you, buddy," he whispered. "One-double-oh."

Khalid turned and sprinted away. Moira adjusted herself into a more comfortable sitting position and took one of Zak's hands in both of her own, resting them on his belly. "This is all going to work out," she said very persuasively. "You're going to be fine."

He didn't believe her. He closed his eyes and lied. "I know I will."

There was no point in either of them telling the truth.

THIRTY

Khalid emerged from an alley onto the middle of a sparsely traveled block. There were more of those odd cars puttering by. Some of them were painted bright white and had signs on them that read FOR HIRE. He figured he'd spotted his first alternate-universe taxi. He almost put his hand up to have one pull over— "Take me to the nearest pharmacy!" he would bark to the cabbie in his very best action-hero voice.

But whatever money he had was waterlogged in his wallet. And probably not worth anything in this universe. He'd noticed the signs by the canal, advertising UPTOWN GONDOLA! for various amounts with the weird $ symbol. His money would be no good here.

His clothes, still damp, clung to him uncomfortably. His shirt was pasted to his chest, and his underwear felt as though it had become a second skin. Two dunks in the water, and even on a warm night like this one, it would take a while to dry out. In the meantime, he was a wet, bedraggled kid standing on the sidewalk by himself, with no idea where to go but no time to dawdle.

Up and down the block seemed to be stores and restaurants, but nothing that looked like a drugstore. He would *kill* for a good old Duane Reade at this point. Maybe they didn't have them in this universe. Or maybe it was called Reade Duane. Or maybe . . .

Stop it. Stop it! Zak's—

He cut himself off. He didn't want to think the words *hurt* or *in trouble* or *in bad shape*, because he knew that those words were just ways for his brain to keep him from thinking the truth, the only word that really described the situation: *dying*.

Time was of the essence, and any forward movement had to be good. Standing around here wouldn't help Zak.

A sign told him he was on Fourth Street. The architecture was similar to that of his own world, except for the strange lighting on everything. He craned his neck to peer up at the facade of a building, feeling like a gawking tourist. In a way, he supposed he *was* a tourist, a visitor to a strange flavor of his own home. It was as though he'd left his apartment and come back later to find that someone had stolen a few things, left most of his stuff, and added some mysterious new belongings.

Eggs and oatmeal, he reminded himself. *This is all about eggs and oatmeal.*

Bad move. The thought just made him hungry.

The buildings were striped at regular intervals with what he now realized were very flat, transparent pipes. They looked like oblong glass tubes, filled with something that glowed. It wasn't neon—it wasn't harsh and too bright. This substance gave off a gentle, warm light, and the overlapping fields of brightness gave nighttime the feel of a pleasant twilight.

He was surprised to recognize Father Fagan Park at an intersection, though the sign called it DRENNAN-YOUNG PARK. It was definitely Father Fagan Park, though—he knew it by sight. Weird. More alternate-universe strangeness.

If he was at Fagan Park, then that meant he had to have walked to Sixth Avenue. A street sign at the corner told him that he was, in fact, at Sixth, though the subtitle read COLUMBIA AVENUE. It should have said AVENUE OF THE AMERICAS.

He'd walked something like eight blocks from the Broadway Canal without seeing anything helpful. Maybe it was time to ask someone for directions to a doctor.

He stood on the corner of Charlton and Sixth, gnawing at his lower lip. He slipped his sunglasses on and felt a little better, a little cooler. He looked around for someone who seemed willing to help a lost kid.

And that was when he noticed something weird. Well, *another* something weird. Even though it was nighttime, it was August and still warm out. All the men he saw wore short-sleeved shirts or T-shirts. But all the women were covered practically from head to toe in long skirts, full-sleeved shirts, high collars. And hats. They all wore hats. Most of them carried small fans.

Even fashion was screwy over here.

He took a right onto Sixth and headed uptown. He actually knew SoHo and lower Manhattan better, but given that the island seemed to be missing a big chunk of itself down there, he figured there would be more opportunities for discovery if he headed north. He vaguely recalled that NYU had a campus not far from where he was. Maybe there was a medical center there.

He tried to pay more attention as he roamed up Sixth, but his energy was beginning to flag. It had been a long, exhausting day. Running from the police in two universes, being tossed into the water twice. He hadn't eaten since lunch, and it was long, long past dinnertime now. The excitement and adrenaline of the day were quickly ebbing, and even the mere eight blocks he'd walked since leaving Zak and Moira felt like a hundred miles. There were some street vendors out, and the smell of cooked lamb and roasted almonds and fresh sausage made his mouth water. He couldn't pay, not with the money in his pocket, but maybe he could *borrow* some food. . . .

A hot rush of shame blasted through him and rattled him awake. His parents would be mortified if they knew he'd even considered such a thing.

He trudged along, more tired and hungry and weak with each step. Even his reading comprehension began to suffer—he imagined strange signs in the windows and doors of the places he passed by, signs that made no sense:

Nⵁ

read one.

♂NLY

read another.

Were there different *letters* in this universe? He dredged up a memory of some boring story Zak's dad had told once as he showed them an old piece of mail from a billion years ago. The *s* had been written as an *f*, so that the word *basket* looked like *bafket.* Khalid and Zak had nodded politely through Dr. Killian's mini-lecture and then spent the better part of the next day at school substituting *f* for *s* when they talked to anyone, which worked hilariously until they had to say *suck*, at which point their parents were e-mailed about their children's "inappropriate use of words."

A million years ago, a caveman in this universe ordered pizza instead of sushi, and now their alphabet has twenty-eight letters. He stifled a nervous giggle.

Different letters. Different fashion. Different accents.

Different lighting. Different cars. Different Manhattan.

All Khalid wanted was a sign for a hospital. Or a doctor. Or a pharmacy.

Where Sixth should have met Waverly Place, he finally got one.

The sign read ART ST., but it should have said WAVERLY PLACE. Khalid recognized the bend of Greenwich Avenue a block ahead, which meant that this was Waverly, no matter what the sign said.

He didn't really care, though. All he cared about was the store on the corner, the one that looked exactly like a good ol' Duane Reade, even though the sign said COHEN & CO., with the two *C*s interlocked like chains. He resisted the urge to dash across the street and run into the store, not wanting to draw attention to himself. He was too tired to run, anyway.

Inside, the cool blast of air-conditioning revived him for a moment. He got his bearings—the place looked like any other drugstore he'd ever seen. He wandered the aisles. Fortunately, there were no additional letters here. Most of the brand names seemed familiar: Advil, NyQuil, and others were all on display. There were others that he'd never seen before: Paramol, NaProx, Bellsyn.

Think, Khalid. Think. You're not gonna find it over the counter, right? It's gotta be with the pharmacist.

He meandered to the back of the store, where the pharmacy counter was. A metal grate—just like back home—had been lowered, and a sign revealed that the pharmacy would be open again at 8:00 AM.

Great. What was your plan, anyway? To ask real nice for some heart medicine?

He mentally kicked himself. He had to do better than this. He had to have a plan. Moira was the genius, but Khalid was good at tricking people. There had to be some story he could tell that would get him the medicine he needed.

But even then, he'd have to wait until morning. And by then Zak could very easily be—

Nope. Uh-uh. Not going there. Road closed ahead. Do not enter.

Taking a new route to the front of the store, he passed a nutrition display. The cardboard cutout showed a guy wearing an impressively expansive Afro and no shirt, revealing huge shoulders and arms. He looked kind of like Barack Obama, which made Khalid shake his head in disbelief. The guy—Obama or not—thrust a foil-wrapped package directly at Khalid, and a word balloon from his mouth read *Try a BarryBar™!* Underneath was a series of cardboard shelves laden with foil-wrapped bars. Khalid groaned quietly at his hunger. Would anybody *really* notice if he swiped one? Would anyone *really* care?

And then they catch you on a security camera and then you get arrested and then you can't help Zak and then everything goes south.

No one was in line at the cash register. Khalid was tempted to beg the guy behind the counter for a BarryBar, for anything at all. But the guy was paying Khalid no mind, instead engrossed in his phone. It was thinner than any phone Khalid had ever seen, no thicker than sturdy cardboard, and it seemed, as best he could tell from his angle, to be all screen.

But there was a familiar logo on the back.

An idea occurred to Khalid.

"Hey," he asked the guy, "where's the nearest Apple Store?"

THIRTY-ONE

Moira found herself hypnotized by the shallow, but steady rise and fall of Zak's chest. *Steady* was the operative word. At least he was breathing, if not deeply. He was in and out of consciousness, sweating, and she could do nothing for him. Absolutely nothing. She'd never felt so powerless and so guilty in her entire life.

She was the one who'd said it was okay for Zak to leave the hospital. With five minutes on Google and her own pride, she'd condemned Zak to dying in an alleyway in a universe not his own.

My darlin' genius lass, her dad crooned often to her, stroking her hair with pleasure at another straight-A report card, another glowing teacher report, another award or prize or commendation. And Moira had liked the praise, slurped it up like soup, even though she'd known a horrible truth her parents had never known: that she didn't deserve any of it.

Oh, she earned the grades and accolades, sure. But it was *easy* for her. Slide a test paper on the desk in front of her and the answers seemed to glow with their own inner light. It was just a matter of picking them. *Easy peasy, play Parcheesi*, Khalid had singsonged in their youth. That was the world of school to her, and she reaped praise for it.

But shouldn't praise come for hard work? Shouldn't it come for something she struggled with and conquered?

But the world kept telling her she was a genius, and so when the time came, she never even considered for a moment that she might read Zak's chart wrong or misunderstand some of the jargon she'd read on her phone. And she'd taken him out of the hospital, and now . . .

Zak coughed and came to, groaning, his hands flapping weakly for a moment as though seeking purchase midfall. She knelt down next to him.

"Don't worry," she said. "Don't worry. Khalid will be back soon."

She hoped. With their phones ruined after their unforeseen swim, she had no way to tell how long he'd even been gone. It was getting darker out, but the omnipresent glow from the buildings around them kept her from telling how late it was.

The alleyway smelled exactly like an alleyway would and should, in any universe. She and Khalid had laid Zak down with his head and shoulders inside an old packing crate of some sort. It wasn't made of cardboard—it consisted of a milky white sort of material that felt like plastic but was soft. Better to have his head in there than on the hard, filthy ground.

The alleyway was so familiar that for a moment she doubted her own hypothesis about traveling to another universe. But the Broadway Canal flashed in her memory, and she knew she was right. Tommy had said there was a special, powerful

178

connection between him and Zak. That connection had somehow been powerful enough to breach the wall between "apartments" and pull Zak through, with Khalid and Moira along for the ride.

Fortunately, this universe was similar enough to their own. She imagined it was analogous to the evolution of marsupials and placentals. Or even the duck-billed platypus. They were all mammals, but they had little tweaks and distinctions because of their environments. But you'd never think a kangaroo wasn't a mammal.

Save it for your memoirs, Moira. Zak needs you here, not theorizing.

She leaned in to blot at the beads of sweat on Zak's forehead with the end of her shirt, which had managed to dry by now.

Zak's eyes fluttered open and jittered back and forth until they focused on her.

"All I want is to see my brother," Zak said, tears gathering at the corners of his eyes. "I just want to see him again. There aren't even any pictures of him in the house, Moira. It's like they erased him. I just want to see him one more time."

"You will. I promise."

Zak sniffled unself-consciously and wiped his eyes. "Can you do something for me?"

She knew immediately what he wanted. She could just tell. She could always tell, with Zak. "Sure, laddie," she said with her mother's brogue.

Zak smiled at that and attempted a small laugh, then without warning closed his eyes and fell asleep.

Or passed out. She couldn't really tell and didn't dare try to waken him to be sure. She figured he needed to rest, and even if he didn't . . . there was nothing else for him to do. Better unconscious or asleep than awake, in pain, worrying.

She wished she could run the streets of Manhattan. Cross the island from east to west and north to south, screaming for a doctor, a pharmacist, anyone who could help. She cursed the summer weather. Neither she nor Zak wore enough clothing that they could sacrifice a piece for her to fashion into a scarf to cover her stupid bright red hair. Maybe it wasn't even anti-Irish sentiment. It could actually just be that hair of hers. There were old superstitions and prejudices about redheads in her own world. People used to think red hair meant someone was evil. Throw in green eyes and they were convinced you were a werewolf, too. Maybe those prejudices lingered here, as crazy as that sounded. Then again, weren't all prejudices crazy and stupid? No reason why this one couldn't persist. Most likely people didn't even remember *why* they hated redheads—they just always had.

She glanced around the alleyway, thinking that if she found something sharp, maybe she could even cut off her hair. Anything to let her go out into the streets and look for a way to help Zak.

"Hey, there," someone said. "What's the snap?"

What's the snap? she wondered, pulling away from Zak and turning around. An older boy—he had to be fifteen or sixteen—sauntered toward her from the mouth of the alley. He wore a red-striped shirt with a patch in the shape of a top hat sewn onto the left breast, and torn gray jeans over boots. He grinned and licked his lips.

"Chap and *chica*, looking for some privacy?" he asked. He pronounced *privacy* the way she'd heard British people say it: *PRIH-vuh-see.*

"We're not hurting anyone," she said with a bravery she didn't actually feel. Who knew what the laws were like in this universe? For all she knew, it was illegal to hang out in an alleyway.

"Never said you were. But the snap's suspish, don't you think?" He kept coming closer. Moira grimaced. She could easily dodge around him and dart out the end of the alley, but that would leave Zak alone. Defenseless.

She stood up as tall as she could, shoulders back. "Leave me alone. Now." She hated to add the next part; it made her feel weak. But she had no choice. "I'll scream."

His eyes lit up. "A screaming *chica*! You go ahead, little red." He stopped three or so yards from her, grinning. He cracked his knuckles. "Scream all you want. Makes no never mind to why tee. The snap's all the same."

Moira clenched her fists and checked around quickly, not wanting him to know she was looking, if at all possible. All the cans and bottles in the alleyway were made of some kind of lightweight plastic that was half-dissolved in most cases. None of them would be useful. But there was a loose chunk of concrete just to the left of her foot. And just beyond *that* . . .

"Leave us alone," she warned. "This is the last time I'll tell you."

He burst out laughing, as though it was the funniest joke in a string of them. She took advantage of his momentary distraction to stoop and snatch up the piece of concrete. It was a wee bit too big for her hand, but she did her best, hurling it at him with all her strength.

She'd aimed for his center of mass, but the size of the chunk threw her off—it struck him along his right hip, hard enough that he hopped back three steps, howling.

"What the snapping hell!" he bellowed, clutching his side. "You *frau!* You better—"

By then she'd already grabbed the second thing she'd seen on the ground, a wooden plank roughly two feet long. It was split at one end, but otherwise looked—and, now, *felt*—sturdy.

The boy had recovered by now and approached her, though as he closed in, she noticed with satisfaction that he limped on his right side. He snarled.

"Best drop that right now," he commanded in the tone of one who was used to being obeyed. "Best drop it *right snapping now!*"

"How about I let you have it instead?" she asked, and swung.

Moira had never really cared much for baseball, but she'd done her share of playing it during phys ed at school. And while sports weren't her thing, physics and geometry *were* . . . and hitting a baseball was all about physics and geometry. The proper stance. The right swinging angle. The correct amount of force.

Aiming for center mass again, she thwacked him along his shoulder. Hard. He yelped and stumbled to his left, a look of pure shock etched on his face. He truly, honestly could not believe she'd struck him.

"What do you think—"

He didn't get to finish, because Moira reared back and smacked him again. This time, the piece of wood glanced off his shoulder and fetched up alongside his head. The force of the blow was so terrific that the wood shattered at that end. The flesh of his cheek ripped; a spike of wood caught there and jutted out like the world's ugliest piercing. The boy howled in abject pain and clapped a hand to his face to stanch the blood. Blood poured from his ear, too.

"What the . . . What are you *doing*?" he whined.

The wood in her hands was shorter by several inches now, but the business end projected with wicked, sharp spikes.

"Teachin' you not to mess with the Irish, laddie," she said.

He backed away from her, still pressing a palm against the gush from his face. "You're in Dutch now! I'll be back! You cow! You stupid, clucking hen!"

Before she could say anything in response, he turned and ran from the alley. Moira actually ran forward several steps, ready to chase him down and re-introduce him to the end of her plank, but she stopped herself almost immediately.

She couldn't go after him. Her hair.

And besides. There was Zak.

"I'll be back!"

She was sure he would be. And this time, she wouldn't be able to surprise him. Despite the warmth, she began to shiver. Who knew what he would return with? A knife? A gun? Maybe just a couple of big friends. That's all it would take.

She rushed to Zak's side. He'd slept through the whole thing. His skin was pale and damp; when she touched his wrist to feel his thready pulse, his flesh was clammy.

"We have to hide, Zak," she said, not knowing if he could hear. "You and me. We have to. I'm sorry."

She pulled him out of the meager shelter she and Khalid had found, and struggled to loop his arms around her neck. After a few moments of trying, he surfaced enough to slur her name. His eyes were slits, unfocused.

"Walk with me," she said, and then, without realizing she was doing it, switched to Mom's brogue. "Can you do that, laddie? Can ya move yer wee footsies for Mama O'Grady?"

Zak scrabbled at the pavement with his feet. That was good enough for now.

She hoped.

They started to move.

THIRTY-TWO

The Meatpacking District looked nearly identical to the one back home, save for the lighting. Khalid's family came to the High Line often, so he was familiar with the area. The High Line itself didn't seem to exist here. An old aboveground train path, it had been converted to a park in his own world. In this one, there was *something* elevated parallel to Tenth Avenue, but it was enclosed and sealed off.

He'd walked another six blocks uptown, then three long blocks west. Subway entrances had tempted him, but he figured his MetroCard wouldn't work in this world. There had also been entrances to something called a superway. Gazing straight up, he saw the tubes running between buildings.

Moira was right. They built a subway in the sky.

Shaking himself, he entered the Apple Store. It was crowded, so he pushed his way to the nearest display table. He planted himself in front of something that looked like an iPad, but one that had been on a serious weight-loss program. Like back home, it was free to use.

Good thing some things are the same.

He thought of what he'd witnessed on his way here—the brand names in the pharmacy, for example. Some the same as back home, some not. A quirk of cosmic chance, maybe. Or—he thought again of Moira's apartment metaphor—maybe it was just that everyone needs a sofa and a bed in the apartment. Maybe some of these things were just fated to be.

Shaking his head, he focused on the task at hand. Leave the mysteries to Moira. He had work to do.

Like the Cohen & Co. guy's phone, the thing before him was all screen, very thin. When he touched it, it gave just the slightest bit, and he realized that it was mildly flexible. A display sign next to it read WONDER GLASS III: STARTS @ $509. There was more, too, but he decided he didn't care.

It took him a moment to figure out which icon on the screen meant *web browser*, but soon he had a window open. It looked familiar enough, loading the default page, which—according to the address field—was tim.apple.bus.

Khalid tried Google.com, but nothing came up. Then he tried tim.google.bus, and a search field popped up. He entered *doctor near 14th street and tenth avenue nyc* and got nothing.

Not NYC. Not here. Manhattan City.

Entering *doctor near 14th street and tenth avenue manhattan* worked. A pin showed up in a map just around the corner.

Hooting with joy, Khalid ran from the store, not caring who he shoved out of the way.

The building around the corner didn't look like a doctor's office or a hospital or anything like that. There was a coffee shop at street level and some stores in either direction, but nothing that screamed *medical.* Khalid wondered if he'd gotten the address wrong or if the online map was outdated.

But then he noticed a sign posted in the window of the coffee shop: DR. VICTORIO BOOKMAN—3RD FL.

There was a door off to one side of the coffee shop with buzzers mounted next to it. One was labeled V. BOOKMAN, MSF. Khalid tried that one and got no response, so he just pressed all of them, over and over, until someone buzzed him into the building. One more similarity to home.

He hauled himself up the stairs to the third floor. He'd walked miles in his own universe, then swum, run, and walked miles more in this one, without a break. His legs ached, and his back throbbed with pain.

On the third floor, there was only one door. A plaque mounted there read:

VICTORIO BOOKMAN
MAGISTER SCIENTIAE FERAE
ALL MAY ENTER

The plaque also listed office hours. Assuming it was the same day and date here as in his own world, Victorio Bookman wouldn't be available right now, but that didn't stop Khalid from knocking politely, then more urgently, then finally pounding on the door with both fists . . . and even giving it a good kick just to be sure.

The doctor was not in.

Khalid turned and leaned his back against the door, then slid down to the floor.

THIRTY-THREE

Moira knew they couldn't leave the alley the way they'd come in. There were still people on the streets, and the sight of her hair might set them off. Besides, she had no idea how long it would take for the nameless boy who'd threatened her to come back, and she didn't want to run into him while shouldering Zak along the sidewalk; she'd be defenseless.

But she and Khalid hadn't bothered going deeper into the alley. Some alleys in New York were blind. Some led through to another street. Some bent. And many of them had back doors opening onto them. Maybe she could find an escape route.

Zak mumbled under his breath, leaning against her as she staggered beneath his weight. It took at least five minutes to get him up, steady (sort of), and moving in the right direction.

She sweated. Her T-shirt sprouted new damp patches under her arms and in a stripe down her back.

Deeper in, the alley darkened as they moved away from the glowing lights of the street. Fire escapes loomed above. "New

York City pergolas," her mom called them. But none of the ladders were within reach. Zak wouldn't be able to climb, anyway.

The alley dead-ended fifty or so feet back. The wall was brick, easily thirty feet high. No way to scale it.

She allowed herself exactly thirty seconds of self-pity. It was a control mechanism she'd developed as a child. She had become upset over some small thing or another, and Mom had clucked her tongue and said, "It's worth bein' troubled over, dear, but not for long." Moira had taken those words to heart.

Thirty seconds was long enough to let a few tears drop and to stomp her feet. Then she clicked back in control of herself and slowly, carefully, lowered Zak to the ground. His head lolled, and she moved quickly to keep him from smacking it as he went down. She dragged some discarded panes of the strange not-cardboard/not-plastic over and arranged them around him in a sort of lean-to, shielding him from the street. Her exploration would go faster without him.

Maybe, she thought as she retraced her path back along the alley, she could hop up, grab a fire-escape ladder . . . get inside somehow, then come down and open a door . . . haul Zak in . . .

She paced deliberately, checking the walls for doors. There were three, all of them metal, all of them closed, all of them lacking doorknobs or handles of any sort. Yeah, she would need to open one from the inside.

"There! There, Jan, like I said!"

She knew the voice and wanted anything but to turn to it. Pretending it wasn't there wouldn't help, though.

Seven different boys—ranging from fourteen to maybe eighteen, she thought—stood in the alley. One of them was her attacker from before. He had a bandanna tied around his head, blotchy with his blood. They all wore the same torn gray jeans with boots, and red-striped shirts with top-hat patches. One of them stood out in front of the rest, fists on his hips. He wore a shiny stud in his nose and a hoop in one ear. He sneered.

"Well, hello there, *chica*. You've gone and run afoul of the Dutchmen."

They certainly didn't *look* Dutch to her. They were a motley conglomeration of different shades and races, a diverse thuggery if ever there was one.

Moira pursed her lips and drew herself up to her full height. She was a little taller than Khalid and the same height as Zak, though dismally shorter than even the smallest of the Dutchmen. She cast about for a weapon, but no lucky concrete or plank lay at hand.

"There was a guy, too," her attacker chimed in. "Layin' right over there." He pointed.

The leader shrugged, his eyes never leaving Moira. "Who cares? We can't do anything about the chap, but we can take the *chica*."

"But the guy—"

"You see him? I don't. He's done scarpered, I'll wager." The leader cupped his hands over his mouth. "Hey, chap! Hey, chappie! If you can hear me, hear this: We're the Dutchmen! Give us your *frau* and we'll let you go."

"The *frau* isn't anyone's to give," Moira said hotly.

The Dutchmen hooted with amusement. "The hair don't lie, boyos!" said the leader, chuckling over his shoulder at his comrades. "Temper like fire! Not bad."

He turned his attention back to Moira. She saw something

that looked like a sharp piece of brick. It was close to the Dutchmen, but she had no choice, so she ran for it. The leader shouted, "Snap to!" and before she'd made it halfway to the brick, there were hands on her, tugging, restraining, a half dozen hot breaths filling the air around her.

She smelled something strange and the world spun like water down a drain and the drain was in her head and she thought, *I'll come back, Zak, I pro—*

THIRTY-FOUR

"What have we here?"

Khalid blinked his eyes open. They were gummy with sleep and seemed to have accreted a layer of lead at some point. It took great effort to open them. A pair of gray men's slacks blurred into view before him. Crisp and well creased. Shoes that looked as if they'd waded through a swamp.

Asleep. He'd fallen asleep. His entire body ached as though he'd been crumpled up like a piece of paper and tossed in a trash can. He had slept leaning against the door, his knees drawn to his chest, head lolling. He could barely move his neck.

But move it he did, looking up. The man standing over him seemed amused. He was older than Khalid's dad, probably, wearing impossibly thin spectacles and a loose jacket that matched his pants in color and condition. His shirt, though, was rumpled and stained. An explosion of dreadlocks erupted from his head and fell around his shoulders like a spider plant. He carried a white paper bag in one hand, keys in the other.

"I say again," he said, "what have we here? Someone come to

see old Doc Bookman?" He chuckled as if the very thought were highly unlikely.

"I need help," Khalid croaked. His throat was clogged and dry at the same time. His mouth tasted like week-old beans.

Dr. Bookman arched an eyebrow. "Are you all right, young man? I thought this was some prank at first—"

"No, sir. No prank." Khalid braced himself and tried to stand. He needed a second attempt, and the second only took because Dr. Bookman leaned down to take an arm and steady him. "I need your help. My friend is sick."

Dr. Bookman nodded very seriously, then smiled. "Well, we can't have *that*, can we?"

"And," Khalid realized with great urgency and great shame, "I have to go to the bathroom like you wouldn't believe."

The office looked like no doctor's office Khalid had ever seen. Appointed in cracked-leather sofas and chairs, with a large walnut desk near the window and floor-to-ceiling bookcases crammed with books, stacks of paper, and thick magazines, it looked more like a college professor's office than a doctor's. Khalid would know—he'd visited Zak's dad's office any number of times over the years.

One thing he'd never seen in a professor's office or in a doctor's office was a large aquarium against one wall, its lid sealed. Instead of water and fish inside, though, it was filled with . . .

"Gross!" Khalid exclaimed. "Cockroaches!" They had weird ideas of what made for pets in this world, apparently.

"Ah, yes. A little experiment of mine. A very delicate and sensitive electroleum assessment. Please don't touch or disturb it."

Electroleum . . . It took a moment for Khalid to figure out why the word was so familiar. *Tommy!* Tommy had told them to use electroleum to bring him back to life. Something like that.

Now curious, Khalid peered closer. There were maybe a dozen cockroaches in the aquarium. Some of them were skittering about. Some were obviously dead, on their backs and still. He noticed that the dead ones had little red markings painted on them, while the moving, living ones had blue markings. Nothing exotic or outstanding; he was disappointed.

"I think you've proved conclusively that if you paint them red, they die," Khalid said.

Dr. Bookman chuckled and showed him into a tiny bathroom off to one side. Khalid relieved himself, splashed water on his face, and drank straight from the tap. He stared in the mirror at the bag-eyed boy staring back at him. He was still exhausted and achy, but he could think, at least.

Out in the main office, Dr. Bookman was methodically emptying the contents of his white paper bag onto his desk, one item at a time. Two bagels, neatly sliced, a container of cream cheese, a bottle of something pinkish that looked like juice, and a tub of something black and pebbly.

"I assume you've not eaten," Dr. Bookman said, "so you can do me the favor of preventing me from eating both of these bagels. With or without roe?"

Khalid's stomach rumbled, and it took everything he had to ignore it. "My friend is dying. I need medicine. For his heart."

Dr. Bookman looked up from his process of spreading cream cheese on the first bagel. "His heart."

"Yes."

"What, exactly, do you expect me to do about this?"

"You're a doctor!" Khalid's mouth watered at the sight of the food, and his stomach contracted so painfully that he winced and bent over slightly. "You can help him."

Bookman finished decorating the bagel and handed it across the desk to Khalid, who crammed it into his mouth and chewed and swallowed so fast he hardly tasted it.

"I'm sorry if you've misunderstood," Bookman said, cutting into the cream cheese for the second bagel, "but I'm not *that* sort of doctor. You'd be better off calling 911."

Khalid inhaled the rest of the bagel. "I'm not sure . . ." It was oddly comforting that they had 911 in this world, but he couldn't call 911, because he had no phone. None that would work in this universe, at least. There was a slab of gray plastic and metal on Dr. Bookman's desk that looked like some species of telephone, and he imagined the doctor would let him use it. But he wasn't 100 percent sure exactly *where* he'd left Zak and Moira. They'd roamed through the night from the Broadway Canal to the alleyway, and he hadn't paid attention to the street signs when he left the alley.

"I can backtrack and find my way back there," he explained, "but I'm not sure how to tell them . . ."

Dr. Bookman nodded. He set aside his bagel without biting into it and rummaged in his desk drawer for a moment, producing a very thin, cloudy sheet of glass. He laid the glass on the desk. "Put your hand on this."

Khalid did as he was bid, laying his right hand flat on the glass. Dr. Bookman touched the edge of the glass and muttered something under his breath that Khalid couldn't quite make out. After a moment, the glass felt warm, too warm to be just the result of body heat. As he watched in amazement, the cloudiness dissipated, clearing the glass until it was almost invisible.

Dr. Bookman spread some of the black, bumpy stuff—roe, he'd called it—on his bagel and took a satisfied bite. "Very well, then. I believe you. Take me to your friend, and we'll call 911 on my phone."

Tears gathered in Khalid's eyes. "Thank you," he said. "Thank you so much."

He just hoped he wasn't too late.

THIRTY-FIVE

Zak's eyes fluttered open, then closed, then opened again.

He was looking into a mirror, but there was no mirror.

He widened his eyes, but his reflection's expression remained impassive.

Tommy? he asked.

Zak.

It's you! He lunged forward—

And he didn't. He couldn't move. He was stuck, frozen in space no more than two feet from his twin. He remembered the reflection in the police station. A universe away. A lifetime ago.

Why do we look the same?

We're twins, Zak.

But you died ten years ago.

I'm still connected to you. I've changed along with you.

He reached out again, but didn't. He *wanted* to, he yearned to, but his limbs wouldn't function.

Tommy, why can't I move?

The rules are different here.

In this universe, you mean?

Tommy shook his head. *No. You're not there anymore. You're not back home, either. You're in a . . . freshet. A current. I'm not sure of the right word. It's a whitecap breaking on the surface of the Secret Sea.*

I don't understand.

Between and betwixt and above and beneath. You're in the no-space, Zak. That's where I am. Where I've been. Dreams come here.

He remembered Dr. Campbell: *"So, we decided to go walk-about, eh?"*

Walkabout . . .

Dr. Campbell, who had lied to him, too, but at least she'd tried to help. She'd tried to explain to him what had happened. More than his parents had done.

"Walkabout is something the Aborigines do in Australia," she'd said. *"They leave their villages or their towns on foot and they wander in the wilderness until they have a vision from what they call Dreamtime."*

Is that where I am? Dreamtime? Is that what I'm experiencing? Are you real? Am I?

Real is not applicable. We are.

Why can I see you now? Why can we talk?

Tommy looked down and shook his head sadly.

You're close to death, Zak. Close to me. *That's how I can talk to you.*

Zak had no body in the no-space, but he felt a shiver none-theless. He'd known he was close to death

—I just want to see him—

but hearing it from the mouth that was identical to his, in a voice so like his own

—I just want to see him again—

made it true.

What do I need to do? he asked.

Tommy shrugged. *Don't trust him, Zak. You know that already.*

Don't trust who?

I can only tell you things you already know.

But before, back home, you said, "They're lying." They. Now it's just him? *I don't understand.*

Zak, you have to go. You have to move. It's not safe for you here.

But I can't move! He tried to lift his feet to prove the point. Nothing. *I'm stuck!*

Not here, there. *Back in the world. You have to leave the alley.*

But I'm . . .

If you don't leave the alley, you'll never finish your mission. And you'll never see me again.

No! I can come back here! If I die, I'll come back here and we'll be together!

It doesn't work like that. I'm tethered to the world. I've been locked in the no-space because of our connection. You're what keeps me from moving past the living world. When you die, there won't be a twin around to tether you. You'll—Tommy grimaced, trying to find the right words—*you'll drift away. Up. You'll leave the Secret Sea and everything it contains. That's death.*

But—

Go, Zak. There's still a way. But you have to go now.

———————

In the alley, Zak kicked away the shelter Moira had built around him.

The night air had gone humid and rank.

Zak began to crawl.

THIRTY-SIX

Moira's head throbbed and her throat was dry. She lay face-down on something cold and rough. The right side of her chest hurt all the way up to her shoulder. As she rolled over, she realized why—the buttons she'd pinned there had been pressing into her for who knew how long. They clicked at her movement.

"Mornin', Red," a voice said.

Moira blinked, then blinked again. The world was fuzzy and indistinct. Her glasses were gone, and everything farther out than two feet might as well have been a smear of paint on a canvas. Figures moved out there in the myopic mist, and she curled her knees in to her chest for protection.

"Here ya go," the voice said, and a chunk of the blur broke off, leaning in, becoming a woman with woefully blond hair tied back in a ponytail and acne pits arrayed along her forehead. She held out Moira's glasses.

Moira took them gratefully and slipped them on. She was in a cage of some sort, something very like a jail cell, as best she could tell. At first she thought maybe she *was* in jail, but the bars of the cell were sloppily welded into metal flanges that had been bolted to the floor. She couldn't imagine an actual police department tolerating such shoddy workmanship.

She pushed herself into a sitting position and forced her attention past the headache that pulsed along the back of her head. There were five other people in the cell with her. All women, she realized now. Which made sense for a prison, but what was the point of *this* place?

Before she could ask anything, she heard the squeak of unoiled hinges. Her cellmates all scurried to the very back of the cell, leaving Moira on the floor up front. She peered around. The cell fit within a slightly larger room, lit by plain old lightbulbs that made her miss home. A heavy metal door at the farthest end of the room had opened, and the leader of the Dutchmen—Jan, she remembered—entered, talking over his shoulder to someone else.

"...decent enough crop. Not promising you anything outstanding, mind."

"I shall adjust my expectations accordingly," said a new voice, this one belonging to the man who followed Jan into the room.

He was tall and slender and caramel-colored, with salt-and-pepper hair slicked back over a high forehead and round, green-tinted spectacles over piercing black eyes. He carried a walking stick with a gold tip and an ornate eagle carved into the handle, but he did not use it, its end never touching the floor.

Moira had a ball of hate lodged in her gut for Jan, but that paled in comparison to the instant revulsion she felt at seeing this newcomer.

Jan stepped aside and gestured to the cell. The tall man

strode over as though only barely tolerant of the necessity of touching the floor, then planted his feet a yard from the cell. His walking stick finally came down, clanging against the cement floor; he folded his hands over the eagle.

"Well, well," he cooed, gazing into the cell. "Well, well." He gave only a cursory glance at the women in the back before his eyes fell on Moira and lingered there.

"What have we here?" he asked, leering. "'One Hundred Percent Girl,'" he continued, reading from her shirt. "'One Hundred Percent Geek.' Of the former, I'm certain. Of the latter . . . Why would one be proud of a carnival background?"

Moira blinked in bafflement. Before she could retort, the man inclined his head toward Jan. "A little younger than the usual for you Dutchmen."

Jan came up beside him and shrugged. "True. Normally, we'd keep one like this for ourselves. Not much right now, but she'll grow up fine. We need cash. For equipment."

"Ah, yes. Word on the street is that you boys are up to something."

"How's that different from any other time?" Jan snorted.

The tall man, clearly bored with the repartee, cleared his throat. "Ladies," he said, "my name is Sentius Salazar." Here he inclined his head, as if too busy for a full bow. "I want to assure you all that you will be well cared for and given every possible consideration while in my possession. I regret that you will need to remain thus . . . discomposed for another half day whilst I complete travel arrangements. Once we arrive at my Nut Island estate, you will be given ample opportunity to bathe, rest, and in general comport yourselves with dignity prior to the companion auction." He smiled in what Moira supposed was to be a reassuring manner. To her horror, she saw—when she checked over her shoulder—that her cellmates had all taken up relaxed positions, nodding and murmuring contentedly to one another.

"Not so bad as all that," one of them said.

"An auction?" Moira couldn't help it. She stood up and grabbed the bars of the cell, staring up at Sentius. "You're going to *sell* us?"

"My dear, what *else* would I do with you? You all were found alone on the streets, uncompanioned, in dire straits. And you, in such immoral attire . . . It would be the very heart of cruelty to turn you back to that life."

Uncompanioned . . . Why would it matter if the Irish or redheads or whichever were alone or in a group? It didn't make any . . .

She paused to turn and spare a moment's gaze at her cellmates. One of them was Asian, another black. They weren't all Irish in here. They were all . . .

And it hit Moira. Struck her like a cannonball, and she chided herself for her earlier idiocy. Stupid. So stupid. If she hadn't been running for her life since hitting the waters of the Houston Conflux, if she hadn't been trying to figure out the physics of their transition to another universe, she would have known earlier.

The cop and the gondolier . . . Their reactions had nothing at all to do with her hair color.

It was her sex.

"Women are slaves here!" Moira breathed, her voice choked with outrage, shock, and sheer terror.

Sentius clucked his tongue. "Tut-tut, dearie. Someone's been filling your head with femalist propaganda and similar rot."

"You can buy and sell—"

"I am not surprised to find that your education in this area is lacking. A little knowledge is a terrible thing. All the more reason to keep it from you. Allow me to elucidate: Slavery," he went on, "was outlawed in the Federal States back in 1782, and all indentured servants and suchlike were manumitted by 1784. Women aren't enslaved—they're *protected*."

"From what?" Moira asked brittlely.

"Why, from themselves!" Sentius exclaimed, as though it was the most obvious answer in the world. "Women are prone to all manner of emotional, hormonal, and psychological traumas. To leave a woman—or even a girl such as yourself—without the support of a man would be the basest sort of villainy. Imagine the horrors of life without shelter, without food or money. Without a firm, guiding masculine hand!" Sentius shuddered. "You're young yet, but fear not—someone will take pity on you. Perhaps to hold in abeyance until you come of age. Or perhaps as a play-fellow for a daughter. Nonetheless, I promise you this: Your nightmare is nearly over."

"Yeah? To me, it sounds like it's just starting."

"Hey!" Jan yelled, thrusting himself toward her. "Back off, *frau*! I'm not gonna stand here and listen to you sass-talk!"

Moira went rigid with intermingled terror and rage. Jan was close enough that she could reach a hand through the bars and gouge furrows in his face with her nails. But she was behind a locked door, with nowhere to run, no room to maneuver. He and Sentius had the upper hand. She gripped the bars tighter and waited for the anger to pass.

"No need for such language," Sentius said smoothly, gesturing for Jan to step back. "I hardly blame *her*. At this age, they are often in the grip of hormones and chemical imbalances. It is the tragedy of the fair sex: As children, so intelligent and so capable, almost the equal of the male. But upon the transition . . ." He *tsked* and sighed with resignation.

"Adios, ladies," he said, and then he and Jan were gone, leaving Moira to stare at the door through the bars of her cage.

To Moira's astonishment, her fellow prisoners seemed relaxed and at ease. One of them—a stunning Asian with a single braid past her shoulders—even took out a nail file from a pocket in her skirt and began touching up her nails.

"What. Are you. Doing?" Moira asked in disbelief.

"Just fixing up," the woman responded. Her voice had the tiniest hint of a Southern accent to it. "I know we'll have time at the estate, but might as well start now, right?"

They just accepted it. They all just accepted what was happening to them, what was *going* to happen to them.

Moira licked her lips. That file . . . It was flimsy, sure, but it could be sharpened to a fine point by rubbing it repeatedly against the concrete floor. She'd done it once before, back home, with a Popsicle stick at Prospect Park. A long time ago. She and Zak and Khalid had decided to build a fort for their LEGO figures, but it kept falling down. Until she'd come up with the idea of staking the Popsicle sticks in the dirt by sharpening them to points first.

That nail file was a weapon waiting to happen.

"So, they just let you keep that?" she asked casually.

The woman boggled at her. "Why wouldn't they?"

"You could use it."

The other woman smiled indulgently. "I *am* using it."

"I mean *against* them."

Silence. The murmured conversations in the room halted, and everyone looked at Moira. Not—as she'd hoped—with interest and cunning, but with confusion and suspicion.

"Why would I do that?" the filer asked.

"Seems a nice enough chap," someone else commented.

"One of the good ones," another agreed.

Are you people insane? she wanted to ask. But didn't.

Because the truth was . . . they weren't. They were caught in a system that, according to Sentius, had existed for centuries. Moira's mind raced. The dates Sentius had given her spun in her mind. She couldn't connect them to any specific dates in the history of the United States back home, but they predated the signing of the Constitution. He'd also referred to "the Federal States." If this country was the Federal States of America, not the United States of America, then maybe that explained the legal distinctions. Somewhere in the earliest days of the founding of the nation, something had gone very right and slavery had been outlawed, eradicated before its grip grew into the tenebrous cancer she knew from history books.

But at the same time, something else had gone very, very wrong. Women had made no gains in their rights since the beginning of the country, and the despicable notions of the past had calcified into the accepted truths of the present.

In some ways—technology, as best she could tell—this world had advanced far beyond her own. But socially, its development had been retarded at some point. She couldn't quite reconcile the two. After all, without women contributing, how could a society advance?

Maybe Marie Curie discovered radiation here, too, but had her work co-opted by men. Or maybe she worked in secret. Or maybe she'd never been born at all. The discovery of radiation was probably inevitable—if Curie hadn't found it, someone else would have, eventually.

She shook her head. No time for this now. It was an interesting theoretical issue, but she had actual steel bars to get through.

The women who shared her cell did not seem frightened. Or angry. Most of them seemed happy. Some bored. One of them—the one who'd given Moira her glasses—seemed resigned to her fate, not upset enough to do anything about it.

Moira would not allow herself to be bored. Or complacent. Or resigned. She was not about to give up the freedom she'd been born into in Ireland and then granted again as an American citizen.

In the fantasy novels she read and loved so dearly, the solution would be obvious, she thought, sitting with her back to the bars. A woman locked in a cell with other mistreated women would find a way to rally them. Together they would overpower their jailers, break free, wreak havoc . . . probably end up out in the forest somewhere, forming a clan of woman-only warriors or something like that.

But *these* women . . . These women weren't warriors-in-waiting. They couldn't even conceive of a world in which they defied men, much less were equal to them. They were so nonthreatening that their jailers hadn't even taken potential weapons away from them. That's how little men feared women in this world.

She ran her hands through her pockets, wondering what they'd left *her* with. But all she had was her useless dead phone and a stick of lip balm. Her house key and MetroCard—shoved into her pocket on the way to visit Zak in the hospital—must have washed out and away during one of her two dunkings.

Great. Maybe the nail-filing lady would let her have the file. Maybe she could . . .

"What's it mean?"

The ponytailed blond with the bad skin had approached her again, settling down next to her.

"What does what mean?" Moira asked.

"This." She tapped Moira's upper right chest. "'I like you ironically.' I don't get it."

Moira looked down.

At her buttons.

Just like looking at a test in school, where the answers glowed and shouted for her attention, Moira suddenly saw the path to her freedom. Or if not her freedom, then at least a noble effort none of the Dutchmen would ever forget.

She cleared her throat and offered her best, friendliest smile at the blond woman. *"Love* your hair," she said.

THIRTY-SEVEN

Zak braced himself against a wall with one hand and tried to push himself up to his feet. His knees and palms burned from crawling along the sidewalk. He blinked sweat away and gave up, slumping instead against the wall, breathing hard.

Where was Moira? Where was Khalid? What had happened to them?

He remembered the gondola, remembered Khalid yelling for them to jump.

And then water. Water, again. Always water. The boat, rocking, tossing him to and fro—

No. That wasn't me. That was . . .

Godfrey.

The memory of Godfrey assaulted him like an electroshock, and he gasped for breath. He'd been reliving Godfrey's last days. In combining their powers to contact Zak, Tommy and Godfrey had been sending not just words but also dreams, images.

Godfrey and then Tommy and *then* the gondola and—

The water.

Vague memories of Moira and Khalid dragging him . . . somewhere.

And then . . . an alleyway? Was that right?

An alleyway, and he remembered speaking to Moira, telling her . . .

"All I want is to see my brother."

Yes.

"It's like they erased him. I just want to see him one more time."

Zak snuffled back tears and wiped his cheeks with the back of his hand. He'd said that, and then he'd seen Tommy, talked to him.

He looked to his right. There, down the street, a flash of blue and red and gold glimmered for just an instant.

Tommy.

Zak's heart throbbed in protest, but he managed to hoist himself to his feet. With one hand braced against the wall for support, he staggered in the direction of the light.

THIRTY-EIGHT

"Young man, if this is a joke, it is most definitely *not* a funny one."

Khalid ran a hand through his hair and paced another circuit of the alleyway. He was *positive* that this was where he'd left Moira and Zak. The buildings out on the street were familiar, and the alley looked exactly the same.

But Moira and Zak were nowhere to be found.

"Right here," Khalid said, forcing his voice not to tremble. It wasn't easy; he wanted to whimper like a baby, the terror and the disbelief clogging his throat. "They were right here. I swear."

Dr. Bookman, standing at the mouth of the alley with his arms folded over his chest, sighed and shook his head. "Is this an initiation of some sort? Are your gang brethren going to assault me once I step into the alley?"

"I swear to God, Dr. Bookman. They were here." Khalid kicked at a loose chunk of concrete; it skittered along the ground until it hit a plank.

"Have you considered that your friends might be playing a prank on you?"

"Zak was *dying*. He's in no condition to play a prank."

"If the situation is that dire, you should just call his parents and be done with it."

Call Zak's parents. Ha! Khalid wished he could do exactly that. If he could call Dr. and Mrs. Killian, then that would mean he wasn't stuck in another universe, away from everything he knew.

And it collided with him then, the enormity of it all, the impossible but undeniable power of it. He wasn't lost. He wasn't in a place where a kind stranger or a cop or the right phone call could fix everything. He was in an entirely different universe, and his best friend was dying, and no one could help. He'd known it before, but there was a difference between knowing something and understanding it. He knew that gravity kept his feet on the ground, but he didn't understand exactly how.

Now, though, he both knew and understood: He wasn't lost; he was trapped. With no way out.

"Oh God," he muttered, and sank to his knees. "Oh my God. This isn't happening. This can't be happening."

Dr. Bookman made a show of examining a bracelet. Maybe there was a watch embedded in it or something like that. "If that is all, I really should return to my office."

"Please don't go." Khalid had meant to shout the words, but they came out as a whisper.

"I've spent enough time on this particular jape, far more time than one should spend on a joke one doesn't get. I'm sorry, young man."

"Wait!" Khalid jumped up, remembering something. "Wait!" He dashed over to Dr. Bookman and grabbed the man by the lapels. "That glass you had me touch. In your office. And then you came here with me. That was a lie detector, wasn't it?"

With a cautious but confident move, Bookman plucked Khalid's hands from his jacket, then smoothed out the creases. "No. Nothing so specific or so crude. It merely ascertains whether or not you mean me harm."

Merely.

"Then you know I'm not trying to hurt you."

"I know you don't intend to hurt me. But someone else could."

"Please. I'm begging you, okay?" Khalid actually dropped to his knees again, grasping the tail of Bookman's jacket. "Please. You have to help me."

Bookman sighed again and rechecked his bracelet. It was slender and segmented, polished silver, and Khalid was convinced it had some kind of watch built into it.

"Very well. Five more minutes."

Khalid jumped up and hooted with joy. He dashed back into the alley and stood off to one side, pointing. "This is where we were. Right here. I remember that standpipe because it's painted blue, which is weird."

"Weird how? Most standpipes are blue."

Not in my world, man. "Anyway, this is where we were. We had Zak propped up a little and sheltered a little."

Dr. Bookman sauntered into the alley and glanced around. He came over to Khalid, studied the ground, and gazed up and down the nearest wall. When he turned around, his foot hit the concrete chunk Khalid had kicked earlier. It rolled against the plank and turned the board over.

"Oh, my," Dr. Bookman said, and took a step back.

Khalid peered around to see what had caused Dr. Bookman's reaction.

On the end of the plank was something brownish, dry, and flaking. It looked like paint at first, but Khalid realized what it was in the instant before Dr. Bookman said, "Blood."

Moira didn't have to wait long, which was good. She was impatient, but more than that, she was worried about losing her nerve. It was one thing to plan an escape and let the adrenaline of it consume you. It was another thing to lose that adrenaline rush and wonder, *Is this really going to work?*

The other women in the cell were either napping or—she couldn't believe this—sharing tips on what Moira could only describe as "auction etiquette." The best way to talk to the buyers. The cues and hints that indicated "a good one." She couldn't believe she was hearing it, and the outrage she felt fueled her conviction.

She had hoped that at least one of the women in the cell with her would offer help, that at least one of them would be more like the women back home. But what were the odds that, in a world of sexist repression, she would happen to be locked up with this world's Xena, Warrior Princess?

Pretty dismal odds.

Some of her cellmates were playing with or cooing over the pins she'd given them. She'd traded a couple of them to the blond woman for what she needed, and then given away all but two.

Her plan. It had to work.

The man—Salazar—had mentioned an estate on an island somewhere. She was probably still in Manhattan, but if she allowed herself to be hauled off to who-knew-where, she would never find her way back. Even if she escaped from the estate, she would be trapped, surrounded by water, with nowhere to go and no way to find Zak.

She had to escape *now*.

Thrill competed with nausea deep down in her gut.

Once, her mom had let her drink half a Starbucks coffee. The sugar and the caffeine had provided a jolt, not only of energy but also of clarity. Everything had seemed obvious; everything had been possible. She'd barely noticed the crawling, vibrating sensation on her skin, the way she couldn't stop tapping her toes.

She was tapping them now. She was alive and quivering.

And everything was very, very clear to her.

Escape. No matter what the cost. No matter what she had to do.

Eyes and neck, she reminded herself. *Eyes and neck. Stay calm. Don't just flail around. Eyes and neck.*

The door squealed open and—joy of joys!—it was the Dutchman who'd started this all, the one who'd first threatened her in the alley. His bandanna had been replaced with a plain white bandage, speckled here and there with bleed-through.

That made what she had to do easier.

"Victuals," he said with a sneer, swaggering over to the cage. He grinned at Moira. "Maybe now you'll be a little nicer? Not such a snapping *chica*?"

Moira didn't respond. She was afraid her voice would betray the thrilling, horrifying excitement coursing through her. She kept her hands clenched tightly.

And carefully.

Very carefully.

The Dutchman put down the tray and unlocked the cage.

Moira told herself to wait. It was tempting to shove the door open—she'd noted already, based on its hinges, that it swung out, not in—but she needed to be patient.

He hauled back on the heavy door, and Moira, watching his struggle, congratulated herself on not flinging herself at it once it was unlocked. As heavy as the door was, that would have been pointless. And embarrassing. And futile.

Once he had cracked it open enough, he gathered up the tray. The women at the back of the cage waited patiently.

He entered.

Not yet, Moira told herself. Her palms went damp, and her breath quickened. She forced herself to breathe more slowly.

He paused just inside the cage, taking it in: The women, clustered together. Moira, alone, sitting against the bars off to one side.

He grinned as though to himself. There was a row of small covered pots on the tray, along with a row of plastic-looking bottles. He put the tray down on the middle of the floor and brought a pot and a bottle over to Moira.

"Now," he said, "maybe say you're sorry for our little snap back in the alley, and I won't take these with me."

Moira stared at him. She wondered if the full impact of the hatred she felt at that moment could be communicated through her eyes.

No, that was impossible. If he could feel her hate, then he would have spontaneously combusted by now. There would be nothing left of him but ash and a blackened, charred skeleton.

"Come on, little hen," he cooed. "Bygones, eh? Say you're sorry and get your victuals."

Still she remained silent. Her palms itched. She prayed nothing would slip, when the time came.

"See them over there?" he asked, jerking his head toward the other women, who were sharing out the other pots and bottles in a depressingly efficient manner that indicated this wasn't their first time in such a cage. "They follow the rules, they do all right. It ain't tough. Even a little *frau* like you should get it." He cleared his throat. "Sor-ee," he enunciated. "Sor-ee. Just like that. Try it. It won't hurt."

Now? No. Not yet. *Wait for it. You'll know the moment. You'll know the time.*

He tried a few more times to coax an apology out of her, then gave up. He shrugged and said, "Well, I'm gonna leave these out there, then," inclining his head toward the cage door. "Next time I check on you, maybe you'll have found your voice."

He turned to go, and that was his mistake.

Now.

Moira pounced, opening her hands. She swung both arms in a wide arc, then brought them together, slapping her hands on either side of his neck. The Dutchman screamed and arched his back, arms flung wide.

Twin gouts of blood spurted from the sides of his neck.

She had bartered with the blond with the bad skin, trading some decorative buttons for the rubber bands that held her hair back in a ponytail. With those rubber bands, she'd then tightly bound two of her buttons to her palms, with the sharp pins standing out. Poor weapons, but the only ones she had. She wielded *I like you ironically* in her right hand and a button that read *To err is humna* in her left.

217

She'd tried to barter for the nail file, but the woman who had it was too interested in her beauty regimen. Oh, well. Improvisation mattered.

The Dutchman gasped and clapped both hands to his neck to stanch the bleeding. Knees buckling, he staggered forward amid choking exclamations from the other prisoners. Moira wondered if she'd punctured anything essential. Carotid? Jugular? She didn't know. But he was stunned and distracted, and she had to act quickly.

A part of her had hoped that the other women would, when given proof of the vulnerability of their captor, join in, piling on the Dutchman and making this whole endeavor a bit easier. But she wasn't that lucky. The women instead shrieked as if with one voice and one set of lungs, then huddled together at the back of the cage, terrified.

So much for sisterhood, Moira thought darkly, and kicked the back of the Dutchman's knee. He went down.

"New York can be dangerous," her mother had told her once, omitting *for a girl,* though Moira knew the phrase lurked there. And so had followed two years of self-defense classes. Which, it turned out, were pretty good for offense, too.

The Dutchman gurgled and rolled over, his eyes alight with the sort of hatred that Moira knew gleamed in her own as well. Angry, not frightened. She hadn't hit anything necessary after all, and she couldn't rely on the shock of her attack to keep him down for long.

She had the advantage, but only for a moment. Pressing it, she jumped on top of him, landing with her knees on his stomach. He *whiff*ed out his breath and groaned, his hands coming away from his neck. The blood flow there was steady but not spurting, so Moira brought both palms down on his face, aiming for his eyes.

She missed, but not by much, hitting him just above the eyes, then raking the pins down. They broke off against the hard bone of his brow, but the jagged metal slashed red trails down his eyelids to the sides of his nose. He screamed again, this time higher, his eyelids cut in half. He thrashed like a storm-driven wave under her, throwing her off, his hands coming up to cover his eyes.

"My eyes!" he howled. "My snapping eyes! You *frau*! You snapping hen!" He kicked his legs with uncontrollable pain. She wondered if she'd punctured his eyes or just scratched them.

Didn't matter. She needed him quiet. She scrambled to her knees just above his head and grabbed his ears. Before he could move to brush her away, she lifted his head as high as she could and then slammed it down with all her strength on the concrete floor.

He thrashed again, and she felt something wet and remembered that the pins were broken but still sharp. She'd cut into his ears. She almost lost her grip on him as he flailed, now his hands coming off his bleeding eyes to snag her wrists as he bellowed curses at her, and she lifted his head and brought it down with all her might a second time. He groaned, and his hands went slack but still held on to her, so she smashed his head against the floor a third time, then a fourth, and then she lost track as her vision went dark and all the sounds of the cage seemed far, far away.

THIRTY-NINE

Zak's legs had gone leaden and numb. He walked like a zombie, shuffling his feet along the sidewalk. Banners that hung from the lampposts read KERMIS PARADE! with an August date that was only a few days away. Zak stumbled along, not sure what "Kermis" was and doubly unsure as to why he couldn't stop thinking the word: *kermis kermis kermis kermis.* He thought of the Muppets and giggled uncontrollably.

Pedestrians pulled away. Some even crossed the street as he neared them.

He was sure he looked terrible. He *felt* terrible. His legs were the least of his troubles. A constant sheet of sweat spilled down his forehead, and he'd given up wiping at it—lifting his hand took too much energy. His shirt clung to him like a desperate child. His heart flapped and fluttered like a caged bat spooked by sudden light.

He stumbled forward two more steps and bit back a muffled cry. Deep in his chest, something was powerfully wrong. He gagged on his own spit.

"Help . . ." He tried to scream the word but could only whisper it as he dropped to his knees.

Zak.

He hadn't the strength to look up. His neck muscles had gone loose and slack, and all he could see was the pavement and his own abraded knees, crisscrossed with bloody etchings and peeled-back scabs.

Zak, I know it's tough. You have to get up. You're almost there.

Tommy? Is that you again?

Zak, please! It's important! Move! Now!

He forced himself to look and realized it wasn't Tommy—it was Godfrey. Leaning toward him, emerging as from a dense, ever-shifting fog. Zak was finally face-to-face with him. After the dreams and visions he'd experienced from Godfrey's point of view, it was strange to see him from the outside for once.

He was white, or at least mostly white. Other details began to filter in through the fog, but then a sharp pain burst like lightning in Zak's chest, drawing a hiss of agony.

I know it hurts. I know you're in pain. Trust me, though—I'm trying to help you.

I thought you were Tommy at first. You sounded like him.

Just keep moving. It's only another block. One more block and you can close your eyes—I promise.

Zak tried to draw in a deep breath, but the sharp, stabbing pain from his heart forced the air out in a harsh gasp. *I can't. I can't make it. I'm dying. I'll be like you soon.*

No. If you die, it's over for you. Tommy and I aren't truly dead. We're trapped in a limbo world. In the no-space. Suspended above the Secret Sea but still linked to it. Me, because of the spell I cast. Your brother because of his connection to you, Zak.

Zak coughed, the motion causing his chest to contract painfully.

"Tommy's not dead?" he muttered.

One more block. That's all.

Crazy. Godfrey sounded so much like Tommy. . . .

Do it, Zak! Come on!

"We're trapped in a limbo world."

"Limbo . . ."

Zak spit something thick and whitish onto the sidewalk.

"Me, because of the spell I cast. Your brother because . . ."

Get up!

Zak's arms trembled as he pressed his palms against the ground.

"Your brother because . . ."

He got one foot under himself and paused for a moment, gathering his energy.

You can do it!

Tommy wasn't dead. Not really. He was in limbo. Because . . .

"Because of his connection to you, Zak."

If Zak died, then Tommy would *truly* be dead.

He couldn't let that happen, no matter how much his heart complained.

Gritting his teeth, Zak forced himself to stand. And then— one hand against the wall and the other pressed to the jack-rabbiting sensation of his own heart—he shuffled farther down the street.

Godfrey was gone.

FORTY

"We have to call the police," said Dr. Bookman.

Khalid had been staring at the blood on the end of the plank. Whose blood was it? Zak's? Moira's? Someone else's? Maybe it belonged to the person who had taken them. They *must* have been taken, right? Zak couldn't have run away in his condition, and Moira never would leave a Basketeer behind. So someone had taken them both and—

"Did you hear me?" Dr. Bookman said. "We have to call the—"

Khalid tore his eyes away from the plank and focused on Dr. Bookman, whose preternatural calm had crumbled. He tapped one shoe on the ground and gnawed at his lower lip as he stared down at the bloody piece of wood.

Officer Cheong. The other cops. The chase.

"No," he told Dr. Bookman. "We can't."

"Whyever not?"

"One of my friends is Irish."

"So? What does that have to do with anything?"

Khalid opened his mouth to explain about the prejudice

against the Irish, but at that moment it all clicked. Everything suddenly made a disgusting sort of sense. He would have seen it sooner if he hadn't been so panicked. Those weird symbols he'd noticed on certain businesses: N♀ and ♂NLY. The foreign characters signified *woman* and *man*. And Dr. Bookman's sign had said . . .

"'All may enter,'" Khalid whispered. "Oh, man," he said more loudly. "It's not that she's *Irish.* It's because she's a *girl!*"

Dr. Bookman startled. "Wait. Is one of your friends a girl?"

"Yeah. Moira. She's not the dying one. She's—"

Dr. Bookman passed a hand over his face. "Oh, my. You're right—we can't go to the police, then. A girl, on the loose with two boys? Do you have any idea what they'll do to her, how they'll punish her?"

It seemed like a rhetorical question, but Khalid had exactly no idea. He couldn't imagine how or why someone would punish Moira for doing precisely what she'd been doing as long as he could remember: hanging out with her friends.

"If the police don't get her, the press gangs—"

"Press gangs?"

Dr. Bookman tilted his head and regarded him quizzically. "Yes. Press gangs. Such as the Dutchmen, the Alphabet Boys, the Chelseas . . ."

"I don't get it. What do they do?"

"Khalid—it's Khalid, right?—where on earth are you *from?*"

North Florida, he wanted to say. A lie would be the easiest way to deflect the conversation, and Khalid's first instinct when cornered by an adult was to, well, to embellish the truth with so much finery and gilt that it was impossible to discern.

But now, he sensed, was neither the time nor the place for

his usual tale-telling. And Dr. Bookman was not the man for it. ALL MAY ENTER, the sign had said.

Khalid took a deep breath. And he told Dr. Bookman everything.

"Zak," he began, "was having these dreams . . ."

Moira wondered how long she'd drifted away from her body. When her vision cleared and the rush of sound returned, she felt as though she'd been gone for hours, but the women around her were still cowering in the corner, and she didn't think even *these* women would stay in one place like that for too long.

Between her hands was the Dutchman's head, now resting on the floor. His face was streaked with blood and tears, and there was a small puddle of blood on the floor as well. Moira couldn't tell whether he was breathing and realized she didn't care. Dead or unconscious, he wouldn't be able to stop her now.

She went through his pockets quickly, discovering some small sheets of a sturdy paper that seemed to be money. She stuffed it all into her own pockets after discarding her now-broken weapons, then added a set of keys that he'd had hooked to his belt loop.

With a deep, shuddery breath, she stood. Wobbled for a moment. The adrenaline rush was wearing off, and the world became thick around her. If she'd had anything in her stomach, she might have thrown up.

The women in the cage had gone quiet now. One of them whispered, "What have you done?"

Moira coughed. Her mouth tasted like hot metal. She didn't bother answering as she headed to the open cage door.

"They'll lobotomize you," someone said. "They won't let you get away with this."

Moira stepped outside the cage and put her hand between her breasts, feeling the rapid and rampant pace of her heart. She took a deep breath to calm herself and then turned to look through the open door at the women inside. They huddled together, though they had nothing to fear from Moira. She wanted to order them to come with her, to smuggle them to safety, but she knew her first priority had to be rescuing herself and then Zak. Both tasks would be impossible with a gaggle trailing behind her.

But she had to do *something*.

"This door is open," she said, "and it will stay open until they send someone else. You have a choice to make. I won't make it for you. But if you stay in there, you deserve whatever happens to you."

"And you deserve whatever you get out there," one of them spit back with a ferocity that, however misplaced, pleased Moira. At least the woman showed some fire. Misdirected, but present.

"I deserve whatever I can *take*," Moira corrected her, and, turning her back to them, opened the metal outer door.

FORTY-ONE

Zak could walk no farther. Everything in him had been wrung out, drained. His mind willed his body to move, to push on, but no matter how forcefully he commanded his limbs to obey, they obstinately refused.

He collapsed at the foot of the stairs to what looked like a brownstone. Did they even call them brownstones in Manhattan? In this universe? He didn't know, and he didn't know why he was wasting the last few seconds of his life pondering this, except that his mind was whirling out of control, thoughts blowing by in a hurricanelike wind. Each one he tried to grasp fled from his fingers.

His heart was like a lawn mower that almost, but not quite, caught with each jerk of the cord.

I'm sorry, Tommy. I wasn't strong enough.

I'm so sorry.

FORTY-TWO

The hallway immediately outside the cage room was dank, ill lit, and narrow. Pipes ran overhead, dripping condensation at irregular intervals. For a moment it felt like home to Moira, like any random basement in any random building in any borough of New York City, but then she saw this spray-painted on the door she'd closed behind her:

♀

It was a Greek symbol, she knew. For woman. It was supposed to look like a hand mirror, to represent the vanity of women, she guessed. Offensive enough in her world, but in this one, it was like a warning sigil for plague.

Get ready, boys, she thought. *Because a snapping-angry* frau *is headed your way.*

Tough thoughts, but she knew that getting out of the cage had been the easy part. She had no idea where she was or how many

Dutchmen she would have to fight through or evade on her way to freedom.

Freedom. It was a tenuous word now, a tenuous concept. For a woman, there was no freedom here. Even if she made it out of the building, she would still be . . . What had Sentius Salazar said? Oh, right—an uncompanioned girl. Without a chaperone or a shepherd to "guide" her, she would immediately be recognized as . . . as what? A runaway? An escapee? A criminal? Judging by the reactions of Officer Cheong and the gondolier, all three were likely.

A quiver overcame her, rattling her so fiercely for a moment that she thought she'd caught the flu. But it was just a momentary shake of adrenaline, and she rode it out. There was too much of import happening for her to be distracted by something so small.

With her hands outstretched, she could touch the rough cinder block on either side as she crept down the hallway, resisting the natural impulse to run, to put as much distance between her and the cage and the possibly dead Dutchman. *Slow and steady,* she told herself. *Like the tortoise.*

The end of the hallway disappeared into murk. Somewhere far, far down in that direction, she made out a glowing green X, hovering up near the ceiling. Part of a broken exit sign, maybe?

Exit sounded good to her. It sounded great. She was surprised to find tears gathering in her eyes at the mere thought of it. The Dutchmen, she realized, hadn't intended on hurting her, back in the alley. She was more valuable to them whole. But now that she'd attacked one of their own . . .

No. She shook her head to fling the thought away from her. She had to stay focused.

She'd come ten or twelve feet down the hallway. There was a door to her left and another to her right. No signage to indicate what might lie behind either one. She frowned. It made more sense to head to the exit, right?

Just then, an echoing, overlapping series of thumps jarred her roughly back to the present. It sounded like—

Feet. Someone walking down a . . . a stairwell.

The footfalls were right on top of her. One of the doors. One of the doors *right here* led to a stairwell. Moira groaned. From the sound of the footsteps, she wouldn't be able to make it down to the exit before they were on top of her. She listened carefully, trying to parse the echoes. It seemed as though the stairs were to her left. So without giving herself a moment for a second thought or doubt, she wrenched open the right-hand door and darted inside.

Fortunately, the right-hand door led to a smallish room, walled with the same cinder block as the hallway. It had probably been a janitor's closet at some point, but now it was crammed with an overflow of rickety shelves and boxes, as well as an old metal desk. On the desk rested a small, thin flask, filled with some kind of thick fluid that lit the room with a soft, pleasant glow.

Moira's heart pounded, and she thought of Zak. *Please let him still be alive. Please, please, please.*

From out in the hallway, the door opposite her banged open. Moira jabbed at the button set into the doorknob. A moment later, the knob rattled from the other side.

"Did you actually remember to lock it?" came a voice. She recognized it. Jan. The leader.

"Of course," said someone else in a tone of self-surprise. Then, with a note of defensiveness: "I always remember."

"Yeah, sure." She heard a sigh and a jingle of keys. "Which one is it?" asked Jan.

Moira allowed herself a three-count of panic—*one, two, three!* she counted in her head—and then scoured the room for a hiding place. Under the desk seemed most obvious, but also *too* obvious. Anyone who came in would look under there. She opted for a corner of the room crowded with boxes. As the key ring on the other side of the door jangled, she pushed one box aside, slipped into the corner, and then—as the doorknob turned—tugged the box back into place. Something tangled around her foot, and she kicked at it for a moment before realizing it was just an old pair of coveralls.

Through a crack between two boxes, she could peer out into the room as the door opened. There was Jan and another Dutchman, this one wearing the same outfit as all the others. Her breath sounded loud and harsh in her ears; she thought of holding her breath, but that wouldn't last long. She settled for breathing through her mouth, which seemed both slower and quieter.

"Damn," the new person said, and whistled. "It's still lit up. How long does this stuff last?"

"Not sure," Jan said. "It's a lot dimmer than it was before. The stuff can be recharged."

They'd closed the door and crossed to the desk by now. The newcomer had picked up the flask, studying it. The light and shadows in the room jittered and leaped with every motion as the liquid oozed around the parameters of the flask.

"Snap it," Jan said. "No one really groks the snapping stuff. Not really. Saw something on the telly 'bout how it's all around us, bein' used in all kinds of ways, but we all just take it for granted. Like, the stuff was invented fifty years ago, but we still don't really know how it works."

"Yeah? So?"

"You hearin' me? Not even the wild scientists *really* get it. That's why it's so regulated. You can't just buy it on the market. It's gotta be tubed and tuned and channeled. They program it when it leaves the refinery so you can't misuse it. They make it less pure or something. I didn't get all that."

"Right. So why bother stealing it before they recharge it? I don't get that part."

Jan snorted. "Of course not. I haven't explained it to you yet. But I need to bring you up to speed. Here. Look."

They gathered at the desk. Jan opened a drawer and produced what looked like a folded sheet of paper, but when he unfolded it on the desk, it lit up like a screen. "This is the schematic of the recycling facility."

A low whistle from Jan's buddy. "How did you get *that*?"

"A lot of dosh, a lot of aggravation, and a lot of patience. Now shutter and listen: The security on the drained electroleum is almost nil. They keep it over here, in these tanks."

Electroleum? Moira's heart leaped at the word. That was it! That was the . . . *stuff* Tommy had told them about. She was looking right at it!

"Who wants drained electroleum?"

"Exactly. Once they recycle it and recharge it, it's valuable, and it goes through all kinds of secure holds, here, here, and here. And then it gets programmed before they ship it out. But before all that, it's just jelly, sitting around."

"I still don't get why—"

"My guy," Jan interrupted, "tells me that if we get the drained stuff, he can charge it for us. Raw, charged, unprogrammed electroleum. And it turns out electroleum can be used for more than lighting, if you get my drift."

Moira watched as the other boy tilted his head, thinking. Then something dawned on him and he grinned, holding up the flask. "You mean this stuff..."

"The one thing they do know: It just absorbs and reflects energy, chap. Handled right, it can be explosive. Can you imagine the looks on the faces of the Alphabet Boys when we come at them with electroleum grenades?"

The other guy hooted. "We'll run everything from Chelsea to midtown! Even the bobbies won't be able to stop us!"

"Well, yeah, that's the idea." From where he stood and where she hid, Moira could only see Jan's back, but she could tell from his tone of voice that he was grinning and had a wicked gleam in his eye. "Look, I've been keeping this all pretty close, but I need you in on all the details. You have to run the recovery team. You'll come up on the facility in a boat on this side. Me and the rest of the boys come through the superway out to the island and distract security while you chaps drain the nonsecure tanks. See it?"

"Yeah. I see it."

"It goes easy as a tart," Jan said. "We suck the tanks dry and we scarper. Half for us, half for the guy who recharges the electroleum. Done."

"And then we take out the Alphabet Boys."

"The Alphabet Boys. The Chelseas. All of 'em, chap." Jan chortled. "We run it all, chap and *frau*, from here to North Park, from Houston to Conflux and back again."

"Snapping right we do," the other said, and they high-fived.

"Not a word to the others," Jan warned as he refolded the schematic and tucked it back in the desk drawer.

"They're already getting antsy," the other protested. "They know something's up."

"We have to wait. We need money to outfit the boat, and we won't have that until we pawn off the *fraus* to Salazar." Here he hooked a thumb right in Moira's direction. She panicked for an instant before realizing he was just gesturing toward the holding cell down the hall. "Once we have the dosh, we bring everyone in. Explain it all. I'm not getting them all het up before we're ready. Not like the Washington Park gig."

The other groaned. "Right, right. All right, Jan."

"Good is good?"

"Good is good."

"Snap it, then. Let's go."

Moira watched them leave. The door clicked shut. She forced herself to count to ten before she dared to move the box aside.

Then she counted to ten again before she stepped out of the corner. She was keenly aware that they could return at any moment. A part of her suspected they would go from this clandestine meeting to the holding cell, where they would find a *frau* missing and a Dutchman possibly dead, certainly mauled. And then what?

And then game over, Moira, without a restart button and with no saved games, so maybe quit actin' the maggot, lassie, and get to legging it!

The voice in her head switched from her own to her mother's. Moira tended to listen to her mother.

She pawed through the desk drawer for the folded sheet of *whatever* and tucked it into her waistband, letting her shirt cover it, and snagged the flask of electroleum as well. Then she cracked open the door, turning the knob with slow, measured rotation. Each minute click of the cogs inside seemed to echo like cannon fire.

With the door open a smidge, she leaned in close, held her breath, and listened.

Nothing. A steady drip of condensation from the pipes, but nothing else.

She opened the door enough to slip out, closed it quietly behind her, and dashed toward the glowing green X down the hall.

FORTY-THREE

Khalid's story took a while to tell. He kept jumping ahead of himself, and then—realizing he'd missed something—he would have to backtrack to explain. When inventing a tale from whole cloth, he could keep all the details and the continuity straight; telling the absolute truth from beginning to end was new territory for him. His brain wasn't accustomed to it.

As he finished, Dr. Bookman leaned against the wall at one end of the alley, staring up at the sky, occasionally nodding and mumbling to himself, tapping a finger along one side of his jaw.

"Twins, you say?" he asked at last. "Identical?"

"Yeah."

"Powerful magic, then. Very strong."

Magic? Khalid shook his head. "I don't believe in magic. I mean, I've seen a lot of weird stuff in the last day or so, but *magic*—"

Dr. Bookman grinned. "Forgive me for using such an outdated term. I'm old enough that I remember the great debates of the eighties. The more acceptable term, of course, is *wild science.*"

Wild science. *"Any sufficiently advanced technology is indistinguishable from magic,"* Moira had said. Well, Moira hadn't really said it. Some old sci-fi guy had said it.

"What's wild science?" Khalid asked, thinking he might know.

"Why, wild science is everything you've described to me! Wild science is what I've devoted my life to studying." He bowed with a flourish. "Victorio Bookman, MSF. *Magister scientiae ferae.* From the Latin for 'doctor of wild science.'"

"So what I described to you is *real* here? It's some kind of superadvanced science that seems like magic?"

"In past centuries we thought it *was* magic, but that term is hardly fashionable these days. Do you truly have no wild science where you come from? No telepathy, no astral projection, nothing of the sort?"

Khalid shrugged. "Not really. Some people think we do, but no one has ever proved it. I never saw anything remotely like it until Zak started having visions. And then we came here and . . ."

"I see," Dr. Bookman said, nodding. "There have long been theories that other universes could exist beyond this one."

"That's what Moira said. Alternate universes."

"Yes. Your friend is very smart. It's too bad most people in this world can't or won't appreciate it," he said darkly. "It's different where you come from?"

"Girls are okay over there." Khalid thought about it. "I mean, there's stuff that goes on, but not like here."

"Given the choice between living in a world with wild science and living in a world with equality between the sexes," Dr. Bookman said gravely, "I would choose the latter. I'm sorry you've come here, Khalid."

It was weird—this world had been frightening at first, but

once Khalid had been able to calm down, it had become something almost magical. The strange, soft lighting everywhere. The canal and its gondolas. The Wonder Glass that was like the world's best iPad times a million. He could have settled in and gotten to enjoy it . . . and that was *before* learning that "magic" was real here.

But now, knowing what he knew . . .

Yeah, he would give up magic to keep Moira safe, too.

"It's a shame for many reasons," Dr. Bookman went on, "beyond even the simple premises of human dignity. Some preliminary evidence suggests that women may have a greater facility in manipulating and understanding some of the concepts behind wild science. Such studies are, of course, suppressed."

Khalid sensed a great sadness in Dr. Bookman, and normally he would have had no problem listening to more of the man's talk. But the blood on the plank was still there, and Zak and Moira were still missing.

"Dr. Bookman? Sir? About my friends . . . ?"

Dr. Bookman snapped out of his melancholy reverie. "Yes. Of course. My apologies. Where were we?"

"Alternate universes . . ."

"Right. Well, as I said, they've long been theorized. There's even a theoretical construct for them. We call it the Secret Sea. The idea is that the multiverse is composed of a sort of quantum foam, with our two universes bobbing in it, almost like corks on the water."

"Or islands in the ocean?"

"Yes, something like that. And it's possible that the laws of physics work differently in each universe. In ours and in yours, we both have what here is called true science. Gravity, electricity, atomic power, and so on. But yours lacks wild science—magic—whereas here, the M-field allows for a different physics. We have supersymmetrical particles like the M-electron and the M-proton, which can bond into M-hydrogen, which is then combined with extracts of interuniversal quantum foam to form the basic building block of electroleum, for example."

Khalid thought about it. M-this and M-that flew over his head, but he got the gist: Science was different enough here that it could seem like magic. "But how could Zak be having visions in *our* world? And how could Godfrey get over there in the first place? How did his ship end up there?"

Dr. Bookman pondered this, but only for a moment. "My universe and yours are only microns apart in one of the compactified extra dimensions of string theory . . . which allowed you to tunnel through in the first place and could account for some leakage of wild science on your side. While most universes are distinct and discrete, it's theoretically possible that similar universes such as ours mutually exert a subtle repulsive force on each other, a force that serves to make them more *diss*imilar."

"You lost me at *microns*."

"Very well. Imagine the two islands in the ocean, our two worlds. Imagine that they are shaped like two capital Cs, facing away from each other." He cupped his hands to show what he meant. "Now imagine that they are close enough that the backs of the Cs have only a small waterway between them. Narrow enough that it can be crossed."

He thought back to Moira's description of an apartment. Maybe most of the walls were reinforced concrete, but a few were just cheap wallboard. That made more sense to him, but since they were talking about a boat, maybe the island metaphor was better.

"You're saying Godfrey's boat went through that waterway?"

"I'm saying that the metaphor may not account for this but that the distance between your world and mine may be narrow in certain places. Especially places of great import or great tragedy. Didn't you say a great many people died at the place where he crossed over?"

Khalid thought of the 9/11 memorial, of the Freedom Tower, of the terrorist attacks that had happened before his birth. "Well, yeah. But that was in 2001, and Godfrey crossed over a long time before that."

Dr. Bookman chuckled. "You think time is linear? That events follow one another like a mother duck leading her ducklings along a path? Not so. Time is simultaneous. Everything that has happened or will happen is happening at the same moment. It's just that we lack the ability to perceive it thus. Time is folded onto itself."

"Okay, sure, fine." Science mumbo jumbo. "But in your world, is it actually possible to bring someone back to life? That's what Tommy said. He said that here we could use that electroleum stuff to somehow bring him back."

Dr. Bookman thought for a moment. "That is the part of your tale that gives me pause. It's been attempted, of course, in the past. Before the wild-science regulations strictly curtailed such things. No one has ever claimed to succeed. But the circumstances you describe . . . a spirit from another universe, connected to the world of the living by an identical twin . . . There are certain theoretical, nearly massless M-particles that could interact weakly with the corporeal world while still retaining a spiritual form. If exposed to the energies of the Secret Sea and then, say, supercharged with some kind of monumental energy release—"

Khalid shook his head. "Look, I have to be honest with you: Science was never my big subject in school. Whether it's true or wild or whatever. I just want to find my friends and get Zak healthy. Everything else is... I don't know. You and Moira can talk about that stuff."

With a self-reproaching frown, Dr. Bookman nodded. "You're right, of course. I'm so sorry. This happens to me: I get so excited by the possibility of something that I forget to mind the *probability* of something. Helping your friends is our first order of business." He gestured. "Come along."

"Where are we going?" Khalid wanted to get moving, but he didn't want to go just for the sake of going.

"Back to my office," Dr. Bookman said with a gleam in his eye. "We are going to indulge in some wild science, my boy."

FORTY-FOUR

The X was part of an EXIT sign after all. At the end of the hallway, Moira discovered a fire door. Fortunately, the wiring up by the ceiling was disabled, and when she pressed the bar to open the door, no alarm sounded.

So far, so good, but what would she do once she was outside? Six months earlier, she could have passed as a boy—maybe—but not now. Taking herself in, she gnashed her teeth and rued the day her mother had looked her up and down and said, "Time for someone's first bra, I believe."

Once she was outside, whatever she did and whichever way she went, she would instantly be identified as a girl. A *frau*. An uncompanioned female, subject to who knew what in this awful world. Escaping the cage and the building did not mean instant freedom.

Think, Moira. Think. You can't just stand around and wait for something to happen. You have to get moving.

Her heart thrummed and her breath quickened, and for a moment the holding cell with the other women seemed almost cozy and homey and safe. She cursed at herself for entertaining the thought for even a fleeting instant. She wasn't like the women she'd shared a cell with. Born free, raised free, she wouldn't let a little thing like an alternate universe with a blinkered attitude toward women get in her way.

Such immoral attire, Salazar had said. She could see his point, from his perspective. Her T-shirt and shorts probably seemed indecent in this universe. They would attract all manner of unwanted attention as soon as she stepped out onto the street. Not good.

Her legs burned to run as far from the Dutchmen's hideout as possible, but her mind braked them. She had to think, not react.

Gnawing at her bottom lip, she made her decision and retraced her steps down the hall. She wanted to run but feared the noise it would make.

Back in the office, she scrounged quickly in her former hiding space, recovering the coveralls she'd kicked aside.

Returning to the exit door, she slipped into the coveralls. They were baggy and hung on her in large, sexless folds, the chest area in particular dragged down by the weight of fabric, covering precisely nothing. She sighed and, not giving into panic, used one of her last buttons to pin back some of the material so that it covered her properly.

There. She looked lumpy, but in all the wrong places. Not feminine at all.

She heaved open the fire door and stepped outside, emerging into a sunken concrete stairwell that led up into an alleyway. The sun was out, and it blinded her for a moment. She cowered down in the stairwell, too aware that if her makeshift camouflage didn't work, anyone who saw her alone—the word *uncompanioned* filled her memory like sludge—would report her to the police. Or maybe try to take her for his own.

Or maybe the Dutchmen had guards and lookouts.

Or maybe . . .

Or maybe you should pull your socks up and not lie about, her mom scolded.

Moira scrambled up the stairs, breathing hard not from the exertion but from the fear. She'd lived in this world for a day and was already terrified of being caught outside by a man. What must it be like for women who lived here all the time? Now that she was almost free, she could allow herself a pang of sympathy for her poor former cellmates, a brief flare of shame for judging them so harshly. They couldn't help it. They were products of the world in which they lived.

At street level, there were no guards that she could see. Certainly no crying for attention or alarms. She scanned the alley quickly—walls rearing up on either side of her, ruts running down the macadam, opening to streets on both ends.

She thought her disguise might work, if not for the smoothness of her face and the length of her hair. A nearby Dumpster overflowed with several bags of garbage. With a wrinkle of her nose, she began pawing through them. The idea of actually wearing anything that had been thrown out nauseated her, but fear of capture trumped the churning in the pit of her stomach.

She found an old ball cap that said *Breukelen Dodgers* in a fancy font. Tucking her hair up into it, she settled it on her head, pretending it hadn't been sitting in a garbage heap for who knew how long.

She smeared some grit from the alley floor on her cheeks

and forehead, soiling the softness of her skin, making it less feminine. It was a makeover in reverse. She tucked the flask into one of the coverall's enormous pockets, slumped her shoulders, and ambled out of the alleyway, onto the street.

Her disguise seemed to work, for the first block at least. People stared at her, but they were staring with surprise and amusement, not with shock or outrage, so Moira figured her "disguise" was working about as well as could be expected. She absorbed the odd glances and stares and smirks. On the streets of this New York for the first time without having to run for her life, she was able to notice the women: dressed conservatively (where *conservatively* equaled *nigh Victorian*) as compared to their companions, with hats, skirts down to the ankles, long sleeves, no matter the heat. They were all too painted, their makeup serving almost as masks, not as enhancement. *Concealer* suddenly had a second meaning.

She tried not to stare at them as she walked, forcing herself instead to concentrate on figuring out where she'd left Zak.

Think it through, Moira. The Dutchmen aren't some secret government agency. They don't have resources. They're a street gang. The first one saw you and left and came back pretty quickly with the rest of them. So they hang out near that alley where you left Zak. Which means you're probably not that far away from him.

In the distance, she recognized the Washington Arch, which meant she was near Washington Square Park. A sign with an arrow pointed in that direction, announcing that it was ART SQUARE PARK here. Name aside, it seemed like she wasn't terribly far from where she'd left Zak.

The glowing lights on the buildings, she realized now, were the same as the substance in her pocket—electroleum. It seemed

245

like some sort of strange hybrid of jelly and neon gas, but based on what she'd heard from Jan and what Tommy had told them at the Conflux, it had other uses as well.

In her mind, she plotted their course from the Broadway Canal to the alley where she and Zak had hidden. She remembered three turns and a few of the street names they'd passed. Fortunately, with the exception of the Houston Conflux (and the missing lower portion of Manhattan) and the Broadway Canal itself, the geography of this Manhattan was similar to her own. She was able to orient herself by the Empire State Building in the distance, though she wondered if it was called by the same name here.

I'm coming, Zak. Hold on. If they don't stop me, I'm coming.

FORTY-FIVE

Zak's vision blurred, doubled, then focused and blurred again. A woman who looked a lot like his father's mother—Nana— peered down at him, her face fuzzy and indistinct, but he could tell she was wearing too much makeup. Her skin was very smooth, unlined, and it made him think of a brand-new leather jacket.

He was in bed, obviously not in a hospital—the smells and sounds and the tin-inlaid ceiling told him that. He relaxed and found that his breath came easily to him. His chest no longer hurt.

He'd passed out at home and now he was in bed, finally waking up from the craziest dream ever. Alternate universes and dead twins and ghosts.

The woman smiled and said, "Oh, good," her voice slightly accented. Almost . . . German? Did that make sense?

Wait.

He bolted upright in bed, and the woman who was not his grandmother hopped back a step.

"He's awake," she called, and leaned in to mop his forehead with a cool cloth.

Zak tried to push her away; she held him down with a gentle but strong pressure on his shoulder. "Not yet," she said. "Soon. Let him look at you first."

Zak looked around as best he could. He was in a small bedroom, on a comfortable bed, covers pulled up to his chest. There was nothing remarkable about the room. Except for the large sheet of thin, clear glass mounted to one wall and the sort of artificial light he was becoming accustomed to, it could have been a room back home, not on a parallel earth. Sunlight poured in through open curtains.

"How long have I been here?" His voice croaked and crackled. He swallowed with difficulty. The woman held out a cup with a built-in straw, and Zak sipped gratefully.

"Not long," said a new voice. "Just long enough for me to fix your heart."

Sure enough, Zak realized that his chest—which had been pounding arrhythmically when he'd finally collapsed—felt fine. At least, he assumed this was what *fine* felt like. He wouldn't know, having had his heart condition his whole life.

The new voice belonged to a small man with wisps of gray hair; all of the lines and wrinkles the woman had avoided creased his chestnut complexion. He pulled a chair over to the side of the bed and sat down. The woman—Zak saw now that she wore an old-fashioned nurse's uniform, but with a skirt that came down to her ankles—stepped back and stood nearby, hands clasped together.

"I'm Dr. White-eagle," the man said. "You can call me Edwin.

Or you can call me Doc, which is what everyone ends up calling me. And I'm going to need to speak to your parents."

Zak's head spun. He was still only half-conscious, and without thinking, he rattled off his dad's name, then started on Mom's. Dr. White-eagle held up a hand and said, "I don't need her name." To the nurse, he said, "Hand me my Wonder Glass, my dear."

The nurse fetched something from a nearby table. It had the surface area of a large cell phone, but only a fraction of the thickness, and was made out of a frosted, translucent substance. To Zak's surprise, an Apple logo was etched into the back of it.

"Find Michael Killian," Dr. White-eagle said, and the gadget responded with a chirpy, "Sure thing, Doc!"

"Where am I?" Zak asked.

"You're in my home," Dr. White-eagle said. "There was no time to get you to a hospital, so I had to help you with what I had at hand. Fortunately for you, you passed out on the doorstep of the one of the city's premier heart doctors, albeit retired." He smiled crookedly and nodded almost apologetically toward his nurse. "Still dabble, of course. Can't keep an old sawbones away from the stethoscope."

Fortunately . . . Zak didn't think luck had anything to do with it. Godfrey had led him here deliberately.

"Four Michael Killians in the metro area," the gadget piped up. "Here are addresses and recent photos."

"This one looks like you," the doctor grumbled, and tapped it. Zak realized—too late to stop him—that Dr. White-eagle was calling his dad. Or some version of his dad who lived in this universe.

A moment later, a familiar voice came out of the Wonder Glass.

"Hello?" said Dad.

For a moment, Zak expected his heart to jump. Or a lump to form in his throat. Tears. Something. But he surprised himself. The only reaction he had to his father's voice was anger.

"Mr. Killian," the doctor charged ahead with no pleasantries, "my name is Edwin White-eagle. I'm a doctor, and I've just treated your son for a life-threatening ailment that you should have—"

"Wait, you what?"

"As I was saying—"

"My *son*? Is this a joke?"

"I assure you . . ." Dr. White-eagle's small, wizened body bunched up in frustration.

"I don't have a son. I don't have any kids." Dad snorted. "I'm not even married."

Dr. White-eagle pursed his lips and stared at the Wonder Glass. He exchanged a glance with the nurse, then quickly made an apology and disconnected the call.

Zak looked away. Now the tears started. Through the anger they came, unwanted guests sneaking in via an unwatched door. He blotted them away with the heel of his palm. Good. It was good that Zak didn't exist here. Good that Michael Killian had never had children.

That way he couldn't lie to them.

"What's going on here?" Dr. White-eagle asked. "Are you a runaway? Is that what it is?"

Zak gritted his teeth, clenching his jaw until the fluttery sensation in his chest abated. It wasn't a heart problem, he knew. It was the feeling you get right before you start sobbing uncontrollably. Like when a car skids on ice, you have one chance to get it under control, early on, and he wasn't about to miss it.

Dad lied to me. I'm not allowed to miss him. Not allowed to get all weepy at the sound of his voice. It's not even him. It's just a version of him. He wouldn't even know me.

After a moment, Zak was able to speak. "You said . . . you said you fixed my heart. You mean you stabilized me for now?"

Dr. White-eagle frowned. "You are aware you have hypertrophic cardiomyopathy, correct?"

That sounded right. Zak had always thought of it as HCM. Other than putting a pacemaker in, there really wasn't much that could be done for his condition. There were surgeries, but they were risky.

"I know I'm sick," Zak told him.

Dr. White-eagle shook his head, and when he spoke again, it was with barely controlled anger. "I'm really going to have to speak to your parents. Or whoever is your legal guardian. Are they Jehovists or something like that?"

"What?"

"A simple procedure!" Dr. White-eagle crowed. "A simple introduction of a nanobionic parasite into your circulatory system and you're fine. You're, what, twelve years old? Thirteen, maybe? It's criminally irresponsible for your parents to know you have this condition and not have it corrected!"

Zak leaned up on one elbow and probed at his chest. It was true. He could tell. His heart, which had plagued him his whole life, was now healed. He had taken his last dose of verapamil, had spent his last day in the hospital.

New tears blistered at the corners of his eyes. He didn't know how to thank Dr. White-eagle. Couldn't find the words.

"Without the resources of a hospital," the doctor went on, "I can't finalize the treatment, but you're stabilized for now. We'll need your parents' permission to finish the process and permanently fix your heart."

Permanently.

Could it even be possible?

In one day, he'd rediscovered his twin *and* laid claim to his health. Zak grinned. What reason was there to leave this place? They had science so awesome that it was practically magic. And no parents to lie to him. Moira had been wrong: They needed to rescue Tommy and then *stay* here. Everything they needed was here. There was no reason to go home. None at all.

Coming to this universe had been the best accident of his life.

He rested some more and woke up antsy. He got out of bed and went to the window, looking out on the city that was both familiar and unfamiliar at once. His heart jumped at the sight, but for the first time in his life, the jump didn't startle him.

If anything, Zak was more aware of his heart than ever before, only now because it felt so indestructible. It was as though someone had opened up a rickety old taxi and stuffed a jet engine in there. Dr. White-eagle had said the treatment wasn't yet permanent, but Zak wasn't sure the doctor was right about that. His heart felt so perfectly normal and so perfectly . . . *perfect* that he couldn't imagine it any other way. Doctors didn't know everything.

He was cured.

My whole life, I was half a person and never even realized it, he thought, gazing out the window of Dr. White-eagle's house. *I was half of a pair and half of myself. Now I'm on my way to being whole.*

If Godfrey was right and there was a way to rescue both him and Tommy from beyond death . . . then that would be the final step. Zak would finally be the person he'd been meant to be. He wasn't sure exactly how he would manage a new life here, in a universe where he hadn't been born, but with his twin by his side, he was sure he'd figure it out.

His twin . . . and his best friends. *If you have to be lost in another universe,* Zak thought, *it might as well be with your best friends, right?*

The skyline of this version of Manhattan was all wrong, of course, what with the taller skyscrapers and the excised chunk of the island below Houston Street. Still, it was familiar enough to comfort him, though he missed the overwhelming presence of the Freedom Tower dominating the view.

It wasn't always there. There were the twin towers first. But they weren't really twins. Not entirely. One had a spire. And of course they were different on the inside.

Like him and Tommy, he realized. Different on the inside. One with a bad heart, one with kidneys that didn't work right. But Dr. White-eagle had fixed his heart, and he was certain that when he brought Tommy back to the land of the living, someone here would be able to help him, too.

Supertechnology. One more reason to learn to love life here.

He pressed his forehead against the window and willed himself out into the city, wishing he could melt into mist and spread himself over the landscape. To find Khalid and Moira. He vaguely remembered them in an alleyway with him, but not much else. They had to be looking for him, which meant he had to be looking for them. Three Basketeers. Simple as that. They weren't his twin, but they were closer to him than anyone else in this universe, his old one, or any others that might exist.

A thought occurred to him: What if something had happened to them? What if they'd been hurt or detained somehow? What if they couldn't find him because they couldn't even help themselves?

Don't think like that. We've made it this far. We traveled from one world to another. There's nothing that can hurt us.

It wasn't true. It wasn't even close to true, and he knew it, but he repeated it to himself anyway, the way children shut their eyes tight against fear and hope for the best.

A buzzer sounded, and Zak looked over his shoulder through the open door. Out in the main room, the nurse—whose name might as well have been "my dear" for all the times Dr. Whiteeagle used it—opened the front door to the house. A smallish, scruffy man wearing beat-up overalls and a baseball cap stood there. His face was round and filthy but somehow familiar. Zak wandered into the outer room and leaned against the wall, studying the newcomer.

"Can I help you?" the nurse asked.

The visitor said nothing; he just stared at Zak. Then, he whipped off the baseball cap, revealing a fall of bright red hair, and said, "Top o' the mornin' to ye, laddie."

Zak flung himself at Moira, throwing his arms around her and squeezing her tight.

FORTY-SIX

On the way back to the office, Khalid paid careful attention to the world around him, this time not allowing himself to be distracted by the surface differences between his world and this one. He noticed for the first time that all the women walked a few steps behind the men, their eyes downcast. Even little girls hung back by a few paces. And no female, no matter what her age, was out on the street without at least one man accompanying her.

The men, he noticed, wore cool, open, relaxed clothing. Exactly what you'd expect guys to wear in August. The women, though, were bundled from head to toe. He half expected them to wear hijab, like in the pictures his parents had shown him from Iran.

But this was America. It was insane.

N♀ and ♂NLY jumped out at him from signs and window hangings, along with another one: ♀NLY COMPANIONED. Women were barred from certain restaurants, from stores of all kinds, from a freakin' *bookstore*. Khalid was surprised to find that he wanted nothing more than to pick up a rock and fling it through the nearest window.

"How do you live like this?" he asked Dr. Bookman. He tried to imagine his mother—a very proud and capable publicist—meandering down Atlantic Avenue in Brooklyn, eyes on her feet, dutifully trailing behind his father.

"It's always been this way." A note of genuine sadness lingered in Bookman's voice. "Not that I'm excusing it on that basis. But no one alive could ever tell you of a different time."

"Hasn't anyone ever tried to change things?"

"Some have. Every so often, someone or other has published a paper or written a book about the capacity of women, their equality with men. But entrenched interests and old assumptions die hard. They've all failed." He sighed heavily. "Surely the same could be said of tragedies in your own world?"

Probably so. Khalid knew there were problems back home, prejudices and bigotries and just plain stupidities that often led to people being hurt or worse. But somehow it felt more aggressive here, thrust into his face with every sign and every window. It was depressing and rage-inducing all at once, and he found he had nothing more to say about it. They fell into silence as they made their way to Dr. Bookman's building.

When they got there, a woman was waiting for them, standing against the wall in the hallway outside Dr. Bookman's office. She wore a neck-to-toes outfit, like all the other women Khalid had seen, with no jewelry. Her hair, blond, was tied up in a tight bun, and her skin was extremely pale. Dr. Bookman sighed at the sight of her.

"Lorraine," he said very gently, "we've discussed this before. You cannot keep coming here."

"Dr. Bookman, you *have* to help me."

"I can't help you." He took her hands and rubbed them as if to calm her. "I wish I could, but I can't. Please leave—you'll get in trouble if you're found out by yourself."

"I have a ticket," she said, and produced from her pocket a slip of something thin and foldable that didn't quite seem to be paper. "They think I'm off to the market, but I came here. I only have a little while. *Please*, Dr. Bookman."

The urgency and terror in Lorraine's eyes and voice momentarily made Khalid forget about Zak and Moira. *Help her, man!* he thought fiercely.

Dr. Bookman unlocked his office door and gestured for Khalid to enter. Inside, Khalid ambled over to the cockroach experiment. Not much had changed. The dead roaches were still dead, and the living ones were still living. He settled into an old, cracked leather chair. He realized it was the first time in two days that he'd sat on a piece of furniture. Every muscle in his body relaxed, and he nearly groaned with relief and pleasure. Through the closed door, he made out Bookman's low murmur and Lorraine's higher-pitched rejoinders. She was becoming more and more agitated, while Dr. Bookman remained calm.

After a few moments—during which Khalid almost drifted off to sleep, so comfortable was he—Dr. Bookman entered, tossing his dreadlocks to and fro as he shook his head.

"You're not going to help her? After she risked coming here?"

Dr. Bookman began gathering things from his bookshelves— papers, books, small trinkets—and placing them on his desk. "She wants me to meddle in a man's mind," he said. "To destroy the memories her husband has of her, such that she never existed."

What could be so bad that someone would resort to *that*?

Khalid gulped and glanced at the closed door. He wondered whether Lorraine still lingered there or had gone. "Can you do that?" he asked. "Is that even possible?"

Dr. Bookman harrumphed and peered at Khalid over his glasses. "I'm not a street performer. I'm a doctor of wild science."

"So you can't?"

"I *won't*. There's a difference. I keep forgetting you're not from around here. You don't understand. Wild science is strictly regulated. Only a small number of people are permitted to study it and perform it. The sorts of technologies that would allow me to breach a man's brain and intrude upon his thoughts are among the most highly regulated. What could be more sacred than our own minds?"

"I see. I guess."

"There are, of course, those who dabble in the wild sciences without a license. Dangerous men, they are. They may be willing to risk their lives for her, but I am not. I took an oath to harm no one with my skills, Khalid. I take it very seriously."

"Even if someone's in trouble?"

"Especially when someone is in trouble. It is in those moments that we are most desperately tempted to commit a small evil in the name of rectifying a greater one. But evil is evil, Khalid. Vanquishing one in the name of another accomplishes nothing."

Khalid wasn't sure he believed that. It sounded noble and high-minded, but it rankled him at the same time. It felt like a dodge, not a principle.

But he did not have the luxury of kissing off Dr. Bookman and moving on to a "doctor of wild science" with a more lax brand of ethics. Zak was somewhere in the city, dying. Moira was somewhere in the city, doing who knew what. Khalid needed whatever help was being offered, whatever was right in front of him. And he needed it now.

Sorry, Lorraine. Really. But my friends come first.

By now Dr. Bookman had a collection of things before him on his desk. Khalid got up and walked over to examine them: Two books—one thick, the other thin—each opened and flat on the desk. A set of papers with lines and circles drawn on them that, when aligned properly to each other, formed a sort of ring on the desk. A small box filled with a reddish powder. A vial of something thick and green and viscous. A chunk of glass with a yellow flaw at its core. And what appeared to be a small, overripe watermelon.

"What's all this for?"

"We'll be using a technique from the voodoo methodology," Dr. Bookman explained.

Khalid looked around. "Where's the chicken?"

A laugh. "So, you have voodoo in your world?"

"Well, yeah. But, I mean, it's not *real* or anything."

Dr. Bookman ran a hand through his hair. "I would like to visit this world of yours someday. This place where they have voodoo but don't have voodoo at the same time. Fascinating. In any event, there is no need for anything so crude as a chicken. That was the historical methodology, before wild scientists came to understand the superphysics behind voodoo. The dead animals, the fresh blood . . . these worked because they were convenient metaphors to focus the mind of the practitioner, permitting psychoempathic manipulation of M-particles. I need no such accoutrements."

He arranged the papers to form a five-pointed star on his desk, then sprinkled some of the red powder along its edge. The green liquid (more like sludge, Khalid noted, as it oozed from the vial) went into the center of the star. Dr. Bookman consulted the thick book, nodded to himself, and chanted something in a language Khalid did not recognize.

Then there was silence in the room. Khalid held his breath, lest his own breathing break the tension-filled air.

"We're ready now," Dr. Bookman murmured, his eyes closed, his hands waving over the ring. "This procedure connects like to like. Classic voodoo. I will communicate with Zak. Give me something of your friend's."

Khalid thought of voodoo dolls back home, and it made sense. A voodoo doll used hair or whatever to connect to a victim, right? So, yeah, with something of Zak's, maybe Dr. Bookman could actually connect to Zak. Only instead of sticking pins in him, he could just figure out where Zak was.

He raced his palms down both legs, feeling for anything at all in his pockets. But other than his useless phone and a few bucks, there was nothing. Certainly nothing of Zak's. Sweat formed along his brow and on his upper lip. Nothing. At all.

"I don't have anything," he whispered fiercely.

Dr. Bookman remained calm, eyes still closed, hands weaving a complicated pattern over the desk. "Nothing? Really?"

"No."

"You are his best friend and you have nothing of his?"

Frustrated, Khalid blurted out, "It's not like we exchanged friendship bracelets or anything."

Dr. Bookman's lips quirked into a flash-fast grin. "You're thinking of the purely physical. Surely you have something of his that is less concrete . . . ?"

Less concrete? What did that mean? Dr. Bookman seemed

to be sinking deeper into a trance, his expression slackening, his body swaying just slightly. Khalid didn't want to interrupt whatever sensation or emotion he was experiencing.

Emotion. Maybe that was it. Maybe that was something "less concrete."

"He's my best friend," Khalid said slowly. But that, he knew, wasn't enough. It wasn't enough to say it. He needed the force of it, the pull of it, the rampant tug and swallow of it. The way only best friends know each other, understand each other. The way only best friends connect.

Dr. Bookman picked up the melon and shook it. Something rattled inside.

"We're the Three Basketeers," Khalid said. "Moira and Zak and me. I've known Zak my whole life. My parents came here—well, came to *my* America—before I was born. Zak and me . . . we played together as kids. Our parents were friends, and I remember when his parents got divorced. He told me it was happening, and he didn't cry or anything, even though he wanted to." Now Khalid closed *his* eyes, surrendering to memory, sinking into what could only be described as his own Secret Sea, a foam of life and remembrance and emotion. It was as real to him now as it had been then: younger Zak, eight years old, his jaw clenched and his left hand gripping tightly to a pole on the playground at the park, saying, *"They said they don't get along. Who cares if they get along? Why is that such a big deal? Why do I have to put up with all this stuff just because they can't get along?"*

"Three Basketeers," Dr. Bookman mumbled, and shook the melon again.

"Zak stayed—" Khalid broke off, realizing somehow that he didn't need to speak the memories; he only needed to have them.

Zak had stayed over at Khalid's house the day his parents divvied up the belongings in their apartment, deciding what would stay, what would go, who could lay claim to what. Together, Khalid and Zak had watched the most horrifying horror movies they could find, speaking not at all, cramming their mouths with popcorn and corn chips and cheese puffs as geysers of blood and mountains of body parts accumulated on the screen. In the morning, they'd both taken turns throwing up, and Zak had seemed better after that, as though he'd gorged himself on bad thoughts and bad memories, then purged them right into the Shamoons' toilet.

"I don't ever want to be alone," Zak had said a few days later. His father had moved out of the apartment, and Zak had come home to a house that felt too empty.

"You're not alone, man. I'm there even when I'm not there."

Khalid squeezed his eyes shut further, crimping down the tears. The air around him had gone cold and stale. Wicked lights flashed and spiraled against his eyelids.

"He's coming . . . ," Dr. Bookman whispered. The melon rattled again and again, louder, faster, and then abruptly stopped. "He's here."

Khalid opened his eyes. Nothing in the room had changed. How could that be possible? How could nothing be different?

Dr. Bookman gritted his teeth; cords stood out along his neck. "Impossible. Too strong. Come to me! I command you!"

"Hey, what's going—"

"I invoke you and I summon you!" Dr. Bookman shouted to the empty air. "You cannot resist me!"

"What's happening?"

"He's resisting." Sweat beaded along Dr. Bookman's brow and slid down his face like rain on a window. "Never happened before," he grunted. "He's strong."

"Who . . ." Khalid began, and then stopped talking at the sight before him.

The air around Dr. Bookman seemed to smear, as though greased. Reds and blues and golds warped the space between them. Khalid blinked rapidly, trying to clear his vision, but the problem wasn't with his eyes; it was with the world itself. The blur intensified, and Dr. Bookman went rigid, dropping the melon to the floor, his arms held out stiffly before him, his entire body ramrod straight, as if he'd been electrocuted.

The sound of wind—far-off wind—filled the room, and Khalid thought he could hear something cracking in the distance.

The colors around Dr. Bookman tightened, sharpened, shrank down into him, and then the wild scientist sucked in a breath that seemed endless, and his shape flickered for an instant, replaced for the space of a blink by a smaller form. He jerked his head back, staring open-mouthed at the ceiling.

"Speak to me!" Dr. Bookman said commandingly. "Speak now!"

And then, garbled: "No, no, no, no, leave me alone. . . ."

"I compel you to speak through me!"

"No." A strangled whisper this time.

"Should I do something?" Khalid asked. He felt completely helpless, useless. A paralyzed appendage.

Dr. Bookman's throat worked, and then he spoke with Zak's voice: "Khalid!"

"Zak!" It took everything in Khalid not to hurl himself over the desk at the sound of his friend's voice.

"No. Not Zak." Dr. Bookman's face twisted and contorted in pain, but the voice sounded calm.

"*Tommy?*"

"You have to—"

And the air smeared again. Khalid leaned forward.

"The electroleum," Tommy said. "*Lots* of it. It's the only way—"

"Right, but Zak's hurt. I have to get to him first."

"No. Nothing else matters. If you can't do that, then you won't—"

Dr. Bookman's brow furrowed, and he shook his head. His body—still stiffened—began to vibrate.

"Speak!" he shouted in his own voice. "Speak true!"

"—rescue us, Khalid!" Tommy said through Dr. Bookman. "Godfrey and me! You have to do it *now*! It's the only thing that matters!"

"Speak!" Dr. Bookman cried. A trickle of blood began to leak from his left ear. Khalid stood rooted to his spot, horrified and mesmerized by the back-and-forth. "Speak! I command it!"

"It's the only way!" Tommy said with Dr. Bookman's mouth. "You have to—"

"Too . . . much!" With a painful, creaking effort, Dr. Bookman moved his right arm an inch, then another, reaching out for something on the desk.

And then Bookman's body spasmed, lashing forward, bent at the waist, then back, and the man screamed a pitiable and horrid scream that nearly made Khalid piss his pants for the first time since that embarrassing day in kindergarten. The smear intensified—blue, gold, red, a vicious turmoil of bleeding colors—and Dr. Bookman danced as if zapped with live current, his body a marionette in the hands of a demented puppeteer. Khalid couldn't move, frozen, watching as the man stumbled backward until he collided with the window. For a terrifying second, Khalid thought he'd hit hard enough to smash the glass and tumble three stories to the street below, but the glass held, and now Dr. Bookman was splayed spread-eagled against the window, his eyes wide and unseeing, his neck decorated with the thread of blood from his ear, a thread that now speckled the shoulder of his jacket.

"So . . . powerful . . ." Dr. Bookman grunted. "Cut loose . . ."

The smear in the air coalesced into a turbulent knot of clashing colors and then flattened out and became a ripple that slowly expanded from its origin at Dr. Bookman's midsection. Khalid watched in awe as gravity stopped working.

Gravity just stopped working.

Dr. Bookman began to slide *up* the window, toward the ceiling, his dreadlocks floating above him. Khalid thought quickly—only Dr. Bookman was drifting up, not any of the furniture, and he began to feel himself becoming unmoored from the floor—

Living things it's affecting living things

—and he grabbed hold of the desk before the wave of no-gravity hit him full force. His feet left the floor, and soon he was nearly upside down, clinging to the desk, his neck craned to see Dr. Bookman floating above him.

"Blow it up!" screamed a new voice from the same lips. "Find a way! It's the only thing that matters! Break down the wall! Tear it down! That's all that matters!"

Godfrey. The new voice. It could only be Godfrey.

"But—"

"Just *do it, Khalid!*" Godfrey yelled. "If you care about Zak and Tommy and yourself, you'll do it! There's too much at stake! There's no time to think about it! Do it!"

Godfrey's voice caught on the *t* at the end of *it*, clacking out the letter over and over again, like a cog turning: *t t t t t t t t t t t t*. Dr. Bookman's hands clenched and unclenched. He spoke in his own voice for just a syllable: "Dis—"

A wind started to howl in the room, and Khalid could swear he felt something wet splash against his cheek. Rain? Was it raining *inside*?

Dr. Bookman screamed again, high-pitched and abjectly terrified. Khalid thought he heard another word: *discon*. Discon? That wasn't even a real word.

Out of the corner of his eye, Khalid caught something happening in the cockroach aquarium. Something was flashing—

"Destroy it all!" Godfrey bellowed, yanking his attention back. Dr. Bookman's mouth strained with the exertion of Godfrey's voice, so much that a small fissure split open at the corner of his mouth. Blood welled up there. "Use the electroleum to bring down the wall! Bring down the wall and restore me to life!"

"I want to talk to Tommy!" Khalid yelled. "Let me talk to Tommy again!"

"Tommy's too weak!" Godfrey roared through Dr. Bookman's lips. "Listen to *me*, Khalid! Too much is happening! We're fading! You have to save us! Do it . . . or I will find someone who *will!*"

Dr. Bookman's throat bobbed and his lips moved, but no sound came out. *Dis . . . con*, Khalid lip-read, and then smelled something burning and realized that Dr. Bookman's hair was on fire. The very tips of his dreadlocks were smoldering, smoke peeling off from them.

He's gonna die. He's gonna burn up.

Struggling to maintain his grip on the desk as his body hung toward the ceiling was like hanging on to the edge of a cliff while wind whipped down the canyon. Khalid focused on his fingers, willing them not to slip.

And in staring at them, he couldn't help looking at the desk. With its powder and its papers arranged just so . . .

Dis. Con. Discon.

Disconnect!

Khalid let go of the desk with one hand. His body lurched upward—it felt as though he was falling, and he immediately grabbed the edge of the desk again. It wasn't far to fall "up" to the ceiling, but it was far enough that he thought it would hurt. And he would be stranded up there on the ceiling.

Speaking of the ceiling—way up there, Dr. Bookman's hair was now burning like a profusion of lit fuses, the flames sparking and crackling as they made their way along the length of the dreadlocks. Halfway now, and soon they would engulf his head. Godfrey was still yelling, exhorting Khalid, screaming at him, and Khalid once again let go with one hand, reaching out to the papers on the desk.

He couldn't make it. They were just beyond his grasp.

Come on, Khalid. You never used to think things through. Just do it!

And he did. He let go with the other hand. His gut clenched as he dropped away from the floor, plunging up with sickening velocity toward the ceiling. But letting go allowed him to twist and stretch out just right.

He had one chance.

His hand brushed against the papers, knocking them out of Dr. Bookman's careful alignment.

Halfway to the ceiling, Khalid hung suspended for a rare instant as gravity rearranged itself. He floated there just long enough to marvel at the sensation, and then the earth was tugging at him again and he fell again, this time down, not up. The sudden and repeated interference with his inner ear churned his stomach, and as he crashed to the floor, he puked up the bagel he'd eaten.

Dr. Bookman slid down the wall and collapsed in a heap, the ends of his dreadlocks still burning as if his head was a keg of dynamite and his hair a profusion of fuses.

Khalid's stomach ached and protested when he unfolded himself from the floor, and not just from throwing up. He'd forgotten about the cop's stun stick tucked into his waistband and covered with his shirt; he'd landed on it when he hit the floor. A bruise already stood out in alarming purplish black on his skin. He pulled out the stun stick and tossed it aside. Then, dancing around the puddle of his own vomit, he dashed to Bookman's side. The carpet squished and he nearly slipped, but he caught himself at the last instant, grabbing a curtain for balance.

Bookman was slumped on the floor, out cold, his head a set of sparklers.

Khalid jerked at the curtain and it popped free from its rod. He wielded the fabric like a matador, smacking at Bookman's head, smothering the flames one by one until nothing remained but charred, crumbling ash, wisps of smoke, and the smell of burning hair.

Fortunately, there was nothing left in Khalid's stomach for him to throw up.

"Dr. Bookman!" He hunkered down and snapped his fingers

in front of the wild scientist's face repeatedly. "Wake up! Come on, man!"

Nothing. He grabbed the man's wrist the way he'd seen paramedics do on TV, then realized he had no idea why they did that. With a groan, he put an ear to the man's chest. Bookman's heart *lub-dub*bed reliably, and Khalid could hear the scientist's breathing, deep and sure.

Maybe he was just knocked out, is all. Maybe he'll be okay when he wakes up.

Khalid rocked back on his heels and realized as he shifted his weight that the carpet was wet beneath him. As he took notice of the area around him, he saw that everything was wet—the carpet was soaked, and puddles covered the surface of the desk. Water had come from nowhere.

Did Tommy bring it? Godfrey? Is it part of the Secret Sea?

He ran two fingers along the top of the desk, then sniffed them. Salt water. From the ocean.

Which was easily a mile away.

Man, I would really like to spend, say, an hour without something freaky happening to me. I've hit my freaky quotient, like, for life.

Depressingly, he realized he was more likely, not less likely, to experience freaky doings in his near future.

He dimly remembered from a school health class that moving someone who was injured was a bad idea, but Dr. Bookman appeared exceedingly uncomfortable, half-propped against the wall, his head lolling forward on his chest. With much grunting and curses muttered in both English and Farsi (the English ones were more fun, truthfully), Khalid hooked Bookman under the armpits and managed to drag him over to the sofa. There, more curses and some sweaty efforts saw the wild scientist arranged facedown on the cushions, arms and legs flung out haphazardly, one hand dipping down onto the carpet. It didn't look comfortable, but it had to be better than the floor.

Khalid inhaled deep and slow. He was out of breath. *Next step: 911. Call the paramedics, right?*

The desk phone was useless, dripping with salt water and shorted out. The whole office was a mess: rancid with salt water, furniture tipped over, the smell and haze of smoke still lingering. Khalid scrounged around for a cell phone. He checked drawers and shelves. As he did so, he came across the cockroach aquarium. He glanced inside, then kept looking for a cell phone . . .

And then went back to the aquarium.

He stared, not believing his eyes. Then, licking his lips, he counted the roaches, whispering each number.

Nine.

There were only *nine* roaches in the aquarium. There had been a dozen before.

And there was no way out. The aquarium had sturdily withstood the voodoo eruption. No cracks that Khalid could see, and the lid was still firmly in place.

That was odd, sure, but it wasn't what had caught his attention. Not really. What had caught his attention was that . . .

Was that . . .

Some of the blue roaches were dead. Fine.

But some of the red ones were alive. The few still stuck on their backs kicked their legs and twitched their antennae, but a couple were staggering around the aquarium as though drunk.

"Oh, man, zombie cockroaches. It gets weirder and weirder. . . ."

He shook himself and pulled away from the aquarium. He had more important things to worry about. He did what he should have done from the beginning: crouched down near the doctor and frisked him. Khalid found in Bookman's inner jacket pocket something that looked like a smaller version of the Wonder Glass III he'd used at the Apple store. But when he tapped and swiped at it, it only lit up with the familiar line-through-a-circle icon and the words *UNAUTHORIZED USER*.

Figures. I get the one guy in the world who actually puts a passcode on his phone.

Dr. Bookman groaned and flailed with the hand that was not pinned under his body. Khalid, crouching, lost his balance and fell backward on his butt. Squish.

"Back and forth . . . ," Bookman moaned. His eyes fluttered open, then closed, then open again, the eyelids twitching. Beneath, his eyes looked but did not see. Khalid waved a hand before them to confirm; Bookman didn't even blink.

"Traveling . . . too much . . . ," Bookman said. "Back and forth."

"Back and forth?"

"The walls . . . are weak. . . ."

Khalid looked back and forth and all around. The office's walls seemed stable enough.

"Godfrey . . . spirit . . . too . . ."

"Hey, Doc? Doc, can you hear me?" Khalid snapped his fingers in front of Bookman's face again, even though it hadn't worked before. Never had he felt so utterly helpless, so powerless. He should be running for help. Or—even better—he should actually be doing something helpful. But all he could do in that moment was stay rooted to the spot, leaning in, snapping his fingers like a moron. A moron with rhythm, sure, but still a moron.

"Stop him . . . Don't let . . ."

"Dr. Bookman? Can you hear me? You gotta help me out, man. I need to know what to do. I mean, do I go after this electro-leum stuff? Is that my play? Or do I keep looking for Zak?" He stood up and wiped his hands on his shirt, which did nothing to dry them. "Oh, man, you're not listening. You can't hear me."

Khalid dropped to his knees next to the sofa. "Zak and Moira are gone and you're unconscious and . . . and . . ." He groaned and threw his hands in the air in frustration. "And I think even your cockroach experiment has gone off the rails, FYI."

And Dr. Bookman's eyes, which had fluttered and danced between open and closed the whole time, suddenly snapped opened long enough to stare into Khalid's for a fixed, terrifying moment.

"It's. Gone," said Dr. Bookman, his voice strong and clear. "Get. Help."

And then he immediately passed out.

FORTY-SEVEN

The clinch lasted longer than they had time for but at the same time not nearly long enough.

"You're alive," Moira babbled, then hated herself for saying it, then figured it didn't matter because he *was*. Zak was alive and looking great.

"Dr. White-eagle helped me," he said, finally breaking the embrace, holding her at arm's length. "I think I'm cured."

"Are you kidding me?" Moira looked over at the woman who'd opened the door, dressed in what appeared to be some kind of medical garb. "Dr. White-eagle?"

"Yeah, over there." Zak jerked a thumb toward a newcomer, a stooped figure ambling into the room.

As soon as Moira saw Dr. White-eagle, her stomach clenched, and her inner voice screamed, *Run!*

Roughly twenty-four hours in this world was all it had taken to make her terrified at the sight of a man. That's all it took.

She grabbed Zak's hand and dragged him toward the door. "We're going. Now. Hurry."

Zak pulled away. "Wait a sec, Moira. I don't even have my shoes—"

Moira growled deep in her throat, more out of frustration than actual threat. She backed up, interposing herself between the woman she now realized was a nurse—of *course*—and the front door, so that she could run if she had to.

"Get your things," she said, "and then we're out of here." Holding a palm up toward the doctor, she said, "Take it easy. I'll be gone soon enough."

"Here, now!" Dr. White-eagle exclaimed. "What's going on here? Who's this girl in my house?" He snapped his fingers and pointed to Zak. "Are *you* her companion? What the *devil* is going on?"

From Zak's expression, Moira realized that he had no idea that women were second-class citizens in this world. He didn't understand the danger she was in just by standing in the doorway, alone.

"Nothing for you to worry about," Moira told the doctor. "We're going to get out of your hair, and you can forget you ever saw me."

"I highly doubt that," the doctor said with some amusement. "A young girl, on her own, comes barging into my house to steal a patient? I assure you, that is something I'll remember for quite some time."

Zak had grabbed his shoes in the meantime and joined her at the door. "Moira, these people helped me. We can trust them."

"Trust *me*, Zak. Three Basketeers."

Dr. White-eagle shook his head, a sad grimace distorting his aged face. "I've known many good women in my day. None of them flouted the law like this, young lady."

"We're going now," Moira announced with supreme confidence. The doctor seemed surprised by the tone in her voice, and the nurse did a double take, clucking her tongue as if to say "for shame." That bothered Moira more than the reaction of an army of sexist men.

"We're leaving, and I'm going to ask you—very respectfully and very politely—not to call the police or report us. As a personal favor. Not as a woman to a man, but as one human being to another."

The doctor crossed his arms over his chest. "That boy is my responsibility. Ethically and legally."

"I really have to go," Zak said apologetically, slipping on his shoes. "It's tough to explain."

He backed out the door with Moira. She jammed her cap back on her head once they had the door closed.

"What's going on?" Zak demanded when they were alone.

No time. White-eagle was probably already on the phone with the cops. "Can you run?" she asked Zak.

"Now? Better than ever, I bet."

"Then let's."

Heaving and gasping for breath, they stumbled against each other as they collapsed into a doorway somewhere along Eighth Avenue. The building was condemned or closed or just not accessible from this side, as evidenced by the thick layer of dust along the door handles.

"I think we can rest here for a second," Moira managed to say between breaths. She pressed herself as far into the doorway as she could, hoping to avoid idle glances from passersby. Her disguise wasn't much of one, she knew, although few people in this world would imagine a woman trying to pull it off. She couldn't risk being recaptured, whether by a street gang or by the police. There was too much at stake.

"Can you maybe tell me what we're running from?" Zak asked.

"Not *we*. Me. I'm the one running."

Zak cracked the first smile she'd seen from him since they'd left the hospital. The sight of it filled her with so much relief and joy that the fear almost sluiced out of her entirely. "Seems like I kept up," he said wryly.

"Not what I meant." She had her breath back now. "I *have* to run. It's dangerous for me here."

Something flickered in Zak's eyes, and he smacked his forehead with his palm. "Irish! I forgot! I'm sorry—I was so out of it in the alleyway that I totally forgot—"

"Not Irish."

Moira explained what she'd experienced since leaving him in the alley—the Dutchmen, and almost being sold to Sentius Salazar and whisked away to an auction somewhere.

"I don't . . . I don't get it." Zak's entire expression drooped. "This world seems so *cool*. They have all this technology and stuff, but they treat women . . . How does something like that happen?"

"The technology is just physics," Moira said. "They got a universe with slightly different physical laws, is all. This world's problem is sociology, not physics. I don't know how it happens. The same way it *doesn't* happen, maybe? Something happened a couple hundred years ago here that got rid of slavery before it ended in our world. Which is great. But then something else *didn't* happen that gave women equal rights in our world."

"But they speak English and they have cars and the city looks kinda similar. I mean, they have Apple stuff, for God's sake! All of that without women being involved?"

"Maybe some things are inevitable, the way different mammals all evolved four limbs. Or maybe there were women behind the scenes. Or, hey, Zak, maybe God is floating above all of this, pulling the strings to make it work out. I don't know, and I really don't care. The upshot is that I don't think I like this place."

Zak nodded. "Yeah," he said after a moment. "Yeah, I hear you. Me neither."

FORTY-EIGHT

There was nothing to say, so he didn't. They were stuck in this world, which wasn't so bad for Zak, but for Moira . . . What could he do about Moira?

"Maybe I could be your—what did they call it?—companion? If you're with me, you'll be safe, right?"

"First of all, I don't think so. You're too young. That's why the cop chased us. And second of all, hey, I mean, you're my best friend and all, but I'm not planning on spending the rest of my life on your arm just so I won't get arrested and sold to the highest bidder."

"Right." Zak grimaced. Just a little while ago, this world had seemed like the answer to all his problems. Was Moira's freedom the price he had to pay for his own health and the return of his brother? More important, what could he do about it?

"Maybe it's just New York," he posited. "Maybe in other places it's safe to be a girl."

Moira shrugged. "Maybe. Maybe it's just this city or this

state or this country. I don't know. You can bet I'm going to figure it out, though. But not right now."

"Why not? Why wait?"

"Because I have a little bit of good news." She fished around in a pocket and brought out a flask of a thick liquid that shone with a very pale light. After a moment or two, Zak realized it was very similar to the light that shone on the buildings.

"This is electroleum," Moira explained. "This is the stuff Tommy mentioned to us."

Zak took the flask from her, expecting it to be hot, or at least noticeably warm to the touch. It was no warmer than the surrounding air, though. The glass was even slightly cool. He tilted the flask and watched the electroleum perform a slow ooze as it settled into a new position.

"This is the stuff that's going to bring Tommy back to life? It looks like glowing snot."

"Apparently, this sample is depleted. You can do all kinds of things with it when it's fully charged and programmed. Here's where it comes from." Moira had produced a folded sheet of something from under her ill-fitting coverall. She opened it silently. It definitely wasn't paper—there was no telltale rustle. Instead, it unfolded into a perfectly smooth surface, its creases melting away.

"What *is* this?" He touched the sheet. It was slick like plastic, but thin like paper. It looked like a blueprint of some sort, but zoomed far out, so he couldn't perceive any details.

"I played with it a little bit on the way over. Watch this." Moira traced her finger around a section of the blueprint, then tapped inside the area she'd drawn.

Before Zak's eyes, the blueprint zoomed in on that area. He gasped and his jaw dropped. It was like watching paper come to life.

"That's . . ."

"I know!" Moira's eyes danced with excitement. "Isn't it incredible? It acts like paper, but it's actually some kind of computer display. Can you imagine if they could make phones out of this stuff?"

Zak thought back to Dr. White-eagle's Wonder Glass gadget. "I think they do."

"Anyway," she said, now rotating the image with an expert twist of her wrist, "it's totally touch-sensitive. And get this." She traced a line on the sheet, following a path along the blueprint; where she touched, the sheet emitted a light, illuminating the trail she had made.

"That's cool," he admitted, "but what are we looking at?"

"This is an electroleum recycling and recharging plant," she told him. "The guys who kidnapped me were planning on robbing it."

"But now they're not."

"Nope. Because we're gonna get there first."

Her face wore the sort of triumphant and self-satisfied smile he knew well, the Moira-look that meant she'd gone three steps ahead of everyone else and figured out the solution to the problem no one even knew about yet. It was incongruous on the dirty, scratched face under the filthy cap with the misspelled version of *Brooklyn* on it. Yet it was so familiar and felt so much like home that he couldn't help smiling back.

"Why are we doing that?" he asked.

"We need this stuff to break down the walls between life and death, right? That's what Tommy told us. To rescue him and his friend. It'll take energy."

"Right. But you said that this place was recycling old electroleum. How much energy could be in *that*?"

"It recycles *and* recharges," Moira reminded him. As though she'd been doing it her whole life, she manipulated the schematic until two different areas were enlarged and glowing. "The Dutchmen were just gonna steal the old electroleum, here. Security is minimal there."

"But we don't know how to charge it—"

"We don't need to," she told him. "They charge it over here." She pointed to the second magnified area. "All the charged electroleum we could ever want."

Zak squinted at the map. "It says 'High Security.' We'd never get in and then get out with the stuff."

"Got a better plan?" She planted her fists on her hips. "Maybe you have an electroleum dealer on speed dial?"

With a sigh, Zak admitted he didn't. "It can't just be as easy as walking into this place, though."

"I'm sure it isn't. But we'll figure it out."

"Will we?"

Moira shrugged and grinned, and for a moment Zak was able to forget how dangerous this world was for her. "Well, *I'll* figure it out. You can watch. Like usual."

Zak had felt like an idiot going into a corner store and asking if there was somewhere he could get on the Internet for free. He felt more like an idiot when the guy behind the counter looked at him, perplexed, and said, "The *Internet*?" as if he'd never heard of it before.

"You know, like a computer?" Zak mimed typing and mousing. "Connected to other computers?"

The guy's face lit up with understanding. "You mean the TIM! There's a TIM café down on Ninth and Thirteenth, but if you just want to get on quick and free, head over to the Apple Store."

The words *Apple Store* just didn't seem to belong to this world, in a world so different in so many fundamental ways. But there had been Dr. White-eagle's Wonder Glass. That etched Apple logo, hovering just above surface of the device.

Different world, similar world. Like twins, after all.

And so he and Moira headed west on Fourteenth, toward what was in their world called the Meatpacking District. According to the signs they saw on the way, it had the same name here.

Moira kept her head down, her hands jammed in her pockets, shoulders hunched, staring at the pavement as they walked. With the sun just setting, Zak felt guilty for enjoying the walk. The air was crisp and less humid than a typical New York August. Just a good weather day, or was the climate different in this world, too?

In any event, *he* could saunter down the street without a care, nodding to other pedestrians, smiling at them. No one would be scandalized by his presence.

He noticed signs banning women on storefronts. Or welcoming them, but only with men in their company.

It was a magic world, this one. A world where his twin could live again. Where his heart could be repaired.

And where his best friend was a criminal.

He wished that this world didn't resemble home so much. Somehow, that made its flaws even worse.

"How did you find me, anyway?" he asked her. He told himself it was to help her relax, but really it was to take his mind off his own guilt.

"Tommy." It was the last word he expected to hear out of her mouth, and it froze him in his tracks, rooting him to the spot. Moira kept walking for a few paces, then stopped and gestured to him in panic. "Keep up with me!" she whispered loudly.

Zak caught up to her. "Tommy? Really?"

"I was backtracking from the Dutchmen's hideout, trying to make my way to the alley. And then I saw you, just standing on the corner. I ran to you and tripped and fell right through you, and that's when I realized I was seeing a ghost." She paused. "I can't believe I just said that sentence."

"Tommy! What did he say to you?"

"Nothing. He just started walking, and I followed him until I got to the doctor's house. He disappeared right on the stoop, so I figured that was where I was supposed to be. When the door opened, I couldn't believe you were right there!" She beamed at him, and her joy both invigorated and depressed him.

"We're gonna be stuck here, aren't we?" he asked.

Her smile dimmed. "Yeah. I think so."

"And you're going to be—"

She shook her head fiercely. "We can't talk about that. Not now. Right now, we have to learn what we can about this recycling place. And find Khalid."

Breaking into a futuristic building they knew nothing about, evading security, and stealing an alien substance they'd never encountered before suddenly seemed a lot easier than finding Khalid. Alternate universe or no, missing chunk of the island aside, this Manhattan was every bit as crowded and overpopulated as the one back home. Without cell phones, finding Khalid would be like isolating a specific drop of water in a lake.

"How are we going to do that?" he wondered.

"One step at a time," Moira said. "We're here."

From across the street, the Apple Store looked astonishingly like one back home, except that it was lit by electroleum, which gave it an unearthly, beautiful haze. Moira couldn't allow herself to be seduced by the pretty tech, though. This world was a minefield for her, a maze with death rays around every corner. She had to be careful. More careful than she'd ever been in her life.

"You go in there and find everything you can online about the recycling facility," Moira told Zak. "I'll be over there, figuring out our next step." She pointed to a rather dingy and darkening alley opposite the store.

"That's crazy. Just come with me."

"No."

He flung a hand out. "There's no sign on the store! Women are allowed in there!"

Moira grabbed his face, pinching his cheeks together. "Be. Quiet!" she whispered. "Don't shout stuff like that!"

"Sorry," he mumbled with his compressed mouth.

Releasing him, she peered around, making sure no one had overheard. "You have to do this part."

"It's better if you're with me. You'll know what to look for. You'll be able to remember—"

"I can't go in."

"Why not?"

She shrugged. "Too crowded. Someone might realize I'm a girl."

"You're being paranoid. No one's even looking at you."

Moira erupted. "Don't you get it, Zak? This is my life now! This is my life *here*. I have to think like this. All the time. I can't just walk down the street or go into a store, like you can. I have to *think* about it. I have to decide which risks to take. Especially if we're going to be stuck here forever. Everything I do has to be calculated."

Zak stared at her for a moment. "I'm sorry," he said slowly, turning away. "I'm being a jerk."

"You're not," she said, mollified. "It's tough to get used to."

He shook his head. He couldn't even look at her. "This is all my fault. I was chasing Tommy, and I brought us here."

"Don't do that." Her voice softened.

"Do what? Tell the truth?" He rubbed at his eyes to keep tears away. "If it weren't for me, you wouldn't be here at all. And you wouldn't have to be afraid all the time. And you—"

"'No use cryin' over spilt whiskey,' my dad says." She chuckled. "'Just figure out how to get it back in the glass!'"

He laughed, and she laughed, too. Until she'd said it, she hadn't realized how much she missed her parents. She could hear her dad saying exactly that, even though he rarely drank anything stronger than a Coke. Her parents seemed to like talking about drinking more than actually drinking.

"We're here," she told him, touching his face gently to turn his gaze back to hers. "And we're going to figure out how to make the best of it. That guy Salazar said something about someone filling my head with 'femalist propaganda.' So there's gotta be *someone* out there in this world fighting for the truth. And if not, maybe I'll get to be the Susan B. Anthony of this universe."

Zak sniffled and laughed. "I don't even know who that is."

"Of course not."

"So you won't go in there with me? Really?"

"Out on the street is one thing. But look at me." She spread her arms wide. "I'm in a dirty coverall, and my face is dirty, and my hat came out of the garbage. Inside, people will look. Besides, it's close quarters in there. If someone realizes I'm an uncompanioned female, I want to be out in the open. Where I can run."

Zak struggled with his words before blurting out, "I don't want to lose you again. I can't stand the thought of it. What if someone comes after you while I'm fooling around in there? You were in an alley before, and the Dutchmen still got you," he reminded her.

"And I got out of that okay."

"Moira." She had told him—after much prodding and annoyance—of her escape, of the bloody beatdown of one of the Dutchmen. "Be real. That wasn't getting out of something 'okay.' That was risking your life and escaping by the skin of your teeth. You got lucky. Really lucky. We both know you're tough, but come on—you won't get lucky like that a second time."

She stubbornly refused to respond to that, saying only, "I can't go in there."

Zak mused for a moment. "How about this: If someone notices you, we'll just say that you got lost and that your dad or your grandfather is somewhere else in the store. They'll spend some time looking for him, and we can slip out."

Moira considered this. "That's not the worst idea I've ever heard." She sighed heavily and studied the Apple Store across the street. It seemed so much like home that she ached inside. And

Zak was right—there was no sign on it declaiming that women could not enter. Maybe it was, if not actually safe, at least safer.

"Let's go," she said.

The Wonder Glass display was crowded, and Zak was antsy, wanting nothing more than to push people aside and get his turn. But drawing attention to himself and, by extension, Moira was a bad idea, so he waited patiently until he had the Wonder Glass to himself.

The person before him had been surfing news sites, and headlines scrolled by on the surface of the Wonder Glass: *Wild Science Conference Hacked—by Alchemy! . . . President Gore Signs Global Cooling Pact . . . Apple CEO Steve Jobs Celebrates 60th Birthday in Territorial Hawai'i . . . Coalition Forces Triumph in Sudan . . . Lunar Olympians Prepare for Winter Games . . .*

Superficially, it was similar to an iPad back home. He had no trouble figuring out the interface or the gestures. The Internet here was something called the TIM, but it worked basically the same way. He started browsing for information on the electro-leum recycling facility south of the city, when he heard Moira, positioned close by, gasp.

Zak spun around and grabbed her hand, ready to pull her away from anyone who would try to snatch her. But then he recognized the source of her surprise.

Khalid.

FORTY-NINE

Zak had truly begun to wonder if he would ever see Khalid again. Near tears, he couldn't help flinging himself at his buddy, enfolding Khalid in his arms.

"Zak?" Khalid murmured in his ear. "Is it really you?"

"Yeah, man."

All around them, the crowd in the Apple Store grinned and *awwed* at the reunion . . . for a moment. It was still New York, alternate universe or not, so soon someone said, "Very touching. You done with this?" and gestured to the Wonder Glass display.

Moira cleared her throat; Zak could tell she was uncomfortable being so close to the center of attention. Together, the three of them headed outside.

"How did you get here?" all three of them asked at once.

And then—for the first time since escaping Zak's hospital room back home—all three laughed as though safety and sanity awaited them out on the street and not a universe away.

It wasn't far to Dr. Bookman's office—a block away, around a corner—and they caught each other up on what had happened as they walked there. Entering Bookman's office, Khalid said, ". . . so I went to get help, figuring I'd look up a hospital or something at the store, and then I saw you guys."

Bookman still lay on the sofa, exactly as Khalid had left him. Moira knelt down by him and touched his neck, then his wrist.

"I tried that," Khalid said lamely.

"I think he's okay," she said. "Seems like he's sleeping."

As if in response, Dr. Bookman suddenly snorted a complicated, phlegmy breath, then rolled over on his side, facing away from them. Moira stretched and actually yawned, then sat on the edge of the sofa. "I can't believe I can finally *relax*. Even just a little bit."

"What's this?" Zak pointed to an aquarium with cockroaches skittering about.

"Dude, don't even ask. It's weirder than you can imagine. You don't want to know. *I* don't want to know. You know that electroleum stuff? He was messing with it. Next thing you know, some of them were dead, then alive—or alive and then dead—and some of them disappeared. It was a cockroach Rapture, man."

"So, now what?" Zak asked. As he made his way across the room to the desk, he kicked something accidentally. Crouching down, he realized it was Officer's Cheong's stun gadget. He tucked it into his pocket and covered it with his shirt. While he was down there, he noticed water underfoot. "What happened here?"

"It was during the whole . . . voodoo possession thing. And believe me, I never thought those words would come out of my mouth. The whole place was just soaked with salt water."

"Weird . . ." Zak armed a sheet of water off the desk, clearing a space. "We need to get online. Does he have a computer or one of those Wonder thingies?"

Khalid held up a rectangle like the one Dr. White-eagle had used. "Yeah, but I can't get it to work."

Without a word, Moira snatched it from him. She studied it for a moment and then, with a shrug, lifted Dr. Bookman's hand by the wrist and pressed his fingertip against the screen. The Wonder Glass made a tiny, clicking unlock sound, and the screen lit up.

"Now I feel like an idiot," Khalid said.

"*Now?*" Moira asked, grinning.

While Khalid and Moira bantered with each other, Zak spread out on the desk the plans Moira had given him. *SOUTHERN CONFLUX ELECTROLEUM RECLAMATION FACILITY*, read a box in one corner. The schematic itself had a number of additions, typed in. When he tapped on a certain box, a keyboard came up for him to type into. The whole thing was like a big, flexible tablet, almost as thin as paper.

"Very funny, Science Girl," Khalid said. "Maybe you're equipped for travel to alternate universes. Some of us aren't."

"You should have read those Philip Pullman books I gave you."

"There were too many zombies needing killing over on Xbox Live."

"I managed to read the books *and* still kick your butt on Live."

"Oh yeah? Well . . . well, imagine how much worse my butt would have been kicked if I'd wasted time with your stupid books."

Something occurred to Zak. He peeled the schematic off

the slightly damp desk and turned it over. Sometimes when he was doing homework, he would jot notes on the back. . . .

Sure enough, there were some sketches and notes on the back, positioned in the center of the sheet so that they weren't visible when it was folded up. Zak scanned them, licking his lips the further along he went. He tapped and scrolled them, finding more information and more sketches. Even a few shaky videos. The "paper" didn't seem to be connected to the Internet (or the TIM, rather), but it clearly had some kind of memory buffer, in which the Dutchmen had stored all kinds of information about their planned heist.

As Moira and Khalid squabbled, he stared intently at the plans. Then he slowly turned to regard the aquarium with its skittering, jittery cockroaches.

"It was a cockroach Rapture, man."

"Guys," he said, "I think we have everything we need."

Moira perked up, but Khalid stared at him with bug-eyed astonishment. "We can't just run off and do this. Godfrey and Tommy *ripped* right through Dr. Bookman. Look at the poor guy."

The poor guy shifted and mumbled in his sleep again.

"I'm sorry that happened to him, but I can't worry about him right now. Tommy needs me. Bookman's going to be okay. Moira said so."

Khalid erupted, flinging his hands in the air. "*Moira* said so? Moira said so? Are you crazy? No offense, Moira, but since when is *she* a doctor?"

"She got me out of the hospital."

"No kidding! How'd that work out for you, Heart Attack Boy?"

Zak touched his chest with the tips of his fingers. Everything was still fine under there. "So far, so good. Never felt better."

"Because you got lucky and stumbled onto a doctor with magic powers!"

"No, Khalid—because Tommy *led me* to a doctor with magic powers. He saved my life while you were off gallivanting around the city, accomplishing precisely nothing. So I'm going to go return the favor."

The wounded expression on Khalid's face almost made Zak apologize immediately. It wasn't Khalid's fault that he couldn't navigate the byways of the alternate universe. But this wasn't about who was right or who was wrong or who hurt whose feelings. It was about life and death. Rescuing Tommy from beyond the veil of mortality, where he'd lingered and languished for far, far too long. While it could still be done.

"Not cool, man," Khalid said quietly.

"Zak . . ." Moira said, gesturing to Khalid in that infuriating grown-up way she had. He knew what she wanted.

He wouldn't give it. Not an apology. Not now. "I'm not sorry."

"Are you joking?" Khalid asked. "You're the whole reason we're stuck in this place! With ghosts and voodoo and—"

"Now you *both* owe each other apologies," Moira said firmly.

Khalid huffed out an outraged breath. "He brought us here!" he complained. "We followed him, and now we're in a world where you can't cross the street without a chaperone. And, hey, might I add that *you're* the one who thought it was a cool idea to bring him down into the subway in the first place?"

Moira harrumphed and crossed her arms over her chest. "Whatever, Khalid. No one put a gun to your head."

"I'm not saying you did. But I'm saying you guys have had your shot. Give me a chance."

The room fell silent. Zak shook his head slowly. Everything Khalid had said, he realized, was true. None of it mattered.

Or rather, it mattered in one way but not in another. Khalid was right: This was *his* fault. Zak had led his best friends here. It was up to him to make it right. To fix things. Like spilling Kool-Aid on Mom's skirt, like all the lies his parents had told him about Tommy, saying sorry wasn't enough.

He had to *do* something.

"There are only two options," Zak said. "Either we go to rescue Tommy or we sit around and talk about it."

"Or we get Bookman some help, and he helps us figure out what's really going on," Khalid insisted. "You weren't here, man. Tommy and Godfrey didn't seem like good guys. They picked him up and set his hair on fire."

"How do you know it was even them?" Zak asked. "How much experience with this 'wild science' stuff do you have? Maybe Bookman screwed up. Maybe he did something wrong. How the hell would any of us know?"

Khalid opened his mouth to respond, but Zak bulldozed over him. "The answer is, we don't. So, what *do* we know? Well, we know that my twin brother is out there somewhere and that we can save him with the electroleum. And we know that we have plans to the plant and a way in. So I say we go ahead and do it, and then we worry about everything else later."

"Look, Zak, normally I'd be all about charging ahead without a plan, but we're in a different *universe*. You're talking about superhero heist-level stuff. Since when did you put on a cape and learn to fly?"

"It's not going to be a problem," Zak said confidently.

"I bet most thieves think that, too. They convince themselves that they'll never get caught."

"This isn't robbing a bodega, Khalid. I'm trying to save someone's—"

"And," Khalid interrupted, "you don't even understand what you're dealing with, with this electroleum stuff. There are ghost things and iPads made out of paper and voodoo and possession and stuff we can't understand. Is it crazy to say let's hit the brakes for a minute?"

"Yes!" Zak fumed. "You said it yourself—when they talked through Bookman, they said we didn't have a lot of time. I don't know what it's like as a ghost, but maybe there's a clock ticking somewhere, and if we don't rescue them soon, they'll be dead for good. So I'm not going to sit around and debate it." Why didn't Khalid understand? No, wait—the question was wrong. It wasn't that Khalid *didn't* understand; it was that he *couldn't* understand. He had no idea what it was like to be a solitary twin, to be missing half of himself. His imagination could stretch so far and no farther.

Don't trust him. That's what Tommy had been saying from the outset. Zak had assumed *him* was his father or a doctor.

He'd never in a million years fantasized that the *him* he was not to trust would, or even could, be Khalid.

"I say we don't go," Khalid said. "I say we help Bookman and get him to do some more research for us. This is what he does. He's the expert."

"I didn't call for a vote, Khalid. I know what I'm doing."

"Oh yeah? You're gonna go hijack a big old factory all on

your own? What are you gonna do, light a match and set the stuff on fire?"

"If I have to."

"Good luck with that."

"He's not going to be alone," Moira said, speaking for the first time in a long time.

They both turned to look at her, still perched on the edge of the sofa near Dr. Bookman, turning over his Wonder Glass in her hands, staring down at it.

"Don't tell me you're doing this," Khalid told her. "I'm supposed to be the crazy, immature one."

"What else am I supposed to do?" she demanded, finally looking up at them from under the brim of her *Breukelen Dodgers* cap. "This place might seem like a fun little party zone for you guys, with cool new toys and all that, but to me it's like being the only mouse at the cat convention. This place is going to kill me, Khalid. And if I'm gonna go, then I'm damn well going to do something worthwhile first."

Khalid shook his head. "Moira, man, come on. This is crazy. You know it is. The two of you? Breaking and entering? Stealing weird magic goo? Getting out without killing yourselves or someone else? It's never gonna work. You're *kids*."

"Joan of Arc was a teenager when she took on the English," Moira said.

"And they killed her!" Khalid howled. "Even *I* know that part!"

Moira stood up and straightened her coverall, then her cap. "Sorry, Khalid. I'm with Zak on this one. We have to do *something*."

"Dr. Bookman might be able to help—"

She shook her head. "Sorry. I don't trust him."

"You don't even know him! Why not?"

"Because he's from *here*. And because he's a man."

The three of them went silent, each of them looking from one to the other. No one spoke. And then Zak nodded to Moira, and the two of them headed toward the door.

"Zak. Moira." They looked back. Khalid gazed at them somberly. "Guys, you have to—"

"We're doing this."

"Zak, man, come on. I'm sorry about what I said before. Three Basket—"

"Don't. Even," Zak interrupted him.

Before anyone could speak again, he and Moira walked out the door.

FIFTY

According to the information on the back of the plans, a super-way led straight to the electroleum facility. A minute or two with Google on Dr. Bookman's Wonder Glass, which Moira had kept, told them that the superway was an elevated subway. *Very* elevated. The tracks ran in sealed tubes between thirty and eighty stories up, connecting the upper levels of skyscrapers. One of the routes—the 10 line, according to the map—ran from Eighth Avenue and Seventeenth Street down past the Houston Conflux and out over the water, where it then tipped and ran down an artificial slope before continuing on to a stop dubbed "Battery Landing" on Battery Island before proceeding to Ellis Island and Liberty Island.

"Better than a ferry, I guess," Moira said.

"They have those, too, according to Google."

Huddled in the lobby of Bookman's building, they cobbled together their strategy, checking their facts against the info jotted down on the back of the plans and comparing them to information available online.

Getting to the facility wasn't a problem—the superway stopped there routinely on its way to Ellis Island.

Getting into the secure facility . . . That was the tough part. But there was a way. Definitely.

Moira must have been thinking the same thing. "Look, Zak, I'm on board, but if we get caught, it's going to be rough on both of us." Worse for her, she didn't need to say. "Even if we figure out how to get in, getting out will be even harder."

"I've got that one figured out," Zak said.

Moira looked stunned at the idea that Zak had outthought her. "Really? How?"

He shook his head. "Later. I'll explain it later."

At Eighth and Seventeenth, there was a massive skyscraper that Zak was certain did not exist in his own world. A sign outside featured an arrow pointing up and the words A.R.T. 8TH AND 17TH.

Moira was more and more jittery with every step they took. Night was falling, but it was early evening and it was New York, so there were still a lot of people milling about. Every single one of them, Zak knew, was a threat to her.

"It's New York City," he muttered to her. "No one's paying attention to us."

"It's Manhattan City," she corrected him, "and I hope not."

All around them was the evidence of this world's cluelessness, from the storefront signs to the overdressed, overly made-up women meekly following their companions along the sidewalks. Zak didn't know how Moira would manage to live in this world, how she would come to any sort of accommodation with a society that saw her as only barely human. Maybe, as he'd speculated before, it would turn out that the woman-hatred existed only here in this city. Or this state. Maybe elsewhere it wouldn't be so bad.

One problem at a time, he thought. *First Tommy, then Moira.*

But that was just a stall, he knew. A pointless, moot stall.

Because if Zak's plan worked, he wouldn't be around after rescuing Tommy.

He would be dead.

Moira wanted to grab Zak's hand as they entered the skyscraper at Eighth and Seventeenth. Up high, they'd spied the sleek matte-gray tube of the superway. Or, as the sign said, the A.R.T.: Aero Rail Transit.

She wanted to grab his hand, and she hated herself for that. She'd never been one to need comfort, or even much in the way of help. To her mother's endless astonishment, she'd taught herself to read at a young age, from then on forgoing nightly parental story time for her own reading. But being out in public, so exposed through her poor disguise, made her feel vulnerable and nearly naked, and holding a friend's hand would make at least some of that go away.

But the two of them holding hands would just draw even more attention to her. So she balled her hands into fists in her pockets instead, biting into her palms with her nails.

Inside, the building's lobby was ornate, with gilded statuary throughout and a grand piano in one corner, where a woman played languid and sad and beautiful music under the watchful eye of one of the three security guards poised near the entrances. It made Moira think of songbirds and cages and the Dutchmen.

A bank of elevators stood at one end of the lobby, with a sign that read GUEST USE ONLY. A hotel. They were in a hotel.

"Over there," Zak said, pointing.

Off to one side, a narrow corridor wended deeper into the building. A sign there read A.R.T. ACCESS.

At the end of the corridor was an elevator. There was an app on Dr. Bookman's Wonder Glass that, when held to a scanner, paid for them and let them in. They wanted to wait for an empty elevator, but they had no luck, so they rode in silence. Moira squeezed herself into a corner and tried to turn invisible, imagining a voice suddenly exclaiming, "Hey, *frau!*" Followed by another. And another. And another. And then hands on her and then—

When the doors opened, they spilled out into another short corridor, this one leading them past floor-to-ceiling windows that showed Eighth Avenue in all its glory. Moira recognized the outline of the Flatiron Building in the distance, as well as the Chrysler Building. It was nice to know that some things didn't change. Or were eternal. Or maybe fated. Whatever.

She wondered again how this world could so closely resemble her own without the free input of women . . . but realized that there was really no way to know. And at this moment, she didn't care. Survival was so much more important than history right now.

They entered the superway station, which reminded her of photos and videos she'd seen of Japanese subway stops. The walls were curved and polished, lit by electroleum; the tracks were clean. After a few moments a train glided into the station, nearly silent. It was low and sleek, not boxy like the subway trains back home. It looked almost like a bullet-headed earthworm plated with ceramic, its undercarriage lit with electroleum.

Zak and Moira hung back, watching people exit and enter the train. This wasn't the one they wanted. They had to watch for—

"There," Zak mumbled, and jerked his head.

Moira followed his direction and saw. Yes. That was what they needed. The next train, then.

The station nearly emptied out. Moira was keenly aware of security cameras mounted on the ceiling, and she did her best to stand like a boy . . . whatever that meant. She observed Zak's posture and tried to imitate it.

"Relax," he said.

"Easy for you to say, chap."

He grinned. "Whatever happened to *laddie?*"

"Maybe while we wait, you can tell me how you plan to get in and out of the electroleum plant without getting us killed or captured?"

"I'm still working it out." He saw the dismay flit across her face. "Don't worry—I'm almost there." He flashed her a grin.

She bit back a retort. She would just have to trust him, as he'd trusted her so many times before.

A second train arrived. Zak and Moira boarded the very front car. They'd noticed with the first train that the operator was up front, not toward the back, as on some subways back home.

The superway train tilted and shifted, then slowly began to pull out of the station. According to what they'd read online, the superway trains moved very slowly when entering or exiting a station, so that track noise wouldn't disturb the people on the upper floors of the surrounding buildings. Once away from the building, a series of sound bafflers and vibration dampeners allowed the trains to accelerate to thirty or forty miles an hour. Not as fast as a subway, but plenty quick.

There were only a few people in the car, and plenty of seats, but Zak and Moira chose to stand at the front of the car.

Just like back home, there was a door here.

A door that led into the operator's cabin.

PART THREE

ZAK

KHALID

MOIRA

TOMMY

FIFTY-ONE

Hey, Tommy, you there? Zak asked.

He waited.

Nothing.

Well, I think you can hear me. Even if I can't hear you. I think that's how it works. I think you've always been around, ever since you died, and sometimes I could see you and sometimes I couldn't. I can't imagine what that must have been like for you, being there all the time, trying to communicate with me.

And I just thought I'd made you up. I thought you were my imaginary friend. So I just dismissed you and forgot you when I was done with you. And I am so, so sorry about that.

But then everything changed. After so long, after trying for so long, you and Godfrey were able to break through to me. Break through the invisible walls between us.

Mom and Dad should have told me. Maybe then I would have figured it out sooner. Maybe then we wouldn't be in this mess.

But they didn't, so I couldn't. And now here we are. But I'm going to fix it. I am.

Listen:

You probably already know what I'm planning. And maybe you're thinking I shouldn't do it. But here's the thing: I have to. Because I was the one siphoning all that blood from you when we were in the womb. I killed you. Indirectly and unintentionally, yeah, but I killed you. And I don't care, can't bring myself to care, that it was indirect and unintentional. I did it anyway.

And then I brought Moira and Khalid here. Khalid apologized for what he said, but he was right. This is all my fault. My fault that he's stuck here. But even worse: Moira's stuck here. Khalid could eventually get along, but Moira will always be miserable here.

So, here's how it'll go, Tommy. I'm going to give you your life. Just like in the experiment in the aquarium. I'm going to use the electroleum, the pure stuff, and we're going to switch places like the roaches did. When we first got here, you told us we needed the electroleum to bring you back. And now I see how it works. It takes life from one of us and gives it to the other. Works for me. One twin comes in; one twin goes out. An even swap.

That's the plan. I can't tell Moira. Not yet. But that's the plan.

I'm going to hope you'll be there for Moira and Khalid. They're going to need a friend in this world, and maybe having someone who looks and sounds like me will help.

Because when I look up, I know there are worlds waiting. When I look down, I know that this earth, this soil, is not a conclusion. And when I look around, I know there are people beyond people.

There's something else. Something extra.

I'm so close, Tommy. . . .

And maybe . . . maybe on my way out and your way in, we'll get a second to say hi.

That would be great.

FIFTY-TWO

Khalid paced Dr. Bookman's office in a futile fury. He had to do *something*, but there was nothing he could think of, nothing within his grasp. He stuttered between the door and the sofa, wanting to chase after his friends, wanting to stay to take care of Dr. Bookman. Life wasn't fair.

Life, right now, sucked. Big-time.

There has to be something I can do. Anything. Zak and Moira are just gonna end up getting caught, and that'll be bad enough for Zak, but Moira's going to wind up as someone's housemaid or something. And when they start asking tough questions, what's Zak going to say? "Sorry, we're from an alternate universe; we didn't know the rules?"

He clenched his fists and planted his feet and screamed to the ceiling, *through* the ceiling, aiming his frustration at the sky and beyond, out to the moon and the stars and the rest of the galaxy.

"Not . . . so . . . loud . . . ," a voice pleaded.

Khalid spun around. Dr. Bookman had pushed himself to his elbows and was struggling to sit up. Khalid ran over to help him. "You're up! Are you okay? We got problems, and you're not gonna believe what I have to tell you. First, it was—"

"Slowly," Dr. Bookman begged. "And some water?"

Khalid scrambled off to the smallish bathroom. He filled a waxed-paper cup with water and dashed back to the main room. Dr. Bookman had moved to the edge of the sofa, where he could lean and peer at the aquarium.

"Yeah, that's weird," Khalid said. "Totally. But—"

"Water, please?"

He handed it over and watched with mounting impatience as Dr. Bookman painstakingly sipped at it. Khalid bounced from foot to foot as the water level in the cup dropped excruciatingly slowly.

Finally, Dr. Bookman finished, sighed, and leaned back on the sofa. "Well, I believe you and I may have quite inadvertently put research into electroleum and psychic phenomena on a whole new path."

"I'm sure your cockroach thing is really important, but honestly, Dr. Bookman, we—"

"You've seen the roaches, yes?" Bookman asked, interrupting. "The dead ones have returned to life."

"Some of them. And are you sure they were really dead? Because . . ." He caught himself. "No, look, we don't have time for this. Things are happening. Fast."

"But . . . but this shouldn't have happened!" Bookman spluttered. "There's nothing in the literature to explain it. It could be a temporary phenomenon, or it could even simply be that the electroleum altered the color of the dye I used. Don't you see?"

"Hey!" Khalid wanted the slap the guy back to the present

but settled for shaking him by the shoulders. "The roaches don't matter, man! Zak and Moira, remember?"

Bookman nodded slowly. "Of course. Yes," he said, speaking with the measured tones of one who has just woken suddenly.

"Let me bring you up to speed first," Khalid said, and proceeded to fill him in on what had happened with Zak and Moira and their plan to use—somehow—the raw electroleum at the recycling facility.

Dr. Bookman groaned and held his head in his hands. "No, no, no! That's not . . . That's very nearly the worst thing they can possibly do!"

"You said before, back in the alley, that if you had enough energy, it could be possible to bring Tommy back to life. I remember *that* part. And, hey, look, it worked for the roaches, right?"

"This will be a disaster!" He stood shakily and closed in on the aquarium, staring into it. "You simply cannot extrapolate from what is now a woefully uncontrolled experiment. Electroleum is, by its very nature, an unstable substance. M-hydrogen, infused with quantum foam from the Secret Sea itself. We only use it in small amounts for experiments, or in larger amounts when it has been carefully altered to control its shifts. This"—he gestured to the aquarium—"proves only how unpredictable it truly is. In the hands of *laymen*, in the hands of amateurs . . . They could detonate . . . Good Lord, they could detonate it all. The explosion . . ." He drifted off, lost in the horror of it.

"Well," Khalid said after a moment of uncomfortable silence, "I'm sure they'll be careful. I mean, they don't want to kill a bunch of people—"

"A 'bunch of people'?" Dr. Bookman studied the aquarium for another moment, then shivered. "A 'bunch of people.' Dear Tesla. Tell me, Khalid—how many people live in your version of Manhattan?"

"In *my* Manhattan?" Khalid shrugged. "A few million. Like, seven or eight. Why? What does that have to do with—"

"Because if your friends do as they plan, then they will be directly responsible for that many deaths."

"Say what?"

"If they blow up that electroleum, they could possibly kill everyone in your version of Manhattan!"

FIFTY-THREE

Zak tested the lever; the door to the operator's cabin was unlocked, which amused Zak. He wondered if the subway doors back home were similarly unlocked—he'd never tried one. He suspected not. Terrorist fears would keep such doors heavily secured. Maybe this world hadn't suffered terrorist attacks. Maybe there was no such thing as terrorism here.

No terrorists. Less crime. Cool tech. Magic, or something close enough. Not a bad place.

He caught Moira's eye. She was turned away from the rest of the superway car, huddled against the bulkhead.

Okay, so maybe not a bad place, but not a great place, either.

They were high up in the air, so Bookman's Wonder Glass worked. A GPS app showed them as a pulsating blue dot moving along a gray line over the city. Zak counted the stops ahead of them. Only two more and then they were out over the open water.

Fortunately, the train's occupancy did not increase much. Some newcomers boarded at each stop, but others left at the same time, keeping the riders in equilibrium. The fewer people on board, the better.

"Now?" Moira muttered.

Zak consulted the GPS again. They were closing in on Battery Landing. He waited a heartbeat; the train began to decelerate.

"Yeah." He tossed glances over each shoulder—no one was paying attention to them. He hoped that would remain the case.

He opened the door to the operator's cabin and let Moira slip in. Now they were committed.

As Moira entered the tiny control cabin, the superway operator startled and swiveled in his chair away from his control panel. He grinned lazily as Zak came in behind her.

"Hey, kids, look, you can't just barge in—"

She heard Zak close the door behind her and reached into her pocket for the stun stick they'd stolen from Officer Cheong. Zak had handed it off to her on their walk to the superway, reasoning that it was better concealed under her baggy coverall. It was waterlogged from their dip in the Broadway Canal, but the operator didn't know that. His eyes widened at the sight of the stick, and he gulped.

"Hands where I can see them," she said. "Don't touch the control board."

"If I don't—"

"Don't touch it," Zak threatened, deepening his voice. "We've modified this stick to be lethal."

Was that even possible? It didn't matter—the operator believed it. He held his hands in the air. "We'll hit the air cushion at the Battery Landing station if I don't signal for anticollision."

He might as well have offered his mother's recipe for stewed wombat, for all the sense that made. "Let us worry about that. Keep your hands up," Moira said. "We'll tell you what to do."

Zak took the stick from her and kept an eye on the operator as Moira approached the control panel. It was a flat touch screen with a series of blinking lights and touch controls. She thought it made sense—readouts for acceleration, a GPS window, pretty much what you'd expect. This whole universe seemed to be designed by someone with exceptionally good taste.

She whipped off her hat to fan herself. The operator gasped. "You're a *frau!*"

"Damn right," she muttered, slapping the cap back on. The board had lit up with a flashing icon that showed a cloud morphing into a crushed puff of air. *Air cushion? Is that what he was talking about?*

She scanned the rest of the board. Off in one corner was a red touch target with a lightning bolt in the shape of an exclamation point within. *That's the alarm.*

"Signal for anticollision," she told him, as if she knew what she meant. "But keep away from that alarm. Unless you want my chap here to fry you with a million snapping volts of electricity."

The operator's fingers fluttered over the board, and soon the cloud icon melted away into the background.

"We're on approach to Battery Landing now," he told her. He seemed frightened enough to be telling the truth. Plus, if he did anything stupid to the train, he would be one of the first to die. He was well incentivized to play this honestly.

Zak jabbed at the back of the operator's neck with the prongs of the unpowered stick, eliciting an anxious hiss of indrawn breath.

"Now we're going to ask you some questions," Zak said, "and you're going to answer them. Aren't you?"

The operator hesitated, and Moira leaned in close to him. "There's a saying I'll bet you've never heard before," she said in a tone as menacing as she could muster. "It's this: 'Hell hath no fury like a woman scorned.' Want to find out for sure?"

The operator hiccuped in fear. "What do you want to know?"

———————

Moments later, as the superway decelerated inbound to Battery Landing, Moira finished tying up the operator while Zak watched over him to make sure he didn't try to escape. They had no rope or cord, so they used Zak's belt and shoelaces to bind the man's wrists and ankles.

Through the windshield, Battery Landing was coming up fast. "Is he secure?" Zak asked.

Moira checked the bonds once more. She wouldn't bet her life on it, but . . . Well, she actually didn't have a choice. "He's good." She stuffed a wad of fabric into his mouth.

Zak settled into the operator's chair. "Microphone?"

"Third tab."

Zak's fingers splayed out on the control board, and he grunted in annoyance. Moira sidled up to him and skimmed the board. "Let me," she said, and found the right icon. A burst of static like a throat-clearing sounded through the superway's PA system.

"Ladies and gentlemen," she said sweetly into a small microphone bud positioned at head height, "this is your new operator. Hi! Bee-tee-dub, this superway has been hijacked in the name of the Feminist Liberation Army."

"Girl power!" Zak shouted into the microphone. Moira arched an eyebrow at him. "I dunno," he mumbled off-mic. "It felt right."

"Now, don't go panicking," Moira said into the mic, "because we have no desire to hurt you. In fact, as soon as we pull into Battery Landing, we expect you all to get off the train and run for your lives. And . . ."

She nodded to Zak, who leaned over and hit the alarm icon. A blaring siren sounded throughout the cabin, as well as the cars.

"That sound you hear means the authorities have been alerted, so they should be on hand to evacuate you as soon as you get off the train." She and Zak exchanged a look. *Is that all?* she asked with her expression.

He shrugged back. *Yeah, that's good.*

"That's all," she said. "Have a nice evacuation, and thank you for riding Aero Rail Transit. Oh, and stop treating women like pets." She clicked off the microphone and slumped back against the bulkhead. If they hadn't been committed before, they were now.

"I'm glad that's over," she said.

"Not yet," said Zak, and when she looked, she saw that he'd stood up and aimed the stun stick at her.

FIFTY-FOUR

Khalid helped Dr. Bookman down the stairs to street level. The man was still shaky—literally, his body trembled with every step. Whatever his voodoo spell had done to him, the effects lingered. Maybe they would be permanent. But Khalid had recovered an older Wonder Glass from one of Dr. Bookman's bookshelves and used it to page a car service. They had to get to Battery Landing.

"He's been going back and forth. For centuries. Constantly exposed to the Secret Sea. To the same quantum foam we use in electroleum. He's attuned to it."

"What are you talking about?" Khalid demanded. "Slow down; make sense."

"He exists outside of physics," Bookman rambled. "The Secret Sea is what remains of the creation of the universe. He's soaked in it. His power is subtle but large. The Secret Sea connects universes and also subsumes them. Each world is a wave. You find our physics strange here, Khalid? The physics of the Secret Sea is the physics of the big bang, of the moment of creation. No one can know what effect that would have on a spirit."

They reached street level. Khalid helped Dr. Bookman prop himself up against the wall and then checked for the car. It hadn't arrived yet. Khalid took a deep breath and made a decision.

"Look," he said, grabbing Bookman by his lapels, "you have to start making sense *now*. Or we're not going anywhere."

Dr. Bookman took a deep breath and steadied himself, both hands against the wall. He still shook and shivered, but he finally managed to meet Khalid's eyes with his own.

"It's the spirit," he said. "The Godfrey spirit."

"What about it? *Him*, I mean."

"That much electroleum . . . that kind of energy . . ."

"Stay focused, man. Talk to me." Out of the corner of his eye, Khalid noticed a car slowing as it came around the corner.

"I was connected to Godfrey, Khalid. He saw inside me and I saw inside him, though I dearly regret it. What he plans to do . . . is monstrous. And your friends are making it possible!"

Khalid clenched his jaw. "Exactly what is he planning? Give me a hint here."

"Electroleum in its raw state is . . . unpredictable. M-electrons and—" He broke off, no doubt distracted by the glazing-over of Khalid's eyes. "Sorry. In any event, it's unpredictable. A product of wild science. Depending on how it has been conditioned, its energies interact in different ways with the world. It can be made safe, as we use it for our lighting. But it can also be dangerous."

"And you guys just leave this stuff lying around."

"Of course not! That's why it's carefully controlled. Regulated.

317

We can control it to a degree, and to that degree, it's useful and safe."

"Until it isn't."

"With enough of it, you could bring down the walls between universes. It could theoretically even break the barrier that separates the living from the dead, as we saw with my cockroaches."

"'Break the barrier.' You make it sound like death is just another alternate universe." Khalid blinked as Dr. Bookman said nothing, but the man's expression spoke volumes. "Wait. Are you saying death *is* just another alternate universe?"

The wild scientist shrugged. "Who's to say? We have after-death phenomena in my world, things that you would most likely call ghosts. And now we have the evidence of Godfrey, evidence that some sort of consciousness can linger after death. We would need vastly more research, but this I know, Khalid: Electroleum in its raw, pure form is dangerous and unpredictable. During processing, specific impurities are introduced to make it function in safe, understandable ways. For purposes of my experiment, I was permitted one milliliter of the raw substance."

"And that was enough to do what it did to the cockroaches?"

"The electroleum in the room magnified the emotion and power Godfrey exuded. I had been testing other properties of electroleum entirely, but apparently the combination of electroleum and all of the energy in the room rejuvenated some of them."

"Wow. That's good, right?"

"How do we know?" Dr. Bookman asked with unfocused aggravation. "How? Without actual testing, how do we know what is good, what is bad? Yes, some roaches seem to have come back to life. Others died. And others simply vanished. To the living and the revived, it is very good. But what about the others?"

"I guess I didn't think of that. To them, it's not so hot."

"No, indeed. Not if you're on the killing end. Or the dying end. And I surmise that in the proper quantities and context, the misuse of electroleum could even kill a ghost."

"Aren't they already dead?"

"Erase every trace of it from the world, the universe." Dr. Bookman flapped his hands. "Semantics."

"So, then, the problem is . . ."

Dr. Bookman flinched in frustration. "The problem is, no one knows, Khalid! No one knows! This is why wild science is so regulated, so controlled. So that people won't try these sorts of things! There are some things we try *not* to learn."

"I don't get it. If it works, then everyone's alive and everything's great."

"No. No. Our worlds are close together, remember?"

"Right." Khalid thought back to the apartment building, to the walls between units. His universe was a next-door neighbor to this one.

"Godfrey slipped through the thin spot in the wall between them three hundred years ago. And died there. He was stuck underground until the event you call 9/11 released him from his tomb. His power helped him survive, but 'survival' is not life. He did not age. He did not progress or change or learn. He only abided."

"And?"

Bookman shook his head. "I saw it all, Khalid. You saw what

he put me through. During the ritual. I was trying to contact your friend Zak. The intersection of Godfrey's rage and the electroleum in my office . . ."

Khalid thought back and shivered at the memory of Bookman levitating, the blood from his mouth, the burning dreadlocks. "The guy was trapped underground for hundreds of years. That'll mess with a guy's manners. He's sort of desperate."

"He's beyond desperate. I have performed that ritual many, many times and never before encountered such . . ." He paused. "I'm uncomfortable with a word that has such nonscientific implications, but: I have never before encountered such evil."

"Evil? Doc, he's going to help us rescue Tommy!"

"No. When he possessed me, I saw it all. It all made sense. I'm trying to explain. . . . Once he was free, Godfrey was able to *move* again. Ever since, he's been going back and forth. He's incorporeal, so he found a way to cross from your universe to mine and back again."

"That makes sense."

"But with each pass-through, he weakened the walls even further. Made them thinner."

Khalid thought about it for a moment. "That's how *we* were able to come through. Before, only a ghost could go through, but now . . ."

"Now actual physical matter can cross over. Godfrey cannot directly manipulate the electroleum. Indirectly, however . . . with a physical intermediary . . . With Zak's help, he plans to *detonate* the electroleum."

Khalid's mouth opened and closed like a dumb fish's. It took long moments before he could speak, and even then he could only whisper, "Detonate? Like blow it up?"

"Yes. The result . . . Well, Godfrey *believes* the result will be an explosion that resonates not merely on the physical plane but on the spiritual one as well. That may very well resurrect Godfrey, given his special connection to the electroleum."

"Well, that's—"

"But at the same time, it will blow open a hole in the wall between our worlds."

Khalid's throat clogged and refused to work. He gagged and stepped away from Dr. Bookman's quaking form. "What does that mean?"

But he knew. What if one apartment was on fire when you knocked down the wall? Or what if the fire was inside the wall to begin with?

He remembered Zak's vision in the subway, the water flooding the tunnels.

And he thought of the teeny, tiny amount of electroleum in Dr. Bookman's office. And what had happened when Godfrey unleashed his power there.

"There's no way to tell what will happen," Bookman said. "The Secret Sea flows betwixt our worlds, and it is not merely water, Khalid. It is the ur-water, the Platonic ideal of waterness. It is physical but also metaphysical. Should that be released into a physical universe . . ." He shook his head. "I cannot begin to comprehend the ramifications."

Khalid swallowed. "Is that what'll happen? Are you sure?"

"No, I'm not. But *something* will happen. Even in the absolute best-case scenario, opening the path between our worlds so explosively will be catastrophic."

Khalid imagined water *everywhere*. Imagined Manhattan inundated with an endless, raging torrent of water sucked out of another universe. All of lower Manhattan, at the very least, covered in the waters of the Houston Conflux.

"Everyone will die," he whispered. "No one will even see it coming. It'll just *happen*."

Dr. Bookman quivered like a toddler with a fever. His teeth chattered. "We have to stop them," he stammered. *"Now."*

FIFTY-FIVE

"Don't test me, Moira," Zak said. "I checked it before, when you were tying him up. It still works."

Under his feet, Zak felt the slowing of the superway, and Battery Landing loomed large in the windshield. He braced himself against the chair with one hand and kept the other pointed, unwaveringly, at Moira.

"What are you doing?" Her eyes had gone wide and staring, her skin fading to an even-lighter shade of pale than usual. "We're in this together!"

"Not anymore. As soon as we stop, you need to get out of the cabin and evacuate with everyone else."

"Are you crazy?"

"It'll be confusing. No one will be worried about your being uncompanioned. You can get on the ferry and go back to Manhattan, then figure things out from there. But you'll be safe, at least."

"Safe? Nowhere in this world is safe for—"

"Better than dead," Zak said.

Better than dead.

She'd heard him right.

Better than dead.

"What are you saying?"

Zak shook his head. "We don't have time."

"Tell me!" she shouted. Stun stick be damned—she wasn't going to let him say something like that without . . . "What are you planning?"

Zak's throat worked, and his lips moved for a moment or two before he found his voice. "I have to die, Moira. It's the only way."

"What?" The stick. Could she grab it before he could trigger it? Were her reflexes quick enough? Were his slow enough?

"I don't know how to sneak into the secure facility," he admitted. "I was lying. The Dutchmen tried planning it out on the back of the blueprints, but they realized it wouldn't work, so they decided to steal the uncharged stuff. There's no way in."

"Then why—"

"I can't sneak in. And even if I could, I don't know the first thing about electroleum. But Tommy told us. Right when we got here, he told us we'd need a 'massive energy source.' So I figured I'd take the direct route. Now I don't have to figure out how to get out, either. All I need to do is floor the gas on this train and plow it right into the secure part of the facility." He grinned lopsidedly. "Boom. Instant massive energy source."

Moira couldn't speak. Words failed her. On the floor, the operator grunted and thrashed against his bonds.

"That'll kill you," she managed at last.

"But Tommy will live," Zak said. "The way it should be."

Moira stamped her foot on the floor—a childish gesture, she knew, but one she couldn't help. "Don't talk like that! Tommy's death isn't your fault! It was a fluke of science."

"I don't expect you to understand. I have to do this. I have to save him." Tears glimmered in Zak's eyes, and if he weren't being such an idiot, Moira would have allowed herself to feel sorry for him.

"What about your parents?" she asked. "Think of what this is going to do to them. They already lost Tommy, and now they'll lose you, too."

"They've already lost me, Moira. We don't know how to get home. We don't know if we *can* go back home. Alive or dead, I'm still a universe away from them."

"So you'll kill yourself? And him?" She pointed to the operator, who groaned pathetically through his gag.

"Don't worry," Zak told him without turning around. "I'll let you go just as soon as you show me how to do it. It's the only way, Moira. The only way for Tommy to live."

"Zak, that's crazy. That's . . . You can't think Tommy wants you to—"

"He probably doesn't. But I'm not asking him. Is it fair that I lived when he didn't? Is it fair that he's been trapped in limbo for all these years, seeing the world but unable to touch it? I've had twelve years. Now it's his turn."

"I won't let you do this," she said, clenching her fists.

Zak laughed. "You're the smartest, most capable person I know, but you can't stop me, Moira."

As though the train had heard the word *stop*, it slowed further and then came to a gentle halt. Through the windshield, Moira could see men in what appeared to be security garb. A chime sounded, indicating that the doors had opened, and the men began pinwheeling their arms, gesturing to a stampede of commuters gushing from the train.

"Time to go, Moira."

"Don't do this, Zak." Tears in her eyes.

"Don't cry for me, Moira. Best thing I've ever done with my life. And I'm sorry you got dragged into it."

"Zak . . ."

"I bet you're going to change this world," he told her. Then he gestured to the door.

She ran all the possibilities through her mind in the two seconds it took her to cross to the door. There were no options. She left or she didn't. She could try to wrestle the stick away from him, but that would just leave them both trapped here. Once everyone was cleared from the station, those security guys would storm the train, she figured. Both of them either dead or arrested. Probably dead. No good.

If she stayed to help, she died. If she left, Zak died.

But Zak was going to die no matter what. It drifted in his eyes, in his posture. He'd approached his death, taken its measure, shaken its hand. He'd accepted it. Nothing she could do would change that.

At the door, she wished for something to say, something profound. But even *Three Basketeers* felt hollow, without Khalid.

"Good-bye," she said lamely, and stepped out into the fleeing crowd before he could respond.

FIFTY-SIX

Zak yanked the gag out of the operator's mouth. "We've only got a few seconds, so let's make it quick. It's really simple." He pressed the tines of the stun stick against the operator's temple, eliciting a whimper from the man. "Show me how to make this thing plow into the electroleum reserve, or I'll shoot a jillion volts of electricity right through your brain." He was 90 percent certain that he didn't have it in him to kill the man in cold blood, but that trailing 10 percent didn't matter, because he'd lied to Moira earlier: He'd never tested the stun stick, and he had no idea whether it even worked.

"You're nuts," the operator exclaimed.

"Sure, whatever," Zak said cheerfully. He'd been at peace with his decision when he made it, back in Dr. Bookman's office. He'd known then that there was no way to save Tommy and keep his friends safe that did not involve his own death. But at the time it had been an abstract problem, a theoretical decision. *Would you be willing to die for your brother? Yeah, sure.*

Now that the moment was right before him, he was pleased

to find that he wasn't going to chicken out. A great and almost holy calm had swaddled him, enfolded him, sent warming waves through him. The world had shrunk to this tiny cabin at the head of the train. He was an explorer on the sea, and this was his craft. Ahead lay the edge of the world, the edge of the world and dragons.

He would live to witness their fiery breath, and not much longer after that.

"Do it," he told the operator, keeping his voice neutral. It was difficult; he wanted to shout in joy. Wanted to explode with elation.

The operator fumbled at the panel. "You have to disengage the safety protocols and put it into maintenance mode, then—"

"Don't describe it—do it."

"ATTENTION IN THE OPERATOR'S CABIN!" a voice blared. "THIS IS PDNY! YOUR TRAIN IS EMPTY, AND YOU HAVE NO MORE HOSTAGES! RELEASE THE OPERATOR IMMEDIATELY."

"Not yet," Zak said. To the cop. To himself. To the operator, whose fingers fluttered over the controls, swiping and tapping. Zak tried to pay attention but found himself fading into reverie.

Soon, Tommy. Soon you get your chance at life. Enjoy it, man. Make the most of it.

"WE WILL STORM THE CAR IF YOU DO NOT RELEASE THE OPERATOR AT THE COUNT OF TEN."

Uh-huh. Whatever.

The operator, trembling, sweating, tapped a few more controls. "Look, you can't steer into the building. There's nowhere to go, no way out of the tube."

"I want to go through the tube, then. Crash right through it."

"You'll hit the air cushion halfway down the tube," the operator said. "The impact will rip the tube open—"

"Show me where that happens." Zak unfolded the schematic of the plant. The operator pointed. Zak nodded in satisfaction. The holding tanks were far from the point of impact, but the bend in the path there nearly guaranteed that the train's momentum would carry it through the broken tube and right into the spot he needed. He would most likely be dead by the final collision.

And then the electroleum would erupt. And swap out one twin for another, just like the roaches in Dr. Bookman's experiment.

Just then a flat, dull crack echoed, and the windshield vibrated with impact. The operator shrieked and dropped to the floor. Zak, stunned, stood his ground, his vision tunneling to focus on the sudden nick in the glass, right at his eye level.

He refocused beyond and through the glass. A security officer with a rifle aimed at him stood at one end of the platform.

Crack! again. This time Zak jerked to one side, though it was ridiculous—he couldn't dodge a bullet. The windshield still held, pocked with another chip. The glass (if it *was* glass) must have been specially treated to resist collisions and the tremendous speed at which the superway traveled. It would take more than a couple of shots to break through.

"Hurry," Zak said to operator, but the man had hit his limit. He shoved Zak aside and dived for the door. Before Zak could recover, the operator had slipped through, leaving it wide open as he tore through the car.

Zak checked the windshield. The cops had stopped shooting, and one of them was waving frantically. A moment later he saw the operator charging toward them, head down, arms pumping. The cops directed him toward an exit, and the man never broke stride.

Now they'd be coming for Zak.

He closed the cabin door and hopped into the control seat. He would have to hope for the best.

Scanning the control panel, he nodded to himself, took a moment to assess it, then stroked a finger along a glowing trail.

The superway lurched and began to move. Zak grinned at the stunned looks on the faces of the cops. They fired at him some more, but soon he was gone, racing down the tunnel to the end.

FIFTY-SEVEN

According to Dr. Bookman's Wonder Glass, the superway's 10 line was currently shut down, making a boat the fastest way to Battery Island. In the backseat of the car, Khalid and Dr. Bookman raced to the ferry stop at the Houston Conflux.

"Godfrey's power is substantial," Bookman said quietly, not wanting to bring the driver into the conversation. They'd offered the man three times his usual fee to ignore as many traffic laws as humanly possible. "But it all exists in the nonphysical realm. He can't actually impact the physical world."

"But he can get *us* to do it for him. Or he can possess people. Like he did with you."

"Perhaps. I don't know if he can do that on his own. I let him in. I *commanded* him in. Without a wild scientist, I'm not sure he can reliably communicate with anyone."

"I don't get it, though," Khalid said, remembering the vision at the Houston Conflux when they'd first crossed into this universe. "If Godfrey is so powerful, then why did we see *Tommy*?"

Dr. Bookman hesitated before answering. "I told you before:

Twins are powerful magic. They have a special connection, and I suspect Godfrey has been able to commandeer that connection."

"I still don't get it. And besides, why would Godfrey want to flood my Manhattan?"

"He's trying to shatter the wall between life and death so that he can return to life. An electroleum explosion might just be able to do that, but it will almost certainly crumble the weakened wall between our worlds, no matter what. And from what I picked up during my ... merging with Godfrey, he fully intends for *your* world to suffer the brunt of the damage. Our worlds are connected, like Zak and Tommy in the womb. If something happens in my world, it will have repercussions in your own. Godfrey will make sure of it."

Khalid's head spun. He couldn't keep thinking about this stuff. Moira would get it, he knew. Zak could probably figure it out, if he let it steep in his brain for a while. But to Khalid, it was all mumbo jumbo. Dangerous-sounding mumbo jumbo, but mumbo jumbo nonetheless. He decided he didn't need the details. He had to stop Zak and Moira. Full stop. Everything else was extraneous information. Let the geniuses do a postmortem later.

Khalid checked the Wonder Glass. This was an older model, slightly larger and thicker, but still more svelte and sweet than anything from his world. It probably ran on some combination of true science and wild science, and it was connected (maybe through voodoo, who knew?) to Dr. Bookman's newer model, the one Moira and Zak had swiped. A positioning app placed the newer Wonder Glass at or near Battery Landing. Zak was probably still angry, but Khalid had no choice—he called the other Wonder Glass.

To his surprise, Zak answered.

"Don't hang up," Khalid said. "Listen, man, you have to listen: Dr. Bookman's up, and he knows stuff. I don't get it all, but you have to be really careful and just get out of there. Now. That electroleum stuff is dangerous. You could get killed. Bookman says Godfrey wants to blow it all up."

"Well, yeah, that's the plan." Zak sounded almost cheerful. "Big blast of energy, just like Tommy told us. It's the only way to bring him back."

"Are you listening to yourself? Do you care about the other people who will die?"

Zak took long enough to answer that Khalid feared he'd hung up. But then: "I'm going to be careful. Everyone will be evacuated. The only one getting hurt will be me."

"No, man. It might not be up to you. And you wouldn't just kill people here. People back in our world, too. It could happen. You gotta rethink this. Please."

"Dr. Bookman doesn't know everything," Zak said. "I'll feel bad if something terrible happens to his world, but at the end of the day . . ."

"Dude, you're not thinking straight. You're gonna be a terrorist. Do you realize that? Do you realize that's what you're becoming?"

"Shut up, Khalid. That's not it at all and you know it. That's not what this is. I'm not trying to hurt anyone, change anyone's mind, scare anyone. If there was another way to bring Tommy back to life, I'd do it."

Khalid had been friends with Zak long enough to be able to tell when he'd made up his mind about something. But Khalid tried again anyway.

"Zak, please, man. There's something off about all of this. Tommy and Godfrey and all of it. Just come back and let's talk about it a little, and then you can do what you think makes sense. Okay? Doesn't that sound reasonable?"

Nothing.

And then:

"It's too late."

He didn't even say good-bye.

"The Godfrey spirit is filled with rage," Bookman said as he and Khalid neared the park. He quaked a little extra at the thought. "I felt it when I was possessed. I've never felt such pure anger in my life. He was able to take over completely. I had to force his presence; he resisted. But once I had him, he took control."

"What about Tommy? When Tommy possessed you, what did you feel?"

Dr. Bookman said nothing. He looked down at his hands, which still shook, as though seeing them for the first time.

"Dr. Bookman? What did you feel? With Tommy. I heard his voice first."

"You have to understand, Khalid: I was trying to contact your friend Zak. That was the point of the ritual."

"Right. And you got Tommy instead. Because they're twins, right?"

Dr. Bookman didn't answer. "Godfrey uses Tommy's connection to your friend," Bookman said. "It's his way of communicating with the physical world. Imagine you are trapped in a room, and a mannequin is bolted in place in front of the only window. You can only stand behind the mannequin and turn its head this way and that and perhaps try to shout loud enough. But all anyone will see is the mannequin, even though it's your voice."

Riiiiight. "I get all that," Khalid said. "But that didn't answer my question. What did you—"

"Nothing," Dr. Bookman said, turning slowly to look at Khalid. "I felt nothing. Because there *was* nothing. There was never a Tommy. I felt only Godfrey."

"But Tommy spoke to me. Through your mouth. I heard it."

"No." It was the strongest word Khalid had heard from the man since before his voodoo ritual. "That was Godfrey pretending to be Tommy."

"Are you sure?" The edges of the Wonder Glass bit into Khalid's fingers as he tightened his grip. "Why would—"

"I am sure. I was possessed by the spirit, Khalid. I know what I felt. It was Godfrey all along."

"But . . . but if Godfrey can pretend to be Tommy . . ." Khalid stared out the window. The familiar yet unfamiliar city, aglow with electroleum, whizzed by. "If Godfrey can pretend to be Tommy, then how do we know when we actually heard from Tommy?"

He turned back to Bookman, who said nothing, staring once more at his hands.

"Dr. Bookman, are you listening to me? How do we know when we heard from Tommy? Did it stop when we got to this universe?"

Bookman drew in a deep breath, steadying himself. "We're almost at the Conflux," he said. "I'll make this quick:

"Energy cannot be created or destroyed. Only transformed.

You have Einstein in your world, yes? Even in wild science, this rule applies. Wild science just allows us to manipulate energy in new ways."

"I don't get the connection." Science. Every time someone started to talk science, it was as though the wind picked up to carry the thoughts and ideas right over Khalid's head.

"There is a connection between Zak and his twin, a connection that transcended death. This connection, to put it simply, is *made* of energy, an energy that flows back and forth between them. Godfrey is able to piggyback on this. He is able to manipulate the energy to his own purposes. He commandeered the connection between Zak and Tommy."

Khalid squinted, trying to rearrange his brain the way he did during math tests. "We went through that already. Am I missing something? *Godfrey* didn't talk to us or to Zak. *Tommy* did."

Dr. Bookman smiled, but it was the smile of a patient receiving bad news. "In your world, there is no wild science. Godfrey had a tenuous existence. Here, he is stronger. Godfrey can manifest in this universe, can appear visible and can be heard, if he wishes, without using the connection between Zak and Tommy."

The Conflux came into view ahead. There were police cars converging there, along with ambulances and fire trucks. Khalid tried to ignore them, focused on the question at hand: Why would Godfrey not speak to them all directly, then, instead only going through Tommy? Why pretend he needed Tommy?

"Oh God," he whispered. "It's because he can *lie*."

He turned excitedly to Dr. Bookman, who was nodding sadly. "Yes, that is the conclusion I've reached as well. By using the twin connection and not his own power to manifest, Godfrey can pretend to be Zak's twin. And convince you of things because you trust 'Tommy,' and 'Tommy' said so."

"Because Zak would listen to anything Tommy said. Oh, man!" He ground his palms into his eyes. "So, wait. Did Zak *ever* really hear from Tommy?"

"I don't know," said Dr. Bookman. "There's a chance Tommy may have been used up and discarded by Godfrey in his desperation to connect to Zak. There might not even be a Tommy at all."

FIFTY-EIGHT

The superway inched forward through the tube. Zak didn't quite understand the entire readout on the control panel before him, but he got the gist of it. The train always moved slowly when pulling out of a station, then picked up speed. Normally, it would cruise along at a leisurely pace while on Battery Landing, but now—as the warning light flashing in the upper right-hand corner of the screen declaimed—the safety protocols had been disengaged. In a few moments, Zak would be able to push the superway to its limits. He would push the engine to its limits to race the entire length of Battery Island, to the recycling tanks, located at the maximum safe distance from the passenger station.

And then the safety air cushion would engage along the tube. Designed to slow a superway moving at a normal rate of speed, the contact between the cushion and a breakneck train would be catastrophic. The tube would be ruptured, and the superway's cars would barrel through the openings, right into tanks of recharging electroleum.

A momentary doubt nipped at him. Was Khalid right? Was he about to become this world's first terrorist?

No. Of course not. He was just doing what he had to do. By the time the superway crashed into the tanks and exploded, the island would have been evacuated. No one would be hurt except for Zak.

And . . .

Boom.

Soon, Tommy. You'll be back soon.

FIFTY-NINE

The Battery Landing Ferry was faster than any ferry Khalid had ever been on, cutting across the water at top speed. Then again, maybe that was because it was on a rescue mission.

The car had dropped him and Dr. Bookman as close to the ferry as they could get. A clot of emergency vehicles prevented them from getting any closer. The driver, who had a news read-out mounted next to his steering wheel, shrugged apologetically when he explained that he couldn't get any closer.

"Someone's hijacked the superway at Battery Landing. The ferry's headed out for evacuation."

"Hijacked? Who?"

The driver shrugged. "I just know what's coming across on the screen. It said something about a 'feminist army,' whatever *that* means."

Khalid had stifled a giggle. The times were too serious for laughter, but he couldn't help it.

He and Dr. Bookman had approached the ferry station on foot. Sure enough, people were being herded off the ferry as cops and firefighters and EMTs loaded on. Dr. Bookman gave Khalid his Wonder Glass.

"You may find this of some help. I will distract the police so that you may slip on board the ferry," Dr. Bookman said.

"Great." Khalid scanned the dock, looking for shadows and easy concealment. He flashed to a moment playing hide-and-seek near Grand Army Plaza. Another world. Another lifetime.

"Khalid." Dr. Bookman rested his hands on Khalid's shoulders and gazed into his eyes. "What your friend proposes to undertake is very dangerous. And what you propose to undertake in stopping him is just as dangerous. Are you certain you wish to do this?"

Khalid felt as though his body hummed with energy. Electricity. Electroleum. Or maybe just nerves. "I don't have much of a choice. He's my best friend. This is what you do."

Dr. Bookman nodded. "Your name. You know its meaning? That it means 'eternal' in the language of your ancestors?"

He'd known, but he'd never really thought about it. "Yeah."

"May your courage be eternal, if not your life. If death *is* another world, I shall look for you when we are both there, Khalid Shamoon."

And then he very gently kissed Khalid on the forehead and, without another word, turned and strode off toward the police, waving his arms and shouting, "Officers! Officers, excuse me! Officers!"

Khalid wanted to absorb everything that had happened, but there was no time, and so he dashed off to cover.

And now he stood at the prow of the ferry as it cut through the Houston Conflux on its way to Battery Landing. No one had spotted him yet—they were all out on the deck, shouting over

341

one another, arranging equipment. He checked the Wonder Glass. According to it, Zak and Moira were moving along the eastern edge of the island. He zoomed in on the dot that represented Dr. Bookman's stolen Wonder Glass and was delighted to find the best satellite image he'd ever seen—it was actually in real time, as he could see the ferry he was on powering through the water. Wow.

The maps showed him nearing what appeared to be a ferry dock at Battery Landing. Good. He would cruise right up and track down Zak, and he would do whatever he had to do to stop him.

Sometimes, being one of the Three Basketeers meant stopping the other two from messing up big-time.

SIXTY

Moira grunted as she was shoved and jostled in the mixed crowd of tourists, commuters, and facility personnel jostling for position at the ferry dock. After leaving the superway, she'd been caught up in the press of people running for the water-bound evacuation post. Klaxons rang from every direction, and a robotic voice on a PA system calmly but loudly urged everyone to "follow the lighted signs to the nearest emergency exit."

Moira didn't know what else to do. Zak's plan was crazy, but she had no way to stop him. And fighting against the flow of people seemed impossible. No matter what direction she tried to move in, the press of humanity bore her in one direction only: to the ferry dock.

And then it happened: Someone jostled her as he passed, knocking off her cap. Her bright red hair spilled out. She cast about for the cap, but it was lost under the stampede of fleeing feet.

Before she could react further, a tall man who was wearing a green jumpsuit with *SUPERVISOR* stenciled on its left chest and a logo that read *Consolidated Tesla Power & Light* caught a glimpse of her and fought his way through the crowd. Moira tensed, but the crush pushed her right toward him.

"Are you alone?" he asked. "Isn't someone with you?"

Oh, crap. "Uh, my dad was here. . . ." She started to move away, but he took hold of her wrist and started pulling her toward the ferry dock.

"Don't you worry, honey," he said to her soothingly. "We'll find your dad once we get you back to the mainland. You won't be out on your own for long."

Gee, thanks, she thought sarcastically. "Gosh, thanks!" she chirped. "I'm ever so frightened." She laid it so thick that any right-thinking person would have convulsed with laughter, but in this universe, the man just nodded gravely and patted her condescendingly on the head.

He maintained a steady stream of nauseatingly infantile comfort chatter as he tugged her along. In this world, any female under the age of thirty was clearly considered mentally defective. And probably the ones over thirty, too. She considered trying to break free, but there was nowhere to go. Before she got back to Manhattan, though, she would have to get away from this guy. Her Good Samaritan very clearly intended not to let her out of his sight until he saw her safely companioned.

As they emerged onto the ferry dock, she was both relieved and disheartened to see a ferry already stationed there. EMTs and cops and firemen (the word was depressingly not exclusionary here) spilled out of the ferry, some of them moving off to one side with medical equipment, still more of them moving into position to guide the evacuees. And some of them pushed into the crowd, heading right for the place everyone was fleeing.

Into the fire, she thought. *No matter what the universe, they go into the fire when everyone else runs from it.*

Just then a group of cops broke away from the pack and headed off to her left, shouting. Moira twisted around to see why, painfully bending her arm.

The cops were chasing someone at the edge of the crowd—a small, slim figure.

Khalid!

SIXTY-ONE

When the ferry docked, Khalid knew he would have to emerge from his hiding place on board. Sure enough, as soon as he did, a cop spotted him, confirming Khalid's long-held suspicion that he would, in fact, make the world's worst ninja.

"Hey!" the cop shouted, and brandished his stun stick. "Get over here!"

Why on earth anyone would go *toward* the person carrying a weapon that zapped you with electricity, Khalid couldn't possibly imagine. He decided not to debate the logic or illogic of it with the cop, though, and instead faked left, then darted to his right, dancing around the cop, who had lunged in the wrong direction.

I can't believe he fell for that! Do they not have football in this universe?

Khalid's glee fueled his mad dash up a flight of tenuous, shivering stairs and out onto the open deck of the ferry. Emergency responders milled all around him, guiding people onto the ferry from the dock. Khalid paused for a second and scanned the crowd for Zak and Moira. Nothing.

From belowdecks came a shout, and the stairs started vibrating as the cop stomped his way up. Khalid briefly considered kicking the guy in the face as he popped up from below, but violence wasn't really his style. Besides, better to put more distance between them.

He raced toward the dock, weaving in and out and around the emergency workers, who yelled out annoyed epithets in his wake. He ignored them. After finding the lifted gate through which the crew was unloading equipment, he jumped through it, pinwheeling his arms and legs madly in the air as he sailed over the gap between the boat and the dock.

Ka-thump! He stuck the landing and bounced ahead, not missing a stride. Behind him a cry went up, and several cops spilled down the gangway in his direction. Ha. Walking was for suckers.

"Stop him!" someone shouted. "Grab that kid!"

Khalid pumped his arms and cut left, diving right into the crowd of evacuees.

Moira jerked her arm hard, breaking loose from the guy who was holding her. "Don't be afraid!" he shouted, and she wanted to yell back, *I'm not, you idiot!* but there was no point. She pushed against the flow of the crowd, moving toward Khalid. Her would-be rescuer gave up as he was carried along by the throng, closer to the ferry.

Three cops were chasing Khalid, fighting the tide of evacuees. Khalid, smaller and nimbler, was able to bob and weave through the crowd, but the cops had authority and weapons on their side—a corridor began to form as people parted, and when it was over, Khalid would be all too easily captured.

"Hey!" Moira shouted, jumping up and down. "Hey, I'm all alone! I don't know what to do! Help me!"

The cops paused for a moment, turning in Moira's direction. She kept jumping up and down.

"My companion isn't here! What am I supposed to do? I'm just a stupid dingbat *frau*, and I'm all alone."

She espied Khalid making his way through a door up ahead as the cops conferred briefly. Two of them kept chasing Khalid, and one of them made his way to Moira. Great. Just one knight in shining armor, when she'd been hoping for three.

"Okay, little girl," the cop said, "you're going to be all right. Don't worry. I'm here now." He held out his hand to take hers, and Moira kicked him between the legs with every ounce of energy in her.

She felt a tiny bit sorry about doing it. No matter how rooted in ingrained misogyny and culturally embedded sexism, his actions really *were* aimed at sincerely trying to help her. But mostly she felt pretty good about her decision. This whole universe needed a good kick in the balls, as far as she was concerned.

The cop's mouth ovaled into a perfect upside-down egg shape; Moira could practically see his uvula. For a single instant there was no sound, and then he grabbed between his legs and howled and dropped to his knees.

All around her, the crowd began moving away from Moira even more quickly. Without sparing a further moment or a further thought for the cop, she charged away in the direction of Khalid and the other police.

SIXTY-TWO

The superway train picked up speed as it plunged through the tunnel. Zak was almost able to convince himself that he was back home on the subway, underground, not encased in a tube ten feet above sea level like a pebble in a straw. Ahead lay only darkness, interrupted by the superway's powerful headlight. The tube was almost preternaturally clean and smooth, frictionless. Unlike a subway, the superway did not bump or stutter or clatter as it raced ahead.

Between the recycling facility's blaring klaxons, the warning voice-over, and the endless bleating from the superway's control panel, Zak's head threatened to explode. Three different sounds, three different patterns, three different rhythms assaulted him on an eternal loop. He closed his eyes and massaged his temples. No need to pay attention. There was only one way to go, and he wasn't worried about crashing, after all.

This was the only way. He knew that he wasn't as smart as Moira, but he had a *good head on his shoulders*, La-La liked to say. His options were limited to staying in this world or rescuing

Tommy. The only choice that made any kind of sense was to rescue Tommy. He couldn't imagine living in this world with the knowledge that he could have helped Tommy and hadn't done so. Maybe, given time, there could be another way. This world was a wonderland of magical science, and Zak had only seen the smallest part of it.

But Tommy had been trapped in the limbo between life and death for too long already. Who knew how much longer he could survive there before pushing on to whatever lay beyond—to a place where not even Zak could reach him? No, all those years of limbo was too much; Zak would not make Tommy suffer one moment longer.

A pang of guilt touched his heart, making it leap like it used to back in the days when it was defective. Leaving Moira and Khalid alone . . . That wasn't the best he could do, but they were resourceful and would figure out a way to thrive here, he knew. Even Moira. If anyone could overcome this world's lunacy, she could.

He allowed himself a few seconds to think of his parents and was surprised to find a deep, dull ache in his chest for them. The anger he'd felt had corroded while he wasn't looking, pieces of it flaking away until what was left was a soft, heavy wad of regret. They had done something wrong, something very bad, but their intentions had been good. He didn't forgive them—he wasn't there, not yet—but he thought maybe he could understand.

Maybe someday I'll see them again, and I can try to forgive them then. We'll see.

The internal warning alarm jumped to a new level of obnoxious aural pain. If it had been a shout before, it was a scream now. He must be getting closer and closer to the air cushion.

He opened his eyes and checked the control panel. What had been a yellow flashing light before was now orange, edging into red. An animated schematic showed the train's resolute path toward the air cushion, represented on the board as a glowing red cloud with an exclamation mark at its center.

RE-ENGAGE SAFETY PROTOCOL! the board advised. A large, pulsating button throbbed next to it, with the word *ENGAGE* bisecting it.

No, thank you, Zak thought.

He looked up to gaze through the windshield again, wondering if he would actually see the air cushion or if it was invisible. His reflection stared back at him. When had his eyes become so haunted? When had his cheeks become so drawn? His heart had been repaired, his health never better, but he looked sicker than ever before in his life.

And then, even though he was standing still, his reflection *moved.*

Tommy?

The thought came to him instantly. The reflection nodded, and the sounds of the alarms, the warnings, the klaxons, all receded, and he could hear only his twin's voice, so similar to his own.

We're close again, Tommy said. *Close like death.*

This is the only time you can see me.

No. It's the only time you can see me. I can see you all the time, Zak. I just can't always communicate with you.

Well, I—

You have to turn back, Zak. Now. There's still time.

No. This is what I'm doing. I've decided. You can't stop me.

Zak, your dying won't solve anything.

It will bring you back. It'll break the wall between life and death. I go one way; you go the other.

No. You've been tricked. By Godfrey.

Zak boggled. It was strange for his doppelgänger in the windshield not to reflect his expression. *What do you mean? You sent me images of the boat. Of Godfrey. You wanted me here. You told me to—*

No. The reflection shook his head while Zak's stayed still. *That wasn't me. I tried to warn you away. I told you not to trust him. But he's more powerful than I am, Zak. He masqueraded as me. He drew you here, knowing that he could use you to break the walls between the worlds.*

What? But wait—if that was true, if Godfrey could pretend to be Tommy ... then how did he know this wasn't Godfrey right now? Maybe Zak's plan would rescue Tommy but not Godfrey, so Godfrey was trying to stop him. Or maybe Godfrey just didn't think it would work and was trying to stop Zak the best way he knew how.

Zak shook his head and turned away from the windshield. None of it made sense. He'd been speaking to Tommy, but it had been Godfrey ... sometimes?

Zak, don't listen to him! said a new voice, the same as the old voice. *He's Godfrey, pretending to me! You have to keep the superway going! It's the only way!*

Zak spun around. His reflection had split in two, one in each pane of the windshield.

We're so close! said the reflection on the left. *You've come this far—don't ruin it now!*

No, said the one on the right. *You don't gain anything if you die. Trust me; I've been there.*

You have to risk it all, Zak. It's the only way. I know it seems crazy, but you have to trust me.

If you die, that's the end. There's no way to get you back. There's no way for me to come back. It's impossible to break the walls between life and death.

It's not only possible, Zak, but you're about to do it! Godfrey is terrified that if you do, only I will come through because we're twins. That's why he's trying to stop you. So that he can manipulate you into freeing him.

Don't believe him! It doesn't work that way. All you'll do is kill yourself and many, many other people. You could rip a hole in the universe, and who knows what that could do?

Zak put his hands over his ears and shouted at the top of his lungs, but the voices weren't in his ears or even in his brain. They were in his soul. He couldn't stop them no matter how much he tried.

—going to kill everyone—

—rescue me without killing—

—no way to change the—

—there's nothing to do but let the train—

—so close to death—

Zak's eyes snapped open. *So close to death. So close to—*

That was it. *So close to death.*

Tommy had told him, back in the alley, that he could only communicate with Zak when Zak was close to death. Like now. And like in the alley, when his heart had been dying.

But then Moira said later that she had seen Tommy, that Tommy had led her to Dr. White-eagle's.

If it was true that only Zak could see Tommy and only when close to death, then how could Moira have seen him?

And if it wasn't true that Zak could only see Tommy when close to death, then why had Tommy said so?

And when he'd seen Godfrey on his way to Dr. White-eagle's, why had he thought he sounded like Tommy? Unless . . .

All Zak knew for certain was that *Moira* had seen Tommy. Because she'd made her way to Dr. White-eagle's.

Moira had seen Tommy. Or Godfrey pretending to be Tommy.

And Tommy had manifested at the Conflux, when Zak had been nowhere near death.

One way or the other . . .

"Someone's lying to me," Zak said aloud.

Khalid. He needed Khalid here to help him figure it out. What had Khalid said? He'd said to think about it. He'd said things didn't make sense.

He called me a terrorist. But—

The warning alarm went from scream to shriek; if a computer could be hysterical, the one controlling the superway was now in a full-blown panic attack.

The two reflections kept shouting. Zak ignored them.

He called me a terrorist, but that's not what I am. Those guys flew planes into buildings. I'm just driving a train into—

Oh, man.

He stared in horror at the control panel, realizing. Finally realizing what he was about to do.

He'd been so sure of himself, and at the same time so distracted. . . .

And now it was too late.

SIXTY-THREE

Khalid figured the cops wouldn't bother chasing someone going *into* the facility. Their job was help people get out, right? But he'd thought wrong. Clearly, they were going to chase him down and drag him out of the dangerous situation, no matter his eagerness to hurl himself into harm's way. Under normal circumstances he'd be impressed by their dedication, but right now it aggravated him. He wanted to stop running, get his bearings, find Zak and Moira before they could do something stupid. And then, ideally, they would all do something else stupid together and get out of this mess and off this island.

He slipped into the building through a door left open by the fleeing, panicked masses. He hadn't lost the cops just yet, but they were still a ways behind him, pushing through the crowd. People kept stopping them to ask questions or request help, and it was slowing them down.

He was in the lobby of what was, just as the Dutchmen's plans had said, the SOUTHERN CONFLUX ELECTROLEUM RECLAMATION FACILITY, according to a large sign just under another sign that read WELCOME, VISITORS! Under the name of the facility was a logo of a *C* and a *T* tied together by a lightning bolt, with the words A CONSOLIDATED TESLA PROGRAM.

The lobby was large, its floor clad in limestone. Along the walls were lighted dioramas showing what Khalid assumed to be the history of the facility or the company or both. Interesting stuff, maybe, but not anything he had time for right now.

Ahead of him, there was a curved, chest-high desk. Some kind of security post or welcome desk. It was, like the rest of the lobby and most likely the rest of the building, unoccupied, having been abandoned when the alarms went out. *The "feminist army" is in the house, and everyone's running scared.*

Frosted glass doors were positioned on either side of the welcome desk. Khalid couldn't tell if they went to different places or joined together once breached. He paused a second to check his Wonder Glass, and just then the two cops caught up to him.

One grabbed him by the shoulder. "Gotcha!"

Khalid struggled against the cop who was holding him, but to no avail. The man was bigger and stronger and just plain meaner—he didn't seem to mind that the bones in Khalid's shoulder were grinding together painfully under his grasp.

"Let go of me!" Khalid yelled. "I need to get in there!"

"Are you nuts? This whole place could blow up at any second. You're coming with us."

"You don't understand!" Khalid said as they dragged him toward the exit. "I need to be here! My friends are in there!"

"Stop distracting us and we'll go *get* them!" the cop with his hands on Khalid shouted.

"Whoa, wait a sec!" said the other cop, and held up a cautionary hand. Both cops stopped, and Khalid saw over their shoulders that someone was sprawled on the floor just inside the door to the building.

Bright red hair.

Moira.

One cop dragged Khalid along and the other approached her, looming over her in that way only cops can loom. Moira pitched her voice low and breathy.

"Help," she whined.

The cop with free hands waved his partner to go through to the dock. "Don't worry," he said to Moira. "I've got you. You're safe. You'll live to have babies."

"I did something to my ankle," she said pathetically, reaching up to him. "You'll have to carry me."

The cop stooped over to scoop her up, and as soon as he was down there, Moira struck.

Moira went for the throat, just as she'd been taught in her self-defense classes. She punched the cop in his exposed Adam's apple. She'd heard once that it was possible to kill someone this way, and she hoped that it wasn't true. She didn't want to kill him, just disable him.

Mission accomplished. The cop, gurgling, went down on one knee, clutching his throat. He wheezed but still managed tortured breaths.

As his partner turned back to help, Khalid took advantage of the situation and broke free. The cop growled and lunged at Khalid just as a heavy, meaty hand clapped onto Moira's shoulder. The cop she'd punched was purple and panting, but he had the presence of mind to reach out to her. She shrieked involuntarily and scrambled backward, but he already had a lock on her, and now his weight was tipping toward her, threatening to fall on top of her.

Khalid, meanwhile, took a jog step out of the reach of his own cop, who drew his stun stick from the holster at his side. The stick arced in the air, spitting blue sparks that danced for moments before burning out. Khalid remembered Officer Cheong's bellow of pain when he'd zapped him back at the park. He wanted no part of that pain. But he wasn't sure how long he could dodge. With every swing and swipe, the cop got closer and closer, and if Khalid turned to run, he would be struck down from behind for sure.

At the same moment, Moira was struggling with the cop who'd grabbed her. Teetering and off-balance on one knee, still choking out each breath, he managed to hold her in place with one hand, no matter how much she kicked and thrashed. She realized that he was about to collapse on her, and then, with that weight pinning her, she'd be caught for good.

"Khalid!" she yelped, not knowing if he could hear or help, but desperate.

And just then the building shook.

SIXTY-FOUR

The ghosts were still shouting, but Zak couldn't allow himself to focus on them. All his attention was on the control panel before him. Beads of sweat slid down his face and dripped from his chin onto the panel, smearing on its surface.

Suddenly his plan to ram the building with the train seemed really, really stupid.

The animation of the air cushion and the train's trajectory had changed, but the cloud at the end was still an orangish yellow, and it still had an exclamation mark in it. He was going to hit. Hard.

Tommy—whichever one of you is *Tommy—I hope I'm doing the right thing.*

He slammed down on the engage button, knowing it was too little, too late, but praying he was wrong.

No!

Yes!

On the control panel, the train was almost atop the air cushion graphic. Zak looked up into the windshield, through and past the ghosts, and saw nothing.

The cushion was invisible after all.

And then he hit it.

Above, the building shook all around Khalid and Moira.

And below . . .

The alarms disappeared for several protracted moments, replaced by the shriek of rending steel and the pebbly rain of broken ceramic falling on the superway. Zak was picked up bodily as the superway whipped to the left and then the right; he fetched up against the bulkhead and screamed silently, the breath knocked out of him. Then the train shuddered in the opposite direction, and he stumbled toward the other bulkhead, catching himself on the operator's chair at the last second.

He clutched it for dear life as the train zigged and zagged, bashing against the walls on either side of the tube. He had the sense that the train had jumped the tracks, or whatever guidance system it had, and that it was bouncing back and forth in the tube.

The windshield—already weakened by the rounds fired by the police back at the last stop—splintered, then finally shattered into thousands of shards, blown into the cabin by the wind force from the tube. Zak shielded his face with one arm while holding on to the chair with the other. Studs of glass slashed at him.

He risked peeking ahead as the storm of glass ended. Through the windshield, he saw a twist in the tube, but the superway was moving too quickly and still jogging back and forth. It wouldn't make the turn. No way.

He bit down hard on a scream as the train plowed right into the wall of the tube. The last thing he saw was a chunk of ceramic peeled out of the wall, flying toward him, and then he saw nothing at all.

SIXTY-FIVE

Both cops paused and looked at each other as the building tremor subsided. Dust filtered down from the ceiling, and lighting fixtures up there swung from side to side. Some of the glass at the front of the building had spiderwebbed.

Khalid took advantage of their moment of confusion to dive at the cop in front of him. The stun stick sizzled as it sliced the air by his ear, narrowly missing his shoulder. A bug-zapper smell permeated the air, and he head-butted the cop, then spun around and grabbed the stun stick.

The cop was bigger, stronger, tougher. There was no way for Khalid to pry the stick loose.

Until he sank his teeth into the man's hand, just below the cuff of his shirt.

The cop's fingers loosened and Khalid snagged the stick, then immediately reversed it and jabbed it into the hand he'd just bitten. The cop yelled and jerked his hand back but didn't go down. Khalid figured the farther away from the brain, the less the impact. So he took advantage of the cop's moment of pain and distraction and thrust the stun stick at the man's neck.

That did the trick. The cop's shout of pain ended with the clack of his teeth slamming together as he bit down. His body stiffened and he stumbled backward, then dropped bodily onto his partner, who lunged forward and collapsed on top of Moira.

"Khalid!" she bellowed.

"Sorry! Sorry!" He zapped the still-moving cop in the back of the neck. The man slumped forward, his head thumping down on Moira's chest.

"Not better!" she yelled, trying to wriggle out from underneath.

"Sorry. Really. Sorry." He helped her get out from under the unconscious cop and—without a further word between them—they hugged. Tightly.

"Good to see you," Khalid murmured.

"Can't believe you made it," Moira replied.

"We're, like, on a crime spree or something." Khalid tilted his head toward the cops on the floor.

"I guess I'll get to be the Bonnie Parker of this universe," Moira said without a trace of regret as she broke the hug. "I'll take it."

"Where's Zak?"

"I think that explosion answers that question."

"I have to tell you something about Tommy. And Godfrey."

"Yeah?"

"Yeah, and you're not gonna like it."

Moira blew her hair out of her eyes. "I don't like much of

anything these days." She took the stun stick from "her" cop's holster. "Let's go find Zak."

Together, they took the frosted glass door on the left and made their way deeper into the building. Alarms screamed and flashed every few feet along the corridor, and the PA voice kept reminding them to evacuate the premises.

The hallway branched off, but they kept going straight. There was a map on one wall labeled EMPLOYEE LOCATION that refreshed Moira's memory as to the contents of the plans she'd stolen from the Dutchmen. The map ended with a door and a label that read SECURE FACILITY/NECESSARY EMPLOYEES ONLY.

"How are we gonna get in there?" Khalid asked.

"We'll worry about that when we get there," she told him, and checked over her shoulder for the millionth time.

"They're not coming after us," he assured her. "They'll get up and they'll go for backup."

"Oh, good. More of them."

"With all the chaos out there, by the time they reach someone and get help, we'll be done."

Moira laughed, short and harsh. "Done. Yeah, one way or another."

The lights flickered overhead and died. Only the spinning red alarm lights provided illumination, filling the corridor with bleeding shadows. They'd been running before, but now they slowed down.

"Hold hands," Moira said, and he felt into the murk until he found hers. "We won't lose each other this way."

"Good call."

They crept along. Now that they'd slowed down, Khalid suddenly had time to realize what he was doing. Sneaking through some kind of combination of electricity plant and magical oil refinery. With all the cops in the world massing outside. And who knew how many security guards still lurked within, looking to help people trapped inside? What about magic protection gizmos? He imagined alchemy guns that could change him to a statue, voodoo electric eyes that would trip him up ten feet past where he'd walked through them.

He told Moira about Godfrey and Tommy and Dr. Bookman's theory as they went, resisting the urge to add a note of haughty self-satisfaction. They rounded a corner—slooooowly—and started making their way down another corridor.

"Are you sure this is the right way?" he asked.

"Yes," she said shortly. "Still here. Still okay. I thought we were in for some sort of massive explosion that was gonna rip holes in the universe."

"Don't be snotty," he said. "Dr. Bookman said there *might* be an explosion. And it's probably still to come."

Her hand went looser in his, but a moment later she squeezed tight. "You're right. I'm sorry. I'm angry. At this place. At Zak for kicking me out of the superway. Sacrificing himself. Either way, if he survived what we just heard, we have to help him. If you're right, he's doing it for nothing."

"Worse than nothing."

"Don't remind me."

Up ahead, a cloud of something filled the hallway, glimmering red in the half light. They stopped. "Can we go around?" Khalid asked.

Moira thought for a moment. "No. The secure part of the

facility is right through there. And we don't have time to go around another way."

So they dropped to their bellies and crawled through, sipping shallow breaths. The stuff in the air tasted like dust, and Khalid soon saw its source—a wall had crumbled off to their left when a ceiling beam crashed through it, and the air was filled with pulverized wallboard.

A small fire burned in the room visible through the hole. An overhead sprinkler rained down on it, containing but not quenching it.

Khalid's eyes stung as he and Moira crawled on. Next to him, she coughed a hard little cough every second or third breath, and Khalid's own throat burned. His eyes watered at the assault of the dust in the air.

They had to pick their way over some fallen chunks of ceiling and buckled sections of wall. The door at the end of the corridor was swathed in a thicker cloud of dust. Khalid took in a deep, gritty breath and risked standing up long enough to try the door. Nothing. Of course. They couldn't get that lucky, that someone would leave a security door open while fleeing. The doors probably locked automatically.

There was a curved black chunk of something plasticky jutting out of the wall next to the door. Khalid rubbed at his burning eyes and hoped his breath would hold out. He inspected what turned out to be a sort of hard plastic sleeve into which he could insert his hand and arm almost up to the elbow. He did so and felt something smooth, glassy, and spherical at the end. He grabbed it, squeezed it, tried rolling it between his fingers. Nothing. Some kind of identification system. Something that used alchemy or astrology or voodoo or Wicca combined with a computer, probably, to identify people. *Mirror, mirror, on the wall* for the digital age.

He dropped back down to his belly. Moira was coughing harder now.

"No way in," he said.

"Always a way," she said. "Back."

Before he could respond, she shimmied backward, rolled onto her side, then turned around and headed back the way they'd come.

Khalid cleared his throat and spit up something that glowed a rotten brown in the red light that filtered through the dust and smoke in the air. Then, of course, he followed her.

SIXTY-SIX

Zak. Zak, get up.

Get up, Zak!

Two voices, but one voice, but two voices. He heard the same voice, saying different things, and it was his own voice.

Behind it all, alarms.

Zak groaned and rolled over. His body ached as though he'd been stuffed into a trash can and sent careening down a steep hill. Every movement caused him pain. He tasted blood, and his face was wet with what he assumed to be more of it.

Get up! There's still time!

Zak! Zak, are you okay? Can you hear me?

Can you hear me?

He pushed himself up to his knees. The world tipped and swayed, just like on a boat, and for a moment he was back on the boat again, back where it all had started. An eighteenth-century ship from a different version of the eighteenth century. A scared boy from an island, making his way to America, caught in a storm, then plunged into another reality.

And then trapped underground. For so long. Alone. Alone
and lost. Dreaming only of himself.

Help me!

Help yourself!

You can do both, Zak! You can save everyone! Trust me!

SHUT UP, BOTH OF YOU! Zak bellowed in his mind, and was
somewhat surprised to find that it worked. The voices fell silent,
and he could think again.

All around him, the cabin of the superway was devastated.
The control board had cracked across its area, with only a single
flickering light remaining. Ironically, it flashed the word *SAFETY*
over and over.

Through the broken windshield, he spied the wall of the
tube, crushed and breached by the now-crumpled and dented
nose of the superway. Lights flickered sporadically in the tube
and in the distance, through the wall. Zak braced himself
between the chair and the control panel and levered himself to
a standing position. His head swam in a fog, and he held tight
to his anchors to keep from falling down.

He tested his legs. Nothing broken, it seemed. His body
ached, but the only sharp, insistent pains came from the multi-
tude of cuts along his body. Flying glass. Glass on the floor. He'd
been struck by it, had rolled in it. He was lucky not to be bleeding to death.

At least, he didn't *think* he was bleeding to death.

Get out of here. Got to get out of here.

His own voice, from his own mind; he was sure of it. And yet
it recalled to him those easier, more innocent days, when he'd
imagined a guardian angel watching over him. The good old

days, when he'd worried only about his sanity, not about spirits and universes and life and death.

Life was so much simpler when I was just crazy.

He dragged himself over the control panel and—carefully avoiding the jagged edges—through the gaping windshield. Pushing debris out of the way, he slid down the nose of the superway and onto the floor of the building. He was in a hallway that was lit only by the rotating red blare of emergency lights. Staggering, he leaned against a wall to rest for a moment.

Zak . . .

Shut up. Whoever you are.

You can still—

Don't listen to him!

Shut. Up!

Using the wall for support, Zak inched down the hall. A chunk of ceiling fell right in front of him, and in the blink of an eye, he saw Tommy standing before him, but then the image vanished.

Close. So close to death just then.

Up ahead, a sign that had once been mounted to the wall lay on the floor. There were arrows pointing in different directions. One said RECLAMATION. Another said RECHARGING. He didn't know which way the arrows were supposed to guide him, because he didn't know which wall the sign had fallen from.

Did it really matter, though? He just had to keep moving. Find help. Figure out the rest of it later.

This way, said the voice, and he blinked sweat out of his eyes, and a light appeared in the air, faint and glimmering for a moment before petering out.

Yes, said the voices.

They were in agreement. For the first time.

Zak followed the path of the light into the darkness.

He stumbled down the hall, stepping around fallen beams and collapsed chunks of ceiling. Through doors and holes in the walls around him, he saw other areas, some of them devastated from the impact of the superway, some of them burning. But he walked straight ahead to a large pocket door that had partly crumpled. It had no hinges, so he pushed it to one side, straining and grunting until he'd shoved it far enough into the wall that he could pass.

Beyond was a large chamber, two stories high. Balconies ran in a ring around the second story, some of them collapsed, some of them dangling overhead from their support structures. At the bottom, where he stood, he spied several desks clustered together, obviously workstations for the evacuated personnel. But the desks didn't interest him. He cared only for the large tanks and drums arranged around the room. The big tanks were bolted to the floor and had wide, thick hoses running in and out of them. The drums were mostly stacked in corners, though many of them had fallen over and rolled hither and yon. A series of Wonder Glass–looking computer terminals were wired together in the center of the room, most of them cracked or sparking with electricity.

One of the drums had split and spilled. A familiar, viscous ooze glowed there. Electroleum.

This is the place, Zak, Tommy or Godfrey said. *You can still use the electroleum to save us.*

Don't do it, said Godfrey or Tommy. *Rescue workers will come here first, to lock it down. Just sit down and wait. You'll be safe soon.*

Zak lurched over to the broken drum of electroleum. He spied another one just past it that had cracked as well; a glowing trickle spilled down one side.

This would do it, he realized. He could still salvage something from this debacle. He could dunk himself in a tank of the raw stuff and let it work its magic. Would that suffice? Is that all he had to do to bring Tommy back? Could it be that easy? No need to plow a train through the place and blow it up. Just . . . take a little dip in the electroleum pool.

Or maybe that would do nothing.

I don't know what to do.

He dropped to his knees before the puddle of electroleum. What should he do?

The two Tommys manifested then, one of them wavering and weaker than the other.

It's time, said the more stable one. *I'm so sorry it has to be this way, but it does. If there were another way, I'd tell you. I swear.*

Zak was exhausted. He wanted to lie down and sleep, but if he did that, he feared he would wake up and the opportunity would be gone. He would be in whatever passed for juvenile detention in this world, and he would spend the rest of his life haunted not just by his twin but also by the knowledge of what he hadn't done.

Don't do it, said the weaker one, fuzzing in and out of view as he spoke. *Just keep yourself safe.*

That's Godfrey speaking, said the strong one. *He knows there's a chance I'll be the only one to come through. Because of our twin connection. And that terrifies him. He's stalling until he can sever our connection.*

Zak laughed. Okay, fine. So neither of them made any sense. Whatever.

Zak, the weak one said, *it's simple: You know I'm your brother because I don't want you to die.*

SIXTY-SEVEN

Moira knew it was only a matter of time before they either suc-
cumbed to the junk in the air or wound up crushed under a
collapsing section of ceiling or stumbled upon by a rescue crew.
They had to move quickly.

She suspected something had gone wrong with Zak's plan.
The explosion that had rocked the building hadn't seemed like
a combustible explosion. It was more the impact of something
fast and solid—say, a superway train—colliding with something
strong and solid—say, a building. The electroleum hadn't been
detonated. Godfrey hadn't gotten his way yet.

Which meant there was a chance Zak was still alive.

Which further meant that he might be hurt somewhere in
the facility. Or—possibly worse—not hurt and trying to blow
the whole place up in some different way.

She didn't know anything about the chemical, physical,
alchemical, and magical properties of electroleum, but she knew
that the Dutchmen had seemed very confident that they could
turn the stuff into an explosive. If it was easy enough for those

dunderheads to do, then she figured Godfrey would have a pretty good shot at it, too.

They had to find Zak. Now.

Back in the corridor, she kept her eyes peeled for the wall that had crumbled—and a beam came falling through it. She jumped back, berating herself for her stupidity. That was the most significant damage they'd seen, so didn't it make sense that the point of impact was nearby?

She wiped dust from her glasses and could see well enough in the gloom to perceive the hole in the wall. The fire burning in there made it more obvious. She hauled herself to her feet. The cloud of dust—and now smoke—was filling more and more of the hallway. She tugged the neckline of her shirt up over her nose as a makeshift breathing mask. It was better than nothing. Barely.

Khalid stood up, too, and after a second's hesitation covered his face as she had done.

"In there?" he asked, pointing. "*Toward* the fire? Really?"

"Three Basketeers," she said, hoping he could tell by her eyes that she was smiling.

"I hate myself for coming up with that," he groaned, but followed her as she scaled a pile of wallboard and fallen ceiling joist into the next room.

SIXTY-EIGHT

Zak roared from the pit of his stomach as he pushed himself away from the electroleum and back on his feet. The stronger Tommy was shifting before his eyes, his colors bleeding and blending together, smearing into blue and red and gold.

And then, as the weaker Tommy faded from view entirely, Zak beheld only Godfrey.

This time, there was no crushing pain to distract him; he saw Godfrey clearly. He had long sandy-brown hair that was tied back in a ponytail, and he wore ragged blue pants, brown boots, a red kerchief tied around his forehead, and a loose, threadbare white shirt with a single brassy button among several dull brown ones.

And he was young. So young. Probably younger than Zak, something he'd never expected.

Just a kid. Still a kid. After all these centuries.

Do. It. Now, Godfrey said, and his eyes burned. They literally burned—tongues of flame licked out from them, and Zak took a step back for fear of being singed.

One of the control panels is still functional, Godfrey said. *You can overload the recharging mechanism and detonate the electroleum in the tanks. You'll finally get your wish, Zak: You won't be alone anymore. You'll be with Tommy. In the land of the dead. Where you both belong.*

Zak shook his head. "No," he said aloud. "Show me Tommy again. Let me see my brother."

Your brother is dead, Zak. He's been dead since his kidneys gave out at age two. I just found his spirit, lingering because of his connection to you. Good fortune on my part. Other spirits, they just vanish, depart, float away above the Secret Sea. But not Tommy. No. Pathetically clinging to the one thing he knew so well in the world: You. Trying to communicate. He would have moved on eventually, would have left the Secret Sea entirely, and all the physical universes. But I reinforced his connection. Kept him tethered to you. All so I could contact you. No one would help a random spirit lost in the world, but a twin . . . Oh, a twin would do anything to help his brother, wouldn't he?

So, really, you owe me, Zak. Because of me, you had your brother's voice in your ear for years. Now's the time to pay me back. Bring me back to life, Zak.

"But it might not work! And Khalid said it could end up killing people back in my world."

Do you think I care? Godfrey raged. *Your world killed me! We could have saved the boat over here, but when we crossed over, we ran aground and I died! Do you have any idea what I've been through? What I've suffered? Imagine being trapped. In the dark. Forever.*

You were a ghost. You could have just come up from underground.

I didn't know which way was up! Picture yourself underground, suspended in the utter dark. And gravity doesn't work on you because you have no mass. Any movement could be the wrong one. You could think you were going up but actually be going sideways. Or down. And you could end up drifting forever in the darkness, headed to the center of the earth.

That still doesn't—

And then, without warning, Zak was plunged into darkness. And silence. There was only the sound of his own breath, and then even that died away, leaving him floating, insensate, deaf, blind.

(I am in darkness.)

(Darkness and quiet.)

(For so long.)

Three. Hundred. Years! Godfrey's voice erupted in the core of Zak's being, like a flare lit in darkest night. And yet still there was no light.

For three hundred years I suffered! Buried underground! Unable to hear or see. A ghost, anchored to the place where I died. Until . . .

(And then there is light.)

(And then there is loud. . . .)

The destruction of the twin towers. Liberating Godfrey from his tomb, allowing him to surface . . .

Centuries of isolation! Only myself! And then, in a thunderclap, I was free! Free! I emerged from under the ground into chaos, into a hell of falling steel, a fog of concrete dust, dead bodies littering the very air. Souls in flight, thousands of them, vanishing into the afterlife.

And I could not join them! I was trapped in the physical world, still bound there. I passed into my own world, then back into yours, but no one could perceive me. I was no longer in the dark, but I was just as alone. No one could help me.

All those deaths—they destroyed me. Brought me over. Made me do this to myself. Unaging. Preserved forever. Trapped underground for centuries.

No, their deaths liberated *you. You cast the spell on yourself. You did that to yourself—they freed you. And look what you've done with your freedom!*

I want my life back! I deserve *it back! It was taken from me too early.*

The boat. The waves. I lived and relived those moments over and over, a thousand, a million times in the centuries before I found your brother. I did nothing wrong! I was a servant boy on a ship, and the ship ran aground through no fault of mine! Why should I suffer such hell?

My spell to save my life had permanently bound me to the living world, even though I was no longer corporeal. I was a living ghost, unable to fully die, unable to live.

Can you imagine the torment? No, Zak, you can't. You're swimming in the black quiet right now, but you have my voice. And you've been there for only a minute or two. You cannot possibly contemplate the torture, the agony, the sheer hell of three hundred years, trapped in the dark. Only to emerge into the world and find no help.

Until your brother. Until I found your brother and used him to bring you to my world, where things were different. Where wild science could provide a way back. A way out. It had to be you, Zak. No one else would do. I had to have a connection to the physical world and a way to force someone to do what I needed. Tommy was the only way to get both.

You're going to kill people! Zak exclaimed. *I know you want to come back to life, but you're going to kill so many people when the walls between our worlds break.*

Do you think I care? Do you think I care at all about your world? Your world killed me! Imprisoned me! I'll drown the whole place in the Secret Sea if I can! I'll flood every last acre of dry land and kill everyone on it if it means bringing me back to life. And even if it doesn't, I'll do it anyway! *My revenge!*

Revenge? Zak asked. *On who? No one did anything to you. It's all a bunch of mistakes and accidents. What's the point?*

My revenge on your whole world! Godfrey screamed. *Your world wrecked my ship; your world imprisoned me. If your world dies so I can live, so be it!*

It made sense and it made no sense. Zak didn't know how much of it was true and how much of it was Godfrey's speculation. Maybe Khalid's friend Dr. Bookman could parse it; Zak couldn't. One thing Zak knew for sure, though—there was no talking to Godfrey. No debating him. No persuading him. He'd been driven mad by his centuries of imprisonment, and nothing Zak could say or do would change his mind.

Tommy! Zak cried. *Tommy, help me!*

I dazzled you when you crossed over, pretending to be your dead twin, letting you think you'd seen Tommy. Your brother tried to get you to run away from the rift between worlds, tried to scare you away from the subway. I needed you to come over. For this. I couldn't wait any longer. I had to get aggressive in order to overcome your brother's meddling.

But Tommy can't help you. No one can help you. Khalid has left you. Moira is powerless in this world. I'm possessing you, Zak. Like I did to that doctor. He forced me to, but the best part is that you just invited me in. Through your connection to your brother. I've been using it to communicate with you, and now I'm just pouring myself into you like water.

Downloading like a virus . . .

Zak screamed again and his eyes opened and he was standing elsewhere in the room, before a glass screen. His body was stiff and he could not move.

As he watched, his own hand—trembling and slow—raised from his side and moved toward the screen. Controls blinked there. The electroleum controls.

He's in me. He's using me.

Go away, Zak! Godfrey chortled. *Back to the dark!*

And then Zak was in the pitch black again, lost in the space under the World Trade Center. Or at least Godfrey's memory of it.

How long was he there? He didn't know. Couldn't tell. He tried counting, but the darkness seemed to swallow his thoughts.

After three *days* of this, he would go insane. Never mind three centuries.

Panic burned through him. Would he be lost like this forever? When Godfrey blew up the electroleum facility, would Zak's body be destroyed, his soul forever consigned to this place, this memory, this nothing?

That's not going to happen.

Sound? Here? In the deadly silent?

And then, out of the endless black murk . . .

A touch.

———————

Zak couldn't understand where the touch came from or how he felt it. He had no body—he was an incorporeal spirit lost in a wash of infinite darkness. But he suddenly had a hand, and that hand touched another hand, the fingertips brushing against each other. It felt like touching a mirror—cool, smooth glass with the character of flesh and bone.

. . . zak . . .

So weak. The voice was so weak. Or maybe it was Zak who was too weak to hear. But he clung to Tommy's voice, like a rope thrown into quicksand, and he walked his fingers up Tommy's until their palms crossed and they gripped each other's wrists.

How many years? How many years since he'd touched his twin? Tears came to Zak's nonexistent eyes, and he focused on them, made them real.

He opened his eyes. He was at the control panel still, his fingers moving of their own accord along the surface.

Get back where you belong! Godfrey howled.

No!

And then, an echo: *. . . no . . . !*

Zak could see both his hands on the panel, moving under Godfrey's control. At the same time, he could feel Tommy's grip on his wrist, somewhere back in the deep black.

The two of you combined are still weaker than I am.

As Zak watched, his hands swiped and jabbed at the controls. A warning klaxon—a new one—sounded once, loudly, blasting like a foghorn with a bad attitude. And then, entirely unbidden, Zak's head swiveled to the left, and he could only watch as one of the conduits into a tank decoupled itself. With a hiss and a mechanical whine, it retracted several inches.

Pure, raw electroleum spilled out of the tank, glowing with hot intensity.

Another conduit disconnected, this one higher up. More electroleum flowed down the side of the tank, pooling and spreading on the floor. Zak felt his lips turn up in a grin.

. . . now zak together . . .

Zak sank briefly back into the black. He and Tommy had both hands clasped together now. He still could not see, but out in the dark he heard his twin's breath and—he imagined, or maybe not—his heartbeat.

Tommy's strong heart. Zak's repaired heart. They beat together in syncopation.

. . . *push!*

Zak grunted and *shoved* as hard he could, tightening his grip on Tommy, pushing with all his might and—

—Godfrey shouted in surprise

—Zak stumbled forward, out of the dark, back to the world

—Tommy cried out

—Godfrey

The air before Zak smeared blue and gold and red. He felt a long, tight, taut string stretched out from his chest, vibrating and pulling at his heart. Godfrey was expelled from him but still clinging to him.

"Get! Out! Of! Me!" Zak yelled. With each word, he felt— heard—an echo from Tommy.

And then, in a rush, the string snapped, and Godfrey hovered in the air before Zak, eyes still ablaze, and Zak—suddenly in control of his body again—stumbled backward and slipped and fell.

Into the widening pool of raw electroleum.

SIXTY-NINE

Khalid and Moira found themselves in a lab or a medical suite of some sort. There were wheeled cots and glass display cases that stood fissured or shattered against the walls. The fire burned in a puddle on the floor. A single sprinkler overhead sputtered and spit at it. Khalid scanned the ceiling and saw why the other sprinklers had failed—the collapsing ceiling joist had severed the pipe in two places, cutting off most of the water supply.

"Look," Moira said in a hushed whisper, pointing at the puddle.

"I've seen fire before."

"No. Look. It's electroleum."

Khalid squinted. Sure enough, the puddle had that familiar viscous ooze. There was another puddle merging with it, something from a broken bottle that lay nearby.

"The stuff doesn't burn on its own." Moira sounded satisfied and relieved at the same time. "Which is good. You have to combine it with something. I bet depending on what you add to it, it burns or explodes or—"

"I love a good science lesson as much as the next guy," Khalid lied, "but maybe we should find Zak?"

Moira shook herself as if waking up. "Right. Over there."

He followed where she was pointing. There was no way out of this room but the hole they'd come through, a door that went right back out into the corridor. . . .

And a hole in the ceiling. Of course. From the collapse.

They maneuvered two cots into position and chocked them with chunks of wall, then climbed up. Khalid went first, then reached down to haul Moira up.

It was darker and smokier up here, with fewer emergency lights. But they didn't need lights—a glow up ahead practically burned through the billowing clouds. They crawled along carefully, wary of more holes in the floor.

"We have to get to where the secure area is soon, right?" he asked Moira.

She was coughing again. Man, the air itself was charred in here! She shook her head and coughed and pointed.

Where the glow emanated, a wall teetered on the brink of collapse. Just before the wall was a massive tear in the floor, a ragged ring that stretched as far as they could see. Down below, a fire burned and crackled, along with the now-accustomed pale glow of electroleum. Khalid wriggled to the lip of the tear. The floor juddered beneath him, threatening to cave in. He froze, then felt Moira's hands on his ankles. He looked over his shoulder. She was sitting up on a more secure part of the floor, clutching him tightly. "Go." She jerked her head forward.

Khalid inched forward carefully. Moira could hold on as much as she wanted, but if the floor collapsed, his weight would drag them both down.

Peering into the hole in the floor, he could see under the wall ahead. There was a fire down there, and a wide, open expanse of floor. Rubble. A series of drums knocked akilter.

And Zak.

Zak was down there.

And he was *glowing.* . . .

SEVENTY

Zak tried to stand up, but the electroleum clung to him and made him slippery. He slipped and fell again, the stuff coating him, glowing. It smelled like ozone and burning metal and too-sweet sugar.

Around him, a wind began to whine in the room, gusting and blowing. The wind was gold and blue and red, and it was Godfrey, a banshee, a poltergeist. Maybe it was all the raw electroleum nearby. Maybe it was his anger. Maybe it was both. Whatever it was, Godfrey was beginning to affect the physical world. Zak held up his arms as papers and pens and other implements from the desks scattered around him got caught up in the wind and began to fly at him.

I can't touch you, but I can move the air! Godfrey crowed. *I can manipulate the physical world now, and you can't stop me!*

A fusillade of pens, pencils, and other debris came at Zak. He curled into a ball on the floor, covering his face with his forearms. Something stabbed into his thigh and stuck there. Something else raked at the back of his hands, drawing blood.

He bit back screams as his body was assaulted over and over, pelted from all sides as the wind spun and howled. Somewhere in there was the gruesome and demented laughter of the boy who'd been dead for so long.

And also—

Zak!

Tommy? Is that you? You sound so strong.

I think it's the electroleum. It's raw and pure. It's acting like a conductor, making it easier for me to talk to you.

A pen glanced off Zak's elbow and bounced away, but he was captivated by the sight before his eyes—his arm. And hand. They were doubled, one offset ever so slightly from the other, the way something looks when you stare at it until your eyes lose focus. But his eyes were focused perfectly.

That's you! I can see you!

I know! I think we—

Zak didn't let him finish. He clenched his hand into a fist; Tommy's hand did the same.

Zak stood, batting a spinning protractor out of the air as he rose, ignoring the bite of its sharp corner into the side of his hand. "Hey, Godfrey! How about a fair fight?"

SEVENTY-ONE

"What's going on down there?"

"They're fighting."

"Yeah, but..."

Moira shushed Khalid, rapt by the spectacle below her. She had come up even with Khalid, the rickety floor notwithstanding. She had to see this for herself.

Godfrey was a swift, half-melted figure painted on the air, his limbs fading and reappearing at whim as he juked and ducked and bobbed and weaved. That was fantastic enough.

But even more amazing was *Zak*.

Lit by the glow of electroleum, Zak went toe-to-toe with Godfrey, somehow managing to land punches. It should have been impossible—Godfrey was a ghost, a piece of the spiritual plane. He should have been untouchable. But Zak was able to touch him. Even as she watched, Zak swung his right fist, catching Godfrey under his chin. The ghost vibrated and shimmered in the air for a moment, reeling backward.

The electroleum. It had to be the electroleum somehow.

Or . . . no! No, it wasn't. Not entirely, at least. As she watched, she noticed that—

"It's like there's two of him," Khalid breathed.

Sure enough, when she focused beyond the glow of electroleum and on Zak himself, she noticed a sort of afterimage, a second, translucent version of Zak superimposed onto her friend. That image, she realized, was what was making contact with Godfrey. Zak wasn't punching the ghost—his twin was.

"This is amazing." Her breath caught as Godfrey kicked up another howling wind. Zak dived behind an overturned desk for shelter.

"Does the electroleum act as a spiritual conductor?" she wondered aloud. "You said Bookman told you it had a spiritual component to it. . . . I wonder if it's somehow psychoreactive."

"Psycho-who?"

"Like, it reacts to emotions or thoughts or—"

"Oh yeah—Dr. Bookman said something like that."

"*Now* you tell me?"

Khalid snorted. "You never asked! You want to analyze it? Maybe later. Right now we should get down there and help Zak. At the very least, we should stop all that junk from leaking out of the tanks. If Godfrey made that happen, it can't be good."

Moira blushed. She'd been so caught up in the magic and science of the fight that she hadn't even thought of that. "Yeah, let's do it."

The balcony below them was none too stable. Khalid insisted on going first, which annoyed Moira.

"Do you really want to be the one to die if it collapses? Will that make you feel empowered?"

She hesitated.

"It makes sense for me to go," he told her. "I'm heavier, so if it holds me, we know it'll hold you."

Even Moira couldn't assail that logic, so she helped Khalid lower himself to the balcony. Clinging to a precarious piece of torn-up floor, he dangled there for a moment, then—with something muttered in Farsi that could have been a prayer or a curse—dropped.

The balcony creaked and groaned and swung to one side . . . but held. Khalid raised a hand to keep Moira from joining him, then—as she watched—jumped from that balcony to the one next to it, landing with a crash that nearly collapsed the second balcony.

Moira's heart stopped dead for a full two seconds, and her vision blurred. Oh. My. God. That had been the most reckless, stupidest, most dangerous thing she'd ever—

Khalid gave her a thumbs-up from his new vantage point, and Moira wanted to strangle him and kiss him at the same time.

She lowered herself to the first balcony.

Below, Zak was moving from desk to drum to counter to drum again, dodging Godfrey's wind and its missiles. He was clearly flagging, and the electroleum near Godfrey was beginning to bubble and darken.

Psychoreactive, she thought. *This is how Godfrey will win. He's pure spirit. When he was summoned by Dr. Bookman, his rage and hate triggered the tiny bit of electroleum Bookman had.*

"*It just absorbs and reflects energy, chap,*" Jan had said at the Dutchmen's hideout.

Godfrey's surrounded by it. How are we supposed to fight that? And Zak's steeped in the stuff—what's that going to do to him?

She looked over at Khalid. He'd already moved to another balcony, this one so crumpled that nearly half of it spilled into the room below. He was scaling his way down, chunks of flooring crumbling around him as he went. But he did not slow down. Moira had to admit that his bravery—even if it grew out of cluelessness—was impressive.

She borrowed a little of his impetuousness and jumped to the second balcony. It shook and complained with a steely series of squeaks, but it held.

All right! Not bad!

Then she scrambled to catch up. And move down.

SEVENTY-TWO

Zak's breath burned in his lungs and throat; he longed to stay still, to catch his breath, but he couldn't afford to stop moving. Godfrey couldn't touch the real world, but he was doing something to the air, like ghosts in bad horror movies. Moira could have explained it, but Zak couldn't.

Watch out! Tommy cried, and Zak ducked just in time to avoid a heavy stapler winging toward him.

Thanks. It was like having a second set of eyes. Or maybe a guardian angel. Zak and Tommy were connected now, united by the electroleum, tied together as tightly as they'd been in the womb. If Zak had had a moment to spare, he would have luxuriated in the sensation.

But overhead, a light fixture—penduluming in the fierce Godfrey-conjured wind—had broken loose and now rained down on him in a shower of sparks, shards of metal, and glops of electroleum. Zak ran, flung himself on the ground chest-first, and slid along the floor until he was under a table.

"You can't avoid me forever!"

Zak didn't know if it was the electroleum, his connection to Tommy, or Godfrey's growing power, but he could hear the ghost in the world now, not just in his head. His voice was incongruously young, not yet broken and deepened. It was the voice of a frightened child.

A frightened child with powers Zak could only dimly understand.

He rolled out from under the table and sprang to his feet. Godfrey hovered over the scene, just out of reach. Zak had managed to get a few punches in before Godfrey came to understand that one ghost could hit another. But Tommy's power came from Zak, and he couldn't leave Zak's body to chase Godfrey. They were stalemated for now, but Godfrey would eventually pin him down with something in the room. And if the state of the electroleum—thickly boiling and popping on the floor, blackening—was any indication, this fight would be over soon enough. Zak didn't understand how the stuff worked, but it was clearly reacting to *something* in the air. How long until it just blew up . . . with all the consequences that explosion would entail?

No way. Not gonna let that happen. You with me, Tommy?

Right with you.

Zak hopped up on the table and took a running start along its length, then jumped. Maybe it was the electroleum; maybe it was desperation. But his jump was longer and higher than any he'd ever attempted before, high enough that Godfrey loomed before him.

Zak lashed out with his fists. He felt the contact of the blows through his connection to Tommy. It was like tapping on flesh that had gone numb, a pins-and-needles sensation along his knuckles. And then his momentum carried him through

Godfrey, and he pinwheeled his arms madly as he crashed into the floor.

Godfrey, reeling from the punches, had sunk closer to the floor. Zak groaned and tried to stand up, but his breath, already so tenuous, had fled him when he'd landed. He lay on the floor, gasping.

Get up! He couldn't tell if it was his own voice or Tommy's. *Get up and get him! Now!*

I can't. I can't stand.

"Need a hand?" asked Khalid from nowhere, and Zak felt hands under his arms, lifting him.

SEVENTY-THREE

Khalid grunted and heaved Zak to his feet. "No rest for the weary, man. You're the only one who can lay a hand on this doofus."

Zak grinned up at him. "You were right. I was—"

"Later." He shoved Zak toward Godfrey.

Moira caught up to Khalid just then. They watched for a moment as Zak tackled Godfrey, the air around them blurring like oil smeared on glass. Zak's fists moved, followed a half second later by Tommy's ghost fists.

"Khalid, look at this." Moira tugged his sleeve.

Leave it to Moira to be present for a ghost fight and find something else more interesting. Khalid followed her direction and noticed something odd: The electroleum along the floor had been turning black, but where Moira and Khalid had walked through it, their footprints now burned bright yellow.

"That's kinda—"

Zak groaned in pain and stumbled backward toward them. Khalid caught him before he could fall.

Above them, Godfrey soared beyond reach. The wind, which

had died down during the phantom fisticuffs, began to rise again.

"You ready for round two?" Khalid asked.

"More like round twenty." Zak's speech was slightly slurred. He'd really taken a beating. Khalid hated to throw his friend back into the fight, but there was no other option.

"Hey, guys," Moira said. "Do you realize you're both glowing now?"

Khalid looked down. It was true; they were.

The wind began to howl. Khalid shut his eyes as debris and dust flew at him.

"I have an idea!" Moira yelled.

It was the footprints that made her realize what they had to do, combined with the hot glow around her two best friends.

Electroleum was wild science, which meant it had a psychic or magical component. Or at least, a component that in *her* world would seem magical. She couldn't really comprehend that, but she could understand the evidence of her eyes. Wild or true, that *was* science.

Zak was covered in electroleum, and it had allowed him to host Tommy in some way she couldn't begin to comprehend. Their twin connection, a rare form of magic in and of itself, exploited the power of the electroleum.

But now Khalid was glowing, too, just from contact with Zak. And their footprints . . .

Godfrey's rage had been corrupting the electroleum all around them, blackening, heating it. When she and Khalid walked through it, though, their impressions reverted it to its normal state.

The stuff is *psychoreactive. It picks up on rage or love or hate or whatever.*

There was no time to explain. Above, Godfrey chortled as the winds gathered. She planted her feet firmly in a widening pool of electroleum and reached out to Khalid.

Khalid raised an eyebrow at Moira but did not say a word. Keeping one hand on Zak, he reached out with the other, stretching as far as he could until he took Moira's hand.

And a jolt—

SEVENTY-FOUR

Zak seized as a jolt of power shot through him. He felt his brother seize as well, the two of them stiffening and freezing at once, Zak's hand tightening painfully on Khalid's.

From somewhere a million miles away, Moira shouted, "Three Basketeers!"

"Three Basketeers!" Khalid whooped.

Zak shook his head. No. "Four Basketeers!" he cried, feeling his brother squirming deep inside.

And then . . .

And then Zak *was* Tommy.

They'd merged. Zak still had his own thoughts, but they jostled for space side by side with his twin's, coexistent with them.

oh*gotta*wow*stop*this*himisbefore*so*he*weird*blows*but*it*cool*up*

zak*tommy*we're*can*in*you*this*heart*together*me

i*think*i*know*what*to*do

*get*him!

And then Zak was in two places at once. He could still feel his hand gripping Khalid's, could still feel the floor beneath his feet.

But he was also in the air. He was Zak and he was Tommy; he was both; he was flying.

He glided up, up, up until he was even with Godfrey, whose eyes widened in terror at the sight of him.

"What are you doing? How are you doing this? This is impossible! You can't do this!"

He ignored Godfrey's panicked babble. Zak was mainlining the power of the electroleum. It should have been impossible. As a spirit, he couldn't touch the stuff directly, couldn't absorb its physical power in addition to its psychic power.

But he wasn't just a spirit. He was tethered along the twin connection to his own physical body, to Khalid, to Moira.

"I can do anything," he said quietly.

And lunged at Godfrey, who screamed in terror for the first time in more than three hundred years.

SEVENTY-FIVE

Khalid squeezed his eyes shut. The wind was ferocious, hammering him, filling his ears with its grotesque song.

He held tight to the hands in his own. "What's happening?" he yelled to Moira.

"I don't know!" she yelled back. "My eyes are closed!"

———

Moira doubled over, clenching Khalid's hand with both of hers now, as the wind built to what she knew would be a devastating crescendo. The gale mounted higher and stronger, and eventually it would rip her right away from Khalid. And he was worried about what she could *see*?

"My eyes are closed!" she yelled.

"Mine too!" came back.

"Well, open yours!"

"You first!"

Not a chance. No way.

Zak hadn't joined in with them. Either he couldn't hear them or—

No. He's doing something. I know he is. I can feel it.

SEVENTY-SIX

Below Zak, the electroleum on the floor, the torrents of the stuff spilling out of the tanks . . . It had all paled to a hot, intense white, a glow brighter than any Zak had ever seen. His body was still down there, still chained by touch to Khalid and Moira. He could hear them shouting to each other, like the sound of a train whistle far off down a tunnel. But he could not spare the attention to listen to them. He was too busy.

Too busy pummeling Godfrey.

He couldn't believe how good it felt! All the frustration and anger, all the loneliness and rage, the disappointment in his parents, the fear of this new world—it all funneled down into his/Tommy's fists as he/they struck Godfrey again and again and again.

Godfrey flung his arms up before his face, trying to ward off the blows. But Zak/Tommy was/were twice as fast, twice as precise, landing blow after blow after blow, forcing Godfrey farther and farther back.

On the floor, the glow of the electroleum began to rise, drifting up like a cool lake's steam on a sweltering early morning.

Zak could see nothing now, nothing but Godfrey before him, his face twisted into sheer terror as the glow ascended and then—as Zak watched—wrapped tendrils of pure light around him.

"No!" Godfrey screamed. "No!"

And for the first time, Zak felt a swell of overwhelming pity for Godfrey.

Godfrey was scared. Godfrey had *always* been scared, Zak realized. Scared of the bigger, more powerful men who controlled his life on the ship. Scared of the storm. Of climbing the rope ladder. Of the sudden juddering halt of the ship. And, yes, scared of dying, so scared of death that he consigned himself to an infinitely worse fate, a liminal half-life that drove him to do anything—*anything*—to return to life.

You were willing to do the same, Tommy whispered. *You were willing to kill yourself and maybe many, many others. For me.*

"Help me!" Godfrey screeched, his voice gone high and tremulous. "Please! For the love of God! In the name of all that's holy!"

But I was doing it out of love, Zak told his brother. *Not fear.*

Does it really matter?

And in an instant, he decided: It didn't. Done for love or done for fear, what Godfrey planned and what Zak had almost done were the same. Their motivations didn't matter. Zak had almost become as bad as Godfrey, thinking the whole time that he was doing the right thing.

"I forgive you!" he shouted, and reached out to take Godfrey's hand. The unholy dread etched into his foe's expression and threaded through his voice was more than enough. Godfrey had contemplated something horrible, planned something monstrous, but the agony riddling him now . . . No one deserved that.

But the heat of the glow forced back his own ghostly hand

before he could clutch Godfrey's and yank him free. And then, as Zak watched, the light pecled Godfrey like a half-molted snake, sloughing off sheets of him as though he were caught naked in a sandstorm.

Godfrey's mouth stretched wide, wider than a human mouth should be able to stretch, and Zak could not look away, staring in horrified fascination, steeling himself for the final scream.

A scream that never came.

The light swallowed what was left of Godfrey without a sound, and then everything went black.

Through the blackness, Zak discerned a wave of light coming toward him, flashing multicolored and kaleidoscopic. Tommy was suddenly before him, drifting and whole.

"We did it," he said, and Zak wept at the sound of his twin's voice.

He extended his hand. "Come on. Come with me."

Tommy shook his head. Zak's hand passed through him.

Which one of us is the ghost now?

"I can't," Tommy said. "It doesn't work that way."

"But why not?" Zak whined. "After everything we went through—"

"After everything we went through," Tommy said, "I'm still dead. That's forever."

"But it isn't. Dr. Bookman's cockroaches—"

"—prove nothing. Do you really think it's the same thing, animating a bug and reviving a person? I died, Zak. Years ago. And you don't get to turn that back. No one does. Not Godfrey. Not me. Not you."

"After all this?" Zak's incredulity was a living thing, and it squirmed and wailed on its way out of him. "I go through all this and I can't have you back?"

"Tell Mom and Dad I love them," Tommy said. "And don't be too hard on them. You forgave Godfrey; you can forgive them."

"I don't want to."

"I know. It's easier to be angry. Do the hard part, Zak. I was there, always. Against the ceiling, along the sky. On the ground. In the air you breathed. I saw them when you didn't, when you couldn't. They were trying their best for you."

"But, Tommy—"

"The Secret Sea is the sum total of everything that lives. I don't belong there anymore. Good-bye, Zak. I love you, brother. And I'm glad I got to know you."

"But—"

"I'm going to miss you," Tommy said, tears clustering and dropping. "I'm going to miss you like that dish you forgot to go back for, the one that would be perfect for guests right now."

Zak wept, his arms outstretched. "We don't have to let it happen! You can come to me! Come to me, Tommy! Come to me!"

And the light consumed Tommy from behind, first reducing him to shadow, then burning him away, burning him through a million pinpoint holes that merged into a single Tommy-shaped outline for an instant before vanishing into the eternal glow.

Zak screamed until he could hear himself no more, screamed until his voice bled itself to death. Even with his eyes shut, he could still see the light, pulsating through his eyelids in a red-white rhythm, a discolored chiaroscuro. The light crashed into him, and the light was water, a tidal wave of it, a tsunami, a monsoon, smashing against him like the fist of God.

SEVENTY-SEVEN

And Zak was in the water and then he soared above it, rising into a dead black sky. Below him was the ocean.

No, not the ocean. The sea. The Secret Sea.

He was above it. In what Tommy had called the no-space. The place near death.

The whole of creation spiraled and spun and thrashed below him. In an instant, Zak saw and comprehended the entirety of it, the crash and wave of the quantum foam, the mingling of realities, possibilities, potentialities. It was an infinite wellspring, the beginning and the end, the alpha and the omega. It was that which preceded the alpha and succeeded the omega.

TOMMY! he screamed into the nothingness.

He looked up—there was only darkness.

He looked down—the world and the worlds spun in eddies beneath him, here swallowed, there revealed by the roaring waves of the Secret Sea. It was vaster than anything he could imagine. The universe was a pinprick within it, tossed and lost on the foam.

He looked all around—the empty blank of the no-space, the limbo between the life of the Secret Sea and the release of death.

He had nothing left in him. No screams, no cries. He hung in the non-air, suspended, watching the play of universes.

This was the Secret Sea, a secret witnessed by Godfrey and maybe by Tommy. And now by Zak. He wondered if to espy this, to perceive the true nature of reality, was to die, like the others. His parents had never forced religion on him, but La-La had told him stories from the Bible, and he thought now of Adam and Eve, of how their sin had been to eat from the tree of knowledge. Their sin had been to *know*, and now Zak knew something no one else knew.

He knew the shape of God. He knew the curve of the unending universe, its warp and its weft.

He cried, his saltwater tears running down his cheeks and then dropping off his jaw to plummet an infinity below into the brine of creation.

And then he dropped down
down
down

SEVENTY-EIGHT

down

    down

        down

           down

SEVENTY-NINE

ever down

until

EIGHTY

IMPACT

EIGHTY-ONE

The shock of water erupted from nowhere and forced Moira's eyes open. She still clung to Khalid's hand with both of her own. Where had all this water come from?

Walls breached in the facility. Zak did something or Godfrey did something or something else caught fire and blew up and now we're drowning.

The water was dirty, briny, and she could barely make out Khalid, reaching for her with his other hand.

His free hand.

The one that had been holding Zak.

EIGHTY-TWO

Khalid didn't know where the water had come from. And, truthfully, he was damn sick and tired of being dunked without warning.

He knew only that he was still connected to Moira.

He knew only that Zak's hand had vanished from his own with the impact of the water.

And that he would drown soon. He knew that, too.

EIGHTY-THREE

Moira thrashed against the current. The water raged all around her, knocking her away from Khalid as she released him. She needed both hands to swim.

But which direction to swim? The murky water made any sort of reckoning almost impossible. She'd been knocked off-balance, and the fluid buoyancy made it difficult to tell which way was up.

Then she felt a current pass her and a hand brush against her. Khalid. He was swimming past her, headed toward something. She didn't know what, but she was almost out of air.

Her glasses had been blasted off her face by the force of the water. She could barely make out his shape through the murk.

It was difficult to move in her waterlogged coverall, but— kicking her feet—she followed him.

EIGHTY-FOUR

Khalid was a middling swimmer. It was probably fair to say he excelled at not drowning, more than to say he was a good swimmer. But right now, *not drowning* sounded pretty good.

Zak was gone. One minute, he'd been there, the next ...

The water shoved at Khalid, commanding his attention. He thought it seemed lighter off to one side. He karate-chopped the water furiously and kicked his feet, propelling himself in that direction.

EIGHTY-FIVE

Moira touched concrete just as Khalid caught up to her. She was faster in the water, and he'd fallen behind. She pressed her palms against the wall and shoved herself in the direction she now knew to be straight up. Khalid followed right behind, breaking the surface of the water an instant after her.

The first thing Moira noticed—other than Khalid's enormous inhaled breath at her side—was the screaming. Lit by flickering lights, people were yelling and crying out. Then came the sound of feet pounding on pavement.

It took her a few seconds to become acclimated to what she was seeing. She was floating in a filthy body of water just off of a concrete platform. The platform was in a tunnel, and people on it ran toward a flight of stairs. Disoriented, Moira blinked grungy water out of her eyes, trying to clear her vision. Without her glasses, everything blurred and smeared and collided into a chaos of indistinct shapes and shadows.

And then someone—a woman—shouted, "Wait! There are kids in there!"

Moira grabbed onto the platform as the current buffeted her. Khalid missed it, slipped past her, then grabbed hold on the other side. Trying to hoist herself out of the water, which rose rapidly to spill onto the platform, Moira suddenly realized that hands were on her, arms straining to pull her out. To her left, Khalid was being helped, too.

After being hauled onto the platform, Moira allowed herself a moment to catch her breath as the water lapped around her.

"You have to get up and run, honey!" the woman shouted, pulling at her.

Moira allowed herself to be tugged onto her feet. On the way up, she couldn't help looking at the woman's legs. They were close enough to snap into focus.

Moira laughed what must have seemed an insane laugh.

The woman was wearing *shorts*.

EIGHTY-SIX

Khalid heard Moira's laugh and shook his head fiercely, throwing off droplets. "Zak," he rasped. "Zak!"

Nothing. The sound of panicked feet. Cries of alarm.

Water, rushing.

"Zak!"

Down on all fours on the concrete, Khalid looked right and left. Where was Zak? What had happened to him? Khalid had managed to hold on to Moira, but he'd lost Zak. Somehow, he'd lost Zak.

As his vision cleared, he could read a sign above him:

EXIT TO
WORLD TRADE CENTER
& 9/11 MEMORIAL

With an arrow pointing toward the stairs. And a familiar capital *E* in a blue circle. For the E subway line.

"What the—"

"Come on, man." The guy who'd helped him out of the water hoisted him to his feet and shoved him forward. "Water's still rising. Gotta get out of here. Now!"

Khalid coughed up some salty water. Moira was being led away toward the stairs by a woman. Other people were crushing their way up and out.

He turned. The subway platform was flooding rapidly as the water filling the tunnel rose higher. Just like Zak's vision way back—

"Come on!" the man yelled, pushing him again. "Move it, kid!"

Khalid broke away from him and ran toward the track. "Zak!" he screamed. "Zak! Where are you?"

The water roared and spumed a sick greenish white, like grassy foam on a dog's lips. Darkness whirled in its depths, but nothing that looked human.

"Zak!" he cried again. "Zak!"

It couldn't be. They couldn't be here, *home*, without him. Not after everything they'd gone through. It wasn't right. It wasn't supposed to work like that. Moira could have said it better, but even Khalid knew: In a story, when the good guys win, they get to go home. All of them.

If I hadn't let go . . . I shouldn't have let him go. I should have held his hand tighter.

"Zak!" Khalid's throat burned; he coughed up more salt water, and then the man who'd hauled him from the water grabbed him bodily from behind, lifting him off his feet. "Come on, kid! We can't mess around!"

"No! No!" Khalid kicked and struggled against the man's too-strong arms. "No! My friend is in there!"

"No one's in there, kid!" Moving toward the stairs.

"We have to save him! He's in there! He's in there somewhere!"

Implacably, resolutely, the man slogged through the rising water to the stairs.

"Let me go! Let me go!" Khalid started sobbing. He beat his fists against his rescuer's back, but the man was solidly built and did not stagger or slow. "Let me go! You don't understand!"

"I understand we're both gonna drown if I don't get us out of here!"

"But I let go of him!" He had to make the man understand. "I was holding his hand and I let go! I have to find him! Please let me find him!"

But the man bore him relentlessly to the stairs as Khalid screamed "Zak!" over and over until his throat felt as if it had ripped in two.

EIGHTY-SEVEN

Outside, Moira blinked against the harsh sunlight. She smelled car exhaust for the first time in two days, realizing only now that she'd missed the familiar stench while in the other New York.

Above her, the Freedom Tower soared, a needle against the sky.

She broke away from her rescuer, who rushed over to a man—husband? boyfriend? brother?—and hugged him tightly. All around her a mob was milling about, people rushing into the street to get away from the subway, cabs honking their horns. All the delirious, delicious chaos of home.

And not a *frau* to be seen.

Moira climbed onto the hood of a parked car, her body exhausted, her mind whirling. Something in the electroleum ... There had been a chance it would rip a hole between realities, and now it had. Their best efforts to the contrary, they'd torn through one of the walls separating worlds. On one side, the World Trade Center subway stop in lower Manhattan. On the other side ...

The Houston Conflux and untold millions of gallons of water, now pouring in.

Who knew how long it would last? Was the rip permanent? The electroleum *could* have caused something so much worse. Why did ...

But she knew. Deep down, she knew.

Psychoreactive. The electroleum picked up on their emotions.

And it took them home.

Them. It was no good to come home if her friends drowned. She cupped her hands over her mouth and shouted, "Khalid! Zak!"

She peered around, shading her eyes. Nothing. Cupped her hands again. Shouted for them again.

Still nothing.

Then she saw a man emerge from the subway, carrying a very still, soaked form that looked familiar. She leaped off the hood of the car, scattering fleeing commuters, and bulled her way through the crowd. The man took a few more steps and then, exhausted, set his burden down on a low concrete parapet.

Before Moira could speak, before she could even think, Khalid charged up the steps, right behind the man. "Is he okay?" he asked. "Is he okay?"

Zak lay on the parapet, frighteningly still.

"Damnedest thing ever," the man said, catching his breath. He gestured to Khalid. "This one just kept fighting me. And thank God, because if he hadn't made me go back, this one ..." He looked down at Zak and shook his head. "Never would have seen him on my own."

Sirens wailed. Police and fire vehicles and ambulances

clotted the street as the crowd, still in a panic, thinned, spilling away from the tower and up along Fulton and Church Streets. Khalid and Moira took each other's hands and stood over Zak.

Who groaned.

And turned.

And vomited a truly epic amount of seawater.

"Gross," said the man who'd rescued Khalid and Zak.

"That," Khalid said with authority, "is the most awesome, best puke I've ever seen."

Moira couldn't help but agree.

EIGHTY-EIGHT

The Shamoons, the O'Gradys, and Zak's parents found them at a hastily erected aid station two blocks from the Freedom Tower, with at least a hundred other refugees of the subway station.

Zak's mother threw her arms around him and sobbed right in his ear. His dad crouched down next to them and grasped one of Zak's hands in both of his, squeezing too hard. Zak didn't have the energy to tell him to let go, especially when he saw the tears in his father's eyes. He didn't think he'd ever seen Dad cry before. But of course, Dad had.

Everyone cried.

Dad had probably cried when Tommy died.

And the thought of it made Zak break down, and he convulsed with sobs against his mother, like a baby, and for a little while, at least, he was just a kid again, just their child, and he was glad to be home.

EIGHTY-NINE

Eventually the water stopped, but not before completely flooding the World Trade Center subway station and more than a mile of track and tunnel in multiple directions. According to the news, the MTA believed some kind of leak was responsible for the sudden onrush of water. It would take weeks to pump out the area, and then the search for the rupture would begin.

Zak knew they would never find the leak. Because it wasn't there.

At least, it wasn't rooted in concrete or steel or earth. Moira and Khalid had cobbled together a theory, based on what Dr. Bookman had said: The leak was in the fabric of reality, where they had used the power of the electroleum to tear through from one world to another, at the spot Godfrey had weakened. And now, thankfully, it had closed, the universe healing itself.

"Universes aren't supposed to interact like that," Moira said. "It's finding its balance, repairing itself."

"We got lucky," said Khalid.

"I don't think so," Moira replied, and Zak agreed. If he hadn't chosen to forgive Godfrey, if he'd combined his anger at Godfrey with Godfrey's fear and rage ... who knew how the electroleum might have reacted?

But it was over now. No need to speculate. The MTA and the Army Corps of Engineers could look and look and look for their "leak" all they wanted, but without a guide like Tommy, they would never find it, for the water came from the Houston Conflux. Or maybe from the Secret Sea itself.

One more mystery in the City That Never Sleeps.

Maybe it never slept because it was afraid of nightmares.

Zak wondered what kind of bad dreams cities would have. He imagined they would involve being uprooted, tenuous and off-kilter.

Like being on a ship at sea, in a storm, with no solid ground for miles in every direction.

PART FOUR

ZAK

NINETY

Zak's parents—like Khalid's and Moira's—were so overjoyed to
see their child back safe and sound after having been missing
for two days that it took a good week before they asked any serious questions. By then, the Basketeers had already agreed to a
short, simple lie. Easier to remember, harder to disprove.

"Tell them we were running from the police, trying to hide
in the subway," Khalid coached them. His fibbing skills were still
top-notch, unaffected by their experience. "They already know
that part, and there's witnesses. And then tell them we jumped
down and followed the tracks into the tunnels to get away. But we
got lost in there. Which is totally believable because it's hella
dark in there, and the tunnels twist all over the place. So we
wandered until the water came out of nowhere and washed us
right into the station."

Incredible and impossible, but the truth was more incredible
and more impossible, so they stuck with the lie. Their obvious
lack of food and the need for medical attention upon their

return gave credence to their lie. And their parents' gratitude—tempered by the grounding—did the rest of the work for them. In the end, all the moms and dads wanted was their children back. How and why didn't matter.

Zak's grounding lasted into the beginning of the school year. He thought it unfair that his parents could lie to him his whole life and yet *he* would end up being punished, but he figured he'd gotten to see Tommy one last time. They never had.

Maybe they were even.

"Don't be too hard on them," Tommy had said. Zak was trying.

He wanted to forgive his parents. It would happen slowly. Right now he felt like he could be angry at them forever for what they'd done, for the lies they'd told. But a part of him knew that nothing—not even ghosts—could last forever.

He wanted to tell his mother what Tommy had said—that he would miss Zak "like that dish you forgot, the one that would be perfect for guests right now." Wanted to tell her because that meant Tommy had been watching, had been with them even though dead. That their family had been, in some way, complete. Most of what Zak had heard and seen during his adventure, he realized, had originated with Godfrey, not Tommy. But that sentence, that emotion: It proved for certain that Tommy had been watching them.

He thought maybe he understood his parents' grief. That he could share it. And they could, in time, share his.

He couldn't forgive, them, though. Not yet. Because somehow he knew that forgiving them would mean explaining what had happened, what he'd seen. And he couldn't explain. Not because he feared that they'd think he'd lost his mind.

But because it was *his.* Right now, his time with Tommy—their merged moments, their too-brief good-bye—was a sacred, solitary trust. A gift from one twin to another, like blood in the womb. His parents couldn't understand because he didn't yet understand.

Someday he would tell them.

Someday.

His punishment ended in late September, right around the time Moira's and Khalid's did as well. They agreed that their parents had probably coordinated this, for mysterious, ineffable adult reasons.

On his first day of freedom, Zak went—alone—to the subway stop near his home. He rode into Manhattan, switched trains, and went as close to the tip of Manhattan as the subway system would take him. Then he walked the rest of the way, past the Korean War Veterans Memorial, past Castle Clinton, until there was nothing between him and the water but a railing at the edge of Battery Park.

His heart skipped a beat. It did that occasionally now. An emergency room doctor had treated him for salt water inhalation on the day he'd returned to this universe, and had told his parents to get him back on his verapamil. Zak had pretended to take it for a while, but now . . .

Dr. White-eagle had said that the treatment was a temporary measure, and now Zak was slipping back into his old life, his heart reminding him it was still there and still fragile.

But he thought that maybe—just maybe—some of its strength would linger. A gift.

Zak placed a hand on his chest and the other tight against his ear. He listened to his heart.

He cast his thoughts out past the confluence where the Hudson River met the East River, out into the Upper Bay, to the horizon, to that invisible line where the sky kisses the ocean. Sunset now reminded him of the electroleum-lit buildings of the other New York, the soft glow along their lines and arcs.

Tommy? he thought, without urgency. *Tommy, are you out there?* he asked, knowing the answer.

He refused to believe—despite Tommy's disappearance—that his brother was gone. Everyone else had thought that, and they'd been wrong. Until he had proof, he would continue to hope that his twin still lived.

And if he didn't? If he was truly lost beyond the fathomless depths of the infinite Secret Sea?

Well, then that would be sad. But Zak would survive. He had come through this much, thinking he was only part of a greater whole, but he realized now that it wasn't a question of fractions. He was doing the wrong math. (He thought of Moira and he smiled.)

It was a question of remainders, not fractions. He was what was left of Thomas and Zakari, the Killian twins. What that meant for him and for the future, he could not know, but he would not forgo the chance to find out.

He knew, in that sun-dappled moment, only one thing, but he knew it for certain. He knew it the way mothers knew they loved their children, the way the shores knew the tides.

Gazing out at the East River as it lapped gently at the bulwark beneath his feet, he knew that he would never look upon the water the same way again.

AUTHOR'S NOTE

Most books—well, most of *mine*, at least—begin with some nugget or kernel of truth, some bit of reality upon which to build my fiction.

In the case of *The Secret Sea*, there were many kernels. There was Hurricane Sandy, which devastated New York City and surrounding areas in 2012. I had a broken foot at the time and couldn't evacuate, so my wife and I crossed our fingers and stuck it out. Until the storm killed the cable, we watched the storm on the news, including a flood washing through a PATH station. I filed the image away for the day I would need it.

TTTS (twin-to-twin transfusion syndrome) is an actual medical condition. Happily, with early intervention and treatment, many babies with TTTS are born safely and can live long, productive lives. I read about it and I paid attention because my wife is an identical twin. She never had TTTS, but it didn't matter. It stuck with me, and that, too, I filed away.

The most exotic, perhaps, of the truth nuggets that formed the basis of the novel, though, is the ship found under the wreckage of the twin towers. People are usually astonished to discover that this wasn't the product of my imagination, that it actually was—and is—real. I first learned about it in 2011 through a *Discovery News* article on Discovery.com: http://news .discovery.com/earth/plants/secrets-of-wtc-ship-revealed -110907.htm. I just stumbled upon the article, purely by accident. Just as I happened to read something about TTTS; just as I happened to be sofa-bound when Sandy pummeled New York.

People ask authors all the time, "Where do your ideas come from?" Sometimes the answer is, "Sheer coincidence."

The boat fascinated me. At the time of its discovery, the scientific community was baffled. The boat didn't adhere to the most common shipbuilding standards of its day. Dating it was difficult, though not impossible—just harder than it should have been. And most important of all: What the heck was it doing under the World Trade Center?

Workers carefully excavate portions of the boat to preserve as much of it as possible. After being underground for more than two hundred years, much of the boat has been degraded and worn away.

Recently (I'm writing this in early 2015), some of the secrets and mysteries about the boat have been sussed out. We've learned, for example, that it was a sloop and that its wood came from the same forests used to build Independence Hall. By examining the tree rings of the lumber, scientists determined that it was most likely built around 1773 (http://news.nationalgeo graphic.com/news/2014/07/140731-world-trade-center-ship -tree-rings-science-archaeology/). The best scientific estimates tell us that the boat was in service for only twenty or thirty years before it sank. There is speculation that worms ate at the timbers, leading to its relatively early demise. Or maybe it was deliberately sunk to add to landfill at the end of lower Manhattan (http://www .huffingtonpost.com/2014/07/30/world-trade-center-ship -mystery_n_5634280.html).

After workers cleared rubble and dirt over three days, the boat's timbers and structure are evident. As hard as it is to believe, this boat once sailed the ocean!

I think what I love most about the boat is this: When I first read about it back in 2011, we didn't know much at all. We know a lot more now . . . but still not everything.

Just like we don't know how to stop another Hurricane Sandy from flooding New York.

Or how to prevent TTTS.

It's the things we don't know that I obsess over, that I seek to explain through made-up stories. Because, yes, I know that Godfrey didn't ride that boat from one universe to another. The truth is more mundane than that, I'm sure. Someday, someone will have explanations for *all* of it.

But I will still prefer my own.

TTTS is real. Subways *can* flood. There really was a boat under the World Trade Center.

The Secret Sea probably does not exist.

Then again . . .

Photos courtesy of the Lower Manhattan Development Corporation. Preservation of and research regarding the World Trade Center Ship Remnant is funded by a Community Development Block Grant from the United States Department of Housing and Urban Development. Used with permission.

ACKNOWLEDGMENTS

Writing is a solitary pursuit.

Except for the small army of other people who make it all possible.

You can't write a book like *The Secret Sea* without some help from the experts. I want to thank Dr. Leanne Magee for consulting on child psychology, Dr. Dave Morgan for being my go-to physics guy (sorry for taking so many liberties with reality, Dave!), Stephanie Kuehn for connecting me with Dave in the first place, Dr. Deborah Mogelof for advising on medicine, and Jack Norris for help with Latin.

And then there are the early readers, who encouraged me along the way: Morgan Baden, who read the book in chunks as I typed it. Eric Lyga, who pointed out an early fatal flaw. Paul Griffin, whose early enthusiasm was like sunshine and rain to a flower. Gordon Korman, who found a hole and suggested how to fill it.

At Feiwel and Friends, I am eternally indebted to Liz Szabla for her faith and vision, as well as to Jean Feiwel. Also, special thanks to Rich Deas, Liz Dresner, Christine Ma, and Christine Barcellona. My thanks go out, too, to everyone in Sales, Production, and Marketing who made this book possible. Thank you, thank you, thank you!

And thank *you*, too, for reading. I'll see you on the waves.

Thank you for reading this Feiwel and Friends book.

The Friends who made

THE **SECRET SEA**

possible are:

JEAN FEIWEL, Publisher

LIZ SZABLA, Editor in Chief

RICH DEAS, Senior Creative Director

HOLLY WEST, Associate Editor

DAVE BARRETT, Executive Managing Editor

ANNA ROBERTO, Associate Editor

CHRISTINE BARCELLONA, Associate Editor

EMILY SETTLE, Administrative Assistant

ANNA POON, Editorial Assistant

Follow us on Facebook or visit
us online at mackids.com.

OUR BOOKS ARE FRIENDS FOR LIFE